UNDER PRESSURE

ROBERT POBI

HODDER &
STOUGHTON

First published in Great Britain in 2020 by Hodder & Stoughton
An Hachette UK company

1

A CIP catalogue record for this title is available from the British Library
Hardback ISBN 978 1 529 35316 7
Trade Paperback ISBN 978 1 529 35320 4
eBook ISBN 978 1 529 35319 8

Printed and bound in Great Britain by Clays Ltd, Elcograf S.p.A.

Hodder & Stoughton policy is to use papers that are natural, renewable and
recyclable products and made from wood grown in sustainable forests. The logging
and manufacturing processes are expected to conform to the environmental
regulations of the country of origin.

Hodder & Stoughton Ltd
Carmelite House
50 Victoria Embankment
London EC4Y 0DZ

www.hodder.co.uk

For Kenneth Meany—
  Mentor.
  Evil genius.
  Grouch.

While in theory randomness is an intrinsic property, in practice, randomness is incomplete information.
—Nassim Nicholas Taleb,
The Black Swan: The Impact of the Highly Improbable

We are all in the gutter, but some of us are looking at the stars.
—Oscar Wilde,
Lady Windermere's Fan

UNDER
PRESSURE

1

The Solomon R. Guggenheim Museum, New York City

Dana Goldrich wondered how many this made. *Five? Eight?* Not that it really mattered, because this was *it*—her last drink. Well, not *the* last one. But the one that would nudge her from not tipsy enough to almost perfectly drunk. It was a fine line of demarcation—one that had taken thirty years of golf tournaments, charity auctions, five-figure-a-plate galas, endless corporate events, and months of homebound COVID-19 boredom to perfect—and she enjoyed the exercise.

But she didn't want to drink so much that she embarrassed herself; her father had taught her that there was nothing worse than a sloppy drunk. So this was it—the final sip at the fountain. And in order to make sure things didn't go south, she needed to make a pledge, so she called up the biggies: *Scout's honor*; *pinkie swear*; *honest Injun* (was that one allowed anymore?); *cross my heart and hope to die.*

The *cross my heart* one ticked the most boxes. It had conviction bolstered by the romantic notion of death being preferable to dishonor.

Cross my heart.

She crossed her heart.

And hope to die.

She hoped to die. But left out the part about the needle—there was no need to tempt fate.

In crossing her heart, Dana spilled a little of her drink, which she found hilarious for some reason. She licked the vodka off her thumb and decided to head up the ramp.

Everyone else was amusing themselves talking shop, which meant one of two things tonight—the Big Rs (Reduce, Reuse, Recycle, Repurpose, Revive) or stock tips. Dana found this particular mix of eco-corporate-dot-com people a hissy fit waiting to happen. Inevitably, one of the natosexuals would insult one of the venture capitalists, things would heat up, and someone would end up with a drink in their face. Maybe get cussed out. But she doubted anyone would throw a punch—as brutal as the Wall Street types liked to think of themselves, they weren't physical people. And the carbon-footprint-obsessed folks? They believed in group hugs, not gang fights.

Her husband, Sheldon, was mingling with some of his hedge-fund buddies somewhere in the atrium below. Dana scanned the sea of evening wear, but there were an easy five hundred people in here, half of them wearing dinner jackets, including the waiters. Throw in that Shelly was not particularly tall and it was like looking for a diamond in an ice bucket. Which was ultimately fine with her; Dana wasn't interested in hearing him pitch another of his funds—this time it was foreign annuities, mostly Saudi backed.

Of course, everyone was talking about the company hosting the event—Horizon Dynamics. Shelly was excited about a rumor circulating among his buddies that they were expecting a big announcement tonight—the kind that would make everyone involved a lot of money when the IPO went live tomorrow morning. And there had to be some truth to the rumor because Dana had already heard a few of the guests discussing various ways to circumvent the tax man.

She moved up the corkscrew gallery with slow, deliberate steps that indicated her blood alcohol ratio was somewhere near perfect. She had read up on this once—it was a matter of basic biology: ethanol passing the blood-brain barrier hijacked balance because humans inherited their inner ear from sharks. It was so simple you almost tripped over it. Which she did. But caught herself on the railing. And spilled a little more of her cocktail.

Dana ran into the wife of one of the account execs in Sheldon's office, a woman with one of those saccharine finishing school nick-names that she could never remember—Muffy or Missy or something. She was with a friend who was rocking the Cruella de Vil look, complete with a two-tone marcel wave.

When Muffy/Missy saw Dana, she squealed and did an excited Pomeranian foot stamp. "Dana! What a lovely surprise." Her facial muscles barely moved, but she was still able to pull her lips into what most people could figure out was supposed to be a smile.

Dana leaned forward, careful to hold her drink to the side, and they metronomed air kisses. "How nice to see you," she said, trying to remember the woman's name.

Muffy/Missy introduced her friend, but the name was lost in the noise. She displayed the same taxidermy procedures—and her mouth looked like an overbaked pizza pocket.

More air kisses.

Muffy/Missy asked about the kids (which Dana didn't have), and wondered when she and Sheldon (only she called him Shelbon) were going to come out to the beach for another fabulous weekend (they had never been there).

Dana indicated a vague spot up the ramp. "I'll be back in a few minutes," she lied. "I promised someone I'd talk to them about an internship for one of their children. I'll see you back downstairs."

That seemed to satisfy Muffy/Missy, and she and Cruella continued their downward trajectory.

As Dana worked her way up toward the skylight and confetti machines, she ignored most of the art on display. The decor—which was all it really was—was a mix of Ansel Adams's iconic photography of the natural world interlaced with Andy Warhol's prints of mass-produced landfill. The Wall Street guys were throwing terms like *juxtaposition, negative space,* and *rampant consumerism* around as if they understood—or cared—about them. Dana worked in the art department at Christie's, and she knew advertising when she saw it. When you looked at Warhol's soup cans beside one of Adams's Sierra portraits, it was impossible to miss the message: too much garbage, not enough forethought. Which was why they were all here: Horizon Dynamics was going to change the world. Or so the seven-story foil banners hanging from the ceiling declared in a classic ad agency focus group slogan: *Today's Solutions for Tomorrow's Problems!*

All of Warhol's work looked like T-shirt art to her. Sure, it was popular. Sure, you immediately knew what you were looking at. Sure, it was a time stamp from an important cultural period. But so what? When Dana looked at the posters and silk-screen portraits, all she saw was a guy who had bothered to show up.

But as an investment? Warhol was a touchstone for both the nascent collector and the uninformed alike; he had *brand recognition.* It didn't matter if it was a Brillo box, a portrait of Jagger overlaid with camouflage, or one of his early shoe sketches—they were all known commodities. Looking up a Warhol piece at auction was so much easier than going through the mental anguish of trying to understand how a small painting could be worth more than a large one. When you purchased a *1969 Campbell's Soup II,* signed in ballpoint and stamped with its series number, all you had to be able to do was read a catalogue.

But Adams was the real deal—an American giant. That his work was hanging here beside Warhol seemed like a snide remark to Dana. But she understood that not everyone got Adams—the biggest obstacle she faced when speaking to clients was getting them to equate his oeuvre to other art forms. It was sad how he had lost some of his relevance to an age where everyone who carried a cell phone camera fancied themselves a photographer. But to Dana, Adams's work was like reading Whitman—and you either got it or you didn't. And most people didn't.

She was halfway through the final turn around the ramp when she realized that her glass was empty. And since she had spilled half of it, she was entitled to one more. But that would be it—a single drink. Then it was quits for the night. Cross her heart.

Dana looked over the railing to the atrium below. The bar was too far away to make in these heels. And she wasn't in the mood for running into Muffy/Missy and Cruella on the way down to discuss children she didn't have and trips she wouldn't take.

She looked around for the elevator just as the lights began to dim. She steadied herself on the railing and looked down into the atrium far below.

The string section began a playful little composition that sounded like birds chirping.

Then foil confetti began to snow from the machines hanging beneath the skylight—fluttering down in a thick, mirrored swarm. The lasers punched into the cloud and it pulsed, developing a heartbeat. It looked alive, playful.

The atrium erupted in applause.

Holograms blossomed from the floor, sprouting up toward the falling foil—three-dimensional tree trunks that grew in accelerated time lapse, branches reaching toward the skylight. The outstretched holographic limbs contorted as they rose and touched the falling foil confetti, and the transformation was complete.

For an instant, the Guggenheim was a lush translucent forest, heavy trunks of computer-generated old-growth trees ascending into the thick canopy of foil foliage overhead.

The gentle chirps generated from the violinists changed pitch and turned into the calls of exotic birds, each voice different.

The room disappeared, and Dana was transplanted to an ancient point in time, before man began to tiptoe toward the happenstance of evolution.

She began to clap with the rest of the partygoers.

Then—

Dana's mind had time to register the flash.

And the initial instant of the explosion.

But everything disappeared when she was destroyed by the shock wave.

2

Montauk, New York

Lucas Page was out on the deck, turning things over in his mind. It was past two A.M. but he had lost track of time to one of those warm fall nights that made him feel like winter might never arrive. He sat in the big cedar chair with a cup of coffee that had passed peak-consumption temperature hours ago. His beaten leather mail bag was on the deck under his chair, filled with term papers that he needed to go through, but his attention was focused on the broad misty strip of the Milky Way. The rhythm of the surf scratched at the beach and he suspected that this was as close to meditation as he could get—something the doctors, in the vague but polished nomenclature of their profession, had tried to convince him could be a useful tool during *times of stress*. But when the voices started up, there was no convincing them to be quiet; they operated on their own schedule. And the hour he spent watching network news earlier gave them all the excuses they needed for a little emotional mischief; there was nothing like a flashback to start the voices chattering.

His head was back on the big deck chair and he focused his

good eye on the stars. Out here, beyond the visual noise of the city, he could get a pretty good view of the sky if the weather was in a giving mood. The telescope was out, but it was really for the kids, part of his oft too-aggressive attempt to teach them a little more about the universe. They had taken turns peeking up at the cosmos after supper, but Lucas was still thinking about the explosion back in the city, and the kids had eventually drifted back into the house. Evidently he was no fun to be around when he wasn't paying attention to them.

Lucas preferred the human eye over the telescope out here because it pulled focus and let him take in the Big Picture without zeroing in on details—a hard-wired problem with his thinking since childhood. His attention wandered from star to star, constellation to constellation, unconsciously and automatically mapping the movements as the minutes ticked by. He was staring at the Seven Sisters and could see five of the girls—not bad with the naked eye at this time of year—when Erin came out.

She sat down in his lap, careful to put her weight on his good leg. "Hey, Mr. Man. I thought you might have gone for a swim."

He smiled into the dark; the water out here was never warm, but this far into October it would be at hypothermia temperatures. Also, with or without his prosthetics, Lucas had all the hydrodynamics of a cast-iron sewing machine. "Can't sleep."

"So you're staring up at the sky?"

"I am."

She nodded over at the telescope. "Why aren't you using your fancy coatrack?"

"That's for the kids. I don't like it. Too much chromatic aberration."

"Of course. *Chromatic aberration.* Silly me."

He smiled and leaned forward, putting his face in the thick red hair that fell over her chest and the blue Wonder Woman T-shirt. She was warm and smelled of that Bvlgari perfume that was a big part of the mental snapshot he carried around. "I'm just thinking about things."

They had both been involved in a silent dialogue from the moment they saw the news, and even though *things* was not much of an answer, it was enough.

"How long will we be hiding out at the beach?" She leaned her head back on his shoulder and followed his line of sight up to the sky.

He reached over to the other chair and took the blanket off the back with his right hand, doing a decent job of covering her. "We're not *hiding out*."

"Okay."

"We're *waiting*. Events like this often come in multiples. Right now I'm more comfortable out here, where statistically there isn't much of a chance of our children being blown up."

Their silence indicated that they agreed on that one point.

Erin pulled her feet up onto his lap under the blanket. "The hospital hasn't called, which means we didn't get any of the survivors."

"That's because there weren't any."

By the way she stiffened, he could tell that she hadn't thought of that as an option. "How do you know?"

The cell phone footage aired on CNN and the telephoto shots of the Guggenheim on Fox had provided the broad strokes: the skylight and front doors had been blown out, but there was relatively little damage to the outside of the building. When you factored in more than five hundred victims so far, it meant that the blast had been designed to affect soft bodies, not hard surfaces. And there was only one kind of explosion that provided those two very specific data points. "Trust me."

"Is that why you're sitting out here, looking up at the sky that you seem to prefer over us humans much of the time?"

He could tell that she had reached the end of her rehearsed

dialogue, which meant that she would either go back inside or ask him what she had been trying not to.

She rested her head on his shoulder. "You think they'll call you?"

And there it was.

"I don't do terrorists. At least not this kind."

"Are you sure this was terrorism?"

"I'm not certain of anything at this point other than a lot of people were killed."

"What humanity needs is a little more humanity."

"What humanity *needs* is to finish what it started and go extinct."

"Don't be a cynic. I can live with your sarcasm, because a lot of the time it's funny. But you're too kind to be a cynic."

"They'll mobilize the entire American intelligence community to nail these people down. They might pull everyone out of mothballs, but this isn't my field. This particular subset of people has a pretty standard operating procedure, and they're not that smart—it's just a matter of time until they get caught. The office might ask me to look at a few things. If that happens, I want you and the kids to stay here." That was as honest as he could be.

"So how about we go to bed?" She got up slowly, using his aluminum leg as a pushing-off point. She held out her hand. "Choose your response wisely."

They went inside, leaving the telescope pointed up at the night sky.

3

The Solomon R. Guggenheim Museum

Brett Kehoe, FBI special agent in charge of Manhattan, paced the length of the Blue Bird command vehicle, overseeing his people as they coordinated with the men on site. But Kehoe was in another dimension, one where nothing—not even the command vehicle—existed; all there was, all he saw, were the video feeds of his team culling the debris inside the building.

The wall of monitors looked like HD cams broadcasting an archaeological dig from the bottom of the ocean. The Quasar task lighting threw focused beams through swirling dust that resembled silt being stirred up. The men in the specialized safety gear could have been deep-sea divers, their chemical respirators not dissimilar to heliox helmets, their movements slow and deliberate. All that was missing were bubbles.

The departments involved—the NYPD, the FDNY, and the FBI—wasted no time wondering if the explosion had been accidental; the Guggenheim was one of the high-visibility soft targets on the FBI's anti-terrorism list and was a well-known quantity regarding accident probability. The building's infrastructure offered no possibility of an event resembling the explosion.

What worried Kehoe was that the creative types tended to compound malice with all kinds of bonus bad ideas: biological and chemical weapons topped the list, followed by the big bogeyman of radioactivity. And if they lacked the funding or smarts for any of those, even the minimally talented could plan secondary events to bolster their branding: kill a bunch of people, wait for first responders to arrive, then set off more carnage.

Their efforts to reverse engineer the explosion were not going well because not a single cell phone or camera inside the building had survived. Even the high-speed security cameras in the museum hadn't recorded anything other than a single blip of white before going dead, their final instant of usefulness stored on the cloud before they had been cooked by the blast.

A couple of surveillance cameras from the park had provided some context. But even when they slowed down the footage, all they had recorded was the skylight and front doors blowing out. Right now all anyone could agree on was that the Guggenheim might as well have been the inside of a volcano.

While the hazmat and explosives crew scoured the site, the bureau did what it did best and went after information. The digital teams were immersed in all manner of social media necromancy, combing message boards, profiles, websites, and accounts. The bureau proper had reached out to the Department of Justice, who were tag teaming with the Department of Homeland Security in search of any group or individuals whose temperament fit the psychological, political, or religious parameters of what had just happened. Email was being sifted; texts and phone calls retrieved from data vaults; passenger arrival lists and recently purchased plane tickets scoured. All in the name of Big Data, which, Kehoe understood, already had these people on a hook.

The Horizon Dynamics gala had 594 registered attendees,

a combination of the rich investor variety and the wealthy eco-friendly *Don't-eat-tuna-if-it-comes-in-cans* crowd. Which meant that a good percentage of Park Avenue's wealth had just been re-distributed through inheritance. There would be teary church services and flowery obituaries and new Bentleys up and down the island.

They had located 32 of the attendees who had left early. Which left 562 souls still unaccounted for. Another 60 victims had worked for the catering company, along with 42 museum employees. Add to that the people by the entrance outside who had been cooked by the burst of flames, along with the pedestrians who had been moseying down the sidewalk and ended up eating the plate glass doors, and the body count was at 702.

The wealthy hung out with the wealthy, and the phone calls had already started. Kehoe had fielded conversations with the mayor, the governor, and the attorney general, all topped off by a very terse exchange with the vice president. The cameras were rolling and the investigation would be a very public display of concern. A bus full of kids on the way to xylophone camp goes in the river, and people light candles and hold vigils; a bunch of rich white people get blown up, and the entire continent mobilizes. This one would show good old-fashioned American priorities at their finest, which, when filtered through the prism of irreducible complexity down to the fewest moving parts, translated to *worship the money.*

Kehoe swallowed the last of his tea and threw the cup into the wastebasket just as Calvin-Wade Curtis, the head of the forensic explosives unit, came in. Curtis had spent three tours with a bomb disposal squad in Afghanistan, where he had become fascinated by the mechanics of detonation. This experience, bolstered by a degree in molecular chemistry, brought him to Kehoe's attention.

Curtis was a small man who looked twenty years younger than

he was, mostly owing to his size and bushy blond hair. His time out in the world had done nothing to soften the country boy twang that made him sound like he was always trying to sell you something. But he was smart. Didn't talk too much. And knew more about explosives than anyone Kehoe had ever met. He was also a consummate blues guitarist—a skill he pulled out from under the bed every Thursday night at a bar down on Houston Street. His only bad habit was a nervous smile that he pulled out at the most inappropriate times. Like now.

Curtis was back in office clothes, but still had a red line around his forehead and nose where the hazmat suit and respirator had suction-cupped to his skin while he performed chemical archaeology amid the charred Sheetrock and human remains inside. Curtis slammed the door, poured himself a coffee from the onboard machine, and dropped into the only empty Aeron in the space.

Curtis took a deep breath and nodded at Kehoe. "Chawla sent me over to talk to you." Samir Chawla was the special agent that Kehoe had put in charge of the investigation proper. "None of the filters, swabs, cultures, badges, or spectrometers picked up anything radioactive, chemical, or biological. There are a few exotics that will take a little more time to test for, but I think we're good." He took a sip of coffee, then reached into his shirt pocket to take out an evidence bag. He held it out. "But I did find this." His nervous smile was tired, but still out of place.

Kehoe held the envelope up to the light. All he saw was what looked like a tiny amount of cigarette ash.

Curtis ran a hand through his hair, then wiped it on his pants. "I sent samples off to the lab, where we'll run it through a mass spectrometer, but under the field scope it looks like a metastable intermolecular composite. I think it was disguised as confetti."

When Kehoe shifted focus from the little envelope to Curtis, the explosives expert continued, "An MIC is a nanothermite—a nanofuel."

"Which means?"

"Which means that this wasn't a detonation; it was a thermo-baric, or an aerosol, explosion." Curtis ran a hand through his hair again. "The roof, windows, and front doors didn't blow out—they were pushed out by the pressure. That's what that initial flash was in the surveillance footage. The people inside had their eardrums, eyeballs, and lungs crushed by a shock wave that sucked all the air out of the room, then used that air to create a pressurized fire-storm. Since the airborne fuel deflagrated but didn't detonate in a traditional sense, most of the vics inhaled burning fuel. And since the initial shock wave would have caused very little damage to brain tissue because it's protected by relatively thick bone, it's very prob-able that many of the victims stayed alive for several seconds—or even minutes—after they were cooked." His smile eased off a little with that last bit. "Not a nice way to go."

Kehoe considered it a point of pride that he never allowed him-self to show emotion at work and even though he was tired, he didn't break character when he said, "Good work."

The building had suffered very little damage—at least compared to the people inside—but it would be closed for months while con-struction crews tried to reset the clock on the damage. The fenes-tration had all blown out, and a few of the interior walls had been pushed in, but it was still recognizable as one of the city's most prominent landmarks. Which was more than you could say for the victims—they looked like castings from Pompeii.

Less than an hour after the bombing, two representatives from the museum's insurance underwriters showed up, asking for a tour. Kehoe didn't bother letting them begin the chest-thumping, he sim-ply told them to leave his command vehicle. But not before showing them the remains of a young woman who looked like a melted tire.

They wouldn't be back.

Kehoe handed the envelope back to Curtis and nodded at the door; he needed some fresh air.

Kehoe and Curtis stepped out into the fall morning, and the light wind was in direct contrast to the humid, cramped environment of the command vehicle. It was state of the art, but when you piled more than the recommended 8.6 human bodies inside (which they had exceeded by 22.4 individuals), the space quickly became a humid closet that smelled of people. Kehoe hit the asphalt and took a deep breath, surprised that the air out here tasted as fresh as it did with a building full of pressure-cooked human beings mere yards away.

They had closed all traffic in the immediate vicinity—from 87th up to 90th, and from Fifth Avenue right across to Park—which meant the sounds of the city were somehow less intimate. Any cars in the zone had been towed, and the only foot traffic allowed inside the wire were residents—which was presenting its own particular set of problems with the NYPD as they checked IDs. Kehoe was proud to be a New Yorker (if only by transplant) because the citizenry were more good than bad. He had seen it during 9/11 and the big power outage of 2003—people donated blankets, handed out free sneakers for the bus and tunnel crowd, and gave away ice cream. But this time things felt different, as if the whole island could go feral. Kehoe (and the analysts he paid to do the thinking) believed that social media was responsible in that it was continually etching lines of demarcation between every discernible demographic, cutting the social fabric into smaller and smaller swatches. And things were getting worse as people started seeing the world in terms of *us* versus *them*.

Samir Chawla, the special agent in charge of the investigation, came up, coffee in hand. Curtis pocketed the evidence envelope, delivered the prerequisite *I'll keep you posted* through the still-present nervous smile, and disappeared without shaking hands.

"Anything?" Kehoe asked his SAIC.

Chawla was a thin, fit man who ran on caffeine and salad. "With seven hundred and two victims, our people are buried under enough information to choke Google. I requested additional agents from the federal pool, and a few from Vermont, Jersey, and Mass have already arrived. We're expecting a hundred more. One of the empty floors is being outfitted with workstations; the math on this one will be considerable."

Kehoe looked up the street. The crowds were not pushing at the fencing, but they were making a lot of noise. The nutjobs had started arriving last night, holding up bristol board placards denouncing the attack as a false flag operation that had been orchestrated by the government. Some wore red ball caps, some wore QAnon T-shirts, some wore Nazi T-shirts, and some were dressed as Muppets. With Halloween a few days off, there was no shortage of costumes in the crowd, which presented its own set of security concerns. Kehoe wondered just when, specifically, postliteracy had morphed into complete stupidity. He wanted to feel sorry for these people, which he resented because they didn't deserve the emotional space. What really bothered him was that they worked tirelessly to connect a bunch of unrelated dots when assembling a working model of even the most basic facts seemed to be impossible for them. Why was it that whenever there was a mass casualty event, the stupid gravitated en masse toward the assumption of conspiracy? Kehoe was not a pessimist—his job precluded that particular muscle—but every now and then he got tired and was tempted to give in.

Besides the rubberneckers, the media was making his life miserable. Every news network on the planet had one—if not several—crews at ground zero. Which translated to almost two thousand individuals from the entertainment corps on site. They had tents set up in the park, but they were being kept away for now. The bureau had yet to issue a comprehensive statement, other than they were in the initial stages of an investigation into what had all the earmarks of a terrorist attack. This concise and factual statement proved to be too complicated for the journalists, and they did what they did, placing blame on either Muslim or right-wing extremists, depending on the source.

But right now Kehoe had problems other than dealing with people who made things up. He crossed the street to the site proper and two of his men eased up on his flanks, doing bodyguard duty. Kehoe stopped in front of the museum and wondered what kind of a human being—or *beings*—were able to justify cooking 700-plus innocent people. Thirty years of trying to outthink society's broken spokes had done nothing to assuage the repulsion he felt at times like this.

Even though all the workers wore matching white coveralls, Kehoe had no problem telling his team apart from the medical examiner's: the bureau people were picking through the rubble, looking for evidence; the medical examiner's minions were carting the dead out of the dust and placing them in vans that had been in constant rotation since last night. Two white-coveralled people from the ME's office were rolling another body out, and as Kehoe watched, he was upset that he was thinking in terms of numbers, not lives.

The ME had two floors of offices and labs downtown, but nowhere near the capacity to handle this many bodies. A temporary facility had been set up in a warehouse earmarked for just such an emergency, where technicians would spend the next month sorting out which body went with what name.

"So what do you need that you do not have?"

Chawla didn't spend any time thinking about the question. "I need more analysts. And more programmers. People who are good with numbers."

There was some sort of a disturbance in the space behind Kehoe, and he turned, his men stepping to his front flanks in a protective measure.

A man in a red ball cap was corralled by two carbine-carrying policemen near the park wall across Fifth. The civilian had a Go-Pro mounted on his cap, and he kept pointing at it. The cops were shaking their heads as he screamed that he knew his rights.

One of the officers reached out and put a hand on Red Cap's elbow and he crossed the threshold from angry to enraged. He spit on the cop and Kehoe knew that signaled the end of the argument—which the officer demonstrated by reaching around to the zip-tie cuffs hanging off his belt.

But Red Cap wasn't interested in complying, and he faked left, then ducked right, scooching between the two policemen like a wiry little monkey.

Up the street the crowd let loose with a roar punctuated by whistles and applause. They began chanting, "Go! Go! Go! Go!"

Red Cap ran toward a stretcher being loaded into one of the vans. "False flag! False flag!" He swung a yellow utility knife.

By this time the two officers were on his six, and he was tackled as he slashed at the body bag, screaming, "It's a dummy!"

But he had made his mark, and the cooked corpse spilled out.

"False flag!" Red Cap screamed again as the cops wrestled him to the ground.

He grinned triumphantly as the corpse's skull impacted with the morning street beside him. "Proof! It's a dum—" The sentence ended when the corpse's skull shattered, spilling cooked brain out on to the ground, splattering him with blood and bits.

Red Cap threw up as the cops cuffed him.

Up the street, the crowd roared.

Kehoe was impressed that the cops hadn't put a bullet into the guy. But their luck wouldn't hold out indefinitely, not with people like that allowed to walk around. Eventually someone was going to get shot—either deservedly or not. And the best way to stave off an accident was to solve this crime.

Kehoe turned back to Chawla, who was shaking his head. "You need more computational firepower?" Kehoe asked.

"Yes, sir."

"Then get Whitaker to meet me at the helicopter pad."

4

Montauk, New York

Lucas was fucking around with the leaf blower, and his prosthetic hand was useless with the pull cord. He had given it a few half-hearted yanks with his good hand, but all he had done was pique the curiosity of the dog, who stood at the door examining him as if he had sprouted feathers. Lucas was about to pitch the contraption through the garage window when he decided that a walk on the beach would be healthier than messing around with yard work that he neither enjoyed nor cared about. As far as he was concerned, they could pave the entire property and paint it green—everyone would be better off. Besides, they had a guy that took care of these things. His name was Mr. Miller and he was about the same age as most of the rocks on the property. He showed up precisely every ten days (rain, shine, or hurricane) to wrestle an ancient gas-powered mower out of the bed of his rust-eaten Ford. Then he mowed over everything on the property—grass, weeds, flowers, shrubs, and the occasional children's toy. Lucas had a strong suspicion that they were Mr. Miller's only clients.

His effort to keep his focus away from the bombing in the

city yesterday would have to be directed elsewhere, so he put the blower down on the floor beside the station wagon. But he gave it a kick, spinning it into the rim of the front tire, which caused the dog to step back, out onto the driveway.

"Well, dummy? How about a walk?"

Lemmy made a noise that was neither all dog nor all human.

"I'll take that as a yes." He closed the garage door and headed around back.

Erin had the big double doors open and the curtains were doing that fall thing they did where they reached into the kitchen as if they knew winter was coming. The kids were off upstairs, no doubt gobbling up data on their devices (they were permitted half an hour each morning on the weekends), Laurie and Alisha probably playing with the dollhouse Lucas had bought them at a garage sale up the road on the Fourth of July weekend.

The house wasn't as large as many of the beachfront monstrosities that dotted the coastline, and every inch of available space was taken up by the kids and their crap. But Lucas was grateful for the weekend home—no matter how he looked at it, they were lucky. The layout had initially been a two-bedroom design, but they had split up the largest room and adapted the attic into a space for the boys. With the two youngest girls in bunk beds in one of the rooms, they were able to keep all five kids relatively happy. Lucas had spent a chunk of his childhood in foster homes, including a six-month stint where he slept in a bathtub, and he still marveled at all the space they had here. The kids were good about it, even when their friends showed up and they were forced to pull out the sleeping bags.

Erin was in the small office off the kitchen, remotely managing her duties at the hospital on her laptop. "Done with the leaves?" she asked, doing a bad job of hiding the ridicule in her voice; it was no secret that Lucas and lawn care had nothing in common but alliteration.

"I went with the 'less is more' approach."

Erin took off her glasses and put them down on the keyboard. "And by *less* you mean what, exactly?"

"In this particular case, *less* means *none*. Besides, it's all relative. My less is more than someone else's more and my more is less than a third party's less. I can argue semantics all day." He came over and leaned on the edge of the desk beside her. "And I can even do it under the guise of quantum mechanics."

Lemmy went to his bowl by the fridge and rudely slurped down almost as much water as he spilled on the floor.

Erin reached out and touched Lucas's thigh—the original one. "You want to go for a walk on the beach?"

He wondered how she was able to read his mind. "I don't know—that leaf blower looks like a lot of fun. Or it would be if I could figure out how to turn it on."

Erin snorted her goofy little laugh. "You don't turn a leaf blower on, you *start it up*."

"Once again I'm happy to go with the 'less is more' approach, and a big yes to a walk. You think the kids are interested?" He realized that there was very little ambient noise in the house. "Are they even here?"

"They're doing homework. And Alisha is playing with her dolls. I think they're worried that you're going back to work."

"Kids?" He yelled into the void. "Who wants to go for a walk?"

Half an hour later, they were below Bluff Lookout. Lemmy led the group, his pack mentality not letting him venture more than twenty or thirty yards ahead before bounding back. Stevie and Hector hunted for Montauk monsters down near the water, their sneakers soaked through and their jeans wet to the knees. Hector had found a sun-bleached crab shell that he insisted was the skull of an alien. Laurie and Alisha collected stones that they socked away in the big canvas tote that Erin had somehow been talked into carrying. Maude and Lucas closed up the rear.

Lucas put two of his real fingers in his mouth and let loose with a sharp whistle, signaling that it was time to turn around; the tide was coming back in and Turtle Cove would soon be full of fishermen in waders and floats, all sporting ten-foot rods, in search of stripers. Sometimes he and the kids fished the tides, but mostly for whiting or mackerel off the beach in front of the house. Lucas hadn't been brought up on outdoor sports and tended to learn along with the kids. But they all stayed away from the weekend fishermen, who came out from the city in hundred-thousand-dollar SUVs and outdoor clothing sporting expensive labels—those guys were wound way too tight.

As they turned, Lucas swiveled his head, focusing out at the ocean with his good eye. "You have to admit, even with all the summer people, this can be a charming place." Mrs. Page had summered out here her whole life, and she had introduced Lucas to the place when he was six. They had managed to spend ten summers on the point before her money ran out, and they relied on the invitation of friends for the occasional sybaritic weekend from then on. Later in life, when he and Erin had had the opportunity to buy the place out here, it had been like coming home. They used the house on weekends and holidays for three seasons a year, renting it out most of the summer, which helped pay a lot of the expenses.

Maude shrugged. "I guess." As much of a young woman as she was turning into, she reverted to the surly teenager act when it suited her. "Are you going back to work for those people?" She had on jeans with no knees and a homemade T-shirt that stated *Eric Clapton Sucks!*

By the way she said *those people*, Lucas knew that she had been talking to Erin. "Not right now. I'm only useful for a very narrow bandwidth of problems, and what happened yesterday—"

"The explosion at the museum?"

"Yeah, the explosion at the museum. That isn't my field at all. I can't see being of much use to them. At least not like last time."

"Did terrorists do this?"

Lucas shook his head. "I don't know. No one does."

"The people on the television seem pretty convinced."

"There's *misinformed* and there's *uninformed*, and the problem is that most people don't let either of those things get in their way when they have an audience—just look at the internet."

Lucas loved all the kids, but he and Maude had some kind of a special bond that he wasn't able to understand. Maybe it was because he'd had to work so hard to gain her trust, or maybe it was because she reminded him most of Erin (which had no basis in genetics, since all their children were adopted), but he had an easier time talking to her than the other kids, as if maybe he understood her a little better.

Maude stopped and picked up a stone that looked as if it might be perfectly round. She handed it to Lucas and said, "So?"

He glanced at it and shook his head. "Elliptical."

Maude took it back and examined it skeptically for a few seconds.

"It's three inches, twenty-three thirty-seconds on the longest axis—three inches, eleven-sixteenths on the shortest."

Maude scrunched up her nose. "If you say so."

"You can measure it if you want," he offered, smiling. But he was never wrong. Not with numbers. And certainly not with measurements.

Maude pitched it out at the water. "How do you do that?"

"It's just a stupid human trick. Like being able to turn your eyelids inside out."

She made her gross-out face. "No it's not; you don't have to be smart to flip your eyelids."

Lucas shrugged again; he had met plenty of what he thought

of as *stupid smart people,* especially in academia. "Maybe." He stopped walking. "Have you figured out what you'd like to do about school?" The school she was at now had succumbed to the classic trade-off between arts and commerce and there was very little in the way of right-brain stimulation—which was where her true interests lay. Everyone concerned knew she'd be better served attending another institution. They had interviewed at a school with an advanced arts program, and they were waiting for her to decide if she wanted to make the switch.

"Am I allowed to have an opinion?"

"Have we ever asked your opinion and not taken it?"

She thought about that for a moment. "I guess not."

"So?"

They had gone through the interview process, and after seeing her portfolio, the school had agreed to enroll her. But time was no longer an abstract concept—they had to decide before Friday morning. The decision was causing her a lot of stress, and Lucas suspected that she was looking at it as an ending instead of a beginning. "You'll probably have to work much harder than you are now, but it's less likely you'll get tired as fast." And he stopped—she knew all of this and it was time to stop selling her. She had to make up her own mind. "But you know all this."

"You said I had until Friday."

"You do."

"But you're probably going away and—"

"We don't know that."

She squinted as she smiled up at him. "We don't?"

"No. We don't."

She eyed him suspiciously. "Well, a few more days won't change anything. So okay. I'll do it. I'll go to LaGuardia."

Lucas turned around and waved at Erin with his prosthetic. "Maude's transferring to LaGuardia," he yelled.

The whole family cheered.

Their voices were still hanging in the air when Hector yelled, "Hey, a helicopter's landing in front of our place!"

Lucas looked down the beach, and the breakers flipped on in his head as a navy blue Jet Ranger touched down, three big yellow letters on the side. It conjured up a cloud of dust and sent subsonic shock waves out over the water.

Lucas swung around to catch Erin in his line of sight. She gave him a soft smile filled with a million sad little meanings.

He turned back to the helicopter. The doors opened and two standard-issue FBI copies emerged, one large, one an XXXL. When they had taken up positions on either side of the bird, the unmistakable form of Brett Kehoe came down the steps.

He was sure the clown car routine was finished, but a fourth figure emerged from the aircraft, a tall black woman who even from two hundred yards out exuded the appropriate mix of pheromones denoting her as a force of nature—Special Agent Alice Whitaker. She was no doubt here as a prop for Kehoe's attempt at emotional leverage.

Beside him, Maude said, "Our day is F-U-K-T."

"Hey, kiddo, what have I told you about that?" He put his hand on her shoulder. "Don't be lazy—use the correct spelling."

5

By the time they got back to the house, Kehoe and Whitaker were on the patio. Three decades slumming with the FBI hadn't smoothed out any of the old-money DNA that was as much a part of Kehoe as the charm, manners, and menace. He had updated his haircut since last time they had been in a room together, but he still looked like a spokesperson for some expensive lifestyle product. He wore one of his tailored suits with the pick-stitched lapels he favored, and even out here on the beach he appeared comfortable.

Whitaker's white linen shirt contrasted with her dark skin and darker eyes, and even in the Ralph Lauren duds, she looked like she could kill a pack of wolves with her bare hands. Like Kehoe, she had changed her hair, and she sported a tight ponytail of Predator braids that could have been designed by a satellite engineer. She wasn't quite smiling, but Lucas could see that she was happy to see him and he grudgingly realized that he felt the same—old war buddies were like that.

Lucas and Whitaker had been paired up last winter during his first stint back at the bureau in almost a decade. She was a field agent, and even though Lucas liked to think that he had chosen her to help him, he knew the truth was Kehoe had set him up—he had intentionally put them in the same general vicinity and let physics pull them together. They had begrudgingly liked each other from the beginning, and quickly developed a weird kind of chemistry that brought out the best in both of them. She was smart and not given to pain-in-the-assery—and she didn't suffer his bullshit, which was a rare trait. They had gone the distance together and she had been added to the very short list of people he trusted with his life—which in a way made her family.

Kehoe's two other men went out front to deal with the twin Southampton police SUVs that arrived with the chopper. The entire performance was dramatic, especially for Kehoe, who was not generally given to theatrics. Or an unnecessary demonstration of force.

Lucas sent Erin and the kids inside. The children ran upstairs, but Erin stayed in the kitchen, leaning against the island, arms crossed, intently watching them through the big window. Lucas wondered if lipreading was part of the superhero plan she was was enrolled in.

The sun-bleached joists of the pergola cast weird rectangular shadows, turning Kehoe into a composite of several portraits, none of them happy. The ever-present Mark Cross briefcase sat on the seat beside him, conveying a sense of significance. Everyone wore sunglasses and looked like they would rather be someplace else.

The pilot was on a folding chair down on the beach, grabbing a few bits of vitamin D and reading a paperback. Kehoe's two extra men were back at either corner of the property, on the edge of the grass overlooking the beach, and the sheriff's men had taken up positions on the other side of the house, up near the road.

Lucas and Kehoe examined each other for a few silent moments, and it was Whitaker who finally cracked the frost with "Nice hair."

Maude had talked Lucas into bleaching his hair as a test run for her Halloween costume—she wanted to go out as Sting and the blond hair was a must. It was supposed to wash out, but that had been three days ago and he still looked like a punk-rock Frankenstein in expensive sunglasses.

Lucas tried out a smile, and by the way that Kehoe shifted in his seat, he knew that his face was doing that scar tissue Karloff thing that scared the natives. "Thank you," he said.

Whitaker shook her head and smiled.

Kehoe filled the empty space by answering a text—the twelfth since sitting down.

The complicated nature of their relationship was no secret. There had been a ten-year span in which they hadn't spoken. Both of them had used that decade to generate a little forgiveness for what had happened—for the things they had both lost. *The Event,* as Lucas called it, had recalibrated his life from the molecular level up and, in some lateral way, had no doubt done the same for Kehoe. But it was still there, in the background, like a deep space magnetic wave that was hard to detect but impossible to pretend didn't exist.

The Event had almost destroyed Lucas physically, and he spent the next few years discovering the new and improved Dr. Lucas Page. When he walked out the other end—with his body cobbled together with all kinds of experimental hardware, his first marriage in the shitter, his job gone, and no friends—he found a man that he didn't recognize but could be proud of. He met and married Erin. They started putting a family together—with children who could not find a place out in the world. He accepted a job at Columbia. Accidentally wrote a book that put him on bestseller lists. And forgot that he had ever worked for the FBI. Until that night last winter when Kehoe had come calling, dragging all the old monsters along with him.

Erin brought out a wicker tray with two mugs of coffee and a cup of tea. She placed it down on the table and went back inside without saying anything.

After Erin was back inside, Kehoe went into lecture mode with his patented poetic cadence. "We won't know the final toll for a few more hours, but right now we're at seven hundred and two victims, including museum personnel, catering employees, and a few unfortunate pedestrians who happened to be walking by when things went south." Kehoe lifted the porcelain cup of tea from the tray and took a sip.

Lucas leaned forward, meshing the fingers of his left hand with those of his prosthetic; even in the warm autumn air, the aluminum fingers were cold against his skin. "I don't see how I can give you any added value on this one, Brett." Kehoe's one unerring rule of management was that he tasked only the right people to a job. And since he was here, he had no doubt worked out all the aspects of his ask.

Kehoe took another sip and put his cup down. "With seven hundred and two victims, the math on this one is going to be a challenge. And then there are the rest of the unknowns: motive, suspect, ideology, logistics, and end game. Right now we don't even have a starting point—no one has claimed responsibility."

That was odd—an exercise this public had to have a purpose, and more than likely it was for PR. "Nothing?"

Kehoe quickly answered a text, then came back with "No one reliable. There were a few tweets from the usual suspects—two from factions of ISIS, one from Al-Qaeda, but it was obvious they had no idea what they were talking about. A few of the predictable nuts tried to get their fifteen minutes—anti-abortion groups, militia types, white supremacists, wrath-of-Godders—the usual dummies. But no official statement from a reliable organization or group."

Kehoe was executing all the proper tactics of investigative warfare. "And the news? How are the networks treating this?"

Kehoe went back to another text and spoke as he typed out a response with his thumbs. "They were getting in our way ten minutes after the dust settled. I've got a good PIO on things, but she can't tell them how to behave—they're more concerned with entertainment than delivering facts, and they are going to be a very big pain in the ass on this one. More than usual, I expect." He finished his text and put the phone back down, continuing without warranting so much as a semicolon in his dialogue stream. "And we have the added nightmare of the online digilantes and conspiracy people. Those hammerheads are making a lot of noise on social media, and they're shaping public perception more than I am comfortable with. We hired a marketing firm to help us get in front of their static, but they are doing damage. Last night two Amish kids visiting the city from Pennsylvania were beaten into comas down on Bleecker because they were speaking German and someone thought they were Muslims. They had been tagged on Facebook as suspects because someone took a selfie in Central Park an hour before the bombing and they were in the background. Their photo circulated via social media and the message boards and the masses did what they do—misinterpret the data." Kehoe took another sip of tea. "And there is going to be more of that kind of thing."

Lucas had nothing to add—he was busy absorbing all the moving parts. "You have your hands full, Brett."

"Which is why I'm here; very few people can guess the number of jelly beans in a jar like you can." There was no emotion in his expression when he opened his briefcase and pulled out a brown evidence file that was as thick as a patio stone. He pushed it across the tabletop without opening it. "Just take a look."

Lucas reached out and put his aluminum hand down on the file. He understood what Kehoe was doing but felt powerless to stop him. When he opened the file, there would be photos of the victims—charred, destroyed corpses that would stir up all the things he had tried so hard to put behind him.

Without meaning to, he opened the cover.

And there it was—a photograph of . . . of . . . what, exactly? It had the general dynamics of a human head, but the skin had been burned to a rippled tar and the only contrast against the burned flesh were white teeth that looked like they had been installed after the fact. It could have been a man, a woman, or a Hollywood mock-up of a demon. Lucas closed the cover without looking at any others—he didn't need to download any more nightmares onto his hard drive. "And?" But Kehoe had him.

Kehoe took another sip of tea. "I need someone who can see patterns where there aren't any. Or identify the correct ones when there are too many."

At that, Whitaker said, "But if you want to sit this one out, no one would point any fingers."

Lucas swiveled his head back out to the ocean and took off his sunglasses, taking in the HD image of the Atlantic. A couple of fishermen were walking the surf, life vests festooned with stainless steel tools, rods overhead. They were looking at the helicopter and the house, no doubt wondering if Snoop Dogg had come to the beach to smoke a little jazz cabbage and snack on Pop-Tarts. The world behind them looked like an old master come to life, heavy on the grays and blues, perfectly preserved with no cracks in the over-varnish. For an instant he wondered if the view held any less magic than when he had his old ocular setup.

Kehoe stood up and crossed into his field of vision. He looked like he was lifted out of a *Life* magazine photo shoot at the Kennedy compound, circa 1962; he had that well-heeled vibe that a lot of the people up here wore on their sleeves, earned the old-fashioned way—through an industrious ancestor. Kehoe was the black sheep of his family; he had turned his back on an agricultural empire in order to bring law to the lawless. "I just want you to do a walk-through and get a feel for what happened. Look at it as an exercise in basic physics and chemistry. That's all—*basic physics and chemistry*. Then look at the data. At the victim list. See if there's a *there* there. One day. Maybe two. Then you're back here getting sand in your socks."

Lucas looked up without moving his head and zeroed in on Kehoe with what he knew was his spooky stare, the one where his eyes didn't align. He thought about the photo of the scorched partygoer. And about the other 701 victims. More than most, he knew what an explosion could do. And the ripple effect it had.

"And of course Whitaker here is your chaperone." He paused and glanced at his watch. "So, are you in or did I catch you in one of your cranky moods?"

"Who did you put in charge of the investigation?"

"An agent by the name of Samir Chawla. He's from the Los Angeles office, transferred in four years back."

Lucas turned to Whitaker and was about to ask if this Chawla guy was smart, but she was already ahead of the question. "Very," she said.

Lucas tried not to smile but it was difficult—he had forgotten about that little magic trick of hers, the way she preemptively answered his questions as if she had a Bluetooth connection to his brain. He looked back up at Kehoe. "Brett, you know I don't play well with others. There is no *I* in *team*. I'm not being facetious, but I know my own weaknesses."

"I don't want you for teamwork."

"Then what is it—*precisely*—that you *do* want from me?"

In an uncharacteristic display of camaraderie, Kehoe said, "Just do do that voodoo that you do so well."

6

Lucas had to concentrate not to let his focus shift from Erin to the helicopter down on the beach. He was going—he knew it; she knew it. They just hadn't figured out how to put it into words without yelling. So they stared at each other for a few moments, Erin doing a bad job of hiding her disappointment, he doing a good job of not looking at the chopper.

Not that it was any secret he would be going back every now and then. But Erin was an optimist, and for her, *every now and then* meant at some undefined point in the future—far off and likely never to arrive. Lucas could no longer play the reluctant antihero; he was back because he needed to do this. He and Erin had discussed it ad nauseam, and they had reached one of those untenable middle grounds where one person got everything they wanted while the other pretended to be happy for them.

Lucas led with the good news. "Two days and then I'm coming home."

"And the schmuck?" Erin asked, jabbing a thumb over her

shoulder toward one of the FBI men parked at the corner of the patio, his form exaggerated by the thick bulletproof vest.

"The *schmuck* will be here until I get back, which will be by to-morrow night. Maybe sooner. I can take the train." He knew he'd get one of Kehoe's men to bring him back, but the train sounded like routine, like it was part of the way things always were in Op-timist Town.

"Which means that you'll be free for Friday so we can register Maude at LaGuardia?"

"I should be. Yes."

She eyed him skeptically but remained silent, and he could see that she was struggling not to say anything that would hurt him.

He walked over and pulled her in. They held each other for a moment, and for an instant their world didn't include FBI men on the patio and a helicopter down on the beach.

Laurie came into the kitchen, holding Alisha's hand. At seven, Laurie had been their resident youngest until Alisha showed up. They worried that there might be a little tension over that, but Lau-rie happily switched into big-sister gear. And now, going on the better part of a year, the two girls were inseparable. They were also the quietest of the kids, and would often show up silently when Lucas and Erin were trying to work something out. Like now.

"Are you going away?" Laurie asked.

"Just for a little while."

Laurie looked over to Erin to see if he was telling the truth, which almost broke Lucas's heart. He squatted down—putting all of his weight on his good leg, and steadying himself on the island with his hand—and the two little girls came over. "I have some work in the city."

Laurie reached out and touched his face in a gentle little sign of affection that she had never used before. "Stopping the bad people?" she asked. It was poignant how a seven-year-old could convert the complex to the simple without missing any of the meaning.

Lucas and Erin tried to talk to the kids about what had happened last year. The conversation had morphed into a discussion about Lucas and his work for the FBI. It had been relatively easy with Maude, Hector, and Stevie—or at least they had understood the general idea. But explaining what had happened proved more problematic with Laurie and Alisha. In the end it came down to good people and bad people and which side they were on.

None of the kids—not even Alisha, who was still struggling with the fundamentals of language—had forgotten what had happened last Christmas. The whole family had their heads candled after that one. All of them except Lucas, who had a pretty defined perception of events that he had worked out in his singularly pragmatic way. Lucas and Erin saw the on-again/off-again struggle with what had happened in all the children as they tried to work it out. Except for Maude; she insisted that she was fine—and she most certainly looked and acted as if she were. She had voluntarily endured a single therapy session. In that one hour her therapist came to the conclusion that the girl was already very good at dealing with trauma and would need a return visit only if she felt it necessary. Score one for the good guys.

That the kids had bounced back demonstrated that they were somehow coalescing into a functioning family. Lucas often wondered how he was doing as a father—a line of questioning that would be completely inconceivable in every other aspect of his life. That he occasionally got it right had to mean something.

Alisha kissed him on his ear, a loud sucking sound that depressurized his sinuses, and hollered, "Can we come, too?" straight into his head.

He kissed her back, and her face rolled into a smile. "Sorry, sweetheart, Daddy can't bring you guys to work."

At that, Alisha's face scrunched up and both Laurie and Erin put their hands over their ears. Lucas even turned away in preparation for the little girl's preprogrammed response. She hollered, *"I ain't no guys!"*

All of a sudden the other kids were in the kitchen. Maude had a sketchbook under her arm, her fingers blackened with charcoal, a single gray fingerprint in the middle of her *Eric Clapton Sucks!* T-shirt; Hector held the dead crab shell from the beach, now painted a black that was beginning to dry; Damien came in and sat on one of the barstools with his guitar. They looked like a bunch of pirate kids.

Lucas opted for the direct approach; you don't lie to pirates. "I have to go back to the city."

Maude said, "That terrorist attack?"

Lucas knew she was asking the question to help him break it to the other kids, and he appreciated the lifeline.

"Yes. It's just a couple of days. Today. Maybe tomorrow. Then I'll come back here. Or you guys will come home to the city."

Damien got off the stool and swung his guitar around to his back like a rifle. "Then break a leg. Well, not *your* leg. You only have the one. Well, you have *two*, but only one *real* one. So don't break that. But if you have to break something, break the prosthetic one. Aw, crap, you know what I mean."

"Watch it with the *crap*," Erin said.

"I'll miss you guys," and even before it was all out, Lucas knew it would be true and that he would regret leaving.

Then he heard the sound of the helicopter's turbofan kicking in and turned to see Whitaker at the door. She opened it, tapped her wrist, and said, "Dr. Page, tempus is fugitting."

It was time to step into character.

7

Long Island

The helicopter banked inland and the lazy undulating surface of the ocean gave way to the thoughtless geometry of suburban sprawl. From this height, the neighborhoods looked tired, deforested, and ready for the Big Darkness (as Erin called Old Man Winter). They were low enough that he could see shrubs bundled up in white Styrofoam dunce hats, shrink-wrapped boats, covered pools, and an army of Halloween decorations waiting to fulfill their purpose before retiring to attics, garages, and basements until next year. The suburban quickly gave way to urban, and the backyards became expressways, parking lots, apartments, and shopping malls—the true core of the American psyche.

His arm was on the rest, his aluminum fingers automatically curled around the plush leather, right pinkie against the bulkhead. As the bird adjusted altitude, the pitch of the engine changed, and a low-frequency hum transferred from the body of the aircraft to his aluminum finger, sending a vibration up his arm, into the transhumeral anchor pin. From there it jumped a few bones, drilling into the base of his skull like a dull dental tool. He pulled his shoulder back and his finger came away from the strut, slowing down his molecules.

Kehoe sat across the passenger bay, his back to the pilot, his focus somewhere out the window. Whitaker was beside Kehoe, eyeing Lucas with what could have been amusement, uncertainty, or both, and her outward friendliness belied the meat-eating predator inside. One of Kehoe's men sat beside Lucas—the big one whose name was Hoffner—on standby while his batteries were being charged. He had the disinterested stare that came with the job, and Lucas wondered if the guy knew how to smile. They had left the other one back at the house as a precaution. Lucas wondered if Erin was giving him coffee and muffins or if she had called him a cab—neither action would be out of character.

Lucas's specialty was numbers. Patterns. Discrepancies where there shouldn't be any. None where there should be some. And he could do some nifty tricks when geometry was involved; he was just a guy who saw patterns where no one else seemed to. But this? Other than a single one-thousandth of a second that had altered his life, Lucas had very little to contribute to a conversation about explosions, at least not on the level he was used to performing at. But Kehoe was right about one thing—an event like this could be reduced to basic physics and chemistry, which meant he wouldn't be completely useless.

He wondered what Mrs. Page would say if she were still alive. Would she approve of his work with the bureau, or would she disapprove of him being around these people? He wanted to think that it would be a little of both, but he had never been good at figuring her out—not from the day she had adopted him to the day she died. And even though he never cared about what anyone thought, her opinion would matter, because he owed everything— his education, his house, absolutely everything—to the eccentric old lady who saw promise in a five-year-old orphan.

After a relatively smooth ten minutes crossing Oceanside, then

Queens, and finally the East River, the chopper dropped down and swung over the East Side, heading for ground zero.

The improvised LZ was two blocks up from the Guggenheim—the closest terrain that could accommodate the Ranger's clearance requirements—at the intersection of East 90th and Fifth Avenue. The chopper centered for a second before dropping straight down onto a freshly painted yellow bull's-eye, shock waves from the Nomex blades spinning litter, leaves, and *DANGER!* tape off into the void.

As the bird shuddered down, the wall of faces lining the perimeter were hidden behind SLRs, lighting, and shoulder-mounted video cameras—journalists here to generate the sugar high of fear that was now as much a part of the American diet as hot dogs, apple pie, and gluten-free muffins. Others held up political signs; some advertised their Facebook pages. There were a lot of people wearing QAnon T-shirts and red MAGA caps. There were hundreds of superheroes in the crowd. Lucas wondered why any of them were here, when he would rather be anywhere else on the planet. But you could always count on a significant segment of the American population to find entertainment in horror. All while dressing like children.

Keeping the citizenry behind the fencing was an army of police officers outfitted in Kevlar vests, tactical helmets, black knee and elbow pads, and small assault carbines cradled in harnesses, fingers over trigger guards. They looked like backup singers for Darth Vader, and even the QAnon people weren't hassling them.

The skids scraped the asphalt and Whitaker was on the pavement before the pilot began to cycle down the turbofan.

As Lucas unbuckled his seat belt, Kehoe said, "I appreciate this," before grabbing his briefcase from the luggage rack and stepping out of the helicopter.

Lucas had to concentrate on his leg as he ducked under the rotors—a necessity whenever he had to move his center of gravity out of its usual orbit.

Out here, without the sound of the helicopter's engine to mute the crowd, the noise was distracting. People were chanting, but there were at least three different contingencies, and they were out of sync in both cadence and ideology. Lucas picked up the terms *false flag, fascist overlords,* and *deep state* somewhere in the mix.

The clatter of cameras was offset by the shouted questions and the glare of the video feeds that were going out live, real-timing out-of-context information to various points on the news and social media compasses. America would have their eyes glued to the tube until this one was long over. And everyone in New York City would want to take a selfie as close to the Guggenheim as humanly possible to show that yes, indeed, they were participating in life.

Kehoe ignored the questions from the reporters and the angry screams from the conspiracy theorists and headed for a bureau van parked at Engineers' Gate, inside a pen denoted by more modular steel fencing.

Hoffner opened the passenger door for Kehoe, then squeezed in behind the wheel. Lucas and Whitaker got in the back. Lucas's beach clothes—jeans, a pair of Vans slip-ons, and a black V-neck sweater over a T-shirt—didn't contrast too much against Whitaker's business casual.

She had been silent for the flight in, but now that they were inches apart and free to speak without headsets, she asked, "So, are you any nicer?" She had her full smile out now, and it looked like she had too many incisors.

"Define *nicer.*"

"That's a no."

The van swung around the helicopter and Lucas watched the faces in the crowd, all turned down the street, cameras up, hoping to capture something that might get them a few more dopamine-generating YouTube hits. Welcome to the future—where everyone wants to be vicariously interesting to the feedback loop of the echo chamber.

Fifth was closed from where they had touched down to two blocks south of the museum—a three-block spread. Traffic control and pedestrian management alone would be a logistical nightmare.

Lucas was no stranger to the mechanics of investigations, but the display of resources was on a level he hadn't seen before—half of the law enforcement officers in the city had to be on Fifth. Uniformed cops were stationed every ten feet and posted at every door, all dressed like the storm troopers back at the LZ. Besides acting the part of security, they were monitoring the flow of citizens and no doubt making certain that people who didn't belong here were kept out. Fifth Avenue resembled a major artery in a police state.

Hoffner kept the speed dialed down as he threaded the blacked-out van through emergency vehicles, various official worker bees—mostly of the law enforcement and medical examiner variety—and all manner of equipment. Lucas knew that the reduced pace had to be pushing Whitaker's blood pressure up; she hated being a passenger almost as much as she hated driving slow.

The ocean liner form of the Guggenheim materialized ahead, a building that opened to derision, evolved into a classic, and was now the location of the incomprehensible.

"You ready?" Whitaker asked.

Lucas wondered if she knew how much meaning was packed into those three syllables.

8

Lucas stood on the sidewalk, staring up at the Wes Anderson geometry of Frank Lloyd Wright's most famous public commission. The structure appeared remarkably intact considering the explosion had killed 702 people and incinerated a billion dollars of banana posters and photographs of an America that no longer existed.

The front door and entry windows had been covered with plywood, but the char marks indicated that plenty of bad things had happened inside. An oversize plastic gerbil tube was installed as an air lock, the kind the CDC used out in the field. The sidewalk in front of the main entrance was carpeted with a grid of electric cables, conduit, and *Danger!* tape. There were bits of glass and garbage strewn about, and a bird was near the air lock, picking at what looked to be insulation.

The medical examiner's people were still carting bodies out— two jumpsuited women were negotiating a body-bag-laden gurney through the outdoor entrance to the air lock, to a line of black vans at the curb.

Cops were everywhere.

Whitaker put her hand on Lucas's shoulder; the action startled him. "I'm at the end of the radio in your pocket if you need me."

Lucas double-checked the plastic zipper on his crime-scene overalls, then shook his head. "If I need you, I might as well leave."

"There's that sweetness I missed so much."

"You're welcome."

Lucas took a breath, then pulled the door open and stepped into the plastic tunnel. The thirty feet felt deceptively long, and when he stepped through the second door into the nave proper, he found himself transported to a familiar place—hell.

They had the Quasar task lighting dialed to equatorial solar mode. Lucas always wore sunglasses—even inside—but they did little to mask what he saw.

He stood by the exit for a few moments, waiting for his pulse to slow the disco beat in his chest. The things he saw, heard, and smelled were driving iron nails into his sensory memory, and he wondered if he could do this.

He leveled out his breath, trying to keep the rhythm even and full, a task directly at odds with how the dust mask was designed; every lungful of filtered air he pulled in sounded like a spider clawing through a rusty muffler, and when he let it out, the mask lifted and the air that escaped tickled his eyelashes.

He closed his eyes for a second, but the darkness and the sound of his own wheezing made it feel like he was buried in someone else's coffin, and a low-grade fear started to snap its fingers. He opened his eyes, pulled off the mask, and wiped his face with his good hand. And somehow he felt a little bit better. So he took a step.

Lucas had been in the Guggenheim dozens of times, and even with its unique layout, it was unrecognizable. Every square inch of surface—from the curved outer walls, to the ceilings of the ramp that wound up to the skylight—was charred and black, with drifts of soot built up in the corners and filling every depression. The now-black floor was crisscrossed with footsteps, gurney wheel tracks, and patterns from the emergency crews. There was broken glass everywhere. Thousands of yards of electrical cable snaked along the walls and over the floor, delivering juice to the lighting and other imported systems. Wright had designed the space with very little in the way of texture, and there was not much in the basic design that was flammable, but if it had a burning or melting point, the explosions had erased it from history in any meaningful form. There were no bodies on the main floor of the atrium, but an easy thirty people in anti-contamination suits were busy packing up the dead on the floors above and Lucas could hear the errant squeak of gurney wheels as they ferried bodies to the morgue.

Lucas started to get a feel for what had happened here.

He walked to the middle of the large room, watching where he placed his feet. Somewhere off to his left, one of the hazmat-suited bureau women said, "Hey, mac, put your mask on!"

Lucas knew she was right—the airborne dust particles alone could clog up a vacuum. But he couldn't take the claustrophobia it caused or the way it amplified the sound of his breathing, so he dropped it and it touched down in a cloud of dust like a dead squid settling on the ocean floor.

He pushed the molten fist of adrenaline to the bottom of his stomach and took in a deep breath to smother it. This one tasted of soot and something sour that he didn't want to think about. He looked slowly around, cranking his neck to the end of its tolerances so his good eye could take in the space.

High above, centered under what used to be the skylight but was now just a hole in the ceiling covered with tarps and plywood, was what looked like a pair of spaceship engines. They were roughly the size of pickup trucks, and four men in harnesses were dismantling them, aided by several winches and a ground crew positioned on the top walkway.

The space was getting smaller and his breaths were getting shallower and he knew that the only way to make it all stop was to get out of here. Which would happen only one way. So he closed his eyes, forced himself to forget where he was, and flipped the switch.

Then he opened his eyes.

He no longer saw color.

Or texture.

Or a room where too many people had died.

What he saw was a space reduced to numerical values. It was an automatic process and it hit him in the brain like a fist of ice. Everything morphed into numbers, numerical representations generated by some hidden mental algorithm that only he recognized as having quantitative values.

He spun in place, arms out, taking in the geometry of the Guggenheim with his one good eye. He downloaded the surroundings into a mental model, bringing the museum alive in a way that not even the genius of Wright could have envisioned—a swirling combination of distances, dimensions, elevations, and volume that was permanently embedding itself in his mental hard drive.

It took a few moments to absorb the environment, and when he was done, he closed his eyes, took another deep breath, and shut the process down.

When he opened his eyes, the world looked as it did for everyone else.

Mostly.

When he felt that all the extraneous mental apps had shut down, he took a few heartbeats to orient his thoughts before beginning the trek to the top of the rotunda.

As he moved through the space, the medical examiner's acolytes ignored him as just another bureau drone. He stepped over broken glass and avoided the little mounds of soot that were scattered everywhere. The art that had been on display was gone—obliterated. There were no charred rectangles on the wall and nothing had survived, which said a lot about what had happened here.

There were a few bodies still in situ on the top two ramps, and more suited minions were hard at work bagging them up. From what Lucas saw, they'd be identifying these people through their DNA, their dental records, and the jewelry baked into their blackened meat.

It took him six minutes to make the top floor. He stood there, watching the bureau's technicians working on the charred metal device suspended below the skylight. It didn't take a degree in stage production to recognize it as a machine used to drop confetti at parties or simulate winter on movie sets; in the film industry it was known as a *snowmaker*.

He calculated the volume of the room, the number of bodies, the available oxygen. He calculated force necessary to undo all these things. The amount of fuel needed. The amount of time it would take. The way it would unfurl.

Then he stopped. And waited for it to happen.

It took a few moments to begin, and when it did, he was almost surprised.

Time stopped, its progress frozen between two ticks of the second hand. The mechanics of the universe ceased. Nothing moved—not the people around him, not the air currents, not even his own heart.

And then a wormhole opened.

It.

All.

Started.

Back.

Up.

In.

. . . *reverse* . . .

In.

Up.

Back.

Started.

All.

It.

The FBI people unwound through time. Some brought bodies back in. Some unloaded gurneys, pulling their occupants out of body bags and replacing them on the floor. Others walked off the set in reverse.

It happened quickly. It happened in slow motion. It happened both ways at the same time.

The men and women in the white overalls kept walking backward into the room, the dust in the air sucked back into their footsteps, the tracks from their gurneys erased as they were undone by time moving against its only provable direction.

The bodies piled back up, filling the space with charred corpses that lay knotted on the floor, woven into a portrait out of Dante's Inferno.

And then Lucas was alone with the dead. They lay silent, the smoke in the air rolling back into their bodies.

Then came the fire. It mushroomed into itself.

The explosion.

Glass flew up from the floor, raining up to the skylight in reverse, where it reassembled into 175 individual panes.

The front doors reconstituted.

Warhol's posters and Adams's prints unburned, refilling frames that appeared out of the shock wave.

And the dead rose up, sucked to their feet in reverse, their skin unburning, their ribs uncracking, their lungs uncollapsing.

Their eyeballs unruptured.

Their eardrums uncollapsed.

Their clothing unburned.

Drinks went back into hands. Smiles went back onto faces. Words went back into mouths.

Silver confetti rose from the floor, floating back into the snow machines hanging high above the crowd.

It was *before*.

As it *was*.

They were alive.

Then Lucas blinked and the clock slammed to a stop and the dead froze in mid-celebration, their laughter and hopes and lives suspended in a slice of time too short to measure in any meaningful way.

Lucas watched them for what might have been a fraction of a second or a fraction of forever. He looked up at the snowmakers. Down at the celebrating crowd. At the sophomore soup can posters. At the banners hanging down from the ceiling that declared, *Today's Solutions for Tomorrow's Problems!*

He blinked. And the clock started back up, this time moving in the direction the universe intended. Time shuttered forward. And caught up to itself.

The world detonated and he was back in the now, with the dead and the dust and the gurneys carrying body bags.

Kehoe was right, this was basic physics and chemistry.

Then his stomach clenched and he grabbed a dented garbage can that had rolled against a wall.

And the taste of soot and death and flesh and time filled his throat and he threw up.

9

FBI Command Vehicle

After dropping his coveralls into the bin marked for the incinerator, Lucas washed his face, doing several passes with the strong disinfectant soap, reaming out his nostrils to scrub away the stink of burned human meat. But the particles wouldn't leave, so he was now pouring coffee down his throat to mask the taste. It wasn't working.

The command vehicle had been cleared out and Kehoe had assembled all his top players for the brief. Lucas knew that it was an audition of sorts, and he was fine with that—the bureau teams were a tight-knit community that had built up trust in one another through performance. He was willing to do a little sleight of hand—but that was it. He wasn't here to be part of a team, he was here as an outside opinion, which required an entirely different approach. But they needed to know that he wasn't dead weight.

Other than Kehoe, the commander of the Fire Department, a small man named Ben Morrison, was there. Morrison rarely blinked, looked like he didn't have a sense of humor, and it was easy to see the little guy complex in the way he carried himself.

When he shook Lucas's prosthetic, his shoulder had torqued—a sign that the guy had one of those handshakes designed to break metacarpals. He looked tired and grumpy and like he had passed *I-don't-give-a-fuck* a long time ago. One of the other people in the room was the special agent in charge—Samir Chawla. Chawla was thin, somewhere in his mid to late thirties, and was a handsome man with grooming that rivaled Kehoe's. He sported a very nice dark blue Pee-wee Herman suit offset by a lavender dastar that matched his tie (and, Lucas strongly suspected, his socks). His eyes were dark and accentuated his avian features, the most prominent being a long thin nose that made him appear more visually interesting than he was. It was easy to see that the guy took himself very seriously. But Whitaker said he was smart and Lucas would give him the benefit of the doubt. After Chawla, Lucas was introduced to Calvin-Wade Curtis, a man with a huge grin who was head of the forensic explosives team. Lucas recognized the military background in the way he stood. And he recognized the southern small-town upbringing in his manners. His slow drawl made him come off as more naive than he was. He looked to be about fifteen and had hands that were too big for his arms, but he was to the point when asked a question. Whitaker was also there. She had rolled up her sleeves and was leaning against one of the desks, arms crossed, the big chrome automatic in the pressure holster on her belt at odds with the neutral fabrics she wore. As usual, Lucas couldn't help feeling like she was watching out for him.

"So?" It was Morrison who opened the dialogue. The tone of his question said that he wasn't pleased at being second-guessed by a nobody. But he came across as smart and focused, even if the handshake hinted at a little insecurity, and Lucas decided to be polite.

Lucas took in another mouthful of dark roast and said, "The cause of the explosion is the easy one."

Morrison didn't seem to like that. "Easy? It took my people—"

Kehoe cut him off. "I would like to hear what *Dr. Page* has to say, Ben."

Lucas continued. "This was a thermobaric explosion."

Morrison's mouth popped open.

Lucas put his coffee down and said, "It's basic physics and chemistry," while nodding over at Kehoe. But his mind's eye was back in the rotunda, cycling through the layout he had downloaded. "The structure is relatively intact, seven hundred and two dead people and a few punched-in walls notwithstanding. Those posters were wiped off the wall by a significant shock wave—the same shock wave that blew out all the fenestration. The snowmaker delivered the airborne fuel—a dust would be too obvious, so confetti or foil is a good guess. Aluminum foil makes the most sense, since it can be bonded with anything you want. I'd go with magnesium since it would accelerate the burn rate. Also, the color would go with the Warhol theme—his workshop, the Factory, was painted silver, and silver is closely associated with his brand. Once the air was filled with the confetti, it was ignited. My guess is that the snowmaker itself was modified to create some sort of spark or flame. Grain explosions are often set off by an electrostatic discharge created by a conveyor belt—an accidental Van de Graaff generator. Either an electrostatic discharge or an actual spark was generated. Probably by moving parts rather than electronics—which would have made it easy to get past in-house security. The spark ignited the confetti, the burn was accelerated by the magnesium, and chemistry and physics took care of the rest. The initial shock wave crushed soft tissue followed by a conflagration that pressure-cooked what was left."

Morrison didn't look like a man used to being surprised. "It took my guys *five hours* to figure that out."

"Then you need more guys." Lucas picked up his coffee and took another sip. "Or *smarter* ones."

Kehoe gave Morrison an *I-told-you-so* expression.

Chawla chimed in with "That's a neat trick, but can you give us any other added value?"

Kehoe stepped into the conversation by handing Lucas a sheaf of pages held together with an oversize paper clip. "Take a look at these."

It was a victim list, a printout of a spreadsheet loaded with various details categorized into columns. Lucas knew what Kehoe was doing, and he resented the performing seal act, but he did it anyway.

He scanned the first page. Then the second. There were forty-five lines per page, each one dedicated to a victim. They were arranged alphabetically, and the columns contained basic grouping criteria such as sex, age, occupation, and address.

Lucas quickly flipped through all seventeen pages, put them down on the desktop beside Chawla, and said, "Okay."

Chawla looked puzzled. "Okay, what?"

Lucas looked back at Kehoe, who nodded, so he began. "Seven hundred and two victims. Three hundred and twenty-four male, three hundred and seventy-eight female, translating to 46.1538 percent and 53.8461 percent, respectively. The largest age demographic was the forty-to-fifty group, represented by two hundred and eight individuals, one hundred and seventeen male, ninety-one female, which, interestingly, is the only segment where males overrepresent females, except for those who were forty-one, of which there were more women. Out of seven hundred and two victims, five hundred and eighteen are residents of Manhattan, followed in descending order by Connecticut, California, Paraguay—that's a country, by the way, not a state," he said pointedly to Chawla. "Then Maryland, New Jersey, Texas, Norway, Germany, England, Canada, and New Mexico."

Everyone was staring, even Whitaker.

Kehoe came in with "How many of the victims had the number seven in their street addresses?"

"One hundred and sixty-one. Thirty-six had seven as a first digit; forty-one as a second digit, which was the largest group percentage-wise; three had it as the fifth digit in their street address, which was the smallest group—although two of those had five digits in their street address, of which there were only nine in all of the victims, so statistically that's the unicorn when it comes to sevens. The most common digit in all seven hundred and two victims was two, of which there were nine hundred and eight, the second being the digit one, of which there were eight hundred and four."

Kehoe would never smile at work, but there was no missing the approval in his eyes. "How many people aged fifty-five?"

"Thirty-eight yesterday. Three of those had birthdays today and two have birthdays tomorrow, making them fifty-six. And three fifty-four-year-olds have birthdays either today or tomorrow, which would bump them into that category."

Chawla shook his head. "Holy shit."

"I can do this all day," Lucas offered, before taking another sip of the now-cold coffee and pushing himself out of the chair. "But I'm not going to. So if you'll excuse me, I have somewhere else I'd rather be."

Lucas stepped out of the controlled microclimate of the command vehicle into the bright fall sunshine, paying special attention to the folding steps that had been set up. Whitaker came out behind him and closed the door, blocking out the conversation between Kehoe, Chawla, and Morrison.

The crowd two blocks up was chanting again, the words *False flag! False flag! False flag!* on loop and he wondered if certain people misunderstood the Pledge of Allegiance to include the line *one nation undereducated.*

He closed his eyes and concentrated on his breathing, trying to ignore the crowd generating a low-frequency hum that rose above the white noise of the city. It wasn't easy to balance the beautiful day against the Gustave Doré scene inside the museum or the imbeciles up the street. He wondered if he was going to throw up again.

Whitaker came up behind him, and even though he wasn't looking at her, he could tell she was smiling when she said, "You know, I've missed you."

10

26 Federal Plaza

Lucas did a quick head count and there were 307 agents in the brief-ing room—which had to be some kind of a record. The auditorium was not dissimilar to the one he used at Columbia, only it was on a smaller scale with lower ceilings. And more guns. There was a podium and a desk at the front, offset by state-of-the-art displays that at this juncture in time were blank—an anomaly for an investi-gation of this magnitude. Evidently Kehoe wanted all eyes on him.

Kehoe was setting the stage for the investigation, but all future briefings—twice a day according to protocol—would be handled by the special agent in charge, Samir Chawla, who stood off to one side. The bureau was a massive bureaucracy, and it functioned on a hierarchal mechanism that was as ingrained as its collegial preppy image. Everyone had a position. And every position had a func-tion. And every function had a purpose. All the way down to the guy who washed the official vehicles in the garage.

Kehoe was in perfect form, the appropriate mix of gravitas and authority. His upbringing was diametrically opposed to the career he had pursued—he had come from a wealthy West Coast family that was prominent not only in agriculture and industry but in politics. He had been a concert pianist by the time he was fifteen, followed by a classical education at Yale that he had walked away from to become a lawman. Lucas understood what money like that could do to a person—he had been raised around it—and very few people could break away from the expectations to take the Robert Frost road. Stories like Kehoe's illustrated that there was something addictive about this business; all you had to do was ask all the agents who had lost their marriages and friendships and health and youth to the questions they couldn't turn off when they went home.

But even a man like Kehoe couldn't fight the clock, and the past twenty hours had taken some of the polish off his chrome. He was in the process of telling everyone to play nice with one another—and he emphasized that this included other agencies: federal, state, and municipal. "I expect a lot of jurisdictional cross-chatter, but I don't want snakes and ladders to hobble our efforts—if things get tied up, I want you to consult Legal to work them out. This is going to chew up all the media cycles for the next while and we can't make any mistakes."

Kehoe stopped the chatter with a raised hand. "The specific cause of the explosion has been determined to be a thermobaric bomb. You might remember the first publicly acknowledged operational use of the MOAB—which is the military designation for Massive Ordnance Air Blast, dubbed the 'Mother of All Bombs' in the media—by our military forces in Afghanistan on April 13, 2017. The device used in the Guggenheim explosion was a scaled-down and custom-made version of the MOAB." Delivery was getting better with each syllable that rolled out of his mouth—exhaustion giving way to instinct.

"A thermobaric explosion is relatively simple to achieve, and functions under the same general mechanics as a grain silo explosion—with a little massaging to increase damage." Kehoe took a sip of tea from his mug. "In this particular instance, the flammable particles were delivered as aluminum confetti dropped from a snowmaker—a device used in movies and television to create weather for the camera." With that verbal prompt, the screens went live with an HD image of the confetti machine suspended below the blown-out skylight. The four massive steel drums now looked like what they were—bombs.

"TEDAC is taking the delivery system apart one bolt at a time, and so far they've confirmed that the chemical composition of the confetti used as the combustible was a thin slice of aluminum backed with a laundry list of other components, mostly tweaked magnesium molecules that accelerated the burn rate, magnifying the pressure wave of the explosion. The banners that hung from the ceiling were also of the same manufacture. The drum gears were modified to create a static charge after a certain number of rotations—about seventy turns—when most of the foil was dispersed." Kehoe put his tea down. "Besides the massive loss of life, somewhere around a billion dollars' worth of art was destroyed."

Seven hundred and two dead people: a ripple of murmurs—lost dollar signs: actual gasps.

Kehoe lifted an eyebrow and all chatter stopped. "Many of these pieces were on loan from private individuals, but there were also corporate loans on the roster. The loss of these works means we can't discount insurance fraud or some complicated confidence scam as a component."

Kehoe put his hands on either side of the podium and leaned forward. A picture of the Guggenheim appeared on the monitors around the room. "The company that was hosting the gala—Horizon Dynamics—is a privately owned corporation that was going public this morning; the IPO was expected to trade at somewhere around half a billion dollars, and the gala was a pre-sale celebration. Horizon Dynamics specialized in environmental risk assessment and the rejuvenation of ecosystems damaged by industry, specifically former petroleum extraction and bauxite mining sites. They lost all of their top people and most of their mid-level management; they will not be bouncing back from this. Because we are looking at a crime that has ramifications in the billions of dollars, we will be closely partnering our efforts with the SEC, the IRS, the U.S. Postal Inspection Service, the CFTC, and the Treasury Department's Financial Crimes Enforcement Network, since they are used to looking at crimes from a dollars-and-cents perspective. So far, all concerned haven't come up with any sort of a lead.

"So until we have evidence to the contrary, we are classifying this as an act of terrorism—with the specific motivating ideology still unknown. Our Joint Terrorism Task Force will be coordinating with the usual outside agencies, and we've reached out to every foreign intelligence agency on the planet through the DOJ and the DHS. So far we're looking for a crime that was orchestrated by people who don't seem to exist, which means we don't know if they are foreign or domestic. The complicated nature of the attack suggests that we are looking for several individuals or a group.

"All the early indicators are that the attack was too complicated and well executed to have been carried out by Islamic fundamentalists; most of the known groups are too unsophisticated to have done this. We're not writing them off, but this looks more like the kind of thing a foreign-state-funded actor would do. Another possibility that has been brought to my attention is that we might be looking at a group of eco-fascists—check the updates." With that he turned to Lucas and eyed him for a moment. "When looking at evidence, a good way to put it is to not only look for the things that are there, but for the things that *aren't*.

"We have teams interviewing everyone from the event planner to museum employees to delivery personnel. We're looking at the confetti supplier, the company that built the snowmaker, and the transport people that delivered it. Our agents are talking to absolutely everyone and anyone in the supply chain for both the gala and the Guggenheim."

Kehoe nodded and the displays cycled up photos of the scene outside the police tape at the Guggenheim—people holding up conspiracy signs and QAnon placards. There were plenty of crazed expressions and spelling mistakes. "These people are going to be the biggest obstacle you face out there—we're combing social media and message boards, chat rooms and comments sections, and they are pumping out disinformation, misinformation, and lies at a rate we can't keep up with.

"We've already had two tourists beaten unconscious after they were incorrectly identified as suspects by online digilantes. Unfortunately, those people are the gift that keeps on giving, and we can expect more problems because of them. You all know how social media clogs up the gears of a good investigation, and with this many victims and so much global curiosity, be prepared for the worst from people. Expect innocent people to be attacked and expect mob thinking. The conspiracy fools at the crime scene are just the beginning—I fully expect their numbers to grow into a sizable problem in both the virtual as well as the actual world. Again, if you're not sure about something—ask." He stepped away from the podium and Lucas knew this was where he would try to make everyone feel like a big family. Kehoe stopped and nodded at Lucas. "Which brings me to Dr. Page, who is standing at the back with our own Special Agent Whitaker."

Lucas didn't bother waving. He just nodded a single time and kept his focus on Kehoe, who continued.

"I am sure those of you who were here last winter during the New York sniper case remember Dr. Page. He is a mathematician— an astrophysicist, actually—and is here as an independent consultant. His methods are not always obvious, and I don't want anyone giving him any grief if he asks for something." He turned back to his people, clapped his hands once, and was back in command mode. "Please keep your phones and computers synced and read all updates. If you don't know something or you need something, ask. From here on out, all briefings will be delivered by the special agent in charge—you all know Samir Chawla." He nodded over at Chawla, then turned off the mic, picked up his mug of tea, and stepped away from the podium.

11

CNN Offices at the Time Warner Center, Columbus Circle

Melanie McGillivray was rounding out her fifth month as an intern in the communications department for CNN. She had a BA in computer science, with an emphasis on systems analysis, and hoped to one day run the IT department for either a Fortune 500 company or one of the lifestyle dot-coms out west. But until she had the experience, knowledge, and connections necessary to climb the ever-greased corporate ladder, her job would lack glamour, living wages, and—hardest of all—self-esteem.

Today, like every day for the past five weeks, she was relegated to one of the lesser spirals of hell—one where she and four other interns managed the insane volume of email on the network server. In any other company, she would spend her hours quarantining viruses picked up on porn sites (she thought that contracting a virtual virus from virtual genitals was a splendid example of the irony her generation was so fond of); fixing pop-up blockers; installing anti-virus patches; updating software; and generally keeping human error to a manageable scale.

But McGillivray didn't work in a typical office. They didn't sell real estate, manufacture widgets, or produce mountains of paper under the guise of contract negotiation. What they did was trade in the most valuable commodity in the realm of human commerce— information. And that core function invariably produced an inordinate amount of correspondence. Which in turn generated all kinds of digital security nightmares.

The bombing at the Guggenheim yesterday had everyone working overtime, the mentally unwell in particular, which meant that the network was inundated with thousands of "tips"—a euphemism for *crazy bullshit*. And this was on top of the usual truckload of troll droppings that they had to wade through every day. The reactor was running at 110 percent capacity.

In the information trade, both journalists and sources alike were continually plagued by hackers, blackmailers, and all manner of social misfits—people intent on sowing discord simply because they could. The end result of this malfeasance was that both the transfer and management of information got exponentially more difficult with each day. Since journalists were a justifiably paranoid group, this resulted in all kinds of complicated password-driven booby traps and encryption software that kept their information locked away. Often from themselves.

Right now, Chad Worthington was standing over her shoulder, screaming about the text he had received asking him about an email he hadn't. The text was from an unknown source, delivered to his tip box. It referenced an email that had been sent to him yesterday and advised him to take it seriously.

"This isn't rocket science, for chrissake!" he said, his volume creeping up. "It's a goddamned email and it's supposed to be there." Chad was a stereotype, a designation he took great pride in fostering, and by some miracle was one of the few straight men occupying an anchor chair who hadn't been #metooed into an early retirement with a golden parachute. He was a lousy journalist, but a decent talking head, a distinction he understood with

uncharacteristic insight. Chad didn't usually take himself too seriously, but today he was making an exception.

McGillivray tried to ignore him as she tapped, typed, clicked,
highlighted, dragged, and expanded. It took almost four minutes,
but she found it. The address was correct, but it looked like an ad
for fertilizer—which was why the spam filter had taken it out. "Is
this it?" she asked.

Worthington leaned over her shoulder and squinted. He smelled
of hair spray and a hint of cologne with some coffee thrown in.
"How am I supposed to know?" He held up his phone. "All I have
is this text telling me to look at it. Why would someone go through
the trouble of texting my secure message box to tell me to look at
a brochure?"

McGillivray tried not to roll her eyes. "Maybe it's not an ad.
Maybe it just *looks* like an ad." She scanned the email with anti-
virus software, and when it was given a clean bill of health by the
digital doctors, she opened it up.

It wasn't an advertisement.

It was a letter.

They both began to read and she stopped half a paragraph in.
"Oh my god," she said.

Worthington was still reading, but he was used to people speaking while he sifted information—it was one of the skills that twenty
years in front of a camera with a producer piping in through an
earpiece had made second nature—and he asked, "Is this real?"

"It was delivered yesterday afternoon at . . ."—McGillivray
checked the time stamp in the metadata—"6:32 and thirty seconds."

"That's thirty seconds before the bombing." Worthington
didn't bother trying to hide the excitement in his voice when he
said, "Which means it's real."

12

26 Federal Plaza

Lucas and Whitaker were in Kehoe's office with Chawla and Special Agent Kathryn Brady. Brady was one of the top people with the Joint Terrorism Task Force, and her specialty was ideologically motivated groupthink. She was part behavioral psychologist, part necromancer, and Lucas wondered if she and Whitaker got along, because he could sense a quiet tension between them. Brady was tall, with a wide face and dark eyes that might have been too large for her face. She exuded confidence and smarts and looked like she had a finely tuned bullshit meter. But all of that was just first-impression takeaways, and Lucas decided that he would reserve judgment—almost anyone could come across as competent for a few minutes.

Chawla's main objective during the brief had been to assign personnel to the appropriate departments. He was engaging and his presentation bolstered Whitaker's assessment, but he let a little vanity poke through the veneer of command and Lucas wondered if he was capable of processing constructive criticism. An investigation of this magnitude was bound to bounce around in the ditch once in a while, and the person leading the troops needed to be able to adapt on the fly.

Chawla was trying to stare Lucas down, which was a losing battle. "And why do you disagree, Dr. Page?"

"I'm not disagreeing. This has all the earmarks of a terrorist attack. But I think you're connecting some dots that might not even be there."

Chawla looked rankled. "Such as?"

Lucas shrugged. "Like Kehoe said out there, this could be insurance fraud or art theft. Stock manipulation. A rival company clearing the playing field. A message to someone. Like the man once said, my crystal ball ain't so crystal clear, but I think it's too early to become wedded to a single line of approach."

It was Brady who said, "Could you be a little clearer?"

He turned to her. "We have seven hundred and two victims, which provides the mass casualty factor. But these weren't a bunch of average folks out at the mall on a Friday night—many of these people were wealthy investors attending a party for a unique company. There was a billion dollars of artwork on the premises. And the explosion had a secondary purpose other than to take lives—it was sadistic. Those people were *supposed* to suffer."

Brady nodded as she took that in. "And you don't think *that* qualifies as terrorism?"

Lucas didn't like being baited like a first-year philosophy student. "Of course it *qualifies* as terrorism. But it could be a number of other things."

Chawla pulled his cuffs so the prerequisite quarter inch was peeking out from his jacket sleeves. "If it's insurance fraud, there would have to be several dozen people in on it to make it worthwhile."

Lucas stared at him over the frames of his sunglasses. "How do you figure?"

"The most valuable piece in there was worth about thirty million bucks. No one would kill seven hundred people for thirty million bucks."

"A woman was killed on the Lower East Side last week for three dollars. Multiply that by seven hundred and two and that room of people is worth precisely two thousand, one hundred, and six dollars to the right criminal. There are people who would cook an entire city for thirty million dollars."

"So you think it's insurance fraud?"

Lucas was getting frustrated, but he made an effort not to let the steam seep through his seams. "What I said was that even though a mass casualty factor lends itself to a terrorism narrative, there are other possibilities."

Chawla smiled at him when he said, "Dr. Page, this is not some pop science book people buy at the airport, this is the real world. With real consequences."

It was obvious by the way he had formulated the dig that he had read some of the less inspired reviews of Lucas's latest book. "Right now the only certainties are that we have no idea who did this or what their motive was. And anyone who claims different is setting themselves up for failure."

Kehoe pushed off the edge of his desk. "Page, Chawla, this isn't getting us anywhere."

Lucas shrugged. "I answer questions when asked."

Chawla leaned forward. "I don't think—"

"I know. Which is why *I'm* here." Lucas took a sip of his coffee and caught a glimpse of Whitaker smiling over Chawla's shoulder. "Sorry, Brett. I'll take a look at the victims list to see if I can come up with anything meaningful. See if there's any signal through the noise."

Kehoe nodded as if that settled the argument. "Coordinate everything through Special Agent in Charge Chawla here. And

Chawla?" There was no missing the command in the voice—this wasn't an ask. "Extend every courtesy to Dr. Page."

Chawla's expression was still frozen between indignation and shock when someone knocked at the door and came in without being invited. It was Kehoe's monstrous assistant, Otto Hoffner. He held up his phone. "CNN just received a letter from the bomber."

13

News of the letter rippled out across the war room like a shock wave, dislodging asses from chairs and generating a murmur that rolled into a chorus of curiosity. Chawla steamrolled through the space with Lucas, Brady, Whitaker, and Hoffner in tow—straight for one of the quarantined conference rooms, this one with opaque glass walls.

Chawla pushed the door open and two men were already at work. He introduced the first as Special Agent Stanley Tranter. Tranter was from the Applied Linguistics department and would have looked at home on any golf course—or ride-on lawn mower— in the country. The second man was from Software Forensics, and his name was Olly Porchnoy. Porchnoy clocked in at somewhere between twelve and thirty years of age and wore a very cheap suit that probably came with the imitation Naugahyde shoes and lavender shirt he wore. The shirt was wrinkled but tucked in, and he smelled of acne cream.

Porchnoy didn't bother trying to shake hands; he just went straight to work. "Okay," he said, and hammered away on one of a dozen keyboards laid out in a line on the imitation wood surface of the conference table. "This was delivered to Chad Worthington's business email at CNN yesterday at thirty seconds after 6:32 P.M. It was disguised as spam, so the network software jettisoned it. After he received a DM on his phone today telling him that he had missed an important email, he went to their in-house people, who found it. They opened it and called us. We're taking it apart downstairs right now, but it's been bounced around a remailer and delivered via a Tor connection. The metadata doesn't have any value and I think it's unlikely that we'll find anything useful hidden in the code." The kid stopped and went to work on another of the keyboards without saying anything. Lucas recognized the body language of someone more comfortable with numbers than people.

Hoffner tapped the tablet in his hand. "The bomber told CNN that if they don't publish his letter, he's going to kill a bunch of children on television. He gave them until the three o'clock slot to air it and put it up on their website."

Lucas checked his Submariner—that gave them a little more than twenty minutes before the world knew as much as they did.

Brady's team was over at the Time Warner Center, texting her updates as they did their part of the investigation. She tapped the screen on her iPhone—which was in some sort of a waterproof case that gave it the general size of a car battery. "Their producer is going out with it. Their legal department has drafted a letter citing their efforts to prevent another attack."

Lucas couldn't see the logic in the demand. "Why the threat? Those people don't need any incentive to go public with something like this."

Tranter directed everyone's focus to the first page of the letter. "I think you'll understand once you read this." And he began to read the letter aloud.

It was two simple paragraphs. There was no salutation. It contained no hyperbole and stuck with clear, concise statements of intent. There was no flair to the language, no passion. But there was no missing the threat it promised.

They wanted a revolution. They wanted the world to join them. In rejecting technology. In reclaiming its humanity. In resetting the clock of history.

And if not, they were going to send the whole shithouse up in flames.

With that, something in Lucas's face must have changed, because Whitaker tapped him on the arm and whispered, "What are you smiling at?"

Tranter had stopped reading and Chawla was doing that irritated thing with his face again. Brady just stood there, looking confused. Hoffner didn't bother to look up from his tablet.

Lucas shrugged. "That letter wasn't written by our bomber."

It was Chawla who said, "How do you know?"

"Because that letter wasn't written by a human being; it was written by a machine."

14

Whitaker jumped into the elevator as the doors closed. "You need to chill."

"I'm tired of people of getting in my way."

"Well, tough shit, and get used to it, because that's the way it's set up. People get in your way, they get in my way, they get in their own way. You're too smart to fight windmills. And I'm not dumb enough to."

Lucas rammed a green aluminum knuckle into the console, and the car began its descent to the garage.

Whitaker adjusted her jacket. "What was that upstairs?"

The elevator dropped through the core of the building, the numbers counting down like the timer on a . . . bomb. "That letter wasn't written by the people responsible—it was written by an algorithm."

"Are you su—" She stopped and reformulated the question. "How do you know?"

Lucas had taught a course titled "Simulation Theory and the Cosmos" for four years now, and the central theorem was that human life was an offshoot of a complicated computer code that dictated the mechanics of the universe. And as much as he liked to deride the quality of the minds the university fed through his classroom, plenty of clever kids had challenged his self-image. He was in astrophysics, but crossover meant that a lot of the computer science students ended up in his auditorium—and some of the programmers were crafty. And like Aziz Shamim had famously tweeted, the acolytes of tech culture operated on one single frequency in response to one direct quesiton: *What is my mother no longer doing for me?* And for some of them, the answer was obvious: *homework.* So every semester he had papers handed in that had been produced by an algorithm. The first few registered as odd, but he couldn't pinpoint what—exactly—was wrong with them. But letters are like numbers and when he finally sat down and took one apart, he figured out what was scraping his bark—the work had been produced by a natural-language generator. "Necessity isn't the mother of invention: laziness is. I've read a lot of term papers written by text compactors, and I've written two articles on the topic. It's pure math. Humans think a certain way."

"And so do computers?"

"Computers don't think, they imitate thought. We no longer have to write a set of rules for machines to follow, where the inherent flaw is that we are not very good at anticipating every contingency. AI perfects itself through trial and error—deep learning—which uses examples, not rules. And a machine can become very proficient at cataloguing examples. Even better than humans—just look at chess or Go or chopping carrots. But we offset that by processing new information in a very different way. Give a carrot chopping machine an onion, or give a chess computer a deck of cards, and they're fucked. They can't adapt. They can't *think.* Look at what happened in March 2018—an Uber self-driving car killed a pedestrian. It saw the woman on the road and registered her presence, but all the examples of pedestrians it had ever been exposed to were at crosswalks, so it ignored her because it didn't understand that she could be there. It couldn't adapt to a task outside of its experience—even though it won't make the same mistake twice.

"But language has a finite number of components and contingencies; there are plenty of examples. *And that letter was written by a machine.* It's content derived from data and produced by an algorithm. A machine can't differentiate the meaningful from the meaningless, and it can't generate any sort of a literary style or voice. It can only perform toward a goal it has been given, even if it is using examples. And I guarantee that the NLG that wrote that letter wasn't particularly sophisticated."

The elevator made it all the way to the garage level without a stop, and the doors opened to three men with carbines at the ready, fingers over trigger guards. Lucas couldn't figure out why they were here—no one was getting this far into the building. And no one would try to come through the garage—too many security points before this particular door. But the precaution said a lot about the siege mentality that had crept into the system—*us versus them* was now a fulltime mindset.

Lucas blocked the sensor for Whitaker, then followed her out into the brightly lit corridor that led to the garage. "So," she said, "how come Tranter couldn't see that?"

"He will. We'll get a call in half an hour after he runs it through whatever software he's used to using and he'll give me an 80 percent chance of being correct, which gives Chawla an 80 percent chance of being wrong. But it will be too late, because CNN is going to run with the story, and the message will be out there. And we both know that there is no shortage of Pizzagate simpletons to buy into the narrative."

"So what *is* going on?"

That was the central question to everything at this point. "Just look at Ted Kaczynski?"

"The Unabomber?"

"No, Ted Kaczynski the children's author."

Whitaker gave him the stink eye as she swiped them through the sally port to the garage. "I only remember the broad strokes from one of my courses at Quantico. He was a . . . holy shit—he was a mathematician, right? He thought that man's relationship with technology was leading society down a path that would eventually destroy mankind. So he tried to start a revolution by sending out letter bombs to various people—computer store owners, university professors—that kind of thing. Tried to blow up an airliner, but the trigger failed and the plane landed. From the late seventies to the mid-nineties he killed three people and wounded two dozen."

Lucas followed Whitaker through the garage. He realized he could still taste soot and something else. "That letter upstairs is a boiled-down version of the Unabomber's manifesto—point for point. There is nothing original in it—instead of naming the system 'industrial society,' the algo called it 'technological civilization,' but that's hardly what I would call originality. It took his basic grievances—leaving out his political bias—and put them in a package that your average attention-deficit riddled citizen could pay attention to long enough to grok. Which is the beauty of automatic text summarization tools—they can parse large quantities of data. And therein lies the joke—a technophobe would never use an algorithm to present that particular argument."

"So they're just fucking with us? They're not really worried about Skynet self-actualizing?"

"Whoever is running this show is smart—you don't cobble together a thermobaric explosion like this without a bucketload of brains—so there's going to be a purpose in everything they do. Maybe it's misdirection. Maybe it's something else." He looked over at her. "And just what, exactly, is Skynet?"

"Don't you take the kids to the movies?"

"All the time; last week we watched *The Sorrow and the Pity*."

"I pictured you more of a *Smokey and the Bandit* kind of guy."

"That was the week before."

Which got a laugh out of Whitaker. "How is the TV brood, by the way? In all this commotion I forgot to ask."

"They're good. Erin is opening a new practice with one of her colleagues, which she's pretty excited about. Maude is a burgeoning artist; Damien is working on being the next Hendrix; Hector doesn't seem to give a shit about anything, so I picture him becoming a barista or maybe a novelist; Laurie and Alisha are the unknowns—they're too young for me to see any trajectory."

"Sounds like things are good in Pageland."

"I guess they are." And he realized that this was small talk and that he needed to contribute. So he did. "And you? How are things? Shoot anyone lately?"

Another laugh. "No. But in my effort to be more domestic I got a cactus. It's plastic, but no one seems to notice."

A Latin dude in cargo pants and a Yankees cap had three Navigators lined up near the washing station. He was singing as he filled a bucket with spray from one of the hoses, and Lucas envied the guy his job for a second.

Whitaker waved over at the man. "Hey, Augustine! Don't you ever stop?"

Augustine waved back and said, "Too much to do!" in heavily accented English.

Lucas followed Whitaker up the main lane, both sides lined with the ubiquitous black SUVs favored by the bureau.

"Why was Chawla talking trash about your book up there?"

"Chawla doesn't read books, at least not without pictures. He probably just Googled it."

"Well, what's your book about?"

The park lights on one of the Navigators flashed as they got close, and Lucas looped around to the passenger side. "It's an examination of Schrödinger's thought experiment on the cat."

"I thought you were more of a dog person."

The doors clicked open and Lucas climbed in. "And Erin wonders why I don't leave the house more."

15

Whitaker's phone rang, and she answered by hitting a button on the steering wheel. "Whitaker here."

Chawla's voice came on in stereo. "Whitaker, you still with Page?"

Lucas said, "I'm here," trying not to sound too irritated.

"Okay, look, you two need to stay in the loop. They're going live with that letter in five minutes, and I wanted you to know what's happening in case you're asked by anyone that matters. We've come up with a name for the bomber, and we'll be using it during briefings and all press releases. It will also be the internal designation."

Whitaker thrummed her fingers on the steering wheel as they rolled up to a stoplight on Broadway two blocks south of Federal Plaza. "Shoot."

"Like we've done in the past, we'll be using the first letters of the target to build the acronym."

Lucas immediately factored the statement out in his head; the Unabomber handle had been manufactured utilizing University and Airplane. He didn't want to hear what Chawla was going to say next, but he couldn't stop the man from speaking.

Chawla continued with "So we're going with the Guggabomber."

Lucas laughed out loud. "You're fucking kidding, right?"

Whitaker hit the mute button on the steering wheel. "Page, be nice. You don't need this job, but I do. Be constructive." She had the stink eye dialed up again.

Lucas shrugged and she unmuted the call.

Lucas leaned into the microphone. "Look, Chawla, why don't you use something that doesn't sound so heavy on the tongue. Maybe something a little less specific, but still in the realm of what's going on."

"Like what?"

Lucas literally threw his hands in the air. "Jesus, I don't know. But not the Guggabomber—please. We'll sound like idiots. Go with—" He compacted everything he had learned about their guy in the past few days into a single stream of code. "Call him the Machine Bomber."

"*The Machine Bomber?*"

"It's just an example. And not a particularly good one. But it's better than the Guggabomber. It fits in with the narrative of that bullshit letter; he claims that he wants to blow up machines. And when it turns out that I was right, and you find out that the letter *was* written by the machine, it will fit the story going forward." Lucas looked over at Whitaker and shrugged—he thought he was handling things diplomatically. "Either way, it's a win-win."

Whitaker was shaking her head fatalistically. She didn't look happy.

Chawla said, "*The Machine Bomber,*" trying it out for size. "The Machine Bomber," he repeated. "I think we'll stick with the Guggabomber." And he hung up.

Lucas looked over at Whitaker, who was still shaking her head. "What?" he asked. "I gave it a shot."

Whitaker held up her hand. "I'm not talking to you except to ask for directions. And where, exactly, are you taking us?"

Lucas pointed straight down Broadway. "Wall Street."

"Why Wall Street?"

"When there's blood in the water, the best place to start is with the sharks."

16

CNN Breaking News

"Good afternoon, I'm Chad Worthington, and this is a CNN exclusive.

"A few moments ago, CNN received a letter from the people responsible for the bombing of the Solomon R. Guggenheim Museum in Manhattan last night. At this point we are unable to disclose how we have confirmed that this letter was written by the actual perpetrators of the terrorist attack, but the claim has been corroborated by the public information officer of the Joint Terrorism Task Force operated by the Federal Bureau of Investigation.

"Please be advised, that the letter has graphic content, and has not been edited for content in any way."

The system is broken, and must be corrected if humankind is to survive. By humankind, we mean a humancentric society, where the value of social relationships should outweigh man's relationship with technology. Technological civilization is an oxymoron and cannot be allowed to continue. We will not allow it to continue. In every war, there must be a first shot. In thirty seconds, an example will be made of a technocentric corporation at the Solomon R. Guggenheim Museum. This corporation states its goal as the betterment of mankind, but it does this with very little humanity and too much technology.

Human history is shaped by large, general trends, not small specific actions. And the destruction of technological civilization is imperative if human society is to survive. There are some positive facets of technological civilization, but they are so completely integrated with the negative aspects that both must be destroyed in order to build a human society worth living in. The citizens must accept that technological civilization cannot be reformed because the system is too pervasive. It must be torn down so that it can be rebuilt correctly. We are going to tear it down by any means possible. The bombing tonight is the beginning of the revolution. All citizens must join us. Burn the technological system down. Reject the machines and embrace our humanity. The only goal is to destroy. And when the destruction is complete, the revolution will be complete. There is no stopping us. We will burn it all down.

"The special agent in charge of the investigation—Samir Chawla—has labeled the author of the letter the Machine Bomber, and the FBI will be using the title for all future news conferences, official statements, and internal designation.

"And that is where we are this hour. After the break, I will be joined by Dr. Melanie Rimbaud, former vice director of the Anti-Terrorism Consortium, a private think tank that aids governments around the world in the fight against political and ideological extremism. Dr. Rimbaud currently teaches diplomatic ethics at Harvard and has a new book out titled *Good Ideas, Bad Ideas: How to Know the Difference in a Complicated and Often Chaotic World.*"

17

26 Federal Plaza

Kehoe was at his desk, trying to put the letter into some sort of perspective. It lacked passion and was light on details, but the message was clear, and it was impossible to miss the promise of chaos shining through the flat prose. And if the Guggenheim was only the opening salvo, this guy would test the whole system.

Beyond the glass wall, the television screens all displayed liquid crystal variants of the same thing—a talking head staring gravely into the camera and offering an opinion on an issue they knew nothing about. It was three minutes past the hour, and even though CNN had broken the story as an exclusive (which didn't make sense to Kehoe; the bombers should have sent it to every media outlet in the country—*that* was how you sowed chaos), it had already migrated to the other networks, and once again he was both impressed and troubled at how quickly information traveled in the digital world. Especially the *wrong* information.

He knew that in the movable feast of news, the letter would soon be replaced with some other cultural sound bite. You couldn't trust the media to handle information responsibly, but you could always trust the media to act like *the media*. Which meant that there was a certain amount of predictability in their behavior.

Kehoe didn't bother reading the letter again, he just stared at the general form of the mini manifesto. Two paragraphs. Not a lot. But enough. When they put this case to bed, the letter would figure prominently in the story—it was their first true lead. Kehoe never forgot that while his people were trying to figure out what a suspect was thinking, the suspect was usually trying to figure out how they were thinking.

Kehoe was still staring at the printout when there was a knock on his door. It opened before he looked up, and a big shadow that could only come from Otto Hoffner canopied his desk.

Hoffner waited for a cue to speak; Kehoe's people knew that just because he was silent, that didn't mean he wasn't working.

Kehoe leaned forward and steepled his fingers under his chin. "What is it, Otto?"

True to form, Hoffner's face didn't play around with any sort of emotion—he was one of those fabled bureau types who never broke character, not even at the office Christmas party. "I just thought you should know Page left."

"What do you mean, *left*?"

"Forensic Linguistics was running us through the letter, and before Tranter completed his takeaways, Page walked out."

"Did he say anything before he left?"

"That the letter wasn't written by a human being."

Before Kehoe could ask him to clarify the statement, Hoffner added, "He said it was written by a machine."

Kehoe ran that through his head. "Did Whitaker go with him?"

Hoffner nodded a single time.

Kehoe thanked Hoffner and the man squeezed back out through the door.

Kehoe sat unmoving for a few moments as he shifted the pieces to the appropriate mental columns. When he had thought things through a few times, he picked up the phone and called Chawla, who answered in one ring.

"Yes, sir?"

"How are you and Page getting along?"

There was a pause that Kehoe knew meant Chawla was trying to find a way to be diplomatic.

"I want the truth," Kehoe prompted.

"He's a nut. He just ran out after presenting some half-baked idea that the letter sent to CNN was written by a robot or an android or . . . hell, I don't even know what he was talking about."

Kehoe remembered something that the celebrated conductor George Szell said about Glenn Gould: *That nut's a genius.* "Don't take it personally, Sam. It's just how he is. You need to find a way to work with him—he'll give you a lot of added value."

There was obvious disappointment in Chawla's voice when he said, "Yes, sir," and hung up.

Kehoe placed the phone down on his desk and went back to his meditative posture, fingers once again steepled under his chin. He had been in the pose less than thirty seconds when his desk phone rang. He punched the hands-free and sat back. "Brett Kehoe."

"Yes, sir, this is Stan Tranter."

"What can I do for you, Tranter?" He tried not to sound irritated, but he had been up for a day and a half and he could hear the tension in his own voice.

"I wanted to let you know that I ran that letter through analytical software to see if we could learn anything."

"And?"

"And there's better than an eighty percent chance that it was written by a text-compacting algorithm."

"A text-compacting algorithm?"

"Yes sir, it's a text summarization tool used to reduce large quantities of data to a manageable size. It's used a lot by lawyers."

Kehoe thanked Tranter before hanging up.

When he was once again alone with his thoughts, he leaned back in his chair and, for the first time in twenty-one hours, almost smiled.

"Welcome back, you nut."

18

Wall Street

Whitaker looked around the elevator, visibly impressed with the posh surroundings. "This is nicer than my apartment."

"It's also bigger."

"No shit. I have to store my shoes in the oven."

Lucas was about to ask her if she had ever forgotten about them when she fired it up, but she hit him with one of her preemptive answers. "I'm more of a takeout girl."

"I see."

She switched gears, going into business mode. "What are we doing here again?"

"We're investigators."

"And?"

"We're investigating."

The car slowed, then stopped, and the bell binged, the old-school brass needle on the dial pointed at the top floor. The doors slid open to a richly appointed reception area. Two women in expensive dresses and even more expensive smiles sat at a desk the size and polish of a vintage Cadillac. Behind them, on an oak-paneled wall, a brass sign read *Knechtel Equity*.

As Lucas and Whitaker approached, both women nodded a hello and in perfect stereo harmony said, "Hello, Dr. Page, it's a pleasure to see you again." They gave Whitaker a shared smile.

Whitaker raised an eyebrow and looked over at Lucas with her *What-the-fuck?* face. His thoughts on bankers were as well known as his stance on guns—he refused to have anything to do with either one.

Lucas said, "May I go in?"

They nodded in unison at some vague point down the hallway. "He's expecting you."

The receptionists stayed with the desk and Whitaker followed Lucas down the hall, past bronze busts of historical figures—the movers and shakers of human history.

Whitaker jabbed a thumb over her shoulder. "Weyland or Tyrell?" She was almost whispering.

Lucas ignored the question and opened a door for her. "Remember, we're investigating."

The next room also had a desk the size and finish of a flagship automobile—this one occupied by a woman who looked like she had been smelted in the same foundry as the two out front, although of an older vintage. "Dr. Page, nice to see you again. Please go right in." Her tone was level, but she glanced up at Lucas's hair twice—which was a new thing for him; people usually got weirded out by his metal parts.

"Thank you, Renée." Lucas led Whitaker through a floor-to-ceiling door that had a brass knob polished smooth from years of use.

The office beyond was something out of the golden age of Hollywood—a fitting home for Captain Nemo. Or at least a swanky place to hang out. It had a corner view of the southern tip of the island and felt like it was somehow suspended in the clouds above the metropolis. The floors were Portoro marble covered with the finest Persian rugs. Other than a massive desk and a pair of silk sofas, the only furniture was a pair of Shagreen armoires by Carlo Bugatti that flanked the fireplace. The rest of the space was taken up with a library that was three levels high, each level with a walkway and banister—the kind of library that took generations to build.

But the real attraction was the taxidermy display in the middle of the room—a giant Kodiak on its hind legs, lips pulled back in a silent roar, facing down a charging aurochs pushing seven feet of horns with sterling silver tips—a metaphor for the bull versus bear philosophy of the modern robber barons. It belonged in a glass diorama at the American Museum of Natural History.

A man came around from behind the desk, his hand out. "Page, nice to see you." He looked like he had been assembled by Edith Head while she was channeling Archie Leach, and it didn't take a lot of imagination to picture him spending a lot of nights at black-tie functions with a bunch of society types.

Lucas and the man exchanged a friendly greeting, and Lucas motioned to Whitaker with his green hand. "Paul Knechtel, I'd like you to meet Special Agent Whitaker."

Knechtel extended a hand, gave Whitaker a warm smile, and said, "It is a pleasure to meet you, Special Agent Whitaker." It was a gentle and genuine greeting.

Knechtel turned to Lucas and said, "I have a meeting in twenty minutes. Should I cancel it?"

"Is it anything important?" Lucas asked.

"With the bombing last night, everything has suddenly become important. Especially tech stocks." He hit a button on his desk. The door opened immediately and the receptionist came in. "Yes, sir?"

"Renée, would you please get me an apple and ginger juice?" He turned to Lucas and Whitaker. "And you would like?"

"Coffee," said Lucas.

"Perfect." Whitaker was watching Lucas for pointers on what was going on.

"Two coffees, then." Knechtel walked over to one of the sofas and pulled the fabric at his knees as he gently folded into the silk brocade. He checked the big gold Panerai on his wrist. "Do I need to cancel my meeting?" He examined Lucas's hair but didn't say anything.

Lucas sat down on the opposite sofa. "I'll make this short—time for a cup of coffee notwithstanding. You can make your meeting."

Whitaker sat down beside him and Lucas opened with "I'm looking into the Guggenheim bombing."

Knechtel's smile faded. "I lost some friends yesterday. The whole street is shook up—everyone knew someone who was there." His focus slipped, and for an instant he was somewhere else. "That letter turned in to CNN is already causing ripples in the market. Tech stocks got a little bump—the brokers aren't happy that someone took a swipe at their city and they're trying to fight back the only way they know how."

Lucas shook his head. "That letter was horseshit. I doubt it has anything to do with what's going on."

Lucas and Knechtel had been friends since MIT, back in their teens when Lucas was working on his first doctorate. Knechtel came from the kind of wealth measured in the number of museums with the family name over the capstone. He had an IQ that was almost supernatural—a gift that he applied toward a PhD in a branch of jet propulsion so theoretical that only a handful of people in the world understood its uses. But school had just been an exercise to limber up his thinking for the eventual step into the family business. Which meant he was a billionaire turned rocket scientist who ran an investment firm as old as Wall Street itself.

Lucas eased back into the sofa. "This is all unofficial, Paul. I'm only here for your opinion. Can you tell me anything about Horizon Dynamics that might not be public knowledge?"

Knechtel's earlier ease was replaced with concentration as he went into recall mode. "They came out of nowhere about eight years ago—small firm built up by a midwestern family. They started cleaning up environmental damage caused by fracking—decontamination and soil rejuvenation. Their approach was next level—nanotechnology, AI-driven solution choices. All very high-tech. They had a captive market because most people are interested in taking out of the earth, not putting back in, and they built up a good reputation. Six years back they decided to cash out and were bought by the Hockney brothers.

"The Hockneys are very private people, and virtually unknown to your average man on the street. But they're a force to be reckoned with on Wall Street. From what I know, it was Seth who instigated the deal, which is unusual—William is known as the decision-maker and the brains of the operation. Also, the company's record on environmental stewardship was in direct contrast to the Hockney track record, so it didn't seem like an obvious choice for them. But they poured money into infrastructure, hiring emerging talent because they were smart enough to know that Horizon's reputation had been built on innovation. William had his fingers in the pie by this point, and the rumor is he's the one who hired a Finnish national named Timo Saarinen to head up R&D.

"Saarinen is smart, and his work in botany had been short-listed for a Nobel Prize about fifteen years back. He still tours and does TED Talks about environmental issues as they relate to big business. He's a known commodity, and if he gives a process or a firm his seal of approval, it's a guaranteed step up for everyone involved. Under Saarinen's direction, Horizon took off.

"Fast-forward to now, and the brothers Hockney decided to go public and cash in. Their IPO today was going to bring in capital to help HD deal with the growing international demand for environmental stewardship—public opinion around the globe is changing. International expansion is something the Hockneys *do* know about—they've always been good at bringing good old American know-how to the world. The party at the Guggenheim was a *Here-we-are* move designed to bolster the IPO. What very few people know is that there was going to be an announcement at the gala last night."

"What kind of an announcement?"

Knechtel leaned forward and his tie dropped out of his lap. "The Hockneys have expanded into nation-state financing—there's money to be made competing with the Chinese Belt and Road Initiative, which is the People's Republic's neocolonial grab at resources. They finance a country's infrastructure using said country's natural resources as collateral, and when payments aren't made—which is what they count on—the borrowing country loses control of its resources. They've been particularly aggressive with this program in Africa and South America." Knechtel paused as Renée came back in and placed a sterling tray down on the burled surface of the coffee table.

She filled two porcelain cups from a Georgian pot before emptying a bottle of mulched sludge into a tall glass that she placed in front of Knechtel. There was something dreamlike, almost ethereal about her, and as she walked out, Lucas realized that she hadn't made any noise at all, not with her heels on the marble floor and not while she had poured the drinks.

By the expression Knechtel was wearing, it was obvious that he was working something out as he picked up his health concoction. He took a sip, pursed his lips as he swallowed, and looked over at Lucas. "I can't tell you how I know this, but the announcement was that Horizon had secured a multibillion-dollar project in

Paraguay—the cleanup of a bauxite mining site. That would have pushed the value of their IPO up by a sizable margin."

Whitaker shifted in her seat and looked over at Lucas, who was lining up all the pieces in his head. "What are the alarm bells I see going off in your head, Paul?"

Knechtel took another sip of his health potion. "The Paraguayans have been in town for a week now, hunting up financing for an infrastructure deal. The IMF has approved them for a seventy-billion-dollar ceiling, which means that they can comfortably be expected to pay back fifty of it before they have to resort to creativity in their payment schedule. The IMF is conservative, and the Paraguayans are here trying to get more money on better terms, because seventy bil won't cover everything they need—it's a big package, and they're looking for everything from roads to airports to a new hydroelectric dam that's going to be the third largest in the world. They need north of a hundred and twenty billion to make that happen. The Chinese don't care about the ceiling the IMF provided, because their goal is to own the country, and they'd love to finance the deal. But the Paraguayan government is making difficult long-term financial decisions over easy short-term ones, and they want to stay clear of the Chinese. They are one of only five countries in South America that have been able to avoid signing on with the Belt and Road Initiative, the others being Argentina, Brazil, Colombia, and French Guiana."

Lucas was staring at his coffee. "Do the Hockneys have that kind of money?" Even though people liked to throw the term *billion* around on television as if it were commonplace, Lucas knew that kind of money was more esoteric than many believed.

Knechtel waved the question away. "They wouldn't use their own money—they'd set up a fund and have investors buy in. Or they could partner with a few banks and have them sell it to their investors."

Lucas stood up and began a slow walk around the room. "So the announcement would have bolstered the IPO, making money for the Hockneys out of the gate." He paused by the taxidermy mount and stared up at the giant Kodiak.

Knechtel finished his drink and pushed the coaster into the center of the table. "Yes. And if they ended up funding the Paraguayan infrastructure deal, they would have lent the money to the country, which would have then given it back to them when it purchased services from Horizon Dynamics. And they have dozens of construction companies under their wings."

Lucas floated the thing through his head. "So they lend the Paraguayans a hundred and twenty billion dollars—money that they get from investors? The Paraguayans then use that money to purchase services from Hockney-owned companies. And the Paraguayans have to pay back the money? With interest?"

Knechtel leaned back in the sofa. "It's not as uncommon as you would think."

"So the Hockneys make a lot of money on the IPO for Horizon, but they make a fucking fortune by beating out the Chinese and financing the infrastructure deal?"

"Yes."

Whitaker shook her head. "I'm starting to resent that my parents were poor."

"So who benefits from the Guggenheim bombing?" Lucas asked. "*Cui bono?*" It was one of the first questions they taught cadets to ask at Quantico, from the Latin, meaning *To whom is it a benefit?*

Whitaker shook her head. "I don't see anyone smiling in this mix. Not the Guggenheim; or Horizon's personnel; the Hockneys; the Paraguayans; potential investors in the IPO; the people who owned the artwork that had been on display at the gala; the insurance companies—everyone loses."

Lucas reached out and put his hand on the flank of the massive bear. There was nothing cute or cuddly about the beast—it looked like it could chew through an entire town in about five minutes. He stared up into the glass eyeballs and said, "Tell that to the people who blew up the Guggenheim."

19

Midtown

"Your pal is very un–Gordon Gecko–like," Whitaker said as she switched lanes like she was auditioning for a gig in *Bullit*.

"He's still a banker."

"So he's *not* your friend?"

Lucas was too tense from Whitaker's driving to shrug. "Bankers can't help themselves—they are motivated by money, which means they can't be trusted except for that one single driver."

"Are you saying we went there to bait him?"

"We went there to get some information. If there's something in it for him, he won't be able to help himself from finding us some answers."

"But he seemed so nice."

"And therein lies the irony." Lucas's aluminum fingers were threaded through the *holy-shit* handle and he relaxed his shoulder, which transferred weight to his arm, mechanically tightening his grip. He had to force himself to keep his eyes open. "You know, I'd be happy to catch a cab."

"Scared of a little speed?"

"It's the rapid deceleration caused by a crash that has me worried."

Whitaker smiled but kept her foot to the floor as she threaded the big Navigator through the afternoon traffic blipping up Broadway. "For a guy interested in the speed of light and the relationship between time and human life, you sure seem to be unadventurous."

"My interest has always been academic."

Whitaker's smile broadened. "Which brings us back to my missing you."

Lucas gave her the only expression that felt natural—a scowl.

"Don't worry, I'm not getting all weepy or anything, but everyone else I meet on the job is nice. Some are even *friendly*. You? Hell, I don't even have to talk to you."

"I like to think of it as an antidote."

"An antidote to what?"

"Toxic positivity."

"Is that even a thing?"

"You don't hang around young people, do you?"

"I'm still surprised that they let *you* hang around young people."

"Someone has to be the old guy in the park screaming at the sandwich in his hand. Might as well be me."

Whitaker nodded. "Noted." She jabbed a thumb over her shoulder. "So what was that back there?" She pulled off Broadway, heading east.

Lucas watched the city outside—any piece of which could instantaneously disappear in an explosive flash. "No system—and that includes a series of crimes—is intrinsically random; the observer just has an imperfect understanding of how said system operates. If you see something that appears to be random, you're missing data. And hidden inside larger seemingly organized structures, you can find smaller ones that look like they're nothing—statistical noise—but they're not. They're just part of a different pattern."

They came to a stop, and Lucas watched the people moving by. There was something different about them, as if their software had been updated with a patch. His fellow New Yorkers were more resilient than any other urban population in the world, but even they had their limits. And the bombing of the Guggenheim was exacerbating all kinds of tension. It wasn't as bad as it had been following 9/11, but the same miasma of malaise was present in the semiochemical signals.

Whitaker pulled through a light, then cut in front of a taxi before glancing over at him and smiling. "I know you're a private man. And I generally don't poke into other people's lives. But I was wondering." She side-eyed him and her mouth cracked into a grin that rivaled Calvin-Wade Curtis's. "What's with the Chev Chelios hair?"

Lucas told her the story of Maude's *Halloween experiment,* as he had named it.

"And you believed her?"

"I did, yes."

"You have a lot to learn about teenagers."

He tilted his head to the right so he could see his reflection in the passenger mirror. He looked like a kook. Or a guitarist out looking for a band. When he hobbled out of the hospital after the Event, vanity had been the first emotional casualty. Most of the world never really saw *him* anymore; all they saw were the replaced parts. It used to bother him, but a decade had helped iron out his expectations. "It's just hair."

"Yes, it is." She was gaining on a big Mercedes sitting in their lane when a pickup tried to pass them on the passenger side. Whitaker hit the gas and switched lanes, punching past the big Benz. There was a serial-killer stick-figure shopping list decal in the back window, representing a mother, two daughters, a dog, and two cats.

Whitaker hooked around the Mercedes with a maneuver that

pushed Lucas against the door and he once again had to resist the urge to close his eyes.

"So where do we go from here?"

Lucas almost ducked as they swerved around a gaggle of tourists rolling suitcases across the street, scattering them like a handful of dice. "We? There is no *we*. You can drop me at the next corner. I'll be walking from here."

"You need to take more risks, my friend."

"Now that's something no one has ever said to me before."

20

The Upper East Side

The house was unusually quiet without the kids. Even Lemmy—his one dependable greeter—was at the beach. The only sound was the high-pitched squeal of the alarm keypad.

Lucas punched in his six-digit code, then stepped into the silence. He did a walk-through of the first floor and wound up in the kitchen, where he placed the new FBI-issue laptop down on the marble island and got himself a glass of milk from the fridge. He stood there for a few moments, listening to the nothing and working on the milk. When he finished it, he rinsed the empty glass and placed it in the dishwasher before stepping out.

The backyard—a luxury in the city, even for this neighborhood—was a small space filled with a swing set, a barbecue, and a picnic table. He walked down the steps and heard the thump of whatever disenfranchised criminal noise Dingo liked to call music coming from the apartment over the garage. Lucas crossed the patio stones, then climbed the staircase.

After knocking on the door to no response, Lucas used his aluminum knuckles to bang on the metal frame. A few seconds later, the music volume inside dropped precipitously, and Dingo opened the door, smiling. "Hey, mate," he said in an Australian accent that ten years stateside had not been able to dull. "I thought you might be back."

Dingo waved him in and closed the door. "Erin and the kids come back with you?"

"They stayed in Montauk." The music was a lot quieter, but Lucas was having a hard time shutting down all the systems in his head and it felt like he was listening to someone kill chipmunks with a tuning fork set to glass-cracking mode. "Could you turn that off?"

Dingo thumbed the screen on his iPhone, and the rodent murder soundtrack blipped out. "Not a fan of the Jesus and Mary Chain."

"I'm not a fan of anything right now. Jesus. Or Mary Chain."

Dingo eyed him cryptically before turning and heading for the fridge. "You want a beer?"

Lucas thought about the milk in his stomach and the work he had to do tonight. "No. Thanks." He dropped into the leather sofa.

"More for me." Dingo got a Modelo and headed back. Like Lucas, Dingo had lost some of his original hardware. He had two prosthetic legs—both replaced below the knee—and today he was in his street feet, as he called them, not the carbon blades he usually sported around the apartment. He was in shorts and a T-shirt with his dojo logo embroidered over the left breast. He dropped into the club chair facing the sofa. "I take it you are back to deal with that business at the Guggenheim."

"That would be correct, yes."

Dingo's eyes never left Lucas as he took a long haul off the bottle. When he was done, he said, "You know, you are one of the dumbest geniuses I have ever met."

"This isn't like the last one. I doubt they'll need me past tomorrow."

"Why? Will you be dead by then?"

"You sound like Erin."

Dingo emptied the bottle and got out of the chair. "That's what people who care about you sound like, I guess." He headed back to the fridge. "Besides, you know how some guys grow into themselves and end up looking like aging prizefighters who have taken their lumps but somehow survived?"

Lucas couldn't jibe the description with the man he saw in the mirror, but he understood the inherent weakness in self-perception. "You think I look like an aging prizefighter?"

"Not at all. I said *some guys*. You? You look like a crash test dummy someone pulled the leg and arm off of, then threw in the ditch."

"Thanks."

"Yeah, well, I just want you to be aware that you're not twelve anymore."

"The bureau has plenty of people to do the legwork on this one— I'm strictly there to look at some numbers. I'm a spreadsheet guy."

"Try to remember that." He took another cold one from the bottom shelf.

"Why did you run around Africa for ten years while people threw grenades at you?" Dingo, whose real name was Martin Hudson, had been an award-winning combat photographer before a dance with a land mine in the Sudan had ended his career of documenting humanity's madness.

Dingo dropped back into the seat and opened the second bottle. "That's easy: I was a moron." The legs of tripods reached up from the umbrella stand behind him, the one incongruous item being the hilt of a broadsword that he'd found in the garbage last year and kept around for sentimental reasons. He was a photographer by trade, but his main energy was put into teaching Brazilian jujitsu to other amputees. "Okay. I'll drop it."

Lucas pushed himself out of the sofa.

"Where you off to?"

Lucas had a hard drive full of data to sift through. "Work."

Dingo eyed him with that weird look again before taking a sip of his beer. "Spreadsheets, right?"

21

West 52nd Street

The bar at the 21 Club could as easily have been located in Madison, Wisconsin—the decor was a cross between rural steakhouse and strip-mall sports bar, put together before irony was a thing. The walls were paneled in stained mahogany and the booths were upholstered in leather, but the tablecloths looked like western shirts minus the buttons, and sports equipment and model airplanes hung from the ceiling. The place had a man cave–cum–Disney set vibe, but the food was consistent (though predictable) and the service exemplary. The patrons came for the history and the implied status, not for the football helmets and plastic fighter planes.

As always, Paul Knechtel was five minutes early for his meeting, a space he filled with his usual pre-dinner snack of Johnnie Walker Blue Label with H_2O croutons. Unlike a lot of people in his profession, he was not welded to his phone and would not answer it while eating any more than he was willing to sleep with it under his pillow. Other people did that for him.

Knechtel was at his usual table, a booth at the back that he knew many other businesspeople, movers, shakers, and Wall Street types considered to be theirs as well. He worked on his scotch while he people watched. The place was emptier than it should have been at this hour. And everyone displayed the forced calm that can come only from alcohol. Evidently the bombing last night had induced communal PTSD, and everyone was trying not to think about it. Knechtel didn't understand the victim mentality, and fear wasn't a big part of his emotional lexicon, but it was understandable that most people were averse to being blown up for no reason other than someone else thought it might be fun.

He was almost finished with his drink and was about to signal the waiter for a second when Zaritski appeared in the door. Even though he had spent a lot of time with the man—and he was staring at him right now—Knechtel had no idea how tall he was or how much he weighed.

Zaritski spoke to the maître d', nodded at Knechtel's table, then came over.

Knechtel finished his scotch in a single throw, then stood up, extending a hand. "How are you, Sasha?"

"I got whiplash from the news. But a call from you means I get to keep busy, so there's that," Zaritski said in heavy Brooklynese.

They sat down and Knechtel nodded at the waiter for two more Blue Labels before stepping into business. "I need you to look into Horizon Dynamics."

Zaritski had been an investigator for the SEC before jumping ship for the private sector. He had no official title, no business card, and no known address. What he had was a new cell phone number every day, a list of connections that he needed an external hard drive to store, and the ability to find the unfindable. "I assume you want this before the markets open in London tomorrow?"

Knechtel waved the question away. "It's not like that."

The waiter came back with their drinks and took the empty highball away. When he was gone, they sat in shared silence for a few moments, working on their scotches.

Zaritski thunked his glass down on the table. "So what *am* I looking for?"

"I don't know. Maybe nothing."

"You're not an *I-don't-know-maybe-nothing* kind of guy, Paul." Zaritski eyed him suspiciously. "Is this proactive or reactive?" Meaning *information gathering* or *damage control.*

"See if you can find anything unusual in their story arc. Try to see if there is anyone behind the scenes that is there for a reason."

"The kind of reason that might lead to their entire executive branch being wiped out in a bombing?"

Knechtel stared at him over the rim of his glass for a few seconds. "That would not be an incorrect approach."

"And you need this when?"

"I need something by tomorrow. If you need to put something else in motion that might take a few days, that's fine. But I need something by tomorrow if at all possible."

"What's this about, Paul?"

"I owe someone."

Zaritski drained his whiskey to the ice cubes and stood up. "Then I better get to work."

They shook hands and he walked away, threading between the tables and ducking out the front door as if he had never been there at all.

When he was gone, Knechtel ordered another scotch, then picked up his phone.

22

The Upper East Side

It was a little past two A.M., and he was tired from scanning countless columns of data—his investigative equivalent of biography. Some of the files were more comprehensive than others; a few contained newspaper articles—gleaned from society pages, from the business section, and even a few from the crime pages (all white collar, of course). Eighty percent of the text could have been replaced with the word *blah* and the general dynamics of the files would have changed very little, if at all.

In the old days he could work at a computer for sixteen-hour shifts with nothing but a little caffeine to prop him up. Now, with one of his peepers blown out and a back that continually overcompensated for missing muscle groups, he found that his limit was about two hours before he had to chow down on a handful of Tylenol.

Lucas folded up the laptop and stood up, realizing that he hadn't eaten since . . . he couldn't remember.

He looked out the kitchen window and the lights were still on in Dingo's apartment, so he took out his cell phone. He was about to dial Dingo's number when the phone rang—it was Erin.

"Everything okay?" he asked, half expecting her to say that she missed him, half expecting her to ask for a divorce.

"The kids saw you on the television earlier, getting out of the helicopter, and they've been worried. I thought you'd call."

He looked at the clock on the microwave. "Shit. I'm sorry, baby. I've been—"

"Busy? I know. But I've been doing damage control all day. They think something happened to you—I lied and said you texted." She was packing his bags for a guilt trip and he resented it. But she was right and that brought even more resentment. She was the only person on the entire planet who could make him feel like a prick.

"I'm sorry." There was nothing else he could say.

"Have you eaten?"

Lying would have been the smart move, but he always told her his version of the truth. "No."

"What would you do without me?"

"*Starve to death* would be the appropriate response." He stretched and felt a few of his vertebrae slip into place. "How *is* the Maude Squad?"

"They're fine. They want to come home. And so do I. Are you okay?"

"Of course. Why?"

"Oh, I don't know." The softness disappeared as quickly as it had visited. "Maybe because you got blown up yourself once upon a time. Maybe because investigating an explosion that killed hundreds of people might trigger some stress or angst or whatever the fuck you want to call it. Maybe because the kids and I were almost murdered the last time you went back to work for these people. You know, the basic reasons married people ask each other if they're okay."

He didn't want to talk about it. Not now. A few seconds after he had stepped into the rotunda at the Guggenheim he had pushed it away, and for a million practical reasons—some of which she had just mentioned—he couldn't allow himself to think about the past.

If he did, he would never leave the house, let alone get involved with another investigation—especially this one. No, denial was an effective tool in the art of self-preservation. "I'm fine. It's just been a long day."

"No shit—I've been watching the news. It looks like people are losing their minds." She paused. "I mean more than usual." Then, in an obvious bid to change the topic, she said, "I'm sorry about what Laurie and Alisha did to the study—I didn't realize it would get so out of hand."

He had no idea what she was talking about. "What's with the study?" He walked down the hall and through the big double doors. He turned on the Tiffany table lamp and the slag glass shade threw a warm green over half the room. There were orange construction paper pumpkins and black foil bats with googly eyes along the shelves, but there was something else new, and it hit him when he scanned the shelving.

He flipped on the chandelier, and the order came to life. "Laurie and Alisha did this?"

"They were in there all day on Friday afternoon before I picked you up at work to head out here."

The girls had shuffled the entire library, three walls of books consisting mostly of rare editions on the history of astronomy, mathematics, and astrophysics—3,212 volumes.

Erin's voice was faraway when she said, "I'm sorry—it seemed harmless and I didn't realize they could do so much damage in a few hours. I thought they'd get bored and stop. But they really mixed your library up."

Lucas wasn't really listening to her. He found their starting point—the shelf in the northeast corner of the room—and he took the book down—a bound copy of George Ellery Hale's first scientific paper at MIT, written in 1886; thirty-one pages in a calfskin binding. He held it in his hand for a second, then looked up at the book beside it.

"They were just having fun," she said, probably thinking his silence indicated disappointment. "They didn't mean to make a mess."

Lucas swallowed a single time. "This isn't a mess; this is organized." He walked down the row of shelving. "Perfectly."

"What do you mean? I saw the room, Luke, they mixed everything up."

"No, they didn't." He stopped at the end of the sequence, at the 2,500-page *Encyclopedia of Astronomy and Astrophysics*—the volumes shuffled around—3, 1, 2, 4. "It used to be alphabetic by author; they reorganized them by number of pages, ascending." He stood there, smiling. "They did this together?"

"Alisha told Laurie where to put the books: Laurie was the muscle, Alisha the brains."

"Go wake her up; I want to ask her some questions."

"You are not going to ask her the square root of self-indulgence at two in the morning. She gets to be a little girl—she deserves *that*. She gets to be three and a half."

Lucas sat down on the sofa, the Hale volume still in his hand.

"So, are you done with the bureau? Are you coming back out here?"

Lucas knew what she was doing, and she was right. "No, I can't." But he slipped the calendar pieces around in his head and found a win-win. "Besides, we have to get Maude registered at La-Guardia. You guys need to come back. If you don't want to drive in, I can have Kehoe send someone out in the morning."

"Forget it. I'll drive us back. I have to go into the hospital anyway to look at the new office." Erin didn't sigh, but she came close. "I saw the news. And that letter. Is this guy really that crazy?"

"That letter is horseshit—he's just trying to fuck with the bureau." *And succeeding.* "We'll hear from him again, but it won't be another letter, it will be another bomb."

"What's happening to people?" she asked.

There were a million ways he could answer that particular

question, and all of them would be true. "The world is a complicated place." He heard the waves in the background and switched conversational gears. "You outside?"

"Yeah. Couldn't sleep."

And he knew that she meant because he hadn't called. "I'll try to be more considerate."

"I'm just being selfish. Which I have every right to be, by the way."

After the last time, he would have understood an ultimatum—the bureau or the family. But she would never do that. "Yes, you do."

"Call Dingo and you two boys go get some food. It will clear your mind. And put some fuel in your stomach."

"I was just thinking about that." He wished that he had stayed out at the beach with his family; in a thousand years, none of this would matter, and he would have spent the only commodity he had—time—on other people. "Smooch the kids for me?"

"Of course. Now go catch some bad guys so we can get back to our baseline."

"I love you."

"I know." And she hung up.

23

Lucas and Dingo stood on the corner of 74th and Madison. Lucas was still in jeans and the V-neck, but he had added a sports coat. Dingo was in his standard uniform of shorts and a hoodie, still in his street feet.

The window of the Apple store across Madison was a pleasing display of aluminum chassis with rounded corners and floating icons of various apps—a noted component in their shift from retail to religion. Which pulled Lucas's focus back to the investigation. And that letter. It was impossible to align the molecules so that the thing worked. Plus, there was no way the people who had come up with that Wile E. Coyote IED at the Guggenheim were stupid enough to think that Americans would ever give up their iPhones.

Lucas eyed the traffic heading north on Madison—all four cars—looking for a taxi. Chance paid off, and an on-duty cab was a block and a half down. Lucas raised his hand.

From somewhere behind him, Dingo's voice said, "You have that *I'm-working-on-a-Rubik's-Cube* look you get when you're trying to figure shit out."

He kept his eye on the cab. And his hand in the air. "I haven't eaten anything since breakfast."

"I've seen you go days without eating. Which is why you're six-foot-three and weigh as much as the average house cat. You look like Jack Skellington. And that hair doesn't help."

He had forgotten about the hair—he really needed to do something about it.

The taxi crossed 73rd, flashed his lights, and threw on the index. "Here's our cab."

"You ever heard of Uber? They're, like, chauffeurs, man. And the cars don't smell like rented bowling shoes."

Lucas held the door open. "Would you please get in?"

Of course the cab smelled like rented bowling shoes.

They charged up Madison, and Lucas wondered if the driver was related to Whitaker. But traffic was sparse, and Lucas settled in when they turned on 79th to cut across the park.

"So why, exactly, are we going across town at two-thirty in the morning to eat poison?" Dingo pointed at the world outside. "It looks like everyone has been Raptured."

"I need a break." He thought about Erin's orders. "And food."

"I have oatmeal at my place. And beer. We could have stayed in, watched *Frankenstein,* and played Yahtzee; I bet you love Yahtzee."

"Is there something wrong with going out?"

Dingo shrugged. "I never leave the house this time of the year; every Halloween some asshole comes up to me, points at my feet, and says, 'Cool costume, bro! Where can I buy those?'"

The canyon of 79th opened up as they crossed Fifth Avenue, then closed in with the dark canopy of the park. Lucas said, "No one's that stupid," but he did a lousy job of selling it.

Gray's Papaya was empty except for an old lady carrying a bagful of umbrellas and a man in a suit who kept slurping from a drink that sounded like it had been empty for a good hour. Lucas ordered two recession specials (both with onions) and two papaya drinks from the little Filipino guy with rockabilly sideburns behind the counter.

They stood by the window, looking out on Broadway.

Dingo poked his hot dog with a finger. "You eat this stuff too much."

"You can't kill me—not with anything man-made." Lucas held up his prosthetic hand to demonstrate his point.

"This, my friend . . ."—Dingo jabbed the dog again—"is *not* man-made. This is sorcery, necromancy, and against the Geneva Conventions."

But Lucas wasn't paying attention—his mind was back in the files, trying to find something that simply wasn't there. Once again he asked himself, *Who would the bombing profit?*

"Ground control to Major Page."

"What? Sorry. My mind is somewhere else."

"I can see that. I assume you're thinking about the techtard who sent that letter."

Lucas smiled in spite of himself and took a sip of his drink, which tasted like a Popsicle mixed with shaving cream. "The only thing I can tell you about these people is that they don't hate technology; they're just fucking with us."

"So you have frat boys blowing shit up." Dingo smiled and gave the hot dog a theatrical sniff. "There, solved it for you."

Lucas realized that Erin had been right—he was hungry. But he didn't feel like eating and he kept staring at his food, as if that would make him want to eat. "This wasn't some dickhead in a Ryder truck loaded up with diesel fuel and ammonium nitrate; this was complicated—*overly* complicated. This target was specific and the people responsible took the pains to do it in a specific—and very creative—way. But how does killing a bunch of people during a gala for a company that does environmental impact assessment and cleanup help the cause of someone who wants a revolution against technology? It's a hundred and eighty degrees against brand." He took a bite.

The dog tasted exactly like it had since he was a child, and suddenly he *was* hungry. Mrs. Page had brought him here the first time. They had pulled up in the Bentley and walked into complete and absolute silence. It was her attempt at finding a child-friendly place; Lucas found out years later that she had heard one of the women at her manicurist promising their son Gray's Papaya if he behaved while she had her nails done. Of course Mrs. Page was horrified that the place had very little to do with papayas. But she tried a hot dog and a drink. And every couple of months after that, they would have supper there. Once, not long after he had started at MIT, Mr. Teach had driven her up to deliver a box of Gray's Papaya hot dogs. Lucas and the girls he shared his apartment with had eaten them for three days.

Dingo leaned over and asked, "Maybe you're asking the wrong questions."

"What do you mean?"

"How the hell should I know? You're the guy with all the answers."

24

Tribeca

Billy Zhang pulled up to the light on the intersection of Harrison and Hudson Streets. It was late now, and he had been Ubering people around since finishing his shift at the restaurant, a little after six that evening. His ass was sore and he had had enough of picking up, driving around, and dropping off drunks—which was basically what his nighttime job amounted to: a shuttle service for alcoholics.

But this was the last one. He had four blocks to go, where he'd drop the drunk kid in the back off at his apartment. Then he'd zip up to the Bronx to get about four hours of sleep before he went to work at his morning job as a real estate agent. No, the American Dream was alive and well, as long as he didn't die of a heart attack before he achieved it.

The kid in the back was mumbling something, and Billy looked up in the mirror. "Sorry?" he asked.

"What country are you from?"

"American," he said proudly. He had immigrated nine years back and was now a proud citizen.

"Where you from?"

"The Bronx."

"No. Jesus, before that. What country? No speak-y Eng-rish?"

The light went green and Billy turned right onto Hudson. "I spea—"

But Billy never completed the turn. His answer was never delivered. And the argument never happened.

Because the Western Union Building they were passing on Hudson Street exploded, blowing the car off its wheels, collaterally taking out a fire hydrant and two pedestrians before flattening it against a concrete wall.

25

72nd and Broadway

Lucas was washing a bite of hot dog down with a jolt of papaya drink when Broadway lit up in one massive whump of white, then blinked out.

Dingo said, "What the fuck was that?"

The few pedestrians who were out all stopped and turned downtown, toward the flash.

"Two . . . three . . . four . . ." Lucas put his drink down as he began to count out loud. "Five . . . six . . . seven . . ."

Everyone in sight turned to the south and looked up.

"Eight . . . nine . . . ten . . ."

With the hot dog still in his hand, he started outside.

"Eleven . . . twelve . . . thirteen . . ."

He stopped at the free newspaper dispensers on the corner. Everyone on Broadway was turned south-southwest, looking up at the sky.

"Fourteen . . . fifteen . . . sixteen . . ."

He followed their line of sight but didn't see anything.

"Seventeen . . . eighteen . . . nineteen . . ."

He stared up at the sky in the general direction the flash had come from.

"Twenty . . . twenty-one . . . twenty-two . . ."

A woman behind him asked someone offstage, "Did you see that?"

"Twenty-three . . . twenty-four . . . twenty-five . . ."

Lucas knew that his calculations were getting close to the end of the island.

"Twenty-six . . . twenty-seven . . . twenty-eight . . ."

Dingo appeared beside him, chewing loudly. "You okay?"

Lucas nodded, but kept counting. "Twenty-nine . . . thirty . . . thirty-one—" And that was when the sound wave came rolling in, like a thunderclap let loose underground.

All of his software fired up and he did the math, calculating the distance from the interval of time between the flash and the sound wave.

Six miles out.

Which meant Tribeca.

He didn't bother worrying that it had been the FBI offices— they were in the general vicinity, but more to the east. This was something else.

A black guy walking toward him scrolling on his phone stopped dead in his tracks. He smacked his cell phone. "What the fuck?" He looked up at them and shrugged. "Fucking technology, man. Never works."

A voice behind him said, "Hello? Bennie? Hello? Hello?"

A woman at the subway stop across the intersection was yelling at her phone and shaking it.

Others were frantically tapping away on their cell phones, as if they weren't working.

Dingo eased up beside Lucas, holding up his hot dog. A monstrous black jellyfish of smoke reached into the sky to the south, its belly rippling with light from the fire below. "What the fuck is that?" he asked.

The question jarred something loose in Lucas's gears, and he remembered what lay in that direction. "Phase Two."

26

60 Hudson Street

The scene around 60 Hudson Street looked like fire engines had been on sale with zero percent financing and no money down. The wire had been set up two blocks out, but the explosion had spread debris beyond the control zone and the wind blowing in from the ocean was carrying smoke up to the Bronx.

The news vans were on site and had probably arrived while Lucas was still counting out loud on Broadway—those people slept in their shoes and kept microphones in their pockets. They were outside the line, but doing their best to convince everyone at home that no matter where they were in the country, they were in grave danger (and that there would be more updates after the commercial break, which was being brought to them by Rascal scooters).

Whitaker honked at the herd of pedestrians milling about in the middle of the street, but they parted only after she hit the siren. Once through the crowd, she rolled up to the barrier and the duty cops—who were dressed in full tactical gear—checked their badges before letting them through.

They crawled up the block, steering around the larger chunks of debris, and parked among the coterie of FBI vehicles behind the big command vehicle. The Blue Bird had its doors open, and windbreaker-clad acolytes scrambled in and out.

There was debris everywhere, from small bricks and dust to garden-shed-sized chunks of burned buildings. Computer parts, insulation, and thousands of feet of cable littered the street, and windows up and down the block were blown out. A hydrant had been knocked off its bolts (no doubt by the car embedded in the building behind it), sending a geyser into the sky that no one seemed to be paying attention to. Hoses crisscrossed the road, and the flame jumpers had three dozen nozzles trained on what was left of the building, sending big belches of steam into the air.

The west and north walls were almost entirely gone, exposing floors and internal organs like a cutaway architectural model. Burning cables dangled from the walls and ceilings, some of them sparking like nerve endings trying to kick-start phantom limbs. All that was missing from the scene was Snake Plissken.

Of the dozen ambulances lined up, only one had the back doors open. A firefighter was seated on the bumper, sucking on an oxygen mask. There didn't look to be any other victims. Or survivors.

Chawla was beside the command vehicle, typing on his phone with his thumbs. He glanced up and greeted Lucas and Whitaker with "Special Agent Whitaker, Dr. Page." He expressed neither surprise nor pleasure that they were here. "The Machine Bomber blew up an internet hub."

"Yes. I know. I'm right here in front of it."

"Which is what he said he'd do."

Lucas took a breath and forced himself to be civil when he asked, "Have you sent a bomb unit over to Eighth Avenue?"

Chawla was in a trench coat and looked like he had been rousted from naptime. "No. Why?"

"There are two main internet hubs on the island." He jabbed

a green metal finger at what used to be a building. "*That* is one of them."

Chawla's expression flat-lined. "And the other is on Eighth?"

"Yes."

Chawla stared at him for a few dead seconds that he didn't bother to fill with any sort of a protest. When he finished connecting the dots, he excused himself and disappeared into the command vehicle.

Lucas turned back to the half-eaten building. Firemen faded in and out of the smoke wafting off the structure. "If that guy ever tries to think, he's going to hurt himself."

"He's right, you know. The guy promised precisely this: *we are going to burn it all down*—his words, not mine." Whitaker narrowed her eyes and tried to peer through the smoke. "Did you see the people with their cell phones? Their shit was fucked up."

"Chawla is only correct on the surface. Go back to that letter, which is entirely ripped off from the Unabomber—Kaczynski wanted to start a revolution by exposing the dangers technology posed to civilization. He was convinced that if he could highlight the dehumanization brought about by what he called the technological-industrial system, there were enough like-minded people out there to join him in destroying it. He wanted to turn the clock on progress back." Lucas pointed at the building. "This fits *that* narrative. But the Guggenheim bombing? It doesn't make any sort of sense. Especially since the corporation hosting the gala was involved in environmental stewardship. He might have disagreed with their approach, but at least their goals toward nature would have meshed with his. It was a half measure."

Chawla called out to Whitaker from somewhere behind them and she slid away, leaving Lucas to stare at the firemen.

Lucas clipped his shield onto his pocket and headed down the block. There was not much he would learn here, and even less he could contribute, but he knew that neither of those things mattered because he was now committed. He would have doubts. He and Erin would probably exchange words—well, he'd offer words, she'd offer silence. He'd butt heads with Chawla. Probably even get pissed off with Whitaker. Definitely get pissed off with Kehoe. But he'd stick it out because that was how he was built.

The scene was busy but not chaotic, and Lucas had to admit that Chawla was effective with logistics, if somewhat stunted in his creativity. But even if the investigation was Chawla's, the bureau was Kehoe's, and the underlying form of the institution would ensure that things unfolded in a certain way. Which Lucas could at least work with. Or make work for him.

The flames were now dead and even the smoke that rose from the charred husk of the building was weak and tentative. Everything that was flammable had been converted into cinders. Firemen scuttled around the scene, but there was no urgency in their movements; there was no need to rush anymore. They still wore turnout coats, pants, and boots, but the oxygen tanks and masks had been shed and a few had abandoned their helmets in exchange for caps.

Along with the firemen, there were a few cops inside the perimeter, and Lucas saw them automatically checking his badge. Some nodded. Some didn't. All of them looked unhappy.

There was debris everywhere and Lucas had to watch where he stepped, paying special attention to avoid puddles, because the New York City streets were famous for potholes that could swallow a hatchback. He stepped over hoses, bricks frosted with mortar, twisted ducting, and lengths of cable. Once he passed the final line of cops, no one paid any attention to him, and he slowly made his way to the corner of Worth and Hudson, to what used to be a parking lot and was now a pile of crushed cars and bricks wrapped in chain-link fencing the shock wave had peeled off its posts.

When he surveyed the damage, Lucas was amazed that there hadn't been hundreds of casualties. If the explosion had been triggered during business hours, the death toll would have been greater by orders of magnitude. Just the people driving by would have totaled an easy two hundred.

It was amazing what igniting the correct molecules could do.

Kehoe's words on the beach a million years ago came back to him: *basic physics and chemistry.*

Basic.

Physics.

And.

Chemistry.

He stared up at the mess and felt himself slip away. Into the space where only he could go.

He was in the *now.*

And then.

He was in some other point in time that could only be the *before.*

And a building that no longer existed in any material way appeared in front of him, pulled from the past by some inexplicable force that he could not command any more than he could ignore. The numbers started creating calculations he couldn't stop, and dimensions appeared, forcing values like mass and volume and distance into their respective places in the equation.

He was at another point in time—one where the building still existed in its entirety—when there was a thunder strike from deep inside and the structure bulged, the far corner near Thomas Street distending like a swollen belly. It happened in slow motion, and for a few beats of his heart the bricks and mortar and concrete simply bent. Then the surface could no longer hold together, and the mortar pulled apart at the seams, and a bright yellow light shot through in a million slices of light.

Then the bulge twitched—actually contracted—before belching out at the speed of sound.

A hundred tons of brick flew toward him, and he ducked, and—

—just—

—like—

—that—

—he was back in the now. In the after.

And it was all over and he was once again standing in what used to be a parking lot surrounded by insurance claims.

A voice from somewhere behind him said, "Dr. Page, you all right?" in a southern accent.

Lucas turned to see Calvin-Wade Curtis standing behind him. Curtis wore white coveralls and an FBI cap. Along with that annoying grin of his.

"Yeah. I was just—" And he realized he had no reasonable response to the question.

Curtis came over. "You were doing that thing, weren't you?" His grin dialed up by ten points with the question.

"That thing?"

"Yeah—the thing you did at the Guggenheim—the one that impressed the shit out of all of us," he said, pronouncing it *shee-it*.

Lucas nodded up at what was left of 60 Hudson Street. "Have you figured out what caused the explosion?"

Curtis stared at him for a few moments before answering with a question of his own. "Have *you* figured out what caused the explosion?"

Curtis seemed like a decent guy, so Lucas decided that he'd play nice. Besides, he needed more allies in the bureau. "Without swabs, I don't know what kind of device was used, but it had a moderate detonation velocity, somewhere around thirty-two hundred meters a second. The explosion originated over there," he said, pointing at the corner of Hudson and Thomas. "Below street level. It was a single blast, but the following fire and black smoke and the smell of the fumes down wind make me think it was bolstered by a fuel of some sort—probably diesel, which makes sense if they have a generator on site. But it would have to be mixed with an oxidizer."

Curtis smiled up at him and Lucas wondered if that grin had ever gotten the guy punched. "Pretty good, Dr. Page."

"Pretty good what?" Whitaker asked as she stepped into the former parking lot.

Curtis smiled over at her. "Dr. Page was sharing his thoughts on the explosion."

"Which means showing off," Whitaker offered.

Curtis nodded back at the building. "Our scanners picked up a little carbon monoxide and nitrogen, which means we're looking at ANFO. Or a refined fuel explosion. There were 80,000 gallons of diesel on site that multiplied the effect. There were about thirty people in the building that we know about. No survivors. Yet. And no witnesses. Yet."

Whitaker held up a hand. "Eighty thousand gallons of diesel fuel?"

"Spread out in thirty 3,000-gallon tanks on three floors."

Whitaker's tone dropped an octave when she asked, "Why the hell would they store 80,00 gallons of diesel fuel in such a sensitive location?"

Curtis put his hand down on the hood of a used-to-be-a-car. "If the power goes down, people need their internet. Everything from alarm systems to cell phones to Netflix needs the web to run. And people can't live without their Netflix."

Lucas was starting to like the man.

Curtis leaned over and spat, and even in the dark, it was the color of charcoal. "And to keep the internet up and running, you need power. So they had a 10,000 amp power plant in there that ran on a pair of twenty-cylinder generators. And those puppies take a lot of fuel. Apparently someone thought that 80,000 gallons made sense."

Whitaker whistled at that. "People never cease to amaze me."

"If this was our guy, he used a charge as a detonator—either TNT or maybe even C-4. It would have ignited the diesel fuel, which, as Dr. Page pointed out, had to have been mixed with some other oxidizing agent, and there you go."

"There we go," Lucas repeated as he looked over at Whitaker. "What did Chawla want?"

"To let me know he put the bomb unit in motion. Those guys have been running all over the city, checking soft targets. They're on the way to the other internet hub on Eighth."

27

111 Eighth Avenue

The bomb squad that arrived on site was a specialized unit that served all seventy-seven police precincts on the island. The twenty-five-man team showed up a few minutes after the security detail, in a command vehicle not dissimilar to the ones used by the FBI.

Besides the humans on the team, there were eight German shepherd K9 units, and a new experimental program—a troop of six giant pouched rats, gifted to the bureau by the government of Belgium. These rats had a unique personality bent that made them easily trained to sniff out explosives (initially land mines—a skill that had been expanded to include other types of devices). Technically, these specific rodents had been banned from entering the United States since 2003, when an outbreak of monkeypox put them on the no-fly list. But this troop had been quarantined under a special grant from the DHS, and allowed entry for their genetically predisposed purpose. The rats and their handlers were affectionately known inside the unit as the Rat Bastards, while the rats themselves were known as HeroRATs.

After the building was secured, and all personnel escorted

from the area, the bomb squad—along with the eight dogs and six trained rats—went to work. The building manager, a solid guy named Mike D'Antonio who resembled a mailbox in pants, pulled the short straw and did the walk-through with them. He didn't bother trying to hide his discomfort at the prospect of being blown up, and the men in the unit were kind enough not to spook him with their usual dark humor.

The team split up—the humans doing a visual scan, utilizing basic tools like mirrors, flashlights, nitrogen swabs, and long-reach exploratory cameras. The K9s were walked through by their handlers, looking for scents too esoteric for their masters to detect. The rats were tethered to long fiberglass poles for the hard-to-get-to places—mostly above and below the endless miles of fiber-optic lines, lower bandwidth copper cables, and utility wiring.

Unlike the hub on Hudson Street, the owners of the building on Eighth did not see fit to store a few swimming pools' worth of diesel fuel on the premises. But that is not to say they did not store any: there were two 3,000-gallon tanks in the basement, and this was the unit's priority.

Donald Jones was the first one in the generator room with his bomb-sniffing rat, whose name was Binky. Binky was no more accurate than any of his compadres—all of them were trained to, and performed to, the same standards. But Binky had an edge in that he was a little smaller than his compatriots. Which meant that he was better suited for confined spaces (his smaller mass also lessened the chances of his weight setting off a land mine out in the field). For some unknown reason, Binky was also faster at his job; the average HeroRAT clearance rate was approximately 3,000 square feet per half hour—a rate that Binky doubled when he hit his groove.

Like any trained animal, Binky was motivated by food—his standard treat being banana chunks and peanut butter. But Binky really lost his shit over green olives; there was nothing that little sucker loved more. Jones gave Binky a small piece as soon as he hit the floor, and the promise of more would have him scampering his little bomb-sniffing ass off.

Jones directed Binky behind the diesel tank between the door and the giant twenty-cylinder generator. He fed the Kevlar line out between the thumb and forefinger of his right hand, feeling the tension for Binky's *I-found-a-bomb* dance. The Kevlar micro braid was specifically designed to transfer vibration, similar to expensive fly-fishing lines, and after nearly two years of working with Binky, Jones felt that the line was more like a nerve ending than an inanimate object.

Jones double-thumbed his training clicker and Binky came out, looking up to him for food. Jones clicked the device again, pointed behind the second tank, and Binky scampered in, looking for something that was completely unimaginable to his tiny brain.

Jones was about to click Binky back when the braid twanged as Binky did his little success tango.

He got down on his hands and knees and shone his tactical flashlight under the belly of the tank. Binky's whiskered face was an inch from an improvised explosive device.

Jones thumbed the clicker three times, and Binky came running out. He sat down obediently, waiting for olives from heaven.

Jones gave Binky an affectionate scratch under the chin before handing his little friend an olive.

Then he sent a text out to his unit.

Binky scored.

28

111 Eighth Avenue

The captain of the bomb squad walked Lucas, Whitaker, Curtis, Chawla, and his wingmen down to the sub-basement, where Binky the rat had earned himself a bagful of olives. The captain's name was Sanchez, and he had the basic presentation of his kind down cold—flat top, yellow shooter's glasses, and arms that looked like they were cast out of discarded mortar shells. Sanchez wasn't big on dialogue, but he explained that they had found an explosive device beneath a fuel tank in the generator room. Calvin-Wade Curtis was doing a poor job of hiding his excitement—at least judging by his smile.

When they got to the generator room, the device was on a fold-out table with a roll of tools. It looked like a Hollywood interpretation of what an improvised bomb should look like—a metal box containing a compact chunk of putty with a blasting cap wired to a receiver that had a cell phone attached. The cap and wires had been removed, leaving the underlying form alone.

"It's a basic IED," Curtis said as they approached the table. "Cell-phone-activated trigger that in turn sets off the circuit which fires the cap, detonating the putty. Once it's back at the lab, I'll run the taggants and we'll know the manufacturer—you don't mix up C-4 in your basement, so that's something. The charge is lens-shaped, which means it was designed to cut through the outer wall of the tank, which in turn would theoretically detonate the contents. You can find instructions all over the web—anyone with mechanical skills, access to the components, and a little patience could build this thing. It's your basic insurgent dummy box, but we don't see a lot of them stateside. This one was built by a right-handed individual."

"Diesel alone is barely flammable, let alone explosive," said Lucas.

Curtis smiled over at him. "It will burn. It lets off a lot of smoke. But you're correct, it's difficult to ignite. And even if it does, it's not explosive. Not unless you mix it with ammonium nitrate or some other oxidizing agent."

"If this had been detonated, would the explosion have been comparable to the one on Hudson?"

Curtis's smile faded out and he turned to Sanchez. "You tested all the fuel tanks on site?"

One of Sanchez's people, a skinny woman whose name tag identified her as Bastille, held up a tablet. "Pure diesel—nothing else mixed in."

Curtis's face scrunched up and he asked, "And you're sure there are no other explosives in the building? No caches of C-4 hidden away? Nothing else that would have multiplied the effect of this device?"

Sanchez was too professional to look offended—he understood that everyone was just being cautious—and he nodded at his team. "We swept the entire building. Other than that one charge, the place is clean."

Curtis pointed at the tank. "And it was hidden underneath the tank, there?"

Sanchez answered with a nod.

Curtis seemed to think things through for a few seconds before he turned back to Lucas. "All this would have done was rupture the tank and add about six inches of diesel to the floor. That much C-4," he said, indicating the open device on the foldout table, "wouldn't even have blown a hole in the wall."

Chawla put his hands into his pockets and rocked up on the balls of his feet, which was a move he had stolen from Kehoe. "Maybe he's not as smart as you think he is and made a mistake." He pointed at Lucas. "And we got lucky."

Lucas looked at Whitaker, who shrugged.

Lucas looked down at the dismantled explosive device on the plastic table and thought about the Guggenheim. And about the building on Hudson that had been reduced to landfill. "Sure," he said. "Lucky."

29

The Upper East Side

Whitaker pulled up in front of the brownstone. It was a little past six in the morning and the city was awake but still an hour off from peak traffic. Lucas felt like he was a hundred years old, in bad shape, and hungry. He sat there with his aluminum fingers threaded through the door handle for a few moments, not saying anything.

Whitaker turned off the engine and hooked her elbow out the open window. "Are you going to tell me the bad news?"

Lucas looked over at her. "Why do you think it's bad news?"

"Because that's the only kind you ever have."

He thought about protesting, but she wasn't wrong. "I'm tired. My back feels like it's made out of bottle caps strung together with butcher's twine. And all I've eaten in the past twenty-four hours is a hot dog, eleven cups of coffee, and some olives I stole from a rat." He stepped out of the SUV onto the wet morning pavement. "I'm going to go inside now."

He tried to smile, but his face wasn't working, and what came out was a grimace that he hid by closing the door and waving her off.

When he walked in the front door, Lucas was again hit by how without Erin and the kids, the place had a different rhythm, a different smell, and a different feel.

He dropped his keys into the vide poche on the big deco console by the hall tree and kicked off his left sneaker, then carefully extracted his prosthetic foot from the right.

After grabbing a club soda from the fridge, he picked up the bureau laptop he had left on the island and climbed the stairs.

He put the can of soda down as he stripped off the day-old clothes, and getting the sweater over his prosthetic was so difficult that he considered cutting it off with scissors. When he was finally naked, he dumped his clothes in the hamper, finished half the can of seltzer, then took off his arm. He saw his reflection through the steamed-up mirror and once again reminded himself that he'd have to do something about that hair—he had forgotten all about it. How the hell was anyone supposed to take him seriously looking like this? He thought about walking over to CVS for some dye, but he'd just screw it up. Fuck it. Tomorrow. Or the next day.

He put the last half of the soda away and stepped into the shower.

As always, it took longer for the scar tissue to heat up, and he hurt in a million places. His entire skeleton was out of whack—no surprise after twenty-five hours on his feet. Welcome to the new and improved Dr. Lucas Page, lucky to still be alive and held together by the finest technology that money could buy—and powered by a stubbornness that money couldn't.

He let the scalding water beat his frame for ten minutes before toweling off and lumbering into the bedroom. He put his arm down on the bed beside him, kept his leg on, and climbed into the Irish linen naked.

He fell asleep almost instantly.

30

Good morning, this is Jolene Quan of WABC, and I am here at Tomkins Square Park.

The park was the scene of a rally this morning in support of the Machine Bomber, a name that has become synonymous with backlash against technological civilization.

After organizing and advertising the demonstration on Twitter, nearly two hundred people showed up to either protest in support of the bomber or demonstrate against the system that he has claimed he wants to destroy. No matter what you choose to call it, the scene was anything but peaceful.

The demonstrators started a bonfire where they burned their cell phones. Apparently all was going well until phones that had been thrown into the fire began exploding. One woman was hit in the neck by what was apparently flying debris and bled to death before paramedics could arrive. Several people reportedly lost eyes and one man had his teeth knocked out. Many more received superficial cuts and puncture wounds.

Authorities are saying that the woman who bled to death would probably have survived had anyone on site had a cell phone with which to dial 911; unfortunately everyone present had thrown their cell phones into the fire. It is unclear if the police will press any charges even though bonfires are against city bylaws. Authorities are reminding people not to burn their cell phones—or anything that may have a battery inside it—because they often can, as you have seen here, become lethal.

And now, Suzie, back to you . . .

31

The Upper East Side

Whitaker picked Lucas up just before ten. With only a handful of hours of shut-eye under her belt, she looked refreshed and ready to attack the day. He, on the other hand, felt like a piece of Ikea furniture someone had slapped together without bothering to consult the instructions. She was kind enough to bring coffee, but it took a stop at a bodega for another before he felt like he might be able to stand up for five minutes in a row. They had been right about that one—getting old was most certainly not for the weak.

Whitaker eyed him in her periphery, doing a bad job of hiding a smile.

"What?" he said.

"Look at you, being all quiet with your new punk-rock hair, all while wearing a suit."

"What's wrong with my suit?"

"You look like a Reservoir Dog." She arched an eyebrow. "Haven't you heard of color?"

"I'm white—this is how we dress. We're grim motherfuckers."

Whitaker broke into her ten-gallon smile. "Not with Evil Sting's hair, you're not."

He had forgotten about the hair—again. "If you'd prefer hanging out with someone who dresses like Nudie Cohn, you can always chill with Chawla."

By the time they parked in the garage and hit the elevators, Lucas could feel the zeros and ones firing through the void. But he was still another coffee away from prime operating condition, and the elevator ride up to their floor was as silent as the commute.

As always, the room was alive with electric current as a million little decisions were being made that would shape the way the investigation unfolded. The ubiquitous monitors were dialed to network feeds, and the rictus-upholstered faces delivering the news looked like puppets with too many teeth. All of them were focused on the explosions of the past two days, and now that they had a name for their guy, they were in full entertainment mode, accompanied by graphics, guests, and former officials.

One monitor was displaying a scene somewhere in Brooklyn, where a bunch of bearded thirty-year-olds dressed like teenagers took turns talking to the anchor, their dialogue delivered across the bottom of the screen on a chyron. They were having a meeting about the Machine Bomber's message. They were thinking about dropping out.

Of what? the anchor asked.

The whole thing, man. Like, all of it. Society. The grid. All of it. Going back to basics. Ignoring the Big Machine.

And to prove it, they had a Facebook group set up. Along with an Instagram account and a web page.

Lucas briefly wondered if earlier generations had looked upon their young people with as much horror. Then he remembered the reaction to the Beatles, then the Sex Pistols, and finally Marilyn Manson and wondered if he was merely getting old. Or if society really was heading into the shitter.

When they got to Kehoe's office, he was on the phone. He waved them in, cut his conversation short with a curt *Okay*, then scribbled some notes on a yellow legal pad with a fountain pen the size of a wrench.

"Page, Whitaker," he said as he capped the pen and placed it on the desktop. He buzzed his assistant, asked for two coffees and a tea, requested that Chawla and Hoffner join them, then hung up.

"Rested?" he asked neither of them in particular; his focus was elsewhere.

Kehoe leaned back in his chair as Otto Hoffner came in, wearing an ill-fitting suit that looked like the seams might blow out if he took a deep breath. The three FBI mugs he carried resembled toys. He placed the tea down on Kehoe's desk, then handed the two coffees to Whitaker and Lucas. They nodded a thanks as Chawla came in—an FBI mug in one hand, a tablet in the other. He took a seat on the window ledge.

Kehoe opened his arms. "Special Agent Chawla, what can we give Dr. Page here?"

Chawla took to his role as SAIC and tapped into his notes even though he had delivered this exact information an hour ago during the morning brief that Lucas had missed. "We've hit a wall with the airborne accelerant used in the Guggenheim bombing. We collected samples from the manufacturer and they don't match the foil that was delivered, so the supply chain was infiltrated some time after it left their facilities in Matawan, New Jersey, and before it was installed in the snowmakers. We just don't know where."

Chawla scrolled through his notes, tapping the bullet points. "We've interviewed everyone in the supply chain, from the shipper that delivered the foil to the rental company that provided the snowmakers, to their driver who delivered the foil and the snowmakers to the Guggenheim, and we've come up with nothing. The snow machines themselves are three years old and are kept in a rented storage locker in Queens. Our forensics guys went over the space and we didn't find anything.

"We've interviewed everyone in the catering company that's still alive. Everyone involved with the company that provided security. All living Guggenheim personnel. We're examining bank accounts and email records to see if there were any payouts, and so far we've found nothing. That foil appears to have been conjured up by a magician."

Lucas held up his hand. "But it's not magic—it's sleight of hand. We just can't find the point our bombers infiltrated the supply chain."

Chawla looked over at him. "We will."

Lucas wasn't so sure. Not if they were now forty hours into the investigation and still had no idea how any of this had managed to take place. "What about Hudson Street last night?"

"That one we have figured out." Chawla tapped the screen. "Three of the tanks were filled with a mixture of ammonium nitrate and diesel fuel."

Lucas eyed Chawla over the rim of his FBI mug. A diesel fuel/ ammonium nitrate slurry was your basic terrorist/right-wing farm boy mix—the most famous use of it on American soil being when Timothy McVeigh killed 168 innocent people at the Alfred P. Murrah Federal Building in 1995—the second deadliest terrorist attack on American citizens other than 9/11.

It could be extremely effective, but it lacked the panache that the Guggenheim device had—as if it were made by someone else. But it played into the Luddite narrative in that it was uncomplicated.

Chawla went on. "All three tanks were filled yesterday. They have 80,000 gallons of diesel fuel on site divided between thirty-three 3,000-gallon tanks—on three separate floors. But diesel fuel only has a shelf life of six months to a year, so they swap it out twice a year. They keep three of the tanks empty to facilitate the swap-out. Everything was scheduled months ago. We checked the fuel company and neither the driver nor the truck came back after the delivery; they reported both missing yesterday afternoon. Going by the surveillance tapes at Hudson, a man in coveralls showed up, connected the appropriate hoses, did the swap, and left. We got zero usable imagery other than that the driver was a male between twenty and fifty who weighs in at somewhere between a hundred and fifty and two hundred pounds. Probably Caucasian, possibly Latino or Middle Eastern. The driver that disappeared was six-four, two-sixty, and black—so he was hijacked after he left his facility and we assume he was murdered. We have teams back-tracking his route, looking for surveillance footage or anything else that might give us some answers.

"As for the explosion itself, the blast pattern and surveillance footage suggest that it originated in the sub-basement, at the corner of Hudson and Thomas. The forensics explosives department believe that the trigger was identical to the one found at the location on Eighth Avenue last night. The forensic explosives people ran the taggants from the C-4 trigger used on Hudson and they were a perfect match for the C-4 used in the bomb on Eighth, so we know that it was the same builder. We've traced the taggants to a Swedish manufacturer—ENF—it was supposed to have been sold to a construction company in Brazil." Chawla stood up. "All the evidence points to someone who is unhappy with, or has a grudge against, *the industrial technological system,* as the letter pointed out. It's our man—the Machine Bomber."

Lucas decided to put it out there. "Why didn't he blow the hub on Eighth?"

Chawla shrugged. "He made a mistake."

"He managed to infiltrate the supply chain for the foil confetti, modify the snowmakers, bypass security at the Guggenheim, then disappear a truck along with its driver after setting up a bomb in the basement of the Hudson Street internet hub. This guy isn't making mistakes." Lucas didn't like equating what was happening with one perpetrator, but even if there was a team on this, there would be one figure playing leader—there always was.

"So how do you explain the unexploded bomb in the basement on Eighth?"

Lucas had been turning that question over in his mind since last night, and there was only one answer. "He wasn't interested in blowing up Eighth."

Chawla tapped the screen on the tablet again. "That's not what the letter said."

"Oh." Lucas rolled his eye. "Then it must be the truth." There was forced calm in his voice when he said, "The undetonated bomb on Eighth is amateur hour all around. There was no mixture in the tank and the bomb was never triggered. Which means that either the internet hub on Hudson *had to* be detonated as part of their plan, or the hub on Eighth needed to be *left intact* as part of their plan." Lucas pointed at Chawla's notes. "They went through a lot of trouble for Hudson. They went through absolutely none for Eighth. They didn't have any intention of blowing it up."

Kehoe was in thinking mode, but he leaned forward, took a sip of his tea, and asked, "What do you think the motive is?"

"It's not about a revolution." He pointed back at Chawla's notes. "That real estate on Hudson clocks in at how many hundreds of millions of dollars?"

"Not including business interruption, it was insured for $4.5 billion."

Lucas opened his hands in a *How-can-it-be-anything-else?* gesture. "It's about money. It has to be."

Kehoe crossed his arms. "How?"

Lucas shrugged. "I don't know."

Kehoe pointed at the door. "Then shouldn't you be somewhere else?"

32

The Upper East Side—Fifth Avenue

Eddie Roberts had been a doorman at the McDougall Arms for thirteen years, and it was a job he enjoyed. The tenants were polite most of the time (with the exception of Mr. Green, who was never nice—*all of the time*). He never had to wait for his paycheck, and every Christmas he got enough in tips to buy the wife something nice, get the kids whatever television had convinced them they couldn't live without, and pay off a chunk of his mortgage. Not bad work considering that the scope of his day involved opening and closing the front door; occasionally helping one of the tenants out of a cab—either because they were drunk or because they had just come back from hip surgery (both were regular occurrences with the tenant demographic); bringing packages in from the trunks of rented Town Cars; and every now and then holding an umbrella while someone got into a car. Like everything in life, there were hiccups in this routine that occasionally had him scrambling, but for the most part he figured that he would ride this job out to retirement.

Fall was behind schedule this year, and the park across the

street was a hundred shades of beautiful since the leaves had yet to fall. Which meant there would be tourists all up and down Fifth today. But Eddie was a glass-half-full kind of guy, and he was just grateful that the weather was nice. Especially with all the shit on the news. It was so bad that his wife hated him coming in to work in the city—if you listened to the idiots on CNN or FOX, they could convince you that the world was ending. Which Eddie knew was horseshit. This was New York. People got killed all the time. But people were born all the time, too. As his old man said, it all worked out in the wash.

He was outside enjoying the day, watching the traffic, and waiting to open a door—of either the vehicular or building variety. Halloween was on the way and a few kids walked by, all dressed up as characters he didn't recognize. His own children were now too old to go out trick-or-treating, but back in the day, they had gone through the classics—ghosts and witches and Mexicans and hoboes. One of his boys had been a Ghostbuster three years running. And one of his daughters had always been a princess. But these days everyone was a superhero of some sort. Or that Harry Potter kid. No one had any imagination anymore.

He was about to go inside when there was an explosion somewhere overhead—it couldn't be anything else. Eddie jumped—literally—before looking up.

Eddie had time to begin a single word that began with the letter F before the corner of the building drove him two feet into the sidewalk.

33

Fifth Avenue

The apartment had all the correct appointments of wealth: superb examples of period furniture; artwork that cost more than many lifelong incomes; a walk-in closet that rivaled any shop on Rodeo Drive; a bar stocked with thousand-dollar bottles of booze. It was nose-thumbing of the finest order and would look equally at home on the cover of either *Architectural Digest* or *What the Fuck Just Happened Here? Monthly*.

The apartment was owned by a Mr. Jonathan Makepeace—hedge fund manager, philanthropist, art collector, cigar aficionado, and deconstructed human being. What was left of him had been collected in Tupperware bins and carted down to the morgue for an autopsy. But it was no big secret what had killed him—the same explosive device that had blown the corner of the apartment out into the street, punching the doorman into the sidewalk, destroying nine cars, and ruining the false sense of security the other tenants used to rely on.

Lucas stood at the edge of the living room carpet—a massive expanse of hand-knotted silk—staring at a crime scene that reminded him of things he had worked very hard to forget. Makepeace had been at his desk overlooking Central Park when the device detonated. Calvin-Wade Curtis's people were invested in the idea that the bomb had been in his humidor, which was as close to a *smoking kills* commercial as you could get.

Makepeace's upper torso had taken the brunt of the explosion, but that was not to say the rest of him had survived intact—his legs had been found in eleven different pieces. His hips and some of his internal organs were discovered halfway across the room. One of his fingers had been stuck to a curtain.

Three separate FBI teams were shuffling around the apartment—almost thirty people—and Lucas could feel the uneasy quiet that comes from fighting an invisible enemy.

Lucas was not happy to be there and it must have been obvious by his expression because Whitaker said, "If this is too much for you, we can go."

Chawla had already left, which was good because Lucas didn't want to deal with him right now.

He gave his first lie of the day with "I'm good." But the air outside had to be a lot nicer than in here—even with the new ventilation hole in the wall. "Who was this guy?"

Whitaker flipped through her notes and Lucas wondered if anyone in the bureau had any memory retention whatsoever.

"Ran a hedge fund, Makepeace Capital."

"What was their market share?"

"A little over sixty . . ."—she looked up—"*billion.*"

"In what?" The bomb had blasted a hole in the floor, tearing through the carpet and marble, exposing joists like denuded ribs. There was a nice little Seurat—or at least what used to be a nice little Seurat—on the edge of the hole, charred and half gone. There was a bloody footprint on the floor beside it.

She held up her phone. "All I have is the Google stuff—we're waiting on the SEC and the CFTC for more. But the guy was a known commodity. Power player for almost forty years. Started with Goldman Sachs before breaking out with his own fund. When he started, he was heavily invested in aviation and aerospace, and he bolstered these with arms manufacturers. Then he got into tech stocks while everyone else was still investing in phonograph needles, and rode the dot-com boom of the early nineties from a $300 million footprint to $2.5 billion, back when that word meant something. He cashed out before the bust and diverted his energies to emerging industrial nations, large-scale agriculture in particular. In 2007, he switched focus to clean and renewable energy, which helped his clients avoid the toxic subprime mortgage burnout, then moved them back into food production. His latest push was for water futures." She looked up. "What are water futures?"

"When the world runs out of water, we'll have to buy it from guys like Makepeace." A pigeon flew in, and landed on the arm of the sofa. "Did he have anything to do with Horizon Dynamics?"

Whitaker shrugged. "I don't know—the SEC will give us anything his books can't. Whatever we can glean from his hard drive is technically ours—the lab boys pulled his computer out of the bedroom wall in there," she said, pointing at a hole through the living room paneling. "But a full summary of his accounts will take a few hours."

"I know he wasn't on the guest list—I've gone over that already." Lucas ran back through her summary. "Agriculture? They use ammonium nitrate in agriculture. Horizon Dynamics is in environmental risk assessment and the reclamation of depleted ecosystems, which fits. And arms? We found C-4 at the hub on Eighth. And in his humidor."

"So is this what you would call a positive development?"

Lucas looked around the apartment. "Not for Mr. Makepeace."

"He was a dot-com guy—which fits with Chawla's narrative."

Lucas realized that she was adopting his us-versus-them

mentality, and he wasn't sure it was the right approach—one skeptic on their team was enough. "Did he always work at home?"

"A couple of days a week—his wife said he had become a bit of a homebody in the past few years. He was trying to smell the roses a little more—her words, not mine."

"We need a list of every single person he has dealt with, or thought about dealing with, from the day he hung out his shingle."

"That'll be covered under the umbrella of our warrants."

Makepeace had had two visitors that morning—a UPS deliveryman and a guy in a blue suit who sported short-cropped blond hair that would have looked at home in the Addams Family. He had arrived with a big manila envelope and left without it.

Two of Chawla's people had interviewed the UPS guy—he had arrived about twenty seconds after the big blond guy and left thirty seconds before—and he did his best to give them a summary of his visit. He was pretty shaken by the realization that he may have driven around with a bomb in his possession. They traced the delivery, and it had merely been an envelope of proxy forms for one of the corporations Makepeace dealt with. He said that the big guy in the suit had stood there in silence while Mr. Makepeace signed for his envelope, then sent him on his way. Apparently the big guy in the suit had made him uncomfortable—*menacing*, was how he had put it.

The big blond guy was the unknown—they were in the process of hunting him down. If he was a known commodity, they'd have something within half an hour. And if they couldn't figure out who he was, they'd put out a BOLO, and the big machine of public surveillance would find him.

Lucas's phone buzzed with Paul Knechtel's number, the Wall Street friend he and Whitaker had visited yesterday. Lucas answered, "Dr. Page here," and headed for the only place in the apartment not populated by FBI people—the kitchen,

"You've been busy since you left my office yesterday."

"You have no idea."

"Actually, I do. Which is why I called. I have some information."

Lucas stepped into the kitchen and went around the island—a big slab of lapis lazuli with four sinks embedded in the top. "That was fast." But success on Wall Street depended on having information before the competition, which meant it operated on a different kind of time than the rest of the world.

"The internet hub on Hudson that was blown up last night is insured by a company owned by the Hockney brothers. Which means they have to pony up for a $4.5 billion payout."

"The people who own Horizon Dynamics?"

"Yes. And in the past two days they've lost a company that was headed for a strong IPO along with a check for $4.5 bil that is not going to make their stockholders very happy. And when it becomes known, a lot of people are going to take a shot across the Hockney bow. They'll weather the storm, but they'll lose a lot of blood.

"And remember when I said that the Paraguayans were in town hunting up infrastructure funding? I can't tell you how I know, but they're thinking about pulling up stakes and heading home. They can get everything they want from the Chinese, and the Hockneys are looking a little wobbly right now. But they're still here, and it looks like they stayed because another financier is willing to float them the necessary funds. Again, Luke, this is not common knowledge and you can't mention my name."

"I won't." Lucas stared down at the deep blue countertop. "This other investor, what else can you tell me about him?"

"Back in the day he and the Hockneys did a lot of business. He started out as a stockbroker and handled a lot of their investments, but they had a falling-out a few years back. He's top tier. Knows what he's doing. You asked who would profit from wiping Horizon Dynamics off the map—he would be that guy. I'd talk to him if I were you."

Lucas turned back to the living room and focused on the crater that extended out over Fifth Avenue. "Is his name Jonathan Makepeace?"

"How the hell did you know that?"

Lucas stared at the hole blown into the room. "Lucky guess."

34

The Hockney brothers had offices at the crossroads of conspic-
uous consumption and overindulgence, just off Fifth Avenue on
57th Street. Bvlgari, Tiffany, Louis Vuitton, Piaget, Van Cleef &
Arpels, and Trump Tower were all there. Whitaker parked at the
curb and Lucas had to wait for a homeless man holding out a paper
cup to move before he could open the door.

Security in the lobby was befitting the main terminal at Ben
Gurion Airport. There were six armed guards by the entry points,
their Kevlar and nylon gear at direct odds with the decor. Evidently the Hockney brothers were taking what had happened at
the Guggenheim—and what had happened to the internet hub on
Hudson Street—a little personally.

Lucas and Whitaker badged past the first desk but had to sign
in at the desk for HWE—Hockney Worldwide Enterprises. The
security officer behind the second desk took his job seriously, and
inspected both of their ID cards after flicking Whitaker's badge
with his fingernail. He photographed them, gave each a still-warm
laminated pass, and had them speak their names into a digital

registry. When they had jumped through the appropriate security hoops, he pointed them in the direction of the elevator.

The elevator was paneled in oak, accented in brass, and scented with Christmas-tree-in-a-bottle. As soon as Whitaker fingered the button, the car shot up into the building; it had no doubt been designed for people who got paid by the second.

They didn't speak on the way up, and Lucas knew that Whitaker was sharing the realization that they were being watched. Lucas adjusted his sunglasses and, after checking his reflection in the big brass panel, ran a hand through his hair so he looked a little less like Billy Zoom.

The elevator slowed, pinged one soft chime, and stopped. The doors slid open to a woman in her twenties wearing a Chanel outfit in a big black and white houndstooth check that made her look like an optical illusion when she stood up to greet them. "Detectives Whitaker and Page," she said.

Whitaker hoisted her shield. "It's *Special Agent* Whitaker and this is Dr. Page. FBI, not NYPD." She didn't break character when she said, "We are here to speak to William and Seth Hockney," in her *Don't-fuck-with-me* voice.

The woman smiled and her outfit came to life as she walked around the desk. "I'm sorry, but you'll need an appointment. They are not in the habit of speaking to just anyone and—"

Whitaker lowered her volume precipitously when she said, "Unless you want fifty agents in FBI parkas to sweep in here in about ten minutes, you get us in to speak to the Misters Hockney *right now*."

The receptionist shifted on her feet, and this had the effect of changing the pattern on her jacket, as if she were a chameleon. "Please have a seat over there while I tell them that you are here." She gestured to a bank of Herman Miller chairs that had all the appeal of airport lounge furniture, then went back to her desk and spoke a few hushed sentences into the phone.

Other than the receptionist-cum-gatekeeper, there were no other visible humans. The desk backed onto a marble wall that stretched away at right angles to points unknown, forming a wide hallway that contained architectural models in glass cases every twenty feet—miniature representations of the jewels of the Hockney empire: office towers, stadiums, ports, railway yards, and factories. But scenes from the natural world were absent—there were no mountains or forests or lakes represented.

The click of leather soles was audible for forty paces before a man turned the corner, into their line of sight.

Whitaker elbowed Lucas. "It's the bad motor scooter from Makepeace's lobby—the one with the Addams family haircut who scared the UPS guy."

By the way he moved, Lucas guessed that he was the head of security or some other such functionary whose sole job was to keep the Hockneys isolated from the masses. Or people like him and Whitaker.

Without looking at—or even acknowledging—Lucas or Whitaker, he went to the desk and spoke softly into the receptionist's ear. Lucas couldn't hear what he said, but the receptionist's outfit changed hue again and she glanced up at them, then looked back down at the glass top of her desk. She nodded, mumbled something, then fell silent as Lurch came over.

"Special Agents Whitaker, Page, may I help you?"

"Yes. We're looking for someone." Whitaker held up her phone, screen out, displaying a frame from the surveillance footage of Makepeace's lobby. "You."

Lurch's expression didn't shift when he said, "And here I am," as if this were simply another minor inconvenience in a day full of them. "I am Mr. Frosst."

"We'd like to ask you a few questions."

Frosst examined her, then shifted focus to Lucas, his attention going down to the green anodized hand, then up to the bad eye behind the sunglasses. "I assume you want to ask me about my visit to Jonathan Makepeace's earlier today."

"Why would you assume that?"

"I'm probably one of the last people to see him alive."

"So you know he's dead."

Frosst smiled, but there was nothing friendly in it. "Obviously."

Lucas recognized a hint of either West Virginia or eastern Kentucky in his accent. He had polished the edges down, but it was still there in the way he almost added an extra syllable to every second word.

Frosst locked Whitaker in his stare. "I would like to do this in front of my employer—I was at Mr. Makepeace's on their behalf. But I am afraid they are in an important meeting right now and can't be disturbed. If you could come back on Tuesday, that would be—"

Whitaker took a step toward him and the man shifted his weight, reducing his profile—the instinct of a fighter. "Just make it happen. I don't want to come back here with a warrant and drag you out in handcuffs."

As Frosst examined her, Lucas knew he was looking for a weak spot.

She said, "I won't tell you a second time."

Frosst kept his cool, but the muscles beneath his jaw flexed. He held the pose for a second, and Lucas wondered if he knew what he was up against with her. But Frosst went through the calculations and decided that this wasn't a fight he wanted. "Please follow me," he said, all traces of his accent now erased.

Like Paul Knechtel's office on Wall Street, everything had been chosen for impact, not subtlety. But considering that these were the flagship offices of a family that had its fingers shoved into the economic pies of every major industry in the world, the hallways had as much traffic as an abandoned Egyptian tomb—all that was missing were a few feet of sand on the floor and ancient Roman graffiti on the walls.

Complementing the scale dioramas of the jewels of the Hockney empire, the walls were adorned with the names of the hundreds of corporations that fell under their control, and Lucas couldn't help making the conscious connection that he knew most of them. Evidently, theirs was a wealth that could not easily be measured. Or, more than likely, taxed.

Frosst delivered them to a door that looked like the portal to Jurassic Park—if Jurassic Park had been populated by billionaires who liked Makassar ebony and Art Deco lines.

When they walked in, Frosst made the introductions and it was obvious that the routine was part of his function around them.

William and Seth Hockney looked just like one would expect old billionaires to look. William, now pushing seventy-five, was tall and thin, with cheekbones that had probably helped him pick up nearly as many women as his wealth. He was in gray wool slacks, bespoke cap-toe shoes, and a very nice blazer. He could have been leading the von Trapp family as they ripped through "Edelweiss."

Since William got the looks, it made sense that Seth didn't. He was small, standing five-two in heels that were too thick, and wore a suit that did its best to mask that one of his arms was slightly longer than the other. He had a heavy-lidded stare that did little to enhance his already iffy looks. But there was no missing the intelligence behind his eyes, and Lucas knew that a lot of people had probably underestimated him.

"And what are you here to help us with today?" William's mid-Atlantic accent was precise and effortless.

Lucas kept Frosst in his peripheral vision when he said, "I understand that you know Jonathan Makepeace was murdered earlier."

William looked at Lucas, then switched focus to Whitaker, then back to Lucas. "Do we need a lawyer present?"

"No, but we would like to ask Mr. Frosst here a few questions—he asked that you be included in the conversation."

William glanced over at Frosst, and apparently the look held meaning because Frosst shifted on his feet and said, "I had delivered an envelope for you."

That did little to shift William's obvious irritation at having to speak to the plebeians, but he knew when he was at a disadvantage, if only theoretically. "Please, make this brief. I am sure you are aware that we have a lot going on today."

Whitaker made a production of pulling out her notebook. "So how long were you at Mr. Makepeace's?" The source media were time-stamped. Frosst had entered Makepeace's lobby at 10:13:42, leaving at 10:22:22. Security footage showed that he entered the apartment at 10:16:07 and left at 10:19:59—an inside time of three minutes, fifty-two seconds. Plenty of time to plant a bomb in a humidor if you knew what you were doing. And Frosst certainly looked like he knew what he was doing.

Lucas could see that Whitaker was gearing up to get angry, so he stepped in. "Why was he there?"

William waved it away. "As he said, he was dropping off some papers for us."

"Would they have been in reference to the Paraguayan infrastructure fund he was about to pull out from under you?"

William had excellent poker skills, but Seth didn't, and his jaw dropped open.

William said, "The nature of our business with Mr. Makepeace is confidential." But he was eyeing Lucas now, and there was a lot going on behind the facade of control.

Whitaker was busy writing in her notebook as she asked, "So, how long were you in Mr. Makepeace's apartment?"

"Less than four minutes."

Which was the answer of a man who had paid attention. Of course the logical next question was: *Who paid attention to how long they were in someone's home?* The answer was: *people who planted bombs.*

"Were you alone with Mr. Makepeace?"

Frosst took a deep breath. "The housekeeper was there. And a UPS deliveryman showed up while I was there. He arrived about thirty seconds after I did and left thirty seconds before." Which squared with the story the UPS driver had told the agents who had interviewed him.

"Did you notice anything out of the ordinary?"

Frosst shrugged. "The housekeeper let me in. I met Makepeace in the living room at his desk. We spoke briefly: *How are you? I am fine*—that sort of stuff. Then the UPS driver showed up. Delivered a package to Mr. Makepeace. Then we both waited in the living room while Mr. Makepeace went to another room, then came back and handed the UPS man two large overnight envelopes. He waited for the driver to sign the waybill and leave. I then gave Mr. Makepeace the envelope Mr. Hockney asked me to drop off, then left myself."

"Where was the housekeeper during your visit?"

"Keeping house."

Whitaker stopped taking notes and looked up at him. She raised an eyebrow and he came back with "Somewhere else. I don't know where. I didn't hear a vacuum or dishes being put away. The apartment was quiet. The apartment was *always* quiet—Mr. Makepeace was a calm, quiet man."

"What was he wearing?"

"Horsebit loafers—brown crocodile. A pair of chinos. A white button-down, the cuffs rolled up." He shifted on his feet and added, "I didn't see the color of his socks or underwear."

William Hockney held up a hand. "The agents are just doing their job. Someone killed Jon, and we all want to find out who. No one is accusing you of anything." He looked over at Whitaker, and turned on the paternal tone. "Are you, Special Agent Whitaker?" The forced calm was still there, and it was pretty convincing.

Whitaker stared at Frosst for a few moments before folding up her notebook and turning to William. "We understand that you and Mr. Makepeace had a close working relationship at one point. In light of what happened at the Guggenheim the other night, do you think his death is in any way linked to your business together?"

William waved a hand at the sofa and his sleeve crept up, exposing a watch that chimed in at a quarter of a million dollars. "Would you please have a seat? I can't stand for long."

Everyone migrated to the sofa and club chairs by a fireplace large enough to roast an entire steer. William and Seth took up position in the club chairs, and Lucas and Whitaker got a sofa. Mr. Frosst stayed near the door. *Still looking like he has a stick up his ass,* Lucas thought.

Whitaker picked up where she had left off. "I know you've been interviewed by other agents regarding the bombing at the Guggenheim, and I apologize for any redundancy in our questioning, but it's obvious that your interests are somehow part of these attacks."

William stared at her for a few cold seconds before turning to Lucas. "You are Dr. Lucas Page, the astrophysicist?"

"Apparently, yes."

William Hockney smiled as if there was some hidden joke in the question. "I see."

Whitaker killed the silence with "When was the last time either of you saw Mr. Makepeace?"

William shrugged. "Three, maybe four months ago. It was in Zurich. I can check the dates should you wish."

"Thank you, that would be good." She held out a card. "Do you know of anyone who would wish ill on Mr. Makepeace?"

Seth answered that one with "All of Wall Street."

"Anyone in specific?"

William waved the question away. "Please excuse my brother, he tends to the melodramatic."

With that, public dominance was now established.

William continued with "But he is not wrong in that Mr. Make-peace was a very aggressive investor. He was also successful. It has been my experience that this particular combination of elements tends to foster jealousy in others."

Whitaker's phone buzzed. She checked the number, then excused herself from the conversation.

While she went over to the window, William reacquired Lucas. "And what, may I ask, is a man of your reputation and upbringing doing with the FBI, Dr. Page?" William looked honestly perplexed.

"My facility with numbers is an advantage."

"Pearls before swine. Should you ever want to challenge yourself, I would be more than happy to discuss a position for you." He held up a hand, palm out. "Not that I am trying to hire you away from your esteemed company here, but a man of your abilities could do so much better with his time."

"Well, that's very condescending of you, but thank you. If I ever feel like being underappreciated, I'll know where to come."

William dead-eyed him.

Whitaker hung up and snapped her fingers at Lucas, who stood up.

As they headed for the door, Whitaker said, "We will be in touch," to no one in particular.

Lucas raced down the hallway, trying to keep pace with Whitaker, and the door closed behind him. "What is it?" he asked.

"There's been another bombing."

35

Pelham Gardens

Lucas stood on the sidewalk, staring up into a tree. A bonsai was jammed into the crotch of a branch fifteen feet up. It was mangled, half of its pot gone, diminutive roots dangling free, small fingers of dirt stuck to them.

"How very meta," he said.

Whitaker followed his line of attention. "Leave it to you."

He turned to her and arched his eyebrow.

"Look around."

So he did.

There were too many emergency vehicles, a platoon of NYPD officers in uniform, and a duplex that had most of the first floor blown out. But she was talking about the bonsai. They were everywhere. All over the sidewalk; all over the street; all over the cars; all over the park *across* the street.

The water from the fire hoses had settled into puddles, but there was still runoff heading for a storm drain somewhere down the street. The FDNY guys were stacking hoses on the back of one of the trucks and two ambulances sat silent, lights flashing with no apparent purpose. A bonsai dragged along in the current, hiccupping toward parts unknown.

No one had bothered with all the little dead charred trees strewn around other than to drive over them, kick them out of the way, or stomp on them. Some were still smoking, and it looked like Gulliver and the Lilliputians had really gotten their drink on before duking it out in a tiny forest.

But the damage to the trees was minor when compared to what had happened to the house. It had been a typical three-story duplex with main entrances at either end, both up identical eight-step stoops. But the first floor on both units had blown out—that the entire building hadn't collapsed was testament to American postwar craftsmanship and building materials. And luck. What was left had been eaten black by flames.

A crowd had assembled at the end of the block. Like the others, this one was populated by people in costumes—mostly superheroes and *Star Wars* characters. They were chanting *False flag! False flag! False flag!* on loop.

Samir Chawla was beside one of the bureau wagons, speaking to Calvin-Wade Curtis, who had his smile dialed up to solar level. Lucas wished he would do something about the habit, like punch himself in the face when he felt it coming on. Chawla saw them and came over.

They exchanged curt but civil greetings.

"What have we got?" Whitaker asked.

Chawla went to work on the tablet that Lucas had come to realize was indispensable to him. "The house is rented by a doctor of some sort—academic, not medical. His name's Timo Saarinen and he's the project manager for Horizon Dynamics. We've had a pair of agents on him just in case the people who bombed the Guggenheim decided to go after stragglers and no-shows. They were parked out front and said it was a normal day. No comings or goings. Saarinen stepped out his front door to walk the dog when the place went up. The dog hadn't cleared the sill and his wife and housekeeper were inside. Wife and housekeeper are dead. Dog too. But Saarinen survived. He's a little beat-up, but nothing a few stitches and some painkillers won't fix. He's down the street in an ambulance—he's refusing to leave the scene until someone tells him what happened. He's not being what I would call *cooperative*."

"Did Curtis have anything to add?"

Chawla scrolled through his notes and Lucas wondered if the guy had any memory to speak of.

"C-4 again. Curtis is on his way back to the lab to see if he can match it to the other sites, but I think we all know what he's going to find. We don't know what kind of trigger. Yet."

Whitaker pointed at the ambulance up the street. "Did you interview the victim?"

"I ran him through the basics but didn't get anything useful and figured you could take a shot when you got here. See if you can fill out any of the blanks—he didn't give me much and I didn't want to push him. He's pretty upset."

Lucas looked up at the house. "No shit," was all he could think to offer.

Whitaker put a hand on Chawla's arm. "Thanks, Samir." She pulled out her phone and gently waved it at him. "I'll record our interview."

Chawla nodded a thanks and walked away.

Lucas and Whitaker headed over to the ambulance, passing a gaggle of firemen putting gear away. One of them smiled over at Whitaker. "Hey, sexy lady, would you like to—"

"How about you go fuck yourself, short bus!"

The fireman's expression went from lascivious to heartbroken, and he turned away.

"And I'm the one who needs to chill?" Lucas said.

"Any asshole who screams at me on the street gets an immediate rejection—it's a principle I have."

"I can't say I disagree." After half a dozen steps, Lucas asked, "What did your ex-husband do?"

"As little as he could to make me happy."

"I meant for a living."

"He's a baker."

"As in 'rub-a-dub-dub, three men in a tub'?"

"Something like that, yeah."

Lucas decided that small talk was too much trouble, so he shut up. But his questions had triggered Whitaker, and she said, "It's not like I'm *not* interested in dating. But I haven't been out with a man in so long my neighbors are thinking about sacrificing me to a volcano. I just don't meet the right kind of men out there."

"Well, maybe telling prospective dates to stick their own genitals into their own anuses is limiting your prospects."

She smiled up at him. "Look at you, being all caring and shit. It's like your dreams of being a real boy came true."

"I quit. This friendship thing is too esoteric."

"You don't have any friends; everyone around you suffers from Stockholm syndrome."

Whitaker flashed her badge at the NYPD man keeping watch over the ambulance. He stepped aside and she knocked.

Someone inside said, "Come in," and when Whitaker opened the back door, the paramedic nodded a hello. Saarinen was staring at the floor and didn't look up. He was shirtless but still in suit pants and a pair of monk straps with bright red socks. There was a dog leash wrapped around his hand and a foot of leather dangled from his fingers, the end charred and tattered. He clocked out somewhere in his late fifties and had one of those frames that can happen only with a lifetime of healthy eating, exercise, and good DNA. He looked more like a tennis pro than an academic. He sat on the stretcher while a tech pulled debris and shrapnel from his back that he dropped into a little plastic bowl dripping red.

"Dr. Saarinen, I'm Special Agent Whitaker and this is Dr. Page. May we speak with you?"

Saarinen nodded in a gesture that could have meant *come on in* or *go fuck yourself* that he punctuated with a grunt.

They stepped up into the ambulance and Lucas pulled the door closed; anyone whose wife had just been blown up deserved a little privacy.

They sat on the gurney across from him. Saarinen didn't look up when he asked, "Dr. Lucas Page, the astrophysicist?"

Lucas said, "Yes."

Saarinen gave another nod as if that made no sense at all. Or all the sense in the world. "I can't help you."

Whitaker was using her friendliest voice. "Could we ask you a few questions? You might know something without being aware of it." She knelt down and looked up into his face. "Please. It's important."

Nothing about his expression said that he had heard her. But he waved his hand—the one with the frayed leash in it—and said, "Suit yourself."

Lucas tried to ignore the singed hair and blood and the stink of creosote and disinfectant because the sensory memory would start fucking with his head. So he concentrated on watching Whitaker try to connect with a man who was somewhere else.

"What happened?" she asked.

"I was taking Bongo out for a walk. I stepped out of the house and I guess my wife opened the back door at the same time, because the wind slammed the front door. Bongo was still inside. I turned to open the door and that's . . ." He hit the consonants a little too hard in an unmistakable Finnish accent. "Then I woke up on the sidewalk. My trees were everywhere. My house was on fire. My wife was inside. Our housekeeper—" And he just stopped, as if he ran out of tape.

"Our people found traces of a chemical compound used in commercial explosives—C-4. We haven't been able to isolate its signature, but we'll know more in a few hours." Whitaker took up a seat beside Lucas, facing Saarinen. "Anything you want to know?"

"No."

"Have you had any visitors in the past few days? Any service people? Any packages arrive with the mail? Anything that might lead us to how this device made its way into your house?"

Saarinen winced as the tech pulled a shard of glass from his shoulder and said, "I was out of the country until the night before last. I came home the night of the bombing at the Guggenheim. I lost all of my friends. My employees. And now . . ."—tears welled up in his eyes—"this."

The paramedic asked, "You sure you don't want something for the pain? Not even topical?"

Saarinen stuck with the less-is-more school of language—another typically Finnish trait. "Just finish." When he shifted focus back to Whitaker, he appeared to see the dog leash for the first time. He unwrapped it from his hand and dropped it to the floor. "All I remember was opening the door to take Bongo for a walk." Saarinen stared down at the leash. "And *boom*." He looked up and Lucas knew exactly what was going on behind his eyes. "How much bad luck can visit a person? The last time was enough."

Whitaker's voice wobbled a little when she said, "What *last time*?"

Saarinen fastened his stare on her. "When they blew up my son."

36

Pelham Gardens

The servos moving Saarinen's facial muscles locked in place for a moment and he looked like he had ceased movement down to the cellular level. Then something inside him relaxed, or simply broke down, and he eyed Lucas for a few long seconds. "One of those things that happen. I was on a project in Nicaragua. Cutting-edge work. Magic, really. But as always, there were *political problems.* The uneducated didn't want us there. And to make their point—" He stopped and pinched the bridge of his nose. "A company bus was attacked. Thirty-seven people were on board. They used an antitank rocket." He looked up. "One of the victims was my son, Jukka." He shook his head. "People too ignorant to realize that we were trying to help them. To better their lives."

"When was that?"

"February 21, 2005." His European education was highlighted when he said *twenty-one* instead of *twenty-first.*

The tech was trying to get a piece of metal out of the nape of Saarinen's neck and Lucas focused on the procedure because it was better than looking at the sorrow on the man's face. "I've seen the guest list and you weren't at the Guggenheim for the gala. Why was that?"

Saarinen waved it away. "I should have been there." He paused for a few seconds. "I lost everyone I knew." He looked up at Lucas. "I was on a plane on my way back from Paraguay. The plan was to make an appearance at the end of the evening, but there was no *end of the evening.*" The paramedic tugged the piece of metal free. It was curved like a fishhook and Saarinen didn't flinch when it pulled his skin, then popped free. "Some madman took it away." He looked down at the leash coiled up between his feet.

Lucas knew all the things that were going on in Saarinen's head. The anger. The sadness. The survivor's guilt. And he knew that they would morph into other feelings—mostly rage. "Do you know a Jonathan Makepeace?"

At that, Saarinen looked up. "Of course."

"How do you know him?"

"He does a lot of work for William Hockney."

Lucas thought back to what Knechtel had said. And about the last time Hockney said he had seen Makepeace in Zurich—*several months ago.* "We just spoke to William and Seth Hockney, and apparently neither has seen him for months."

Saarinen shook his head. "Not William *Senior*, William *Junior.*"

Lucas saw the lights go on in Whitaker's head, but he stuck with questioning Saarinen—any minute now he was going to close up. "Dr. Saarinen, do you know of anyone who would profit by disrupting things for either Horizon Dynamics or the Hockneys?"

"Social progress is always hindered by the ignorant who feel they are being left behind. Some village farmer killed my son for no reason other than he was terrified that the world was evolving without him and he wanted to stop it from happening. This is America." Saarinen's eyes narrowed and he looked over at Lucas, then to Whitaker, then back at Lucas. "There are plenty of people who feel they are being left behind."

37

Lucas was trying to focus on something other than the emotions their conversation with Saarinen had stirred up. "Do you have spare handcuffs?"

Whitaker jabbed an index at the glove compartment. "In there."

Lucas found them tucked in between typical Whitaker glove compartment emergency gear—which meant a few packets of ketchup, a chocolate bar, one bent straw, three spare magazines of 9mm, and a hunting knife.

He held the cuffs up and shook his head. "I can't believe that we're still using shit like this in the twenty-first century."

"You were expecting space handcuffs or something?" Whitaker pointed back at the glove box. "You can always put them back."

Lucas forced the strands though their turns a few times, each rotation accentuated by the cicada click of the ratchet. He slid the cuffs into the hip pocket on his suit jacket. "Not until we catch this guy." As a scientist, he had spent his life trying to be an unbiased observer, but this one was testing his abilities.

Whitaker's cell phone rang over the Bluetooth system. She hit the hands-free button. "Whitaker."

"Yeah, Special Agent Whitaker, this is Calvin-Wade Curtis."

By the way Curtis's voice unfolded from the speaker, Lucas could tell the guy was smiling. Which with him could mean good news, bad news, or neutral news.

"Hey, Curtis. What can I do for you?"

"You with Dr. Page?"

"I'm here."

"Okay. First off, the C-4 used to murder Jonathan Makepeace and to kill Dr. Saarinen's wife and housekeeper matched the batch used at the internet hub on Hudson Street and the undetonated bomb we found on Eighth. Same manufacturer—ENF in Sweden; same batch—which was apparently sold to a mining company in Brazil." Curtis rustled some papers at the other end of the line. "I had our financial people look into ENF, and I just got a call back. ENF is a publicly traded company, but it took our guys a day and a half to track this down because it's hidden behind a mile of paperwork, three dozen shell corporations, and a whole lot of dead end conversations—but guess who the majority stockholders are?"

Lucas leaned into the mic. "The Hockney brothers."

There was silence at the other end of the line for a few seconds before Curtis came back on with "How did you know?"

Lucas let Whitaker say it.

"Lucky guess." She hit the asshole lights and flipped on the siren, then pulled the big SUV around in a tight arc of smoking rubber that left a phalanx of honking cars in their wake.

38

57th Street

William Hockney looked up from his desk with an expression that could loosely be described as amused irritation. He took off his glasses, folded them up, and slowly placed them down on the leather surface. "Ah, Dr. Page and Special Agent Whitaker. What a lovely surprise." Evidently, old William's sarcasm wasn't too rusty.

Mr. Frosst stepped away from Whitaker and Lucas. "They insisted on seeing you, sir."

William waved him away with a flutter of his fingers. "Of course they did." The old man stood up and steadied himself on the corner of his desk as he stepped out from behind it. "So what can I do for you two this time?" The amused irritation was back, but Lucas knew it wouldn't last long—people like William Hockney valued their time.

Whitaker stepped forward. "Someone just blew up Dr. Timo Saarinen's house."

"His wife, housekeeper, dog, and miniature tree collection were killed," Lucas added.

William stared at him and all the emotion drained from his face. "And Timo?"

"He's banged up. And none too happy. But he's alive."

Whitaker pulled out her notebook. "He sustained minor injuries. He's down at Federal Plaza, giving us a statement."

William nodded as if that were the appropriate action and walked over to the Art Deco cabinetry that filled out one wall of the office. He pushed a button beneath one of the moldings and a pair of floor-to-ceiling doors slid back, exposing a selection of scotches and whiskeys that rivaled the Imelda Marcos shoe collection. Hockey cracked a bottle of whiskey with a Japanese label and poured three fingers into a silver-rimmed highball.

He walked over to the seating area around the fireplace and lowered himself into one of the club chairs. After putting a belt of booze away, he waved at one of the sofas. "Sit." He stared at the whiskey in his hand. "Please."

The ease and polish had worn off a bit and he didn't bother with his poker face as he mulled things over.

Whitaker looked at Lucas and he shrugged. So they sat down facing Hockney.

"I assume that there is more bad news," the old man said as he stared intently at Lucas.

"The explosives came from a company that you own."

Hockney nodded as if he had expected that. "Of course it did."

Whitaker tapped her notebook. "It was an explosive putty—C-4. The same batch was used at the bombing of the internet hub on Hudson Street last night and at Jonathan Makepeace's apartment this morning. We haven't released this to the press yet, but another device was found at the internet hub at 111 Eighth Avenue. It failed to detonate, but it contained the same C-4."

Frosst came back in, accompanying Seth Hockney and another, younger man who looked like he had been built out of William's genetic building blocks—no doubt William Junior.

"Why are they back?" Seth barked.

William said, "Someone tried to kill Timo," into his highball. Then he pointed at the other man with Seth. "Dr. Page, Special Agent Whitaker, this is my son, William." He didn't look up with the introduction.

Junior nodded twice and Lucas half expected him to click his heels as he did so.

William held up his glass, and without being told, it was Junior who went to the bar instead of Frosst, which surprised Lucas. The younger Hockney poured another three fingers into the highball and returned it to his father's still-upheld hand; evidently the old man's drinking habits were routine.

William took another sip of whiskey, then looked over at Seth. "It was an explosion. Timo's wife and housekeeper are dead."

"Don't forget his dog." Lucas wanted to pry a few seams open to see how these people reacted, because the only certainty up to this point was that the Hockneys were somehow in the mix.

At that, William Hockney gave him the same look that Erin gave him when he was prickly out in public, and it had only one meaning—*shut the fuck up.*

Hockney put the glass down on the table. "Apparently the explosives used in the attempt on Timo's life are identical to the ones used to kill Makepeace this morning and in the attack on the internet hub on Hudson Street last night." He didn't mention the undetonated device found in the building on Eighth.

"So you're looking for one suspect? One group? These aren't coincidences?" Seth asked.

William Hockney let the irritation come out when he said, "Dr. Page, would you please explain the statistical probability of these attacks being coincidences to my brother."

But Lucas kept quiet and tried to absorb the dynamic. Whitaker was no doubt doing the same.

"There's more." William's focus was still on his drink, but there was a lot going on behind his now-sullen expression. "The explosives were manufactured by a company that we own."

At that, Seth came over and dropped into the other club chair.

Junior leaned against the mantel. He had his father's looks and fashion sense, but the command was somehow missing from his movements as if he had been pulled out of the oven before he had finished baking. But it had to be tough being the only son of a man like William Hockney—who had nine daughters from his five different marriages—after all, character is built on personal accomplishments, not inheritance.

"Which company?" Junior asked.

William gave him the same *shut up* look that he had given Lucas earlier.

Whitaker tapped her notebook again. "ENF."

At that, the elder William looked over at his son for a long hard moment. "That is a company that we bought on Mr. Makepeace's say-so when we were still doing business with him."

Lucas decided on one last kick at the tires. "Apparently you're still doing business with him. Or at least Junior here is."

William looked up at his son for one angry moment before turning his attention back to the drink. "If you have any more questions, Dr. Page, please direct them to our lawyers. Mr. Frosst will now walk you and your partner out." And with a flutter of his fingers, they were dismissed.

39

The Upper East Side

Whitaker stopped in front of the market on the corner of Madison. Lucas sat there for a moment, his aluminum fingers wrapped around the polished handle.

"You really think that Randolph and Mortimer will turn out to be our supervillains?"

Lucas smiled at that. "In today's world, with twenty-four-hour surveillance, the only people who *can* be bad guys are ancient billionaires." There were so many moving parts to the equation that he didn't see a through line in the narrative. "The only thing I *do* know is that their friends are really unlucky."

"What are the possibilities?"

"It's certainly not a revolution—I don't even know why anyone is still entertaining that idea." He thought things out for a few quiet seconds. "But if I wanted to blow a bunch of shit up, Frosst is exactly the kind of guy to do it."

"What are the odds that Frosst killed Makepeace?"

"I don't know. He was one of the last people to see Makepeace alive. And that UPS guy certainly didn't kill him. Maybe William

Senior found out that the sprog was working with Makepeace and he didn't like it. But that doesn't fit in with the Guggenheim bombing. At least going with what we know."

"Such as?"

Lucas shrugged. "How do the Hockneys profit in a situation where a company they're about to take public goes up in smoke? I'm not an accountant, but I don't see an upside. And the internet hub bombing? If they have to cut a check for $4.5 billion, it's a kick in the balls, not a boost to the bank account. And if Frosst killed Makepeace, he's the same guy who tried to blow up Saarinen."

Lucas went to open the door but paused again. "That Frosst guy scares me. If he did punch Makepeace's clock, he'd know that he'd get picked up by the surveillance camera—and he doesn't strike me as the careless type." Lucas stepped out and saluted with his aluminum hand. "Now if you will excuse me, I am going to scrounge up something to eat, then take a nap."

Whitaker stifled a yawn. "Don't rub it in."

Lucas closed the door and she pulled out into traffic, heading up Madison to turn east two blocks up, where she'd head over to Fifth.

He walked into the market on the corner. He had been shopping here for four years now, and the place felt like his. The prices were creeping up by increments, but in a neighborhood where the rental fees per square foot were some of the most expensive in the world, he didn't begrudge the owner trying to pay his bills.

Oscar was in today. He had emigrated from Italy twenty years ago and had gone from the fashion business of Milan to a market on Madison—a lane change that he attacked with panache. He was always perfectly dressed, and today was no exception. He wore slim jeans, red Prada flip-flops with a matching belt, and a blue linen shirt—the cuffs rolled up precisely one turn, exposing a gold Rolex. Lucas saw him around the neighborhood after hours with various women, and Erin joked that he had more sex than all of One Direction put together—which Lucas couldn't argue because he had no idea who (or what) One Direction was.

"And what will it be today, Dr. Page?" Oscar asked in a stage-worthy Italian accent.

"A couple of sandwiches. Any suggestions?" Which was a rhetorical question; Oscar loved making recommendations about everything, from the precise temperature at which to store fruit to which mascara held up in the rain. The kids called him Mr. Wikipedia, because he always sounded so convincing. The kids humored Oscar by asking his opinion on everything—a habit that many of his other customers went to great lengths to avoid. Even basic research revealed that most of the time he was full of shit.

"No-brainer today—chicken cutlet with Muenster and grainy mustard on ciabatta, or the croque monsieur." He added an extra syllable to the word *monsieur,* almost managing to make it sound Italian.

"One of each, then. To go, please." Maybe Dingo was hungry—he still owed him dinner from last night when he had abandoned him at Gray's Papaya.

As Oscar slid the sandwiches into the press, Lucas thought about the Hockneys and the sibling rivalry that was visible within the bespoke exterior. As has been true of firstborn children since time immemorial, William obviously thought of himself as the boss. And there was certainly tension between William and his son—Lucas would have to look into that. The only certainty was that William was no dummy. Seth was the unknown. Along with Frosst—just how did that guy fit into the little mélange?

Guys like Frosst got things done for the people around them. And the one characteristic that unified them on every permutation of a Venn diagram was their loyalty; they did things for the people they worked for with a fealty that often went beyond reason.

Lucas thought back to Mr. Teach, Mrs. Page's valet. She had

met him at a golf club in Jamaica. He was young then, in his mid-twenties, working as a caddie. One day he was assigned to her, and by the seventh hole she had offered him a position as her valet—a post he would occupy for almost four decades. And in that time, Mr. Teach had done things for Mrs. Page that could be explained only through the prism of love. Of course it was in no way a romantic version of the emotion. But what else could you really call it? Loyalty? Responsibility? It was both those things, but it was also kind and protective. And although Mrs. Page never would have asked, Lucas had no doubt that Mr. Teach would have killed for her.

Did the Hockneys foster that kind of loyalty?

Lucas paid for the sandwiches, wished Oscar a pleasant evening, and headed out after being told that it would no doubt rain.

It was early in the week, and Madison was customarily quiet in the hours after dinner. He walked by the belt store (the kids always got a kick that there was a store that sold only belts—no buckles), and the saleslady tinkering with the window display looked away as he nodded a hello. It no longer upset him, but sometimes it pissed off Erin. The new improved version of Dr. Lucas Page was hard for some people to put into context—they simply saw him as broken.

He passed the Apple store, and Lucas had come to the firm conclusion that there would indeed be a revolution over technology. But in the end people would not abandon their apps—they would abandon their humanity.

He turned down his street and there were limousines stacked up the block, all the way to Fifth—no doubt another party at the French embassy. Americans could bitch all they wanted about the French, but they knew how to enjoy themselves. Lucas had been invited to a few functions, but he had never taken them up on the offer and eventually they stopped asking.

He threaded through a few young people on the sidewalk in

expensive evening wear—black cap-toe shoes and dinner jackets offset by little black dresses and patent leather clutches. They were staring into their phones.

He keyed in the front door and was immediately hit by the sound of music somewhere in the house—it sounded like ABBA. Lemmy came ripping over from the kitchen in his trademark off-balance gallop.

Lucas dropped the sandwiches down on the Art Deco console and Lemmy poked him in the stomach, leaving a big wet slobber mark on his shirt. He scratched Lemmy behind the ears for a few seconds, then hollered a *Hello?* into the void. The kids all hollered back and feet pounded across the floor upstairs.

Erin was on her laptop at the island in the kitchen, beside a big vase of fresh-cut tulips. She took off her glasses—were those new frames?—and came over, sinking into his hug. Lemmy did circles, his tail whacking against Lucas's aluminum leg with each rotation. Then the kids blew into the kitchen.

And the past two days disappeared.

40

The Upper East Side

The crew was in particularly fine form tonight, and no one was bitching. Maude cleared the table; Lucas rinsed the dishes (he had modified a dish brush to attach to two of his fingers); Hector loaded the dishwasher; Laurie cleaned the table; and Damien put leftovers into Tupperware—which was unusual in that the kids usually ate everything put out. Even Alisha was contributing, sitting in her chair happily singing about an ant moving a rubber tree plant with the kind of vigor only a three-and-a-half-year-old can muster. Erin leaned against the island, going over files regarding the new office she was opening with Shapiro, oblivious to all the moving parts in the space around her.

While Lucas rinsed bits of noodle salad down the drain, he realized that as happy as he was to have them here, he would have been more at peace if they were still out at the beach house.

"Can we walk over to the park after supper?" Damien asked, forcing a blue plastic lid down onto a tub with a pop.

With one of the few words he understood still hanging in the air, Lemmy got up from his place on the small prayer rug by the back door. His head seesawed back and forth as he listened with the concentration of a safecracker to hear his favorite word again.

Maude, who was putting plates down on the marble beside Lucas, said, "Well?"

Lucas knew that staying inside, afraid of the world, wasn't going to give them any exercise. Or teach them to deal with life. "Anyone have any homework that can't wait?"

Damien raised his hand. "Apparently I *always* have homework that can't wait."

Maude punched him in the arm—she struggled to maintain a C average and took any flaunting of his natural talents as a personal snub. Damien never did any homework, yet he brought home solid As in pretty much everything—the one exception being an F in phys ed last semester after an archery mishap on Roosevelt Island resulted in the school's bus needing four new tires.

Damien held his arm, feigning injury. "Now I can't finish cleaning up."

Maude said, "Use your teeth."

"I'm not kidding. Look, my bone's sticking out."

Maude held up a ladle. "If you don't quit it, *this* will be sticking out of your *head*. Hashtag *stop being a baby*."

Lucas didn't bother getting in between them—they were just goofing around and he liked to let them work out their own shit. He watched how some of the kids who came through his classes dealt with conflict, and it bordered on psychotic.

Without looking up from the files she was immersed in, Erin said, "Hector has to finish his model rocket for physics and Laurie has to read a story."

Hector held up a hand like it was all a big misunderstanding. "All I gotta do is glue some fins on. Give me ten minutes with the super glue and I'm golden."

Laurie didn't say anything; she knew she was busted.

Lucas turned off the water, pulled the brush out from between his metal joints, and wiped his hands on a towel. "So we go for a walk. When we get back, I'll read with Laurie, and Hector can go nuts with the super glue."

Lemmy was moving in tight excited circles at this point—or at least as tight as a hundred and twenty-five pounds of Great Dane mixed with Mastiff possibly can. His tail hit the cabinet door on each rotation, rattling it on its hinges.

Erin shook her head. "The last time Hector used super glue, I had to pry his fingertips off the dining table with a butter knife. I'll read with Laurie and *you* can watch Captain Sticky here."

Maude held up the ladle triumphantly. "Therefore we go for a walk!"

Lucas had changed out of his suit and was in jeans and a pair of Chucky Ts—the only sneakers he liked beside Vans that he didn't kill in a few days; it was amazing how his prosthetic foot chewed through shoes. Erin walked beside him, her arm around his waist and her thumb threaded through his belt loop. They walked like this sometimes, but only for short stretches—she usually gave up after he stepped on her foot the second time.

The kids were moving with enough energy to burn off their supper calories and Lemmy was in mosey mode, stopping at every third or fourth lamppost for a sniff—the doggy version of social media. Lucas often wondered how he chose where to stop—it seemed completely random—but he had long ago decided that this was one of the mysteries of the universe that he just wasn't smart enough to unravel.

They hit Fifth and turned south. The kids preferred walking on the west side of the street, but the roots under the cobblestones turned that stretch of sidewalk into an ankle-breaking stunt for Lucas. He did it every now and then, but it really slowed them down.

The sun was setting beyond the park, and the green oxidized schooner atop the clubhouse on the sailing pond looked like it was on a sea of fire. The seasons seemed a month behind this year, and most of the leaves in the park still clung to the trees. The warm wind blowing up Fifth gave the false impression that winter might not make it, and Lucas allowed himself to enjoy the illusion.

But most of his mental universe was occupied by their guy. That both the Guggenheim and Makepeace's apartment were on the same street he was now walking along with his family wasn't lost on him, and with each step they took down Fifth, neither crime scene felt far enough away.

How was the string of bombings laced together? How did the attempt on Saarinen, Makepeace's murder, and the Hockneys mesh into a cohesive pattern?

Then there was their boy Frosst. Had he really walked by a bank of security cameras, planted a bomb in Makepeace's humidor, then walked out? If he had, it wasn't at the Hockneys' orders, because they could be called a lot of things, but stupid was not one of them. At least not William.

The only thing that was a given was that the Hockneys were part of the formula, even if they didn't know it.

This was not about a revolution. It was not about abandoning technology. Or turning your back on the system. It was about something else. Maybe money. Maybe some other plot point. But it wasn't a revolution.

"Would you stop working?" Erin said.

"Sorry." Lemmy had his nose to the base of a tree, intently picking up esoteric information with the deep sniffs of a sommelier.

The kids were waiting at the light at 72nd. When it went green, they looked back. Erin glanced up the street, then nodded, and they headed across Fifth, Maude holding Laurie's hand, and Laurie holding Alisha's hand. Damien and Hector ran ahead.

Lucas, Erin, and Lemmy followed them across Fifth, into the

park. Terrace Drive was closed, and the kids ran off for the play-ground.

Erin grabbed Lucas's hand and her fingers were warm. "Okay. So talk to me. How's work?"

"Pointless."

"That's not the confidence I fell in love with."

They walked through the gate to the 72nd Street playground, which was technically closer to 71st, something that the kids loved pointing out almost every time they came. They circled the little concrete tower and Lucas headed for the green painted benches set down in a spectator semicircle around the cubist concrete play-ground.

The space was empty, which was anomalous for a warm night in the fall. Evidently the bombings, and the television reporters cry-ing wolf 24/7, were having an effect on the population.

Lucas tied Lemmy's leash to the bench and was about to sit down when his phone rang. He took it out of his pocket, intention-ally ignoring Erin's arched eyebrow, and saw that it was Kehoe. He walked away for some privacy.

"Dr. Page here."

"Page, have you got a minute?"

Lucas turned back to the park, to the kids ripping around the cement clubhouse and Erin sitting alone with Lemmy. "One min-ute." He wondered if Kehoe had slept at all in the past two days.

"I want you to go talk to Saarinen. He was in this afternoon and we took his statement, but it was all useless. I know that his wife and housekeeper were blown up today—"

"And his dog."

Kehoe ignored him. "But he's the only targeted survivor we have, and he might have some information without knowing it. You were right, and this thing is starting to hang together, but none of the analysts can figure out how. If anyone knows which knobs to fiddle with after something like this, it's you." Kehoe was going for the direct approach, something he did only when expediency was important.

"The guy didn't look like he was interested in talking. What do I do, show up with flowers and candy?"

"Maybe not flowers and candy, but you can show up with something. His favorite sandwiches or something—drop by unannounced just to check up on him. Tell him you were wondering how he was doing. Play the kindred spirits card, use your injuries as an in."

"Jesus fuck, where do you come from?"

"I'm sorry if your sensibilities are hurt, but we need this to move forward. And we need it to happen *now*. Drop by his place. Have a coffee. Hold his hand. Take him a little gift. And do it tonight."

Lucas looked over at Erin, who was eyeing him suspiciously. Then she turned away.

Lucas said, "Text me the address," and hung up.

41

Lighthouse Park, Roosevelt Island

Jody Pinkerton and her sister Marny watched Frederick Dobel read the letter from the Machine Bomber.

Dobel was a tall black man in his . . . forties? fifties? Jody had no way to tell; everyone over twenty looked the same to her— *ancient*. But Dobel did a lot with what he had. He was dressed in a classic trench coat that he had topped off with a frayed Paul Smith scarf and accented with polished Frye harness boots. His look was vintage and, like, *so modern* at the same time. And Jody would know—she had a street fashion gram called Urban Wearfare. She wasn't rolling in money yet—but she did have almost a thousand followers, and one of her posts had been liked by Selena Gomez, so she was going places. But until she made it, she was working at the Gap.

Dobel was standing on a bench, holding the letter at the top and bottom, reading it as if it were a royal decree. It was from the guy—the revolutionary guy—who had been blowing things up because he was so sad for humans. Because machines were doing everything.

And, when she thought about it, they kinda *were*.

Because the world was getting really techy. Scary true. Last week there had been a power outage, and they couldn't operate the cash registers at work. People wanted to buy things, but they couldn't ring up the sales. And even if they could, the credit card machine had been down. And she had seen this show on Netflix about how a self-driving car had killed a guy—just killed him—because he was reading a book instead of driving. But it was a self-driving car, so what was he supposed to do? So no, technology was most definitely becoming a problem. She had spent the day reading about it on her phone.

And her sister, Marny, had texted her that they should go to this demonstration to learn what they could do. And they were committed to helping out any way they could. Last year, her and Marny had done the ice bucket thing. Twice! Both times she had worn a nice little Alfred Sung top and she had looked so cute because she had bangs back then (she looked great in bangs, all of her friends said so). And her and Marny had dumped buckets of ice water on their heads twice. Well, actually, only Marny had done it twice; Jody figured that once was good enough. Apparently, every time you dumped ice on your head, some guy gave a bunch of money to some charity in your name. But it was *a really good* cause. Which was why everyone was doing it. Well, everyone except her upstairs neighbor. His name was Mr. Warren and he had some disease he liked to blame for not going out—it was Parkin's son's disease—but he was just lazy. Probably a drunk, too—he was shaking all the time. Just a drunk old man too lazy to help out crippled kids by dumping a little ice on his head. Probably thought it was too cold. Boohoo, sucks to be him.

Dobel finished reading and held up the letter. "And now we burn our phones!" he said. He pulled out a lighter and touched the flame to the letter. When it was burning, he dropped it into the garbage can beside the bench, which went up with an angry *whump!*

And people began chucking their phones into the fire. Like, brand-new and everything! Some were on. Some were turned off. Some were old flip phones. One lady scuttled forward and dumped a whole shoe box of phones into the fire, then spat on them.

Jody looked over at Marny, who had her new iPhone clamped to her chest. Their eyes met and Jody could tell that Marny thought these people were *insane*.

Jody and Marny got the fuck out of there.

Immediately.

42

The Upper West Side

The doorman looked like a scarecrow dressed in a uniform stolen from a marching band; all that was missing was straw sticking out of his collar and a pair of cymbals. He eyed the box and paper bag Lucas placed on the desk as if they were contaminated with the coronavirus, but he called up, then nodded at the elevator at the back of the foyer. "Penthouse."

When Lucas picked up the box, the Windex came out and the scarecrow began furiously spraying the marble top.

The hallway to the penthouse matched the foyer downstairs, with a strong period Art Deco flair expressed with black lacquered paneling and chrome fixtures. It was easy to find the apartment—it was the only one with a federal agent in front of the door.

The bureau man was a twenty-first-century off-the-shelf variant of Joe Friday. He smelled of Old Spice and looked like he spent his weekends in the garage tinkering with his boat. Lucas had to put the box and bag down to pull out his badge, and the man examined it, called it in, then handed it back with zero fanfare. He rapped on the door with the back of his knuckles and stepped aside.

Saarinen opened the door and took a step back, visibly surprised. He stared for an indecisive second before saying, "Come in." He held a glass half filled with ice cubes and, judging by his breath, vodka.

The apartment was outfitted with straight lines, a lot of beiges, and a collection of art glass spread out on every flat surface. There were ten-foot ceilings and a view of the American Museum of Natural History across the street. The patio doors were open and the sounds of the city supplied the ambient noise.

The focus of the room was a bottle of Finlandia and a glass ice bucket on the coffee table. The bottle looked like it wouldn't make it to midnight. Saarinen had two framed photographs out—one that had to be his wife, the other presumably his son. Lucas suddenly wished he hadn't let Kehoe talk him into coming.

Saarinen nodded at the glass in his hand. "A drink?" Three separate prescription bottles—painkillers for the shrapnel wounds—were on a side table, two knocked over and their pills spilled out. An open copy of Lucas's last book lay open beside the pills, text side down.

Lucas sat down on the sofa, still holding the box. "A water would be great." There was something missing in the space, and it took him a few seconds to realize what it was—there were no bonsai.

"I am usually distrustful of anyone who doesn't drink." Saarinen pulled a bottle of water from a Knoll console and handed it to Lucas. "But tonight it means that there is more for me."

Lucas wondered if the man was intentionally morphing into a Bergman character but when he factored the two photos on the coffee table into the conversation, he decided that he had no right to pass judgment.

Saarinen moved around the coffee table, and for a man who was well on his way to killing a quart of vodka, his footing was better than Lucas's. "So . . ."—he topped up his cocktail, then put the bottle down on the table with a percussive thud—"why are you here?"

Lucas thought about lying, but it wasn't in him. Not with a man who had spent the night looking at photographs of his dead family. "My boss asked me to come by and talk to you. See if you knew anything that might be helpful to us."

Saarinen eyed him for a moment. "That is very transparent of you."

Lucas put his hands on top of the box. "And I thought this might have some meaning for you."

Saarinen just stared at him.

Lucas peeled back one of the flaps of the box and lifted out a little bulldog puppy that was snoring tiny piglet snores.

At the sight of the dog, Saarinen did the last thing Lucas expected—he smiled.

Lucas held the little guy out. "Sometimes a dog is the best medicine. But if you don't want him, he goes back—he has a nice family waiting, so he's going to have a good life one way or the other."

Saarinen pushed himself out of the chair and took the fat little biscuit into his arms. He spoke to the dog in his native Finnish, but there was nothing cutesy about his tone—he sounded like he was giving orders.

"He's ten weeks old and he's housebroken and piddle-pad-trained. There are pads, a leash, and some food in the box—I wasn't sure you'd be equipped." He looked around. "But I might be wrong." The place was obviously well stocked, even if there were no miniature trees. That there might be dog food in one of the cupboards was not much of a stretch. Lucas knew that the place belonged to the Hockneys—it was one of several *hôtels particuliers* they owned in the city.

Saarinen nosed the dog. "I like living in Pelham Gardens. It's close to the zoo and the botanical gardens; Bongo and I used to walk the park before closing every night."

Lucas held out the bag. "I also got you some food—soup.

I Googled Finnish food, and apparently soup is a big thing. I couldn't find any pickled herring."

Saarinen nodded at the bottle of Finlandia on the table. "I've been drinking my dinner."

"How very Teutonic of you."

Saarinen leaned back and put the puppy down in his lap. He stood on the man's knees with wobbly legs, looking at the floor, which might as well have been three stories down. He mewled and Saarinen scratched him behind his ears.

Lucas could blame this on Kehoe, but part of the reason he was here was because he understood what Saarinen was going through. After his own very personal Event he didn't have much of a support group. Kehoe had visited once. Hartke, his old partner, had visited twice. His first wife, Nancy, had visited a handful of times until it became evident that he would live, then she had sent a bailiff with divorce papers. And that had been about it; no one wanted to be reminded of what could happen on this job. He had a sneaking suspicion that test pilots probably had a similar relationship with one another. "I just wanted to see that you were . . ." He paused, searching his lexicon for the appropriate phrase. "Not too terrible."

Saarinen smiled at that. "Are you now going to tell me that things will be fine? That I'll get over this?"

"You will never get over this."

"Honesty. A *rare* trait."

"You've been through this before."

"My son's murder killed our entire family; my wife and I both died with him. Somehow it was worse for her, I don't know why. Maybe it was that maternal bond women speak of. For ten years I lived with a corpse. So did she, but at least the dead man in her midst got up, went to work, and tried to continue living." His eyes unfocused, and Lucas could see him slip through the wormhole to yesteryear. "In a way, that bomb did her a favor this morning. I just wish it had done the same for me." He upended the glass and stared at it, as if seeing it for the first time. "I'm sorry. It has been a long day."

Saarinen leaned back in the chair with the dog still in his lap. The pup had fallen back asleep, but wasn't snoring this time. "I have spent my life trying to save nature for people who don't care. And today at the scene of my wife's murder, the crowd chanted that it was all a lie; that it hadn't happened; that it was part of some elaborate fantasy and I was a crisis actor." For the first time, emotion bled through his features, and it looked as if he would cry. But he swallowed, took another drink, then let out a sigh. "A crisis actor? It is the twenty-first century and we still have to deal with flat-earthers and anti-vaxxers and moon landing truthers. This is what you get when guns are more important than books—a nation of sociocultural primitives." He stopped and focused on the glass in his left hand. "Please forgive me—like I said, it's been a long day." He took a swill of Finlandia. "Ask the questions you came here to ask, Dr. Page."

"What is your opinion of Mr. Frosst?"

Saarinen scratched the puppy's belly. "I don't spend much time with him. He works for the Hockneys."

"Do you think he might have something to do with these bombings?"

Saarinen shook his head. "Mr. Frosst is a lot of things, none of them very attractive, but he would protect the Hockneys with his life if it became necessary. He is not a man you want in your blind spot."

"And William Junior. What can you tell me about him?"

Saarinen smiled at the question. "Edgar Bronfman once said that a wealthy family is shirt sleeves to shirt sleeves in three generations—if he had met William Junior, he would have changed it to *two*."

"Not as smart as his father?"

"Not as smart as this dog here." He softly tapped the puppy on the head.

"You've been with Horizon for five years now?"

"Yes."

"I don't know the Hockneys all that well, but you and they don't seem all that compatible. They have spent their life destroying nature; you've spent yours trying to heal it. I can't square the conflict."

Saarinen shrugged as if the answer was self-evident. "There's an old Finnish saying: Sometimes you must take the devil's money to do God's work."

"Will Horizon recover?"

Saarinen shrugged and swallowed more vodka. "Horizon wasn't a company in the usual sense—it owned no real estate or machinery—its strength was its people. It was a brain trust, a think tank. And the brains were all destroyed in the Guggenheim bombing. They are all gone. My employees and friends."

"What was the IPO valuation figured at?"

Saarinen shrugged. "Half a billion dollars—without the prospect of the Paraguayan contract. With the contract, it could have reached a billion dollars. More, possibly."

"Are the Hockneys the kind of people who can lose a billion dollars without it affecting their sleep?"

Saarinen smiled at that. "Dr. Page, the one thing I can say about William and Seth Hockney is that they don't know how to forgive." He put his hand back on the puppy. "And the people responsible for these bombings better hope that you find them before the Hockney brothers do."

43

The Upper East Side

He was somewhere in a deep slumber when his phone started to dance across the nightstand, bringing him back to the living. He reached for the glow in the dark before all of his systems were up and running.

He was certain he had instructed his mouth to say *Dr. Page here,* but all that came out was *"What the fuck!"*

"Were you sleeping?" It was Whitaker.

He squinted to see the glowing hands of his Sub. "That's what us old busted people do at three in the morning."

"Yeah, well, tough noogies. Look, Chawla just called. Frosst wasn't alone in the Mercedes when he went to Makepeace's; we found footage from a ground-floor security camera at another building on Fifth that put someone else in the back seat of the Benz with him. The other person didn't go up to Makepeace's, but he was definitely in the car. Which makes him a witness to Frosst's activities just before and just following his visit."

Lucas was awake now. He sat up on the edge of the bed, which wasn't easy with one hand holding the phone and his leg and arm in storage for the night. "Without any proof that Frosst planted the bomb, it just makes them a passenger."

"We can still question him."

Lucas reached over and flipped on the light with his hand holding the phone; for a second, Whitaker's voice was reduced to a tinny squawk. His side of the room lit up.

"—age? Page?"

"I'm here. Why couldn't this wait until morning?"

"Because the man in the back seat with Frosst was Seth Hockney."

Lucas saw the opportunity in the information. "And we're entitled to question him, and since we were instructed that all further questions go through his lawyer, we can bring him in."

"Yep."

"When?"

"He's flying in tomorrow, nine A.M."

"That's in six hours."

"What's your point?"

"I'm going back to sleep." He hung up, put the phone back on his nightstand, and snapped the light off. He lay back down and Erin said, "I love getting woken up at four in the morning."

"It's only three." He reached over and put his hand on her hip.

She yawned. "Oh, okay. My bad."

44

26 Federal Plaza

Lucas stared into the sun, and the city to the east looked like a green screen image against the chemical sky. He wanted another coffee, but it would be in poor form to greet Seth Hockney with a mug in his hand.

Chawla, in his role of the Big Cheese, stood near the landing pad, today sporting a bright orange dastar and matching tie. One thing Lucas could say for the guy, he knew how to dress.

Lucas and Whitaker wouldn't take part in the interview; Kehoe didn't want it to look like an interrogation. But that was not to say that Lucas would not be involved—he still had value as an agent provocateur.

Whitaker nodded into the sun. "His chariot arrives."

The bird came in from the east, cutting over from the standard civilian path down the East River from points north—probably Seth Hockney's home on Long Island. Lucas doubted that even a man as rich as Hockney would bother to take a helicopter in from his pied-à-terre on the Upper West Side.

It was a sleek, expensive craft and probably made the rest of the Manhattan billionaires jealous. From head on, it barely looked wide enough for one person, but the illusion was broken as it banked, exposing a very sexy profile.

The helicopter hovered for a moment before the landing gear extended, and it touched down in a perfect three-point drop.

The door opened mechanically and a set of steps rolled out of the body of the machine with the precision of a Swiss watch. Chawla ducked below the rotors as he ran up, his hand on his turban.

Frosst stepped out, buttoning his suit jacket as his feet hit the membrane of the roof. He ignored Chawla and turned to help Seth Hockney out of the bird as the turbofan shut down and the rotors began to slow.

The impression Seth gave yesterday still held, and even Frosst with his warfare school stride looked more polished. Frosst helped the old man down the steps and led him to the edge of the landing pad, a bright yellow circle in a field of beige.

Another man exited the aircraft behind him, this one a lawyer type, wearing a very good suit and carrying the requisite barrister's briefcase. He was maybe sixty, with silver hair, and a face that you wouldn't remember if your life depended on it. One look at the guy told you he had a sailboat somewhere with a woman's name slapped on the transom. Or the name of his favorite cocktail.

Everyone on the roof passed through the access door manned by two junior agents in suits that looked poor in the current company. They filed down the single flight of stairs to the main elevator and rode in silence to the floor where they'd hold the interview.

Lucas and Whitaker broke off from the group and headed to a conference room where Kehoe was waiting for them. A junior agent sat at the desk, a laptop in front of her.

Whitaker delivered the news. "They're *he-ere*," she said, drawing out the word as if she were pointing at a static-filled television screen.

Kehoe turned to the wall of monitors—six different camera

angles in the interview room. Chawla, Seth Hockney, Hockney's lawyer, and the bureau's lawyer entered. They sat down, Hockney and his counsel on one side, Chawla and the lawyer on the other. Frosst was in another room—Kehoe wanted Seth questioned without him in the background, just in case he was involved in the mix.

"All right," Kehoe said to Lucas. "Let's see if you're as smart as I tell everyone you are." He pointed at the four men in the room. "So go make yourself a nuisance."

45

The interview room was on the small side, but it was clean and the furniture was law-firm quality. Special Agent in Charge Samir Chawla, the bureau lawyer—a man by the name of Martin Brotsky—Seth Hockney, and his lawyer—one Alexander Stogner—were the only ones present. Kehoe would send Page in—he wanted the old guy to dance a little to see if anything fell out of his pockets.

Seth Hockney looked like he was both present and absent at the same time. He was watching Chawla, but he might as well have been looking through him; his expression was dialed into bored and irritated, which was a hard mix to pull off.

Hockney's lawyer was one of the partners at Stogner, Pruitt, and Gibson, a law firm that had the sole directive of handling the legal dealings of the Hockney brothers. Chawla didn't know what these guys charged, but when you represented billionaires who came to work in a helicopter that cost more than a nice beach house in the Hamptons, it had to be a shit ton of cash. Which was probably why the guy looked so smug.

Page came in and circled the table with the slow deliberate

movements of a creature scenting blood in the water—all he was missing was a dorsal fin. He didn't bother saying hello, he just made a circle around them, before stopping at the one empty chair.

Chawla sat back to watch things unfold.

The lawyer was trying to establish dominance through eye contact and Page allowed him the attempt. He smiled, took off his sunglasses, and stared down so his eyes were off at different angles. The lawyer shifted in his seat: score one for Page.

After another fifteen seconds of the stare-down, Page introduced himself. "Mr. Hockney, thank you for coming in. Mr. Stogner, I'm Dr. Lucas Page." He didn't extend a hand.

Page acted like he was considering sitting down, but then his expression changed as if he had remembered he left the stove on at home, and he said, "Just so we're clear, no one is being accused of any wrongdoing. We have simply asked you here to help clarify a few things that we're having difficulty lining up. As you know, Mr. Makepeace—your stockbroker—"

Stogner held up a hand. "For the record, Dr. Page, Jonathan Makepeace was not Mr. Hockney's *stockbroker*. Mr. Makepeace had previously handled some investments for the Hockney brothers, as did many other financial advisors; there was no exclusivity in their relationship."

"Of course." Page nodded.

Chawla knew that this was where Page would pretend to have forgotten something, and politely excuse himself. When he came back, he'd come at Hockney with the video of him in the back of the Benz a few moments before William Makepeace was converted to nonmoving parts.

On cue, Page said, "Would you please excuse me—I forgot something. I'll be back." He walked over to the door.

Chawla opened his hands. "As I am sure you can understand, we are very busy this week and your cooperation is very much appreciated—the whole world has its eyes on us."

That seemed to appease the lawyer, who nodded as if he had just earned his pay. "Before we go any further, I would like to present you with a prepared statement." Stogner picked his briefcase up off the floor.

Page opened the door.

The lawyer popped the catches.

Page stepped out into the hallway and closed the door behind him.

The lawyer smiled at Chawla and began to open the case.

Which was when the device within detonated.

And the room was deleted from the world.

46

All he heard, all he felt, was the siren chewing through his eardrums. It was raining, and the air was filled with smoke and he wondered if he was dead.

He rolled over.

Water filled his mouth and smoke billowed over the ceiling above, rolling in a poisonous cloud.

"Page!" It was Whitaker's voice.

He felt her hands on his shoulders.

She pulled at his jacket.

Screamed his name again.

He tried to get up.

Slipped.

Fell.

Got his good leg under his mass. Tried again. Pushed up. Whitaker helped.

And he was standing.

"You okay?" she screamed from somewhere behind him.

He nodded and maybe answered, maybe didn't.

The explosion had punched the door to the interview room off its hinges. It was embedded in the Sheetrock across the hall like a magic trick gone awry. It was on fire.

Lucas took one wobbly step forward.

The water running out of the interview room was black with blood and Chawla's turban snaked out in the wash, torn and covered in bits of dark hair.

Lucas's system recalibrated, and he went from dazed to operational. He pulled the fire extinguisher off the wall.

Frosst materialized out of the smoke like a Polaroid in a suit. Two agents screamed at him to get back. One grabbed his arm and Frosst leveled him with a solid punch that put him into the wet carpet.

Frosst stepped into the interview room and Lucas blasted the portal with fire-retardant foam.

Inside, Frosst tore the room apart.

Lucas kept his hand clamped around the trigger of the extinguisher, aiming at the bright spots in the smoke.

He stepped into the room, sending foam off into the water and steam and smoke and fire. He saw Frosst at the edge of his visibility; the sleeve of Frosst's jacket was on fire. Lucas hit him with a jet from the extinguisher.

Lucas kept the trigger down, blasting indiscriminately in a panic that he couldn't control. The room hissed under the water from the sprinklers and the foam from the extinguisher.

And then the emergency lights came on, and the flames were gone, and all that was left was the familiar stink of cooked flesh.

Smoke wafted off Frosst in slow motion and he held what was left of Seth Hockney in his arms.

47

His suit smelled like it had been stored in a barbecue for ten years. Even if they could purge the stench, the best tailor in the world didn't stand a chance against the charred holes or the stains left by the chemical foam. No one was bringing this back from the dead any more than they could reassemble Special Agent Samir Chawla, the bureau lawyer, the dead billionaire, or his very expensive lawyer.

The explosion had stripped the room down to the studs—obliterating the Sheetrock and taking the suspended ceiling out in one raging gulp. Curtis took a cursory glance at the space and said there had been a pound of C-4 in the IED. They had examined the taggants in the putty, and it was of the same manufacture and batch as the other devices—made by ENF. The only reason they hadn't lost half the floor was because the walls up here were solid-core cinder block, two layers thick.

No one who had been in that room would have an open casket. That there had been enough left of Seth Hockney for Frosst to pick up had been dumb luck.

Lucas was on the roof, watching the bomb squad go over the helicopter; it was a reasonable assumption that whoever had rigged Stogner's briefcase had taken the extra measure of hiding a backup device on the chopper.

Lucas didn't know a thing about aircraft, but in the past hour he had learned that the Eurocopter AS365 Dauphin clocked in at about ten million bucks—before you added things like cup holders and colored stitching.

Lucas leaned against one of the railings that zigzagged across the roof, separating traffic areas from utility zones. He was in an alcove near the HVAC units, and the membrane under his feet was splotched with the telltale scars of dead cigarettes—a hangout for nicotine junkies back when smoking had been an acceptable vice.

He was facing west, into the warm wind still massaging the city. No matter how many ways he tried to spin Seth Hockney being mulched into meat confetti downstairs into a positive development, he failed.

Footsteps crunched on the grainy deck behind him and Whitaker eased up, putting her foot on a lower rung of the railing and hanging her forearms over the top. "You okay?" she asked.

He didn't say anything.

She converted a deep breath into movement and turned around, leaning back on the rail in an Old West saloon stance. "What's going through your head?"

"Has it made the news?"

"Our information desk put out a statement saying that there was an incident and we will release further details shortly . . . blah . . . blah . . . blah."

It was the perfect response; vague and noncommittal. "And Kehoe?"

Whitaker said, "Ask him yourself."

Lucas didn't bother turning to meet Kehoe's slow, measured

pace. Even after what had happened downstairs, the man wasn't stepping out of character. He moseyed up to the rail, and the impression that the three of them were preparing for a gunfight was hard to miss. "Any thoughts?"

Lucas had been running this through his head on loop for the better part of three days and all he had were questions. "Whoever is doing this is creative; every device so far has been unique. If Frosst killed Makepeace, it would have been under orders from either one or both of the Hockneys. But now Seth is dead, and we know that Frosst didn't kill him—he didn't know that the lawyer's briefcase was wired because he was pissed that we wouldn't let him into the interview room with his boss. And he doesn't strike me as the suicidal type. So there's every reason to believe that Seth Hockney and Frosst visiting Makepeace just before he was killed is a coincidence.

"If Frosst planted both bombs—the one at Makepeace's and the one in Stogner's briefcase—who ordered it? Who wanted Seth Hockney dead? Was it William? Or was Frosst acting alone?"

Whitaker held up her hand. "Don't forget the lawyer."

Lucas waved it away. "I can swallow the lawyer as collateral—he's just a lawyer and they're like house cats, replaceable. Unless, of course, he was the prime target, which is not an unreasonable assumption. Maybe he fell into the same victim category, whatever that is." If he wrote down all the questions Seth's murder had generated, he could fill a hard drive.

"Is William Hockney behind all this? Was he sealing up the information chain between Makepeace's death and himself? Or had Seth done something in the chain without William's blessing, and William found out? Saarinen said he is not the forgiving type. But blow up his brother? William could have hired outside personnel to sneak into Seth's house and help him slip in the shower—which wouldn't look suspicious. I don't buy it; like the Guggenheim, Seth's death was a PR move."

It was question after question, which amounted to a handful of maybes.

"And how *does* Seth's murder connect to the Guggenheim bombing? If William Hockney was responsible for that, why bomb the gala of a company that was going to bring him a billion dollars? I can think of better ways to piss money away." Lucas ran a hand through his hair, and it felt dry. "It's the unknowns between the other unknowns that are troubling." Lucas still had the stench of burnt plastic and fried human being in the back of his throat.

Whitaker said, "Example?"

"If Frosst planted the Makepeace device, who directed him to? If it was Seth, and William found out and was displeased, did he order that hit on his brother downstairs? Or did William want to distance himself from Frosst after having him kill Makepeace and the plan snafued and his brother got killed?"

Setting off a bomb in FBI headquarters took the kind of balls very few people had. The act was more than arrogant—it was a personal and public fuck-you to the bureau.

Whitaker asked, "You think Seth Hockney blew up the Guggenheim and then the internet hub and this was some kind of silencing?"

"All I know is that they're connected. There are too many things spinning in the same gravitational field for them not to be."

Whitaker was shaking her head. "Any other possibilities?"

"Sure. Maybe someone is trying to send a series of very personal fuck-yous to the Hockneys. Maybe they made enemies of the wrong people. It's the easy money."

"What about Frosst?"

"If the Hockneys are involved, so is that fucker." Lucas looked over at Kehoe. "Where is he right now?"

"We're holding him downstairs. He's finishing up with the paramedics and he's not happy about it. But we're running out of reasons to keep him from speaking to his boss."

Lucas thought back to how Frosst had reacted to the explosion, how he sprang into action. "You need to look at Frosst's background in an entirely new way. Take him apart right down to the molecular level."

"And what are you going to do?" Kehoe asked.

Lucas pushed off the railing. "First, Whitaker and I are going to go talk to William Hockney. Someone needs to tell him that his brother and one of his lawyers are dead. And he should hear it from someone other than Frosst."

"We can send someone else."

"I want to see how he reacts. Just don't let Frosst go until we've spoken to William."

Kehoe pulled a cuff and looked at his watch. "You have one hour." He looked like he was thinking a dozen different things at the same time. "Why do I get the feeling that you're not telling me the bad news?"

Lucas took off his sunglasses and rubbed the bridge of his nose. "Because I don't like guessing."

Kehoe's eyes stopped moving and he gave Lucas his *Don't-fuck-with-me* look. "If you did, what would you say?"

Lucas headed for the access door. "That we're looking at more than one bomber."

48

57th Street and Fifth Avenue

Lucas and Whitaker brought twelve agents with them—a group of men and women who looked spawned from the same lab in the basement that produced almost everyone who walked the halls of the bureau. They had nondescript clothing that complemented their similar features and haircuts. But they were window dressing—all that Lucas really wanted out of them were the three big yellow letters stenciled on the backs of their windbreakers.

Lucas, Whitaker, and their backup people blew through security this time, not bothering with more than a perfunctory flash of their badges and a blast of pheromones that told people to get out of their way.

When they arrived upstairs, Lucas and Whitaker didn't bother with the receptionist—this one different from that of the other day in height only—Whitaker just held up her badge and turned right, toward William Hockney's office. The receptionist ran after them for a few paces, but turned back when she couldn't keep up. Lucas heard her pick up the phone.

They were almost at the Jurassic-Deco doors when four men

who clocked in at an average height of six-five stepped in front of them. They all had the heavy-lidded stare and impassive features of their ilk, and there had to be twelve yards of fabric between their suits.

Whitaker held up her badge and said to the agents in windbreakers, "Shoot them if they don't get out of our way."

The certainty drained out of their faces as Whitaker pushed through. Lucas could smell the aggression, but they parted.

Whitaker and Lucas pushed past Hockney's secretary, who was on her feet, waiting for them. "Mr. Hockney is—"

"Going to want to see us," Whitaker delivered without a hint of give.

They opened the door and Mr. Hockney was in his chair by the fire, talking to three men who were split between the sofa and the other chair. Voices were raised and everyone's body language was agitated. They all looked up when the door opened.

Whitaker led the way, but it was Lucas who got the most attention—no doubt because of his spiffy duds with all the holes burned in them.

If William Hockney felt any surprise, he didn't show it. Which Lucas realized was the difference between the rich and the poor—to the rich, law enforcement is an inconvenience, not a threat. "Special Agent Whitaker, Dr. Page," he said in perfect monotone. "I assume this is important." It sounded like he was ordering a glass of water from a waiter, which was a quick recovery from the heated conversation of only a few seconds ago.

Whitaker stepped forward. "We need to speak to you."

Hockney took a deep breath and nodded toward the man in the middle on the sofa. "Please tell Mr. Molinaro that I regret this interruption, but it cannot be helped."

The man—an interpreter—turned and spoke softly in Spanish to Molinaro, the oldest man in the group. Molinaro responded, and the interpreter said, "We understand and will be happy to pick this up at dinner tonight. Mr. Molinaro is looking forward to dining at your apartment—your chef was a surprise the last time, and he hopes that he is still in your employ. He is also looking forward to seeing your son again."

Hockney smiled and nodded. "My chef has something special planned." He paused, glanced over at Lucas, then finished up with "Unfortunately my son William is away on business and won't be able to join us."

Everyone stood, shook hands, and the Spanish speakers left. As they walked by, Lucas saw that Molinaro's cuff links were striped in rubies, diamonds, and sapphires, and there was something familiar about the motif. Then he made the connection—they represented the flag of Paraguay.

After Hockney's visitors had left, the old man turned to Lucas. "To what do I owe this displeasure, Dr. Page?"

Whitaker nodded at the other agents and they left the office. Hockney mimicked her and nodded at the security men, who pulled the door closed when they left.

Hockney looked Lucas up and down. "Are you all right?" But there was zero concern in his voice.

"Mr. Hockney . . ."—the tone in Whitaker's voice got the old man's attention—"I have some bad news."

Hockney didn't say anything, but Whitaker, with her preternatural ability to sense questions before they were asked, said, "Yes, it's your brother. He and Mr. Stogner were killed."

His facial muscles went rigid, as if he were a bust of himself.

After a few long seconds, his engine started back up. "I see."

Hockney went to his fancy hidden bar and pressed the secret button. The wall slid open, and without looking at his hands, he reached for the nearest bottle, cracked the top, and poured three fingers into a glass.

He returned to his chair and sat down without touching his drink.

After a moment of silence, the old man opened his mouth to ask a question.

Whitaker preemptively answered with "We're still investigating, but it appears that Mr. Stogner had an explosive device in his briefcase. It detonated when he opened it."

Hockney no longer looked like a captain of industry—he was just an old man who had received bad news about someone he loved. Or at least that was the impression he was selling. "Was anyone else hurt?"

Whitaker nodded. "The special agent in charge of the investigation was killed along with one of our lawyers. He was interviewing your brother and Mr. Stogner at the time."

"And Mr. Frosst?" There was nothing in the question that gave his feelings away. He might as well have been asking about the time. "He accompanied Seth."

"Mr. Frosst has some minor injuries. He will be released soon."

Mr. Hockney nodded once. Then some errant command blipped through his software and he raised the drink to his lips. He held it up for a moment without looking at it, shook his head once, then put it away in a gulp that would choke a weekend drunk. At that point he seemed to see the tumbler for the first time, and he placed it gently down on the end table beside the coaster.

Without turning to look at them, he said, "Dr. Page, judging by your appearance, I assume that you were close to the blast."

"Mr. Frosst ran into the room when it was still on fire and I followed him with an extinguisher."

That seemed to please the old man. He smiled, but it was a sad, distant expression. "Mr. Frosst is—*was*—fond of my brother." He looked up. "Is there anything else you two have come here to tell me?"

"Do you have any enemies?"

William Hockney didn't look up when he said, "I would think the answer to that question is obvious by now, Dr. Page."

And with a flutter of the old man's fingers, they were once again dismissed.

49

26 Federal Plaza

Whitaker spent less time in her office than in any other routine location in her life except the front door of her ex's apartment, where she picked up her son every second weekend. The space did not fit the criteria for either a cubicle or a proper room because it was neither of those things—it was simply an alcove on one of the general task floors, hidden away behind a support wall. There was no door, but there was a line across the floor that implied an invisible barrier. Some of her fellow agents—the ones who felt friendly enough to do so—often mimed a knock when they came to see her. The gag had lost any of its humor a long time ago, but that didn't seem to stop anyone. Lucas was right about that—people didn't grow.

While Lucas was downstairs, trying to flow-chart the events of the past few days with the bureau's various departments, she was going over field agent reports. The bombings hadn't been carried out by phantasms—there were human beings out there doing this. And human beings made mistakes, you just had to recognize them. More of Lucas and his patterns.

The file on Frosst was bolstered with some general Big Data

information—it was amazing what you could add to a file just by hitting the search engines. Whitaker was already half an inch into the binder and it was doing nothing to soften her dislike of him.

Unlike the files on a lot of men of his type, Benjamin Frosst's was replete with all the prerequisite details, including date and location of birth, addresses growing up, educational background, and health history. There was nothing remarkable in the building blocks of his life—they could have belonged to a parts manager at a car dealership or a high school teacher anywhere in America. And even his transcript from the University of Montana, where he earned a Bachelor of Arts under the general discipline of business, showed him to be only an average student. But he had somehow escaped the predictable and moved on to the remarkable when he was hired by a Japanese banking consortium a week after graduation.

He disappeared into their corporate maze for a decade, where he bounced around various parts of the world, first under the heading of *general security,* later as *specialized security,* then finally as *head of security—personnel.* His passport records, gained through a request to the Department of Homeland Security, showed him making nine hundred trips to foreign countries during his time employed by the Japanese, most of them to well-known dictatorships around the world—some to countries that no longer existed. The only known routine he had was a yearly two-week vacation that he spent in California.

And then, for no apparent reason, he was back in the States, working on Wall Street as head of security for one of the investment banks. He spent eight years with the firm, and again the only routine in his life was his yearly two-week sojourn in California. His tenure ended during the subprime mortgage crash of 2008, when the company was disassembled. Remarkably, the enterprise hadn't succumbed to the greed and mismanagement associated with that particular historical block of financial bloodletting—it had fallen to a hostile takeover by the Hockney brothers, who were using the chaos in the markets to shore up their empire. Three weeks after the firm shuttered its doors, Frosst showed up on the Hockneys' payroll.

Frosst's occupation was listed as head of security on his business card, but his income tax returns declared that he was a personal assistant—the truth was probably somewhere in between.

Whitaker went through some of the photographs in the file, and in every single one he was with one or both of the Hockney brothers. He was always dressed impeccably, and his expression never varied off the asshole setting by more than a few degrees. Lucas was also right about his hair—it always looked terrible (not that Lucas had any right to pass judgment in that department).

Frosst had an apartment in the same building as the Hockneys—a twenty-six-story Renaissance Revival on the Upper West Side that overlooked the park. William occupied the penthouse—which translated to the entire top floor; Seth occupied the floor below; Frosst had a three-bedroom flat on the third floor. He had no wife or significant other. He owned two cars—a Range Rover and a Ferrari. His credit card statements showed very little in the way of extraneous spending, and he didn't appear to have any vices other than his tailor and an account at Tourneau that he used to stock up on high-end wristwatches.

There was nothing remarkable about the man. He didn't seem to have any interests outside of work. He didn't gamble or own a boat or chase women. Lucas was right—without the Hockneys, Frosst wasn't even there.

So why did he set off all of Lucas's alarms?

Whitaker closed Frosst's file and pushed it aside.

If you factored in the Guggenheim and the internet hub and Makepeace and Seth Hockney as parts of the same puzzle, it all seemed cockeyed. Like something was wrong.

Was it Lucas?

50

Medusa, New York

The house was there.

And then it wasn't.

In its departure, it punched a flaming crater into the field that slowly chewed its way through the dry fall leaves and unmowed grass in a widening circle that the wind quickly sculpted into an ellipse.

The Medusa Fire Department arrived on site fourteen minutes after the explosion scared the shit out of the neighbors. There were no fire hydrants this far out of town (or even in town), but the volunteers ran a pump into Tenmile Creek. But by the time they started on the house and the barn, both were little more than insurance claims.

It took an hour of dousing the two outbuildings with four hoses pushing water at 400 pounds per square inch to completely subdue the flames, but everything went well and no one was injured. When a final inventory was done, the farmhouse and barn were gone, one 1999 Jeep Wrangler had met its demise, two toolsheds had been eaten by the flames, three utility poles had been lost, and the field was black.

At this point the neighbors were involved in a dialogue with the attending experts—a euphemism for *volunteers*. And even if you didn't believe in eyewitnesses, it was pretty obvious that there had been an explosion. Which was odd, because there were no propane tanks on the property and no natural gas lines out here. There had been no barbecue found on the premises—not near what was left of the porch, and not anywhere in the field around the house. The neighbors said that the occupants, Hazel Rich and her son, Donny, weren't gun owners—so it was unlikely that a stockpile of ammunition or gunpowder on the premises (a natural assumption in any rural enclave, even in a state with relatively strict firearm laws) had accidentally gone up.

The sheriff collected details. Ms. Rich was fifty-one, Donny was twenty-six. Based on known schedules, it was believed that both mother and son were home at the time of the explosion.

They found Ms. Rich in a ditch across the gravel road, under a tree. There were bits of plaster and shingle in her hair—from when she had been blown through the roof—and her clothes had been torn off as she had come zipping back down through the trees. Most of her bones were broken and her head was facing the wrong way, but she hadn't lost any parts other than her nose, which was some kind of a miracle considering the ride she had taken. Her shredded nightgown hung in the branches overhead, bloody and attracting flies.

Proof of Donny's death was found dangling on a barbed-wire fence at the edge of the property, more than 800 feet from the house. It was a foot, still clad in a white tube sock stuffed into a blue rubber Croc in a man's size 11.

This was a small town where they were not used to investigating explosions, but the local authorities thought things through and

then called in the New York State Police. A coroner from Schenectady was sent over.

One of the troopers, a man named Eli Benson, had been in the
first Gulf War as part of a bomb disposal unit. This is not why he had
been called, but it turned out to be a nice little bit of synchronicity
when he was the one to discover the trigger for an improvised
explosive device embedded in the mailbox down by the road—no one
else on site would have recognized it for what it was. Or bothered to
call the FBI.

Benson did both.

51

Whitaker had come down to check on him a few times, but for the most part he had been left alone. He called Debbie, and she would take over his classes for the next couple of weeks—or however long he still had a job. He had chosen her as his assistant because she was impervious to the jet engine whine of the student need turbine.

His attention swiveled back and forth from the bank of monitors mirroring his reflection to the wall of printouts spider-webbed together with red Sharpie lines. It looked like a conspiracy theorist's bedroom, minus the pushpins, yarn, tenuous deductions, and poor judgment. There was order in the mess, and he saw a dozen underlying patterns when he looked up at what most people would see as chaos.

He was staring into the void when Whitaker came in, holding up her phone. "There was an explosion upstate—town called Medusa. Two people killed. They found an IED trigger on site—it looks like the same kind we found at the internet hub on Eighth. C-4 again. We don't know the manufacture or batch yet, but Calvin-Wade

Curtis's team is already on the way and Kehoe wants to know if you think it's worth our time going up there."

"How far is it to Medusa?"

"It's near Schenectady. Two plus hours by car. An hour in a chopper."

Lucas thought about the bomb that Seth Hockney delivered to Federal Plaza aboard his personal helicopter. "Who was the victim?"

"*Victims*—plural. Fifty-one-year-old woman and her twenty-six-year-old son."

"What was her occupation?"

"She was a cashier at a gas bar."

"And the son?"

"Worked for the local agricultural board doing some kind of computer gig."

Lucas was about to wave her away when something came to him. "Where was his degree from?"

Whitaker punched into whatever file she had up. "SUNY Cobleskill."

Lucas pulled up some facts about the school out of his memory chip. "In?"

She bit her lip as she scrolled through the file. "Started out in cellular biology, but graduated in computer programming."

"Okay."

"Okay, what?"

"Okay, it's worth our time."

She snapped her fingers. "Then pack your bag, Mr. Grinch—we're going on a road trip!"

52

The Hockney Building

Dr. Saarinen was in his office on the floor that had been occupied by the management team of Horizon Dynamics but was now home to only him, two receptionists, and a roster of ghosts. He was looking out the window without seeing the city when William Hockney entered. Mr. Frosst was with him, but he stayed by the door, his face flat and emotionless. He didn't make eye contact.

Everything William Hockney did had presentation to it; he didn't come into a room—he *entered* it. But even a man like William couldn't lean into the wind indefinitely, and the past few days had dulled some of his poise. Saarinen knew grief was like that—it aged those left behind while stopping the clock for those it had taken, and they remained inaccurate fireplace mantel portraits grinning back with unfulfilled promise. And even though Seth had been in his seventies, he was still William's *little brother,* which had to carry all kinds of baggage.

Saarinen understood how grief could sculpt a person. His son's death had very nearly destroyed him. But he had been lucky with his work. His ideas were bigger than he was, and even though it wasn't enough, it mitigated the pain. At least some of the time. But his wife had never found a balance, and for the past ten years he had been living with a thin projection of the woman he had known. Sometimes, when he caught her from a certain angle, she hadn't even been there.

But William Hockney had always seemed impervious to the machinations of human emotions—it was almost his trademark. It was Seth who had been the dreamer.

It was impossible to deny that William Hockney was one of those fabled figures that dotted the history books. And not because he had been born with a silver spoon in his mouth. No, he was one of those rarefied beings who possessed the intangible x factor of greatness. It was not something you could buy. It was not something you could inherit. And it was not something you could imitate. In truth, it was not even something you could define. But it was easy to recognize, and one look at William Hockney told you he had it. Which was maybe what made his son such a disappointment to him—even through the optimistic lens of fatherhood, it would have been difficult to miss the lack of promise.

Hockney headed straight to Saarinen's bar and poured three fingers of whiskey—one of the obscure Japanese brands that he liked—into two tumblers. He placed them on the coffee table and sat down, facing the other sofa—which was his way of telling Saarinen that he was expected to take a seat.

Saarinen was still feeling a little foggy from last night's dance with the bottle of Finlandia, but now was not a time of restraint.

"How are you, Timo?" Even in his grief, William was tastefully dressed. But he also looked tired and preoccupied.

Saarinen didn't know what to say, so he sat down and they drank in silence for a few moments.

There were pleasantries they could exchange—sympathies and understanding nods—over their respective losses. But they didn't have that kind of relationship. Seth had been the glue between them, and a mutual acceptance of awkward silence was their form of conversation. Now that Seth was dead, any dreams of bringing Horizon's magic (and therefore profitability) to the world were over. So there was not much to tie them together, other than their own very different versions of grief. This was going to be the *Enjoy-the-rest-of-your-life* conversation. Saarinen couldn't see things unfolding any other way.

Saarinen had come to the office today only because sitting in the guarded penthouse overlooking the museum would just be wasted time. And there were still things to do.

After his liquor was consumed, Hockney said, "I came here to ask you what you want to do with Horizon."

Which was the last thing in the world Saarinen had expected—William Hockney never made business decisions based on emotion. And trying to salvage Horizon was a foolish dream. All of the management was gone—and they were not the kind of people you could replace on an unemployment website. It would take years of recruiting at universities and poaching from other top-tier companies. And they would have to rebuild the corporate ethos—all in the shadow of what had happened at the Guggenheim. They would no longer be industry leaders; they would be playing catch-up with new companies that filled the vacuum left in their wake. No, Horizon was more than dead—it was cremated and its ashes were scattered in the wind.

"Horizon is over, William. I am over. I don't have it in me anymore." He looked over at the old man. "And neither do you."

"Timo, Seth talked me into buying Horizon, then talked me into putting you at the helm. And a handful of years later we were about to launch an IPO with a billion-dollar potential. We did it once, we can do it again." He slowly pushed himself out of the sofa, picked up the bottle of whiskey, and poured them each another drink before placing the bottle down on the marquetry top. He slowly folded back into the leather.

Saarinen held the glass up in a half toast. "Thank you, William. But I am not interested. I have been fighting with . . ." He stopped because it wouldn't serve any purpose.

"People like me?" The old man waved it away. "I have spent my life playing the devil, Timo, and I have no problem with the epitaph I leave." He took a sip of whiskey and pulled his lips back over his teeth.

"Then yes . . ."—Saarinen again raised his glass in another half-hearted toast—"people like *you*. I don't have it in me anymore."

"So Horizon is dead?"

Saarinen knew why he was asking—a lot of money hinged on the Paraguayan infrastructure deal. And without Horizon, they would have to restructure. But Saarinen wasn't going to continue. "I am afraid so, William."

The old man nodded over at him. "Then I thank you for your service and wish you well in your future endeavors."

Frosst came in and helped the old man out of the sofa. And as he did, he looked over at Saarinen and smiled—it was a gesture that William Hockney did not see. And there was nothing kind in it.

53

County Route 357
Upstate New York

Lucas had opted for Whitaker's driving instead of a ride in a helicopter. Not that he misunderstood the statistical safety of the sky over the road, but the idea of Seth Hockney flying over the city with explosives in his lawyer's briefcase was still fresh in his sorting software. So for one of the few times in his life, he went for gut over brain.

They were Pac-Manning the backcountry roads west of Schenectady and he could not stop himself from hearing the imaginary *wonka-wonka-wonka* sound of the vehicle icon on the GPS screen.

Even with the imminent arrival of Old Man Winter, it was beautiful up here. Autumn was Lucas's favorite season, and he knew a lot of it went back to that night at his last foster home when Mr. Potts had driven him out to observe the stars for the first time. And some of it no doubt had to do with that very first conversation he had with Mrs. Page on the stone terrace the day she had adopted him. But all that could very easily have been outweighed by the Event—which had happened one day in late August.

They rounded a gentle curve in the road and the world slipped back into focus as they arrived at what looked like a country fair but which the GPS announced as their destination.

The road was clogged with pickups and SUVs, all stopped, engines idling, brake lights staring them down. People were walking on the shoulder in both directions. It was a slow kind of walk that you didn't see back in the city—not even in Central Park on the weekends. No one yakked into cell phones.

"What the fuck?" Whitaker asked, and pulled into the oncoming lane to get around the line of vehicles. She didn't bother with the lights or siren. One errant pickup's driver decided that she was trying to cheat the system, and he began to pull out, so she hit the asshole lights and blipped the siren for three chirps. He eased back into his lane.

The cops at the roadblock eyed them suspiciously as they approached, but they kept talking, neither one coming over or moving the traffic gate. Whitaker cranked the siren for a second and that got their attention. The lower man on the totem pole came over with an irritating slowness.

Whitaker rolled down her window.

"Sorry, ma'am, but no vehicles allowed beyond this point." Up ahead, the road was filled to capacity with emergency vehicles and law enforcement cruisers and SUVs.

Whitaker stretched her face into a smile, but there was nothing remotely friendly about it—she looked like she was gearing up to bite someone. She pulled out her badge. "FBI."

"Are you supposed to be here, ma'am?"

Lucas turned to watch because he didn't want to miss this; Whitaker was nothing if not predictable.

She pulled the smile off her face and said, "It's Special Agent Whitaker, not ma'am. Now open the fucking gate."

The officer stared openmouthed for just under the too-long time stamp, then closed his mouth. "Yes, ma—I mean Special Agent . . .

um, *Whitamcallit*. Right away." He nodded at the other country cop by the barrier, who dragged it out of the way, leaving an arc of painted pine splinters on the road.

"I fucking hate the country," Whitaker said a little too loud as she rolled up her window.

"I'm sure the feeling is mutual."

"Oh, it is. Why do you think they don't have black people out here?"

"They have black people out here."

Whitaker waved a hand at the windshield, indicating the world beyond. "Yeah? Where?" Pedestrians were allowed past the first barrier, but the crime-scene line was still a few hundred yards farther up. People milled about—the bombing was obviously the most exciting thing to happen around here in a while.

"Well, maybe not *right here*. But they're here. This isn't Sweden."

"I went to Sweden for a basketball tournament in high school. They have more black people there than they do here. And by here, I mean *right here*."

People walked in the road and Whitaker had to flash her headlights or tap the horn to get them to move.

"I lack the sufficient data to either agree or disagree."

"Three hundred people outside, all of them white, and you lack the sufficient data? This is why we don't work together more."

Lucas did an instantaneous head count. "First of all, there are only precisely eighty-three individuals that I can see right now. Second, we don't work together more because I can only take you in small doses. And it's not because you're black."

"So you're on their side."

"*Their* side? That sounds a little paranoid."

"Really? Because all the white people are now looking at the car and pointing."

"No one is looking in the car and . . ." Lucas stopped because some of the people *were* pointing. "Maybe they're pointing at me." But they weren't; they were pointing at Whitaker.

Daylight Savings was in a few days—but that was only to roll the clocks back an hour. Outside it looked like they had been rolled back a hundred years. "What the fuck?" he said.

"Maybe I should have you sit in the back—they could take that."

Lucas was grateful when they arrived at the second barrier.

The man at the gate had obviously been notified of their arrival via radio, and the barrier was immediately dragged open, this particular cop smiling as they pulled through, his attention laser-focused on Whitaker.

The scene was a quarter mile up, in a field.

Two of the bureau's vehicles were on site—one belonging to the bomb squad and the second to the forensics team. Two local fire trucks were on the shoulder, away from the house, along with an ambulance; six or so pickup trucks; two Econolines that had county crest magnets on the doors; two semitrailers—one carrying a backhoe, another a bulldozer; a dump truck; two garbage trucks; and what looked like a snowplow.

"Looks like they called out everyone except the Marines."

"Small towns. People pull together." But they did that back in the city, only it took a larger catastrophe to unfreeze the neighbor bone.

Whitaker pulled onto the shoulder about a hundred yards from the driveway, a ribbon of gravel that ran four hundred feet from the road to between a pile of burned-out rubble that had been a house and a smoking mound of cinders of what might have been a barn.

A skinny country cop in body armor came up, his shoulders swinging like he had just come from the gym. His sleeves were rolled up, exposing bright ink on both arms that stopped at his wrists, and he had a phone in his hand. He looked like he would rather be somewhere else. "You more FBI?" he asked, his question directed at Lucas.

Lucas nodded.

Whitaker stepped up and the man stuck out his hand. "I'm Deputy McCoy—Owen McCoy." He was wearing sunglasses, but Lucas could see him give her a full appraisal.

"Special Agent Whitaker, and that's Dr. Page."

Lucas gave a small wave with his prosthetic. He caught McCoy's eyes lock on the metal fingers for an instant and the cop asked, "Iraq?"

"No."

"Afghanistan?"

"Nope."

He looked a little embarrassed and Lucas didn't bother offering him an out, so he turned back to Whitaker. "Your people have been here for about an hour. I'll walk you up."

Lucas watched McCoy fall into step with Whitaker and he wondered if she had noticed the way he had looked at her. Maybe it was a thing only guys could see, but it was obvious that he was attracted to her. Lucas hoped he was good at handling rejection. Or at least not crying in public.

McCoy walked them through the last security check, which was for the immediate vicinity of the crime scene, and Lucas waved down Gail Simcoe, one of Kehoe's people from back in the city who was the SAIC out here. She excused herself from a conversation with a space-suited acolyte who had soot and char marks on his white disposable coveralls.

McCoy said goodbye to Whitaker and told her that he was around if she needed anything. He handed her his card with "You know . . . just in case."

Whitaker waved him away with an irritated flutter of her fingers that Lucas knew she had stolen from William Hockney. "I'm good." And she turned her attention to Simcoe.

Simcoe was a short woman that Mrs. Page would have called

thick-boned. She had her FBI windbreaker and cap on and obviously took herself seriously.

Simcoe closed the gap in ten clunky strides. "Page, Whitaker. You made good time." She held out a field tablet. "Here's what we have on the victims so far. The explosives team is going through the place now." She nodded at the pile of rubble up the driveway. "We're hoping to have some more answers this side of an hour."

Lucas took the tablet and Whitaker asked, "Anything stand out about the vics?" They now had a silent agreement that she would do the talking and Lucas would open his mouth only when he wanted something—that way, no one got their feelings singed.

"Hazel Rich: white female, fifty-one years of age; Donny Rich, male, twenty-five—her son. She was divorced. Employed at the Gas Smasher over in Greenville. Neighbors said she was quiet. Enjoyed gardening. Had a boyfriend who works at a car dealership in Albany. We checked on him—no record, no priors. Also divorced. No red flags. No obvious enemies." Simcoe had her lecture delivery down, which was an important skill.

"And Donny?" Whitaker asked.

Simcoe nodded at the tablet. "Some kind of computer gig working for the local agricultural board, converting data to text for their financial reports."

Whitaker looked over at Lucas. "The right skill to create the letter from our guy?"

Lucas nodded. "Could be."

"What was his background?"

Simcoe had a good command of the file. "Did three years at SUNY Cobleskill; started out in cellular biology and switched to technology and communications middle of his second year. Graduated seventeen months ago. Neighbors said he had friends over on the weekends. He did chores. Took out the garbage, mowed the lawn and the field there, did all the laundry and cooking, and sold action figures on eBay to make a little money. Neighbors said he was a good kid and really helped his mom out. Didn't drink. Besides his work for the agricultural board, he did some off-the-clock computer work for people—had an ad on the local craigslist and put up flyers. Hardware repair. Teaching oldsters the difference between the cloud and an operating system. No priors or record. Everyone said he wasn't the kind of kid to get into trouble. No known enemies."

Lucas swiveled his head, taking in what had been a home a few hours earlier. "Did the neighbors have anything to add? Any strange guests or comings and goings?"

"Not a thing."

Lucas nodded up at what used to be a house. "What happened?"

Her tone didn't change when she went into the details. "The plans for the house are there," she said, pointing at the tablet. "Hazel was blown through the roof; we found her across the street, under those trees." She pivoted, swinging her arm like a weathervane. "She was mostly intact." Then she clicked around another ninety degrees and pointed to the eastern edge of the property. "We found one of Donny's feet hanging off the fence over there. We took the dogs out but didn't come up with anything else—it looks like his foot is all that's left, although we did find a molar in the driveway that might be his."

Lucas examined the house plans on the tablet's screen. They were digital blueprints with the county surveyor's label in the bottom corner. He flipped through the two pages, memorizing the layout, then handed the tablet back.

Simcoe nodded at the unmistakable form of Calvin-Wade Curtis up near the chimney. "The forensics explosives team may give you something useful."

Even from here, Lucas could see Curtis smiling. "Anything we should know?" he asked as they walked toward the crime-scene tape.

Yeah," Simcoe said seriously. "Let us know if you find any more body parts."

54

It was hard to imagine that the field had once framed a rural house, a shed, and a barn; it looked like a steampunk satellite had plummeted from the sky, scattering wood, brick, and glass when it detonated against the crust of the earth. Other than the chimney, very little had survived the explosion in any recognizable form, the notable exception being a kitchen chair that was sitting in the field a few hundred feet away, as if someone had placed it there for star-gazing. It was near the border where the scorched lawn met the tall grass. Every other element of what had once been a household had been reduced to its basic components, which meant splinters and broken glass.

The local rubberneckers were far down the road, held back by the local sheriff's people. But there were no news crews on site. At least not yet. And everyone seemed to be behaving themselves. Only a few people held up cell phones, which were pretty much useless at this distance.

Curtis walked Lucas and Whitaker around the perimeter, outside the yellow line staked to the ground. He looked like he belonged out here in the country, and his southern accent was a little thicker, as if the terrain reset his translator. The nervous smile was on full display, which still weirded Lucas out.

Curtis's men were scuttling around the debris, de facto crime-scene crabs culling what was left for useful morsels. "We found taggants on site that match our guy's batch of C-4 that was manufactured by ENF."

The remains of the house were still smoking, but the bureau men were nonetheless sifting through the charred chunks in search of anything that would help them figure out who, precisely, had done this. They had two white plastic tempos set up beside the driveway to protect the folding tables they were using to catalogue evidence. There were Tupperware bins spread around the property, and hundreds of small flags in bright yellow plastic for the photographers. In the old days, the photos would simply go into a folder, to be flipped through and analyzed with the medium of experience; today they were geotagged and fed into a program that generated a three-dimensional model of the environment so they could go back and walk the crime scene in virtual feet.

Curtis held up a polyethylene evidence bag with a twisted piece of metal inside. "Standard DIY trigger—you can find instructions for fifty variants on the web in half an hour—for 'educational purposes,' of course. I saw a lot of these in the Middle East. Which is why one of the state troopers was able to identify it—like me, he spent time over there disarming IEDs. He gave us a jump on the investigation, which was a nice little piece of luck."

Lucas took the bag and examined what looked like a partially melted cabinet hinge. He did a little mental Photoshop to reconstruct the piece and said, "This is the same as the one we found in the unexploded device inside the building on Eighth the other night?" He shook the bag. "Cell phone trigger?"

Curtis nodded and grinned.

Lucas examined it for a few more seconds, focusing on the way one of the wires had been fastened, then cut—at a forty-five-degree angle. "Other than being easy to put together, can you tell us anything about it?"

Curtis's smile changed. "Even though it's the same C-4, it was made by a different builder than the one we found on Eighth, the one that killed Makepeace, and the one that took out Saarinen's wife and housekeeper. I can't be sure about the Hudson Street bombing, because we didn't find any of the pieces—they were vaporized."

Whitaker peered at it. "How do you know it's a different builder?"

"This one was made by someone who was left-handed. The other ones were built by a right-handed individual." He nodded at what took a lot of imagination to picture as a house. "We have samples of both victims' handwriting from their driver's licenses, and they were both right-handed. Other than that, it's the same—made with components you can find in any hardware store."

Lucas handed the piece back to Curtis and shifted his attention over to the pile of debris the bureau men were fine-tooth-combing with various devices, instruments, apps, and eyeballs. He wondered if they would find any more former occupants. Or parts of them. That was the beauty of being hit with a massive shock wave—it deposited parts of the victims all over the place, so first responders could play a game of Where's Waldo? as if it had been designed by Jeffrey Dahmer. "What size of a charge?"

Curtis smiled like he was glad that Lucas asked that question. "A shitload. I'd say five pounds. Maybe more."

"Five pounds?" Whitaker asked, not even trying to hide her shock. "You could take out an aircraft carrier with five pounds."

Curtis gave them his smile again. "*Two* aircraft carriers, if you knew where to place the charges."

One of Curtis's men whistled and they all looked over. He was pointing into the rubble, near a single spindle of wood rising from the charred timbers. "Stairs to the basement are clear!" he yelled.

Curtis excused himself and stepped under the tape to see what he was needed for. More smiles, maybe.

Lucas headed away from the tape, into the field. They had what they needed to figure this all out—there was more than enough data. But he wasn't seeing it. At least not in any meaningful capacity. He needed some distance from his thoughts, at least metaphorically. So a trip out into the field seemed like the right thing to do. If for nothing else, to get away from people who smiled around the dead.

"Are you looking for anything special?" Whitaker asked. "Because the blown-up house is over there." She raised her arm and pointed in the direction Curtis had gone.

"I'm just trying to get a little distance on this."

"I thought Calvin-Wade's smiling might be bothering you."

"It's not a habit I'm fond of."

Lucas watched where he stepped. The forensics people had already swept the field and Lucas wasn't concerned about stumbling over a lost body part—the grass fire had wiped out all the hiding places—he was concentrating on the uneven footing.

He headed out into the field, toward the kitchen chair sitting in stark contrast to its surroundings.

Whitaker said, "Nice talking to you, too. I'll wait here."

Lucas took his time as he walked in the black grass. All manner of household items were strewn about, from kitchen utensils to books to at least three separate computer keyboards—all bent, broken, charred, or barely recognizable. The house was on ten acres, most of it fields that bordered forest on two sides—a mix of coniferous and deciduous. Burned leaves were laced in with the incinerated grass and a light wind gave them a voice that was a little above a whisper. Lucas listened to the sounds of the field as he turned it all over in his head.

Cellular biology before switching to technology and communications.

Some kind of computer gig working for the local agricultural board, converting data to text for their financial reports.

Did some computer work for people. Ran an ad on craigslist.

Didn't drink.

Had friends over on the weekend.

Lucas reached the chair. It was pointing away from the house, but perfectly level in the burnt grass, its legs blackened but the seat somehow untouched by the fire or explosion. He picked it up by the backrest and swung it around to face the house. One of the legs got caught in the scorched grass and he had to lift it up a little higher to make the rotation. He set it back down, then levered into the seat.

Over at the house, Curtis climbed out of the basement on a collapsible ladder. He pulled off his gloves and headed the long way around the debris toward Whitaker, who went to meet him. He was grinning like he had sucked down a quart of nitrous oxide. *What's with that guy?* Lucas wondered.

Lucas watched them speak for a few moments, Whitaker asking questions and Curtis smiling too much while he answered. He really needed to work on that. At least when he was on site.

Lucas went through Donny Rich's background again as Curtis and Whitaker talked.

Agriculture program before he switched to technology and communications.

Some kind of computer gig working for the local agricultural board, converting data to text for their financial reports.

Did some computer work for people. Ran an ad on craigslist.

Didn't drink.

Had friends over on the weekend.

Lucas didn't will it to occur—it just happened.

Time stopped.

The second hand froze.

The world ceased spinning.

And the unthinkable, the unnatural, and the impossible happened as the gears of the universe meshed with the transmission of his mind and it all started up. In reverse.

The clock.

And the earth.

And time itself.

All rewound.

The winds crawled back over the field, picking up leaves, carrying them toward the trees. Birds at the edge of the field flew in reverse. Fire erupted at the edge of the burnt grass; it crawled under his chair and pulled back toward the driveway, unscorching the yard as it went. The debris—the splintered timbers and shingles and bricks and glass—lifted off the ground and wove back toward a center. Hazel Rich's naked body soared out of the ditch, through the trees, flying into her nightgown as she cleared the branches, arcing through the sky, through the roof, and back into her bed. Donny's foot unhung itself from the barbed wire at the edge of the property and punched through the cloud of fire to disappear into the explosion that then collapsed into itself, like a star imploding.

And the house was there.

And the barn was there.

And the jeep was there.

And they were both still alive.

And the tall grass in the field was moving with the wind and it smelled like fall.

Then Lucas blinked.

And he was once again sitting in a chair in the middle of a scorched field that smelled of fresh flames.

By himself.

Whitaker and Curtis were at the end of their talk and she was waving Lucas back. He stood up and the movement pushed one of the pieces floating around in his head into place. And with the first step, another one slid home. By the time he was back at the tape, a few more had clicked into position, and he knew what they were going to say.

Lucas decided to hit them preemptively just to see how it sounded out loud. "Donny had a workbench in the basement? Bomb-making equipment? The extra supplies magnified the explosion, which is why the damage was as extensive as it was. But he didn't blow himself up; he wasn't in the basement when the explosion occurred. There was another device. Probably under the kitchen counter, which was facing the driveway. The shock wave blew in the side of the jeep and sent that chair out into the field. It also launched Hazel Rich through the roof—she was in bed, and her room was on the other side of the house. But Donny's room was right above the kitchen, and he got the worst of it. Which is why you only found that foot over there, past the chair."

Whitaker examined him with that look she had when she was trying to figure out what to say. Sometimes Erin had that exact expression.

Curtis simply stared, his grin put away for the moment. "We didn't get that far with our models but, um . . . yeah."

Lucas turned to the road and headed back to the Lincoln.

"Where are you going?" Whitaker asked.

"Back to the city."

"But we just got here."

"And now we're leaving."

She came after him, and on the uneven ground it didn't take long for her to catch up. "Care to tell me what's going on?"

"There's going to be more."

"More what?"

"More of everything."

55

Forest Hills, Queens

It was a quiet tree-lined street that looked like it had been plucked from the pages of a postwar American novel about a father who taught his son how to be a decent man through their common love of baseball.

Rebecca Woolsey was taking her twin daughters for a stroll on what she knew would be one of the last nice days of the year. Fall had been generous, but it couldn't stay in a giving mood forever. The weather app on her phone was promising rain later in the day, so she was playing a little game of Beat the Clock with Olivia and Aurora. They were bundled up in matching pink down jackets and tucked comfortably into the new pram that her girlfriends had chipped in to get her as a baby shower gift. It was the deluxe model, equipped with a smart system that sent a text to her phone when one of the girls needed her diaper changed. There was an onboard health monitor that displayed both girls' vitals and it had a built-in GPS so Rebecca could clock her daily mileage. The carriage had a Bluetooth stereo and built-in temperature control to keep the twins comfy and happy.

She passed under a big maple, its leaves every shade of orange and red imaginable. She pointed up, cooing softly to the girls, and they smiled up at Mommy.

Rebecca sang, "If you're happy and you know it, clap your hands." And clapped her hands.

The girls smiled and waved their hands up at Mommy.

"If you're happy and you know it, clap your hands."

She clapped again, and on the second beat there was a big explosion somewhere behind her.

She jumped. And spun. Down the block, wood and shingles and glass were raining down from the sky. Half of a house was gone, and the part that was left was on fire. Car alarms were going off. Smoke billowed into the air.

A man walked out of the house, stumbling slowly as if he didn't know the place was on fire. But so was he.

He walked to the middle of the road. Fell to his knees. Then flopped face first into the asphalt.

Rebecca started to scream.

Brooklyn

Juan Delgado had just started his shift and was on his first delivery of the night—a jumbo with half pepperoni and mushroom, half pineapple and anchovies, along with an order of buffalo wings, Cheesy Bread, two-bite brownies, and a big bottle of Mountain Dew.

If you looked at the order without knowing the client's history, it would be easy to think that a couple on the verge of divorce over irreconcilable differences had called it in. But Delgado had delivered to the man in 4E many times—the guy smoked a lot of dope, which helped explain his *todo loco* order—he always ordered weirdo combinations. Delgado thought that the foundation of his diet was some kind of a dare.

Delgado stepped into the elevator and pressed four. He was careful not to tilt the pizza—the guy was a good tipper, and every now and then Delgado stayed for a joint and a slice. The dude's name was Enrique Cristobel, and he was a UPS driver—he was always in one of those ugly brown uniforms that the company still hadn't thought to update with something a little cooler, like Nikes and a tracksuit. Maybe a hoodie with some gold lettering. But the dude was sick, and they kinda shared a heritage—both of their grandmothers were from Oaxaca—so it felt more like a friendly visit than work. The joints didn't hurt, either.

The elevator pinged open and Delgado turned right.

As usual, there was music playing inside. It was some heavy metal bullshit and Delgado decided that he wouldn't stay; he was more a hip hop kind of guy.

He knocked loudly, and someone inside turned down the volume and footsteps headed for the door. But they stopped as Delgado heard a cell phone ringing somewhere off in the apartment. The footsteps receded and he heard Cristobel answer.

"Yeah?"

Pause.

"Yeah, I'm at home. Right now. Yes. Why—"

And that was when the explosion tore out the corner unit of 4E, killing the occupant, one Enrique Cristobel, along with the man delivering his dinner, one Juan Delgado.

Hoboken, New Jersey

It was rush hour, and traffic on Washington was slower than usual due to the lights on 12th Street being down. They had a cop directing traffic, but he was doing a crummy job and everyone was honking. And swearing. And wishing they were somewhere else.

And in all the tension, no one saw the third floor of the five-floor building blow out.

But they heard it.

All the drivers looked up from their phones just in time to see the bricks come raining down. Several vehicles lost windshields. A pickup truck was taken out by a section of fire escape that had been launched into the sky. And some guy on a bike got a brick in the teeth.

But no one had been paying attention enough to actually see the moment of the explosion. Although everyone who was in a two-block radius at the time would later claim that they had.

Castleton Corners, Staten Island

Raymond Fields was watching the evening news with his wife, Brenda. And judging by the panicked faces, you'd think that nothing else was happening in the world other than that Mr. Machine Asshole blowing shit up. Why were people so freaked out about this guy? Fields had served his country in Vietnam and had seen the real damage that human beings did to one another. Don't get him wrong—he had sympathy for the people whose lives this asshole touched—but dying at a gala with all your rich friends was a fuckuvalot better than bleeding out in a fucking field while little chinko bastards in black pajamas stripped off your wristwatch before sticking a rusty knife slowly up your ass.

No, if you asked Ray, America had gone fucking soft. All you had to do was look at the way kids dressed today. Back in his youth, when the protests against the war had started, the old people said they couldn't tell the girls from the boys. Which Ray knew was bullshit. Sure, they had long hair, but they were real men. These days, guys wore gauchos—fucking gauchos! Men carried around emotional support animals and they worried about hurting other people's feelings—their fucking feelings! Jee-zus, what had happened to the country?

Ray got up from the sofa and went to the fridge. As he opened the door, he asked Brenda if she wanted another PBR. She said nope, so he just grabbed two—that way he wouldn't have to get up in another five minutes.

He closed the fridge and walked back into the living room with two cold ones. He popped the top.

But he never got to take a sip because the house next door blew up, taking out the propane tank at Ray's side door, which blew him and Brenda and the whole fucking place to smithereens.

56

26 Federal Plaza

Kehoe stood transfixed, his feet held to the floor via a magnetic phenomenon that refused to release him. He stared at the news teams feeding on tragedy, looking grave and concerned as they filled time between the commercials that sold blood thinners and reverse mortgages. But even in his paralysis, he was plugged into the central nervous system of the crime-solving organism he directed, and he could feel different parts of the beast coming to life

The talking heads were in fine form. Three days of this had been enough time for them to pull out their thesaurus apps and memorize different terms for *bomb, explosion, fire,* and *victim*—in that general order of importance.

But they were ahead of the bureau right now, and had dispatched the makeup-and-rictus-grin squads to the latest explosions, all four of which had occurred less than fifteen minutes ago, and all within what appeared to be thirty seconds of one another. The police were already on site at all four locations, but the bureau's people were still at least five miles out on two of the locations and ten from the third and fourth.

A journalist from CNN—an Asian woman who looked to be about fifteen years old sporting the worst pair of glasses Kehoe had seen in a while—was in the Forest Hills neighborhood of Queens. It was a beautiful tree-lined street displaying some of the nicest turn-of-the-century real estate to be found in all five boroughs. The journalist—one Emily Chow, according to the chyron—stared seriously into the camera, index and middle finger pressed to her ear to accentuate that she was speaking live to the studio. She was nodding and shaking her head and pursing her lips and doing her best Lon Chaney as she answered all manner of idiotic questions from the anchor back in the studio—a man so poorly up to speed on this particular topic that it sounded like he was trying out for *SNL*. But Chow held her ground, didn't break out laughing, and never lost the appropriate gravitas or her good manners.

One of the nicer homes on the street—this one a big stucco-and-wood pseudo-Tudor—stood behind her. It looked like the kind of place that sold cuckoo clocks or cheese, and it reminded Kehoe of Solvang, California, where he had spent summers as a kid. Half of it was gone, spread out all over the street, and partially into the next if Emily was to be believed. The half that was left was on fire, and two dozen turnout-coat-clad firemen were attacking the blaze with hoses, foam, and determination.

Authorities had yet to release the names of the victims, but Chow had been informed that three people had died in the house—a couple in their sixties and their son, who was twenty-four. Chow was certain that since there were no natural gas lines on the street, this explosion was in some as-yet-unknown way connected with the Machine Bomber, an invisible enemy that the FBI had been unable to stop.

Kehoe's single rule of not giving in to open displays of emotion at work cracked at that last little bit of stupidity and he threw his mug of tea at the wall. The mug did not survive.

One of the other giant monitors was tuned to Fox News. They

were splitting the screen between the studio and Hoboken, New Jersey. Technically, Jersey was outside of Kehoe's purview, but that did little to alleviate the mixture of anger and embarrassment he felt. Tonight it looked like the anchor was having a harder time than usual understanding things as he spoke to one of their men in the field—a pudgy guy in an ill-fitting imitation Brooks Brothers blazer that had one too many buttons. Mr. Too-cheap-for-a-decent-sports-coat was standing in front of a mound of burning rubble that the chyron said was a multifamily rental property that had exploded mere moments ago. The chyron was moving slower than the one on CNN or MSNBC, presumably due to the older viewer demographic, but they made up for this by using all the right language—notably *inferno, terrorist,* and *immigrant.*

Authorities had yet to identify the victim, but it appeared that he was a man in his mid-twenties.

Like the scene in Forest Hills, firemen were pumping half a dozen large jets of water into the conflagration. Police cars and ambulances were on scene. What was missing was an FBI presence, and Kehoe was grateful that he had no more mugs to throw.

The anchor was repeating the same question using different words, as if that would sell the idea he was pushing. He wanted the field man to confirm that yes, indeed, this was the work of the Machine Bomber, the man responsible for blowing up the Guggenheim; the internet hub; Dr. Timo Saarinen's wife and housekeeper; Jonathan Makepeace; Seth Hockney, his lawyer, Samir Chawla, and the bureau's lawyer. Apparently the network's people had not figured out that the explosion Kehoe had sent Page and Whitaker on was also connected to their guy—which was at least something. But the anchor kept hammering the point, slipping the word *Muslim* in here, and the word *Mexican* in there. All couched by the term *unconfirmed* to avoid any legal jeopardy.

A local affiliate—this one WABC—was broadcasting from Brooklyn. The anchor was an overweight middle-aged man who looked like he smelled of last night's booze. He had a complexion that appeared to be built out of toxins, and his eyes were red and set in deep sockets. He was morosely reporting on another bombing, this one an apartment in a thirty-unit low-rise. As with the others, smoke billowed from what used to be a dwelling. The curtains hanging out the blown-out windows were still on fire. No one knew how many people had been injured or killed. The anchor looked like all he wanted was a drink.

MSNBC was on another screen, this one at the far end of the war room. A man—or was that a woman?—with a baseball cap and a script grimaced into the camera. Kehoe settled on *they* and quickly read the subtitles that were up. They were in Castleton Corners, Staten Island, where an explosion had leveled a small single-family home. Apparently the only person home at the time was a renter who lived in the basement—a twenty-four-year-old man—but there was no doubt that he was now dead. This time not only was the entire building gone, but it had taken the house beside it out as well, killing the older couple who lived there. They kept turning back over their shoulder and nodding at the firemen, who were hard at work trying to put out the flames licking into the sky. And like the other reporters, they wondered when—if ever—the FBI was going to catch the person or persons responsible. Then they went to interview one of the firemen on site.

Kehoe knew that he had spent no more than a single minute absorbing the chattering morons on TV, but the exercise had driven his oil pressure up and he felt the hoses starting to vibrate. He turned to Lawrence Braithwaite, one of his agents, and snapped his fingers.

Braithwaite, a small black man who pushed the dress code boundaries with his shoes and hair, looked up. "Yes, sir?"

"Get Whitaker and Page on the phone and tell them to get back here."

Braithwaite gave him a thumbs-up and asked, "What's the reason I give them?"

And that was when Kehoe's clamps finally let go. *"Because someone is still blowing people up in my fucking city."*

57

Palisades Parkway

Whitaker was uncharacteristically quiet after she hung up with Braithwaite, which allowed Lucas a little time to focus on all the numbers dancing on the head of the pin. There were so many digits at play at this point that one miscalculation could send the whole thing spinning off into deep space, where it would implode. So he concentrated on keeping the equations simple. Some of the figures were missing; some were in the wrong place; some were even the wrong value. But it was building itself.

It was dark now, and if he had been back in his old life, he'd wonder where the day had gone. But when he worked for the bureau, time became a contorted commodity that had a way of bending in half. Or unfolding so that an hour felt like a month in a closet. Not that he didn't get lost in his own head when he was unpacking the mysteries of the universe, but somehow the real-world consequences of hunting down killers opened up tiny wormholes that his wristwatch couldn't compensate for. He wondered if there was a physiological explanation for it—he'd have to ask Erin. Or at least Google it. That morning felt like weeks ago. Which made no sense at all, since he still smelled burnt plastic and smoked Chawla at the back of his throat. Or was that from his time on the chair out in the scorched field?

Whitaker interrupted his silence as a garbage truck pulled out from behind them, passing in the left-hand lane—an unusual occurrence, since Whitaker had the heaviest foot Lucas had ever seen outside of a Coors Light commercial. "What's going on?"

The picture was incomplete at best, completely wrong at worst. "William Hockney is the linchpin. I don't know if he's responsible for all this, but he's the number holding the whole equation together. Without him, there is no equation."

"So Medusa and the bombings in Queens, Staten Island, Hoboken, and Brooklyn straight-line back to Hockney?"

"Nothing in this straight-lines anywhere. But this is somehow tied to him."

"What about Frosst?" She pulled into the slow lane and opened her window. The warm wind pressurized the Navigator with a big breath.

Lucas thought about him for a second and something was off. "Maybe."

Whitaker indexed, then pulled out behind the dump truck to pass an ancient Volkswagen Jetta with a Jay Peak sticker on the trunk. The Volks was piloted by a hippie more immersed in whatever was transpiring on his cell phone than in the traffic around him. Lucas wondered what the guy's life expectancy would look like on the appropriate actuary table. "If I wanted to plant a bomb, Frosst is the guy I'd use."

Traffic heading back into the city was sparse, but lights from the northbound lanes blinked through the trees. With the way things were going, he wouldn't have been surprised if the entire city decided to empty out. Another few days of this and people would be building big boats and collecting pairs of animals in the park. Sure, the citizenry were resilient in ways that no other populace on the planet could even hope to approximate, but even New Yorkers would take only so much before they said *fuck it.*

"So what's next?"

Lucas answered with the body language of the lazy, which was not lost on him—he shrugged. "I talk to William Hockney."

"About?"

"About why someone is intent on squeezing his nuts in a vise."

They spent a few moments in silence, each absorbed in their own thoughts, that Whitaker eventually ended by saying, "Tell me about your book, about Ricky Schroder's cat—that's the one where the cat is both dead and alive, right?"

Lucas had always been amazed at how people missed the point of Schrödinger's thought experiment. "Think about it for a second—a cat cannot be both dead and alive. A cat is dead. Or it is alive. If you can't figure out which, it's because you're missing information. It's not very complicated."

Lucas looked over and Whitaker wasn't listening anymore. Her attention was on the rearview mirror.

"What?" he asked.

"There's a Range Rover on our ass; it's been there since the I-87 off-ramp. Two guys in suits."

Lucas resisted the temptation to turn around, and before he could ask if she was certain that it wasn't a coincidence, she answered, "They were waiting for us on the shoulder." She kept her eyes on the rearview mirror as she passed the Jetta.

"What do we do?" Lucas asked.

The interior lit up as the Rover lurched forward, almost touching their bumper.

She pulled out her pistol. "Try pointing with your finger and going *pow, pow, pow.*"

58

26 Federal Plaza

Kehoe came out of his private bathroom to find Otto Hoffner standing in front of his desk. He held a single sheet of paper in his hand and there was no missing the import in his body language.

Kehoe didn't waste time asking why he was here. He just opened his hands in a give-it-to-me gesture.

Hoffner took a step toward him, the paper extended in an arm that looked like it had been transplanted from Conan the barbarian.

Kehoe took the printout, but Hoffner went into information delivery mode without being prompted. "We're on site at those four residential explosions and we have a pretty good line on who died—we'll know more once the bodies make it to the ME. But I think we can rule out coincidence. The man blown up in Forest Hills was Steve Whiteman. He was the driver for the event organizer at the Guggenheim—he delivered both the snowmakers and the foil bags. The man killed in the apartment in Hoboken is Tony Iannantuono. Iannantuono was an intern at Stogner, Pruitt, and Gibson—the law firm that employed the Hockney lawyer blown up in our interview room with Special Agent Chawla. The guy killed in Castleton Corners was Barnabas O'Hare. O'Hare was a mechanic with the company that maintained the generators at the internet hub on Hudson Street. The guy blown up in Brooklyn is Enrique Cristobel. Cristobel was—"

"The UPS driver who was at Makepeace's apartment on Fifth Avenue along with Benjamin Frosst the morning that Makepeace was killed."

Hoffner nodded. "Yes, sir."

"What about the victim upstate that Whitaker and Page went to check out. What was his name?"

"Rich, sir. Donnie Rich."

"Does he factor into this?"

Hoffner shrugged—a nearly imperceptible movement that his trapezius muscles barely allowed for. "We don't know, sir. Page might have something to offer."

"And we interviewed all of these people?"

Hoffner would have nodded if his neck had been flexible enough. "All but Rich, sir. And they all checked out. All had been on the job at least eighteen months. No records, no reason to suspect they were involved at all. We did cell phone and internet checks. We looked into family members and known friends. Social media accounts and bank records. They were all clean."

No, they weren't. "Let me know as soon as Page walks in."

59

Palisades Parkway

Whitaker pushed the big V8 into the task and they looped around a line of cars. "And you still refuse to carry a gun." It was a fatalistic observation. "I hope this isn't one of those *I-told-you-so* moments."

Lucas focused on the side mirror.

The Rover had pulled out and was closing the gap. There was no way it wasn't following them.

Whitaker glanced into the rearview mirror. "We can't outrun them in this beast." The road opened up and was empty of vehicles except for the garbage truck that had passed them earlier. It was a hundred yards up, hogging up the right-hand lane.

Whitaker was picking up speed and about to overtake the garbage truck, when it braked and swerved, fishtailing. And slowly began to drift.

"Fuck." There was nothing but resignation in her voice.

Tires squealed as its profile took up the entire road in slow motion.

The right side of the garbage truck filled the windshield with a wall of metal.

Whitaker pounded down on the brakes. The truck slid sideways, blocking both lanes.

She swerved and hit the gas, trying to pull them around the back bumper. But the rig's tail dug into the cement wall bordering the shoulder, blocking their path and throwing out a fan of sparks that bounced off the road.

The truck was completely sideways, and the wheels facing them lifted off the pavement and it looked like it was going to roll.

Lucas reached out and braced himself against the dashboard.

Headlights from the Rover filled the cabin.

The garbage truck teetered for too long, then dropped back to earth, bouncing and coming to a stop.

Whitaker pounded both feet into the brake pedal, and they skidded.

"Hold on!" Whitaker barked as the Rover rammed them in the back right corner, spinning them around in a full rotation.

Before they stopped moving, Whitaker was out of the car.

She had her pistol out.

Lucas turned and the two men were out of the Rover. They both had small carbines.

He ducked and spun back, facing the garbage truck. Frosst was climbing out. He also held a small rifle.

From somewhere to his left, Whitaker screamed, "Drop your weapons!"

Lucas pointed at Frosst and yelled at her, "On your six!"

Whitaker was facing the other way and she opened up with her semiautomatic pistol, squeezing off two three-round bursts.

Lucas wanted to turn. Wanted to see what had happened behind them. But he couldn't take his eyes off Frosst ahead.

"Whitaker!" Lucas yelled.

And over the ringing in his ears from the punch of her six shots, he heard her shoes scrape on the asphalt and knew she was turning.

All he could do was stare at Frosst. He was on the pavement now. Raising the big snout of the ugly weapon.

And then Whitaker's gun punched in the dark—another three-round burst.

The fabric on Frosst's suit erupted and he slammed back into the truck's front fender.

From somewhere off to his left, Whitaker said, "Page? You okay?"

He wanted to answer. Wanted to speak. Wanted to say something to let her know that he was fine. But all he could do was watch Frosst stand back up and raise the rifle.

Somewhere behind them cars slammed on brakes. Skidded to a stop. Honked.

He found the strength to turn to her. Their eyes met. "Whitaker!" he yelled. And she understood. And began a turn. Started to raise her pistol.

But Frosst had her.

The first round hit her in the neck, vapor-trailing a black mist out behind her.

The pistol flew from her fingers, clattering away somewhere in the dark.

Whitaker's hand went up to her throat.

The second shot hit her in the chest, punching through her body and zipping off into the dark. There was an instant of hang time where she stood there with a surprised look on her face. She tried to say something, but all that came out was a big black bubble of blood that popped down her chin.

And then the puppet master cut her strings, and she collapsed.

Lucas reached out and shots punched through the windshield as Frosst opened fire on him.

60

26 Federal Plaza

Kehoe was in his office with the door closed, and he felt like an insect in a terrarium—only less relevant, which was not his natural set point. Beyond the glass, the hive operated at full capacity, workers and drones and soldiers moving with the preprogrammed tasks of their caste. Calls were being fielded; data collected, analyzed, and collated; tips were being vetted; leads followed; suspects questioned. And yet here they were, with four more bombings to deal with.

He had reached the point where, for the first time in his career, he understood how some of his predecessors had been desperate enough to try mediums, paranormal investigators, and all manner of quackery. After all, desperation was the breeding ground for foolishness. But Kehoe was an educated man and knew that what he needed wouldn't be found in carnival confidence scams; he needed his people to do what they had been designed to—their jobs.

Like anyone in life whose vocation involves solving an endless string of riddles, Kehoe was hardwired to believe that solutions were, in some way, always achievable. But Page insisted that the only certainty to a problem was an outcome, which did not necessarily equate to a solution. Kehoe believed that there was an acceptable reality at the end of all this—and it involved finding the person or people responsible. Page believed that was magical thinking, and that Kehoe was limited in his outlook. Page said that one way or another the bombings would stop, but it might take old age or a meteor to put the problem to rest—an outcome, not a solution.

Which, at this particular place in time, was just too much abstract masturbation for Kehoe to take. He needed to believe that they would stop this joker. He had to, because his entire life had been built around that specific directive. Or solution. Or outcome. Or whatever Page chose to call it.

Kehoe needed Page in here because he needed to shake up the cage. And if there was one thing that rude son of a bitch could be counted on for, it was a little disruptive motivation. And that antisocial prick knew how to think. It came across as navel gazing, but it produced, which was all that mattered.

Page hadn't said anything, but Kehoe could see that machinery in his head moving pieces into place, and he wanted access to the printouts. Page wasn't a man prone to sharing until he had all the answers, but right now Kehoe needed anything that would give his people a direction, even if it was the wrong direction. Because what they had pulled in so far wasn't working. One thing his tenure at the bureau had taught him was that barring action, movement was the best option. It often took you in the wrong direction, but like Albee said, sometimes it was necessary to go a very long distance out of the way in order to come back a short distance correctly.

Kehoe picked up the phone and dialed Whitaker's cell; he wanted to know what their ETA was.

When it went to voice mail, he hung up.

Then he dialed Page's number.

And got the same result.

61

Palisades Parkway

Whitaker was on the pavement, staring up at the sky, a hand clamped around her throat. Blood was pissing out everywhere and the pavement beneath her was black.

She looked over at Lucas. Tried to say something. But all that came out was a god-awful fucking noise that sounded like a child's made-up language in which the words were horrid shrieks.

He reached for her.

Black hydraulic fluid pissed from her neck. She was crying. And making that noise.

More rounds hammered into the SUV.

Lucas ducked. Covered his head. Screamed.

Whitaker was stretching, reaching for her gun. Trying so hard.

Frosst fired.

The round hit her in the foot and she howled again. Flopped around like a hammered fish that didn't know it was dead.

Some part of Lucas yelled for him to hit the gas.

He stretched over the transmission hump with his leg.

Rounds zipped into the four-by-four. Drilled through the

windshield. Popcorned him with glass. The seat beside him barfed white foam. All he could hear was the world coming apart at the seams.

More shots hit the car. An endless *Chunk! Chunk! Chunk!* of metal-eating insects.

He pulled the shift knob and pounded down on the gas. The engine went dinosaur and the Lincoln lurched forward.

Heading for the truck.

Lucas kept the gas to the floor.

To call what he did driving would be an injustice; it was the desperate act of a dead man.

Glass peppered his face. He kept his foot welded to the floor.

Peeked up over the dash.

All he saw was Frosst zeroed in the Lincoln's hood ornament.

There was impact.

And then the space filled with the sound of the two vehicles becoming one.

The universe cracked open and Lucas hit the windshield.

The oxygen around him was swallowed by the center of the sun. The heat ate his skin and his lungs filled with fire.

He tried to scream one final time, but it was taken away by the explosion.

Everything disappeared.

And then even the nothing was gone.

62

26 Federal Plaza

Kehoe was standing beside his desk with the phone in his hand when Hoffner came in without knocking.

"You better have news," he warned.

Hoffner paused, an action that did, indeed, have news all over it—the *bad* kind. "We just got a call from the Palisades Interstate Parkway PD—something happened, sir. Special Agent Whitaker and Dr. Page were in an accident. There was a shootout of some sort. It looks like they were ambushed. Palisades PD isn't sure yet because the vehicles are all still burning and they haven't been able to recover all the bodies."

"Page and Whitaker—what's their status?'

"I can't get a straight answer out of anyone. The initial reports are that there are no survivors."

And for the second time that day—which meant the second time in his entire career—Brett Kehoe lost his temper.

This time it was the telephone that did not survive.

63

The Upper East Side

They were done with supper. She had been playing catch-up with work since fleeing to the beach house, so tonight she opted for the easy money and they ordered Indian. Most of the kids weren't picky eaters—which was a major stroke of luck—and they generally enjoyed anything put in front of them. At least most of the time. Hector was the lone exception and would rarely step out of chicken strips or macaroni and cheese territory. But he tolerated anything in batter, so they had managed.

The children were doing homework and backpacks were spilled out onto the floor of the den.

Alisha, who was still a few years from school age, always felt left out after supper, so Luke had come up with activity time for her. But that loose directive certainly had not been meant to include rearranging his library, and Erin was impressed at how well he had taken it. He wasn't good with surprises, and he certainly wasn't good with disorder with his work, but there had been no disguising the pleasure he had derived in seeing what the girls had done. He hadn't grilled Alisha like she knew he wanted to, which meant that he was making an effort.

But tonight it was back to crafts for Alisha. Sometimes it was coloring (which often ended with crayon wax in her teeth); sometimes it was craft time (she could paint a pinecone like nobody's business); and sometimes it was just sit with Lemmy and scratch his belly. Tonight it seemed like the last, and that was fine with the dog. For some reason he put up with things from the children that no other beast would. Not that they were ever cruel to him—the kids loved and respected Lemmy—but he had been lipsticked more times than Erin could count. His toenails had even been painted a couple of times. But the big goof didn't seem to mind. And he was very protective of the children, sometimes to the point of wonder.

Damien had hauled his guitar and amp down from the bedroom and wanted to show off the new song he had learned. Luke had bought him the guitar for his birthday, and the kid was taking lessons and practicing seriously. Damien enjoyed the instrument, and since neither Luke nor Erin were right-brain people, they did their best to foster artistic aspirations in the kids—it helped them step out of their own expectations.

Damien looked the part in ripped jeans and a Beastie Boys T-shirt. He plugged his guitar into the little Fender Champ, flipped the rocker switch, and waited a few seconds for the amp to warm up. After the prerequisite not enough time, he gave it a big open E, fiddled with the tuners until the chord stopped warbling, then turned to the five-person-plus-a-dog crowd. Everyone was seated in a semicircle, committed to the viewing experience; one of the benefits of five kids was that they had a built-in audience.

Damien pulled out the grin he reserved for Diet Coke and Mentos explosions, then went into a heartfelt rendition of "American Idiot," singing included. Lemmy sat up and began howling with the song, totally off-key. Alisha joined in. Then the other kids.

And by the end of the song, Erin worried that they would start breaking furniture.

Damien finished, said, "Thank you, New York!" and took a bow.

Everyone clapped. Maude and Erin added a few whistles. And Lemmy went over and licked him.

"That was cool!" Hector looked honestly impressed. Which was the appropriate reaction toward a kid who hadn't touched a guitar before three months ago.

Erin put a hand on Damien's shoulder. "That was great, kiddo. Even without more cowbell."

"Why would I need more cowbell?" Damien looked up at her, unsmiling. "Huh?"

"Never mind. I'm getting old."

"No crap. Especially if you can't tell the difference between a guitar and a cowbell."

All the kids stopped in their tracks as the walls of the room lit up with flashing blue and red.

Erin froze in place.

The kids instinctively ran for the front window.

"It's two cars of FBI guys," Maude said. She turned back, and her eyes locked on Erin. "Luke isn't with them."

Erin told the kids to wait in the study as she went to the front door.

They heard the door open.

They heard men's voices ask a question.

They heard her respond.

They heard one of the male voices say something else.

And then they heard Erin begin to sob.

64

Columbia University Medical Center
Fort Lee, New Jersey

Kehoe hated these talks, almost more than the events that forced him to have them. Loved ones were never very understanding about sacrifice and duty and loss. They couldn't afford to be because it forced them to accept that the people they loved felt it necessary to serve a different cause. If there was one supreme bit of knowledge he had gleaned from all of his years doing this, it was that most people couldn't handle the truth—especially about their own lives.

The two agents with him stood as far behind him as the space allowed—which was more than most elevators in that this one was designed for the horizontal as opposed to vertical passengers. It was painted a horrid robin's-egg blue.

Kehoe thought about what he would say. How he would say it. And how he would respond to the things that would most likely be said to him in return. It was a game of probabilities, and over the years he had developed a pretty keen sense of how things would go.

The elevator stopped and the doors slid open, exposing a long hallway with windows down one side. But even with the natural light, it reminded him of a 1970s Soviet airport.

Kehoe wasn't sure if the two agents with him were consciously walking in step with him or if it was an unconscious action, but he changed his pace. And so did they. It was a known phenomenon called spontaneous synchronization, and Kehoe always found it unsettling.

He had never been to this particular hospital before—it was nowhere near his regular routine—so he followed the directions he had been given at the front desk, taking the blue line to the orange line, where he turned left, to the yellow line that took him to the hallway he wanted. He entered the doors at the end.

In keeping with the Soviet airport vibe, no one was at the desk. Kehoe played a quick game of *Let's Make a Deal* with the three anterooms, and walked through the first door to his left, where he almost tripped over Erin Page.

She was sitting on a bench, head back, eyes straight ahead. She wore jeans and a white cotton shirt—home clothes, not surgeon's clothes. She was staring through the window in the wall in front of her.

Kehoe knew what she was staring at but didn't look over. He needed to appear like he was here for her, not himself. "Hello, Erin."

She didn't seem surprised by his voice and she didn't look up. Or shift focus. Or say anything. She just kept staring at what was happening beyond the window.

Kehoe turned and looked at the two agents with him, and without being told, they left to take up position out in the hallway. He sat down beside her.

From this vantage point, it was impossible to ignore the activity on the other side of the glass. Page was laid out on a table, covered in a thin cotton sheet spotted with blood. He was missing an arm and leg, as if Frankenstein's monster was not quite yet assembled. He was bruised, and banged up, but he was alive. Which was the only thing that mattered at this juncture in time.

"How are you?" Kehoe said quietly. With someone like Erin he'd have to go in easy; otherwise there would be screaming.

Erin didn't say anything.

Kehoe went with "I'm sorry about this."

He paused, expecting her to say *Me too,* but she continued ignoring him.

Kehoe swallowed and said, "Is there anything I can do?" He expected a reaction at that one and was hoping for an angry *Fuck off!* because it would at least give him some stage direction.

But Erin kept ignoring him, which was a sensation he was unused to.

He wanted to ask her if he should go in for her. If he needed to talk to anyone. If everyone was being helpful. If there was anything he could do for Lucas. But none of those things seemed to be the right approach.

The technician on the other side of the glass pulled the camera down and placed it over Lucas's face, which made Kehoe focus on the obvious. This was his fault; if he hadn't come knocking at their door last winter, they wouldn't be here.

The technician grabbed Lucas's jaw with a gloved hand and turned his face to the left. He took a few photographs, then moved Lucas's head to the right, snapping a few more. Lucas remained inanimate during the process, as if his batteries had been disconnected. Kehoe wondered if he was heavily sedated, past giving a shit, or just beat up.

Kehoe looked away. "Erin, I need to talk to you about some things."

But she just kept watching the tech, her arms crossed, her eyes somewhere far away.

The best thing for him to do would be to leave. But he had a responsibility to Lucas to keep Erin and the kids safe, and that wouldn't happen if he left. Erin had enough on her plate and Lucas was in no shape to help anyone. "I understand you are angry. But you need to listen to what I am going to say. The people who did this might not be finished yet."

Erin didn't say anything, but the vein on her neck pulsed beneath the freckled skin and the muscles in her jaw flexed.

Kehoe continued. "I want you and the kids to go away. Just until we sew this up. And before you tell me that you can go out to the beach house, you know that it's not hard to find you out there. I can send some agents home with you. Pack up the kids and they'll take you to the airport. We'll put you on a bureau jet and take you somewhere safe. You can pick the place. But it can't be anywhere near friends or family or someplace you've been before. My people in the witness protection arm will handle the flight manifests and accommodations. It won't be for long, I promise."

Erin didn't even twitch, and it was impossible to miss what had attracted Lucas to her—this woman was forged out of very rare elements.

Kehoe had one last move, and he decided that it was worth the play. "Your being here isn't going to help him. You have to think of the children. About keeping them safe."

At that, Erin turned her head. She looked up at him. Then slapped him across the face.

Behind the window, the technician put the camera aside and disappeared through a door. A moment later he was standing in front of Kehoe, just a little too close. "Dr. Page, is everything all right? I can call security." He was a big man with a mustache stained yellow from extracurricular smoking. His name tag said *Willeford*.

Erin turned back to the room behind the glass.

Kehoe decided that he wasn't doing any good by being here. "It's okay," he said, and stood up. "I was just leaving." And with that, he walked away, leaving Erin staring at her husband beyond the window.

65

Bleecker Street

Michael MacDougal, known to his YouTube subscriber army as
MightyMikey, considered himself the Charlie Chaplin of his day.
All three Marx Brothers rolled into one. Larry, Curly, and Moe
in a single package. Jerry Seinfeld conjoined to Chris Rock. He
was a YouTube sensation and made a little more than a quarter of
a million dollars a month by pranking authorities. MightyMikey
was—in the parlance of his time—a First Amendment auditor. He
pushed the boundaries to see how those in positions of authority
reacted. He liked pranking cops the most because America wasn't
a police state, and he wouldn't let it become one.

His brother, David, was his cameraman; he was known to
MightyMikey's followers as McFly, because he was able to film the
sickest situations without losing the shot.

Today MightyMikey was going to see how close he could get
to the cops with what looked like a suicide vest. It was nothing
more than a fly-fishing outfit from Walmart, eight road flares, a
broken digital clock, and a controller from a Nintendo console, but
it looked legit. Or at least it would to your average cop.

It was dark now, which would help if they needed to run; MightyMikey's video exploits often ended with his making a dash for it. It was amazing how cranked people got with a little foolishness—twenty-first-century Americans were wound way too tight. Especially the cops, who were not known for their patience or sense of humor—which was precisely why they needed to be exposed as the crypto-fascists they were. Besides, his cop videos got the most views. MightyMikey sold three thousand T-shirts a month with his catchphrase on the front: *Better the cops get pissed off than I get pissed on!*

There were a few television appearances after his last one—when he had tried to confiscate babies from Latino mothers, claiming he was with ICE. None of the women had pressed charges. And a little SJW outrage on Twitter notwithstanding, it had cracked a lot of people up.

McFly was behind a pile of cardboard boxes and some office chairs that were heading off to a garbage barge. MightyMikey stripped to his underwear, put on the vest, then crossed the street and put himself on a trajectory straight past a parked cruiser where two uniformed cops were drinking coffee. Probably having dough-nuts.

McFly had a hard time not laughing while he zoomed in on his brother. The guy was a comedic genius—his body language was Jim Carrey on Molly. People loved shit like this. YouTube was a gold mine; they both drove 911 GT3s and next year they were moving up to Lambos—everyone wanted to be them.

McFly kept the camera steady as MightyMikey, internet impre-sario and virtual star, pranced right by the two cops in the cruiser, shaking his tighty-whities.

The doors flew open on cue.

The cops were both big guys and blocked the shot, so McFly came out from behind the boxes. But he kept low.

MightyMikey had a mic on the vest, and he wore a small button camera that they'd never see—it saved everything to an onboard SD card.

MightyMikey was doing great. Acting all nuts and pointing at the sky and talking about the voices in his head. It was a classic example of a man with mental illness facing down cops. They had done shit like this enough times that they knew they'd get more slack than a black dude; the cops couldn't do anything to him—he wasn't touching the control—his hands were reaching for the sky as he ranted. He was no danger to anyone. And if the cops tried to mace him, MightyMikey had them cold. This was America, and they couldn't get away with—

The cops had their guns out.

MightyMikey screamed something about knowing his rights, then lowered his hand and pointed at one of the cops.

And that's when they shot him.

Ten fucking times!

MightyMikey stumbled back in a few jerky strides before tumbling through the coffee shop window.

McFly popped up and yelled.

The cops spun.

McFly called them fascist pigs. But kept the camera rolling.

Their pistols came up.

McFly kept the camera on them; they would never shoot him on film. They wouldn't shoot an innocent white—

But they did.

66

Columbia University Medical Center
Fort Lee, New Jersey

Lucas didn't look incomplete; he looked destroyed. His chest was bruised and bloody and stitched back up—offset with burn marks from the explosion. His hair was singed. The right side of his head had been peeled open, the skin from the top of his skull—both the auricularis anterior and auricularis superior—had been yanked back, tearing behind his ear, all the way down to the occipitalis, like a gore on an antique globe. They had stitched it back together, his right ear in the middle of the sewn-back flap, but they hadn't even bothered with the pretense of aesthetics. His prosthetic eye was gone, lost somewhere in the conflagration on the parkway. If they found it, they'd deliver it to the house in a little evidence bag; her husband's ceramic eyeball, dropped off like a pair of cuff links. The people delivering it—FBI agents? Cops? FDNY?— would look embarrassed. They'd place it in her hand and leave without ever looking her in the eye. Things like that made people uncomfortable.

His arm and leg were gone; she was the only one who ever saw him like this. It wasn't modesty; most people simply got the heebie-jeebies when facing someone missing parts that their mind told them should be there. Lucas said it was a brain thing—that particular piece of biological machinery was able to function only because it ran on certain directives, mostly in the fill-in-the-blank department. He tried not to let the kids see him without his prosthetics. It was a little vain, but he said they would stop seeing him as Mr. Can-Do soon enough, and he didn't want to accelerate the process.

"Jesus fucking Christ, Luke," she said, and reached out to touch the stub of what used to be his right arm.

She didn't want to cry.

She had promised herself that she wouldn't cry.

And now she was fucking crying.

Why had he crashed the car into that man? But she knew. He had done it because someone he cared about—had a responsibility toward—had been in trouble. And there were a lot of things you could call Lucas Douglas Page, but selfish was not one of them. Not when it came to the people he wanted to protect. And he had most definitely wanted to protect Whitaker. Even if it was a lost cause.

And now here he was, in the hospital after playing a game of chicken with Mr. Death. How was she going to explain this to the children?

"Would you stop crying?" His voice sounded like it had been generated at the far end of the world, then shipped over in tin cans, one syllable at a time.

Erin wiped her eyes. "If this had happened to me, wouldn't you be crying?"

"Is it bad?"

"You look like a Sebastian Krüger painting of yourself. You look . . ."—she paused—"*lived in.*"

"Something tells me that I look *died in.*"

She said, "You, Mr. Man, are one lucky dude," through the tears.

"Only because I landed on my brain."

"How do you feel?" She wiped her eyes with her cuffs.

"There are people out there having autopsies performed on them who are in better shape than I am."

"You almost nuked the fridge this time."

The doctor came back in, carrying his chart. "Okay." His name was Joseph Levine, and he had worked with Erin during her internship at Mass General. He had the no-nonsense delivery of the terminally occupied along with the lousy bedside manner to match. "You'll need a couple of days here and then you need to take it easy for a while. Except for the scarring, you'll be as good as new." He looked down at Lucas and smiled; there was nothing convincing about it.

They had already gone over the damage he had sustained in the crash, subsequent explosion, and flying-monkey trip through the windshield. He had broken three ribs going over the dashboard, and his head had done battering-ram duty on the laminated safety glass, which had peeled the side of his noggin off on the way through. The explosion had sent a ball of fire into the sky that singed his eyebrows and clothing as he passed through it. But the silver lining was that the broken ribs had stopped his breathing for a few seconds and he hadn't seared his lungs when he went through the flames. And the whole circus display had ended when he hit a tree off the shoulder. A retired schoolteacher put out his burning clothes, CPRed him back from the land of nuts and cake, and called 911.

"And the hearing in my right ear?" he asked a little too loud. His ear canal was packed with something.

"The damage to the side of your face is all aesthetic—your ear was peeled off and it tore the canal in the process. We've reattached it, but it will take some time to heal. The eardrum is fine. You'll have reduced sensation until the capillaries and vessels regrow a work-around, but I think you have a pretty good understanding of what to expect. We'll have to change the bandages daily, but we should be able to take the packing out of your ear in a week." He looked down at Lucas. "You've got more character now."

Erin rolled her eyes. "He already has enough character."

It took all of his energy, but Lucas smiled over at her. "What can I say? The omnipotent narrator in my life is occasionally given to hyperbole."

The doctor double-clicked his iPad. "All right. The orderly will take you back to your room. I understand you've brought him new prosthetics," he said to Erin. The ones Lucas had been wearing were mangled and probably irreparable.

"They're up in his room."

Lucas went to hold up his hand, but he wasn't wearing it and the stub of his right arm pulled at the sheet. "I don't want to go to the room. I want to see Whitaker."

He didn't like the way Erin and Levine exchanged looks.

"Now," he added, and even with mono hearing, he couldn't miss the panic in his own voice.

67

Whitaker's arms were across her chest. Her eyes were closed. She was swathed in bandages and looked like an ancient Egyptian princess in the process of being prepared for the afterlife. Except that she was alive—theoretically speaking.

She had the prime bed in the surgical ICU, where Humpty Dumpty's doctors had reassembled all the damaged women and men—none of whom had come in with less of a chance of making it off the table than Special Agent Alice Whitaker.

That she had lived until the EMT people arrived on the scene was in itself a minor miracle. That she had survived the various medical catastrophes that befell her in the ambulance on the way to the hospital—including a myocardial infarction—could be considered more of a mid-level miracle. And that she had made it through five hours on the table—where they had kick-started her heart three more times in between rebuilding damaged organs and repairing shredded arteries—nudged her into divine intervention statistics. If she lived, there would be no reason for her to buy a lottery ticket ever again; no one wins that kind of jackpot twice.

But the doctors believed the lottery question to be purely academic—they were certain that she would die.

There was a woman at her bedside. She looked a little like Whitaker, but smaller and rounder. When she saw Lucas in his chair at the foot of the bed, she snapped out of whatever faraway place she had been in.

She looked at him and tried out a smile that didn't make it to her tear-filled eyes. "You must be Page."

Lucas tried to sound jovial when he said, "How did you know?"

The smile almost made it into her eyes at that one. "Angie said I had to watch out for you."

He was about to ask who she was, but she said, "I'm Toni—with an I. Al's sister." Evidently Toni had the same witchy thing as her sister when it came to questions.

Lucas tilted his head back, indicating Erin. "This is my wife, Erin."

The two women shook hands. And once again Lucas noticed that instant sister thing that all the women around him effortlessly plugged into.

"Any updates?" Lucas asked. He was going on fifteen-minute-old information.

Toni dropped back into the chair. "They said to prepare for the worst. Which is about as vague as you can get. I cornered one of the nurses and she was kind enough—or mean enough, I'm not sure which—to tell me that no one here expects her to make it. And if she does, she was without oxygen for a long time. Maybe the EMTs should have left her alone. I don't want her ending up a crip—" And she stopped herself.

Lucas held up his hand. "It's okay."

"I'm sorry. I didn't mean . . . it's just—" And she stopped. "I'm just sorry."

Lucas tried to smile, something that in the best of times never really worked out. Toni's reaction said that it was better if he didn't try. "Look, I don't do greeting cards all that well, and if the doctors say that she's probably going to die, then there's a chance that's true. But I also know that if anyone has the mojo to kick probability in the nuts, it's your sister. She's special."

Toni's eyes rimmed with tears and she nodded and they shook loose and ran down her cheeks and she wiped them away. "She never said you were nice."

He let loose with his imitation smile again. "I'm not. I just hate doctors."

Toni looked up at Erin. "Aren't you a doctor?"

Lucas said, "She's only a doctor to her patients. With me, she's just my wife. The rest of them? Dullards and quacks." He felt Erin squeeze his shoulder.

Toni tried to smile. "You know what she calls you behind your back?"

"No."

"The Tin Man."

It was Erin who said, "Why?"

"She said he's still looking for his heart."

"What about her kid?" he asked. "Stan, the little man?"

"Her ex brought him by this morning. Willy's a good dad, no matter what Al says. They just had one of those bad marriages that all the counseling in the world couldn't save. He's a good guy, he just wasn't good *for her*." She put her hand on her sister's arm. "Not everyone can be married to an FBI agent. It takes a special kind of denial."

Erin's hand tightened on Lucas's shoulder. "No shit," she said.

68

Lucas said, "I'm sorry about Kehoe."

"Me, too." Erin didn't look like she was buying whatever he was selling.

"He's not what you would call a *people person.*"

"*You're* not what I would call a people person; Kehoe's not what I would call a *human being.*"

He shifted in the bed, and he was grateful that she had brought his spare prosthetics from home—he was always uncomfortable without them and it was worse out in the world. And after the flashback package of the explosion, they were better than comfort food and a security blanket rolled into one. He wanted his old ones back, no matter what shape they were in; they weren't just scrap metal and carbon fiber, they were *his arm* and *his leg.* Even if they were destroyed, he didn't want them simply going in the dumpster. If they couldn't be repaired, maybe he'd turn them into table lamps. "It's what he does—gets people to do what he needs from them. It's never personal, it's a Big Picture thing." The leg was fine—it wasn't torquing anything and it helped him from falling over in the bed. But he couldn't put the arm on yet; the broken ribs on that side couldn't take getting thumped by pointy aluminum parts.

Erin pretended to be busy filling a glass with water and Lucas wondered if it was going to hit the wall or him. But she placed it on the wheeled dinner tray and did her best to sound like she didn't care. "I don't want to talk about Kehoe."

"That doesn't mean we don't have to." He reached out, put his hand on her arm. The movement hurt his whole body, and he wondered if the ringing in his ears would ever subside.

She pulled away, like a wave rolling off the beach, and crossed her arms. "So talk."

"What did Kehoe say?"

"That me and the kids need to go away. He said something about the people in Witness Protection handling logistics."

"He's right." Lucas tried not to look worried, but judging by Erin's expression, his acting chops were lousy.

"Luke, we went through this last winter. I'm not doing this to the kids again. Besides, you killed the guy."

He held up his hand as if he were auditioning for a Diana Ross video. "I killed *a* guy. Not *the* guy."

She gave him one of her patented wife faces. "So you're killing random dudes now?"

That was her second *dude* of the day. "What are we, Bill and Ted?"

"Don't do that to me. You know what I mean. That man you killed, the one you drove the fucking SUV into, the one you blew up—that asshole—wasn't he *the guy*?"

Lucas had had plenty of time to put things together in the little spaces of black that had been part of his life since the impact. "It's the guy who put Frosst in motion that I need to put in a box."

All the color drained from Erin's face, leaving the freckles on a pale background. "But Kehoe's been on the television telling everyone that they know what happened and that they're putting the case to bed."

Lucas shook his head, and it knocked his gyroscope out of whack and he got dizzy. He paused and waited for things to normalize. "Unless Kehoe's come up with something I don't know about—which is possible—he's wrong."

"Can't you just stop? Please? For me?"

"Stop what?"

"Having to be right all the time. It's exhausting. They think they got their guy, let them. You don't always have to be the smartest person in the room, Luke. It's all right to be wrong every now and then. No one will hold it against you."

"I will."

"And therein lies the problem." Erin took another step back and opened the blinds a little. The bright afternoon sun cut the room up into spears of 1980s Michael Mann art direction. "Okay. Get to the bad part."

He closed his eyes and for a minute the room stopped spinning. When he opened them the carousel started back up and he had a hard time focusing on her. "Kehoe's right. Take the kids and go away. Let him handle things so you don't make a mistake. I don't think you're in danger and I don't think I'm in danger. But I don't want you and the kids here. *Just in case.*"

Erin was doing a pretty good job of hiding the anger he knew was starting to percolate just below the surface. "The kids will miss Halloween."

"When's that?"

"In two days."

Lucas tried to wave it away. But he didn't have an arm. "You can take them out wherever you go."

"They've been looking forward to this."

What could he say? Tough shit? That they needed to get used to being disappointed? No, their kids had ended up with them precisely because they were too used to being disappointed. "They'll get over it." He knew it sounded insensitive, but this wasn't about giving them Halloween, this was about keeping them safe.

"And what about you?"

"I've been through this before—I can change my own bandages, wash my wounds." Lucas once again waved her question away with a hand that wasn't there, and the irony wasn't lost on him. "And I can do it more effectively if I'm not worried about *you*." Most of that was true.

"Will you be safe?" Which was a good question. Maybe even an excellent one.

Lucas nodded in the general direction of the hallway. "Kehoe's got a guy in front of the door—I'll be fine." But even as he said it, he wondered if it was just magical thinking; the people with the explosives had been pretty good at sneaking up on their victims so far.

She looked like he had just punched her in the stomach. "And you're staying with the bureau? You're going to—"

"No. I'm not."

She didn't say anything to that. She just stared at him.

"I am done. Quit. Going back was a mistake and I never should have done it. I thought I needed this, but I don't. I don't want it and I'm done."

"Why is there a *but* coming?"

"Because there *is*." He looked up at her. "Like Hartke last winter—I *owe* Whitaker. And I owe it to the other people who will get hurt if I leave now. I fucked up and I can't leave my mess for anyone else to clean up. This is on me. And when I'm through, it's over." He felt the tears in his eye and he didn't try to push them away—Erin and the kids were more important than anything he could imagine being allowed to be part of. "I quit." He reached out for her.

"Pinkie swear?" she asked, and her tears shook loose and rolled down her freckled cheeks.

"Pinkie swear."

69

ABC 7 Eyewitness News

We are here at the intersection of Kingston Avenue and Park Place in Brooklyn, where earlier today a young man was violently murdered. You can see the scene behind me in Brower Park, where police officers are still trying to piece together the precise chain of events that led to the death of the as-yet-unidentified victim.

At ten A.M. today, approximately five hundred people showed up for what authorities are calling a flash-mob demonstration. They were here to voice their support of the Machine Bomber, something which has become common-place since the bomber published a letter a few days ago.

Authorities were not aware of the demonstration, and did not arrive until after people from nearby housing reported the large fire in the park. By which time one young man was already dead and several more were injured.

Shortly after the Machine Bomber's supporters arrived,

they started a fire and began to burn items of technology that they brought; everything from cell phones to printers to toasters and electric toothbrushes were tossed onto the pyre. The fire quickly began letting off toxic smoke, which killed several birds that were in nearby trees downwind. But it is not the loss of animal life that is most tragic, it is the death of a young handicapped man.

According to witnesses, the victim was rolling down the sidewalk in his electric wheelchair—past the entrance to the park visible behind me—when he was attacked by several demonstrators who allegedly screamed, "Kill the machine! Kill the machine! Burn it! Burn it!" As many as thirty individuals rushed forward and attacked him. They apparently carried him to the fire and tossed him and his wheelchair into the flames, where he was burned alive.

We are now going to show you exclusive video of the incident, taken by one of the demonstrators in the park at the time—Marta Kovacevic. In exchange for this video, Ms. Kovacevic has asked that her Instagram profile and account information be watermarked in. You can also DM her directly on Twitter, where she can be found under her name.

Please be forewarned, there is graphic content . . .

70

Columbia University Medical Center
Fort Lee, New Jersey

He had been staring up at the acoustic tiled ceiling for months now.

Or maybe it was only weeks.

Possibly days.

Or even just hours.

Maybe minutes.

And then he realized that seconds were a possibility.

Fuck it.

It felt like forever, and as long as he lay there, calculating the number of holes he was looking up at (18 holes east-west by 18 holes north-south per tile—324 holes total—multiplied by 352 tiles in the room—equaled 114,048 holes per room—131 rooms per floor, 16 floors in total—translating to 239,044,608 holes in all) the world was moving on without him.

He thought about taking another jolt of happy juice from the dispenser—*for the road,* as they say—but if he hit the morphine button, he'd never get out of here. He stared at the machine for a minute, thinking that maybe one more boost couldn't hurt. After all, they made that button look like a bull's-eye for a reason—as if missing it was a shame. A crime. A goddamned tragedy. Besides, if they wanted you to take it, it couldn't be bad, right?

Fuck.

This.

Lucas took the needle out of his arm, which was no easy task, since they had plugged it into his left. But it was close to his elbow, which enabled him to get it out with his teeth. He spit it out and it whipped over the side of the bed like a dead tentacle.

He pushed up off the mattress with his good arm and his ribs lit up with ten thousand volts at almost enough amperage to knock him over. He lay back down, took a breath.

Fuck.

This.

Erin had left the bed railing down, and he pushed up again, sliding his prosthetic leg over until it slipped off the edge of the mattress and the pendulum action pulled his hips around, lifting his spine, giving him the momentum he needed. And it didn't hurt his ribs as much. It wasn't easy. But it was bearable.

There.

I'm sitting on the edge of this bed.

Not bad.

He sat there for a few moments, sending little signals out to his parts to see if he could count on them. Other than his broken ribs, and that he could barely hear out of his bandaged ear, the rest of the shit could be relegated to the category of minor inconveniences. Not that they didn't add up; sometimes a bunch of little nothings made more of an impact than one big something, like the death of a thousand cuts.

He slid off the bed until he felt the floor under his bare foot. Then he heard—and felt—his carbon-fiber foot hit the linoleum. He reached back with his hand and pushed off the bed. His body swung out, and for a second he thought he was going to overshoot his center of gravity and take the closet door in the teeth.

But he didn't.

And just like that, he was standing.

Miracle Number Two out of the way.

He stood there for a few moments, figuring out how he was doing. And it was pretty good. Everything seemed to be working. At least if he stood still.

But standing still was no way to catch bad guys.

After the Event a decade back, he got so used to falling that for a couple of months he wore a mouthguard—he'd be doing fine, and then he'd miss a tiny little muscle adjustment in his back or his arm would swing too far out and he'd topple over. It was never a graceful fall; it was six-foot-three of mechanical man clattering downstairs or windmilling into a table or slamming into a wire garbage can like a drunk. Thank god YouTube had been in its infancy back then—the thought of some dickhead with a cell phone camera retiring off the revenue from his embarrassment would be a hard one to take.

He looked down at his feet, making sure not to let his head go too far forward.

They were both there—different colors, but there.

Okay.

Move your feet.

So he did.

The prosthetic first.

Then his original biological machinery.

It worked. He moved.

One small step for man; one giant leap for Dr. Lucas Page.

Holy.

Shit.

So he tried another.

Then another.

And with each inch covered, his confidence grew. By the time he put his hand on the locker, his internal gyroscope was back on-line.

Miracle Number Three taken care of.

Inserting the pin in his humerus into the collet on his prosthetic went smoothly, and it felt good to be all put back together.

Miracle Number Four? Check.

He stood there for a few moments, feeling better, with only little pulses of pain coming from his ribs, timed to his breathing, like a badly designed machine.

By the time he started contorting into his clothes, he was confident that he could make it over the wall. More or less. He creaked. And he hurt. And he was bleeding. And he couldn't hear for shit. But he was better than he could reasonably expect. He didn't feel any guilt knowing that he had escaped Whitaker's fate, but he did feel gratitude, which then brought the appropriate mix of conflicting emotions into play. He understood that there was no logic to the way events unfolded—they just did. You either accepted them or you didn't.

He looked around the room, wondering if there was anything he should take. There were a few vases of the obligatory we-hope-you-don't-die flowers from colleagues and assorted ass-kissers. Way too many, considering he had been in here a little more than twenty-four hours. And a bunch of bloody bandages and a crappy sippy cup. No, he didn't need any of this shit.

The agent watching his room jumped to his feet when Lucas opened the door and limped out into the hallway. "Hey! What? Um. Look. I . . . uh."

"Great vocabulary. No wonder they have you guarding dead people."

The agent was young, maybe twenty-seven or -eight, and looked like he couldn't muster up a beard without resorting to Chia Pet tactics. "Sorry, sir. I was told that no one was supposed to go through that door."

"I think they meant *going in*." Speaking made him cough, and he tasted blood at the back of his throat that he swallowed.

The kid just stared at him. "You don't look so good."

Lucas turned away and limped on down the hall. "And you don't sound so smart."

71

Fort Lee, New Jersey

Lucas caught a taxi in front of the hospital. The cabbie stared at him in the mirror a little too long—evidently he looked more like a drop-off than a pickup. But he gave the driver the address in a none-too-friendly tone, and that seemed to shake the guy into action. Judging by the way he took off, he wanted to get Lucas to his destination before he expired.

Every bump, pothole, lane change, acceleration, deceleration, swerve, and corner told Lucas that he should have taken that final shot of morphine. But he was tired, and when they were on the George Washington Bridge into the city, he put his head back on the seat and—miraculously—fell asleep.

He woke up a few blocks from the office, and he could feel that blood from the bandages on the right side of his face had leaked out and dripped down, pooling in his collarbone. He wiped it away with his pocket square, and when he looked up, the driver was watching him in the mirror with an expression somewhere between terror and horror.

"You don't look so good." The cabbie's permit identified him as one Zigfriedo Gomez.

"Thanks."

"No, seriously, man—you *don't.*"

"I'll be fine."

"You want me to take you to a doctor?"

"I just came from a doctor."

"Did he beat you up?"

"Ziggy, pull over."

"Let me take you through the light, so you don't have to walk. I won't charge you." He reached over, and threw the meter. "It's on me—"

"*Pull. Over.*"

The sudden maneuver pinched his arm between the door and his ribs, sending a bolt of pain through his internal organs, and he wanted to puke. But he held it in and was embarrassed that it took him four tries to get his wallet out of his coat pocket.

He ran his card through the touch-screen process, and when he looked up, the cabbie was holding out a box of Kleenex. "You're bleeding."

Lucas took it and grumbled the closest approximate thank you he could fake, then got out and slipped his sunglasses on over the eye patch.

He didn't have to wait for the light, then was double lucky in that he didn't lurch across the intersection like Johnny Cash after a bender. But New Yorkers are notoriously impervious to weirdos in their midst, and he was grateful that no one gave him more than a cursory glance.

Armored vehicles and police cars were on the street in front of the building and dragon's teeth had been planted every three feet around the perimeter; it looked like they were expecting a rush by hostile infantry.

The armed tactical men at the concrete barrier gave him a

thrice-over, and he pulled his badge and ID. They had extra agents on duty—a paramilitary arm that looked like they should be kicking down doors. There were a dozen K9 units, all outfitted with tactical vests denoting them as FBI personnel in big yellow letters.

The counterpart to the armed bureau people were the crowds that had come down to demonstrate, or protest, or whatever you wanted to call a bunch of adults dressed up as superheroes and *Star Wars* characters waving signs advertising their ignorance. A lot of the placards said that there was no bomber. Others said the FBI itself was fake and didn't exist outside of its own mind. Some accused the FBI of being staffed by traitors who were intent on destroying the country. Lucas could forgive stupidity on occasion because it wasn't intentional, but he found willful ignorance like this revolting.

One of the security people at the door proper took a long hard look at his credentials. And the sign-in officer came over when he swiped through the turnstile and asked to see his identification. Evidently bureau personnel weren't used to seeing the freshly sewn-up come into work with IV bags dragging behind them.

Miraculously, the elevator didn't stop until it hit his floor, and he took a deep breath as it slowed, willing himself to stay upright. The doors slid open and he walked into the war room.

The second hand locked between two ticks of the clock.

No one moved.

Or talked.

No one breathed.

Or laughed.

No one sneezed.

Or made a phone call.

No one touched a keyboard.

They just stared. Mouths open, like a gaggle of shocked federally employed law enforcement emojis.

Lucas headed down the middle of the room, between the rows

of desks. As he made his way, a sensation from the past jumped the void and he could feel it wafting off the agents: pity—they felt sorry for him.

Kehoe was in the middle of a phone call that he ended with a quick "I'll call you back" as soon as he saw Lucas.

Lucas gingerly lowered his frame into one of the Corbusier club chairs and closed his eye, trying not to feel the pain fingering his organs. For the first time in a very long while, he felt like he could die at any moment.

"Are you okay?" Kehoe sounded concerned, which was out of the norm.

"Swell."

Kehoe examined him for a few moments that he ended by leaning back in his chair and crossing his arms. "Because you don't look good."

"So people keep saying."

"You're supposed to be in the hospital."

"No, I'm supposed to be home with my family, but they're gone."

Kehoe didn't register a facial expression. "Is this the part where you act like this is all my fault, we argue, then realize we're on the same side and wrap up with a hug?"

Lucas nodded at the teacup on Kehoe's desk. "This is the part where you have one of the minions bring me a cup of coffee."

Kehoe leaned forward, punched into the office line, asked for a coffee and a sandwich, then resumed the forced casual of before.

"Where is my family?" Lucas asked.

Kehoe had folded his arms across his chest again. "California—Big Bear. I sent two people I trust with them."

At that, Lucas felt the tears start to sizzle, but he pushed them away. "Thank you."

"Why are you here? You should be relaxing in the hospital, eating Jell-O and enjoying Turner Classic Movies."

"Where are you with the investigation?"

"I can have a summary delivered to your home if you would like."

"What I would like, Brett, is an answer to my question."

Kehoe nodded at the war room beyond the wall of windows. Lucas didn't turn to look; he didn't need any more vertigo. "We're going through Frosst's life piece by piece. And we haven't written William Hockney off—his brother's death puts him at the helm of a very well funded retirement."

"William Hockney is past the point of actually caring about money—it's become an existential reward to him." Lucas realized that he was sliding to one side, and he pushed himself up in the chair. Where was that fucking coffee? "It's not William Hockney."

"Seriously, Luke, are you okay? Because you really do look like shit."

"I could have done without the *really*. But thank you for the manufactured concern."

Hoffner came in with the coffee and sandwich, and Lucas was grateful he placed the mug in his hand—if he had put it down on the desk, he wasn't sure he'd be able to get to it. "Thank you," he said, meaning it. He took a sip and it tasted of medicine and blood. When they were alone again, Lucas asked, "Have you talked to William Hockney?"

"We interviewed him twice and we've got a line open to his lawyers. He's been around the block enough times that he wasn't shocked, but he *was* surprised. He was worried that his son might be in the guy's cross hairs, and he's grateful that you put a fork in his ass."

"Where *is* his son?"

"Beijing, bringing capitalism to communists—the world is a many-splendored thing."

"You think Frosst did all this?"

Kehoe opened his arms. "What's important is that we have

everything under control here, Luke. You were a big help. You rattled a lot of trees. And you pointed us in the right direction."

"Have you tied the bombings in Medusa, Forest Hills, Hoboken, Castleton Corners, and Brooklyn to Frosst?"

Kehoe shook his head. "Not yet. The IEDs in those bombings were all cell-phone activated, and they detonated one after the other, seconds apart. The cell phone we found on Frosst didn't make any calls around the time of the detonations, but it's possible he had a burner and disposed of it before he tried the hit on you and Whitaker. But we assume that Frosst carried them out. He used those five young men to advance his agenda, then erased them—it's not an uncommon tactic. Like I said, I have a whole department going after him. We'll find the connection."

"Not if it's not there." Lucas tried to pull in the scent of coffee, but all he got was the medicinal smell of antibacterial ointment. "It's not Frosst. Not entirely. There is too much money revolving around this. And there's a personal angle that I can't find; the bombing at the Guggenheim was too barbaric to have the simple goal of erasing those people from the gene pool. Our guy is sadistic—he wanted them to suffer. This is personal, Brett."

"That's not what Behavioral Sciences is saying." Kehoe took a breath and it was obvious that the past week had taken its toll on him the way he said, "Look, Luke, you need to get some rest. The doctors said you'd be in the hospital until Monday, and that was being optimistic. Look at you, you're—"

And by the way he let the sentence hang open, Lucas knew he was trying not to state the obvious.

"There's nothing wrong with my mind, Brett."

"It's not your mind I'm worried about. Human bodies can only take so much. How about I put you on a plane to your family? Spend some time with them until I get all the bolts put into this. Go to Big Bear. Have Halloween with your kids. Sit by a fire. Read a novel. But you're not coming back."

Lucas almost threw the coffee at him. "Not coming back? You fucking came to me, Brett. I didn't ask you for a job. *You* showed up at *my* door last winter with Hartke's death as a carrot and had me come in here because your computer models—I'll repeat that: *computer models*—couldn't figure out that shot. So I came back. And we both know what that was like for me. You cut me loose before, you're not doing it again."

Kehoe nodded at the door. "I just did."

72

The Upper East Side

A junior agent drove Lucas home—another kid who looked like she wouldn't know how to use a rotary phone if her life depended on it. Her name was Vasquez, and she was polite and quiet. Lucas sat in the back, trying to stay upright and to think—which felt like mutually exclusive tasks. Every now and then he'd see a poster or a flyer or a sign taped to a lamppost, stapled to a fence, or plastered onto a wall, and they all seemed to be a call to the citizens to join the Machine Bomber in rejecting technology and joining humanity. He thought about it for a moment, and in absolute terms it was an alluring premise. But then he remembered the protesters/demonstrators down at Federal Plaza and worried that there was very little humanity to rejoin.

Lucas asked Vasquez to drop him off at a corner on Madison. She went through the same routine as the cabbie had earlier, telling him that it was no trouble to drive him all the way. But this time Lucas didn't feel the need to fake civility and simply told the girl to fuck off, which got the desired effect.

He went into the market and Oscar was behind the counter—this time in a bright orange V-neck T-shirt and a perfect five o'clock shadow. When Lucas walked in, Oscar did a *What-the-fuck?* but didn't say anything because a fedora-wearing hipster with a little girl in a tiger Halloween costume was at the cashier, buying diapers, an off-brand box of macaroni and cheese, some microbrewery IPA, and a pack of Parliament Menthols.

Lucas didn't crowd him—if the guy didn't see him and stepped back, the whole Erector set would come crashing down. And the way he felt, he might never get back up.

The guy paid for his stuff while the little girl, who was about Laurie's age—maybe eight—stared up at him. Her face was painted with whiskers and she was beautiful, and the way she stared suggested he looked like he had been shot out of a cannon. She pulled on her father's pant leg and pointed up at Lucas.

The man turned and, seeing Lucas's aluminum hand and bloody bandages, said, "Great costume, bruh. But can you smile or something? You're scaring my kid."

Lucas did his best and a dollop of blood leaked out of the corner of his mouth and spilled down his chin.

The girl screamed.

"Asshole," Hipster Dad snapped, and left with his diapers, macaroni, smug beer, packaged cancer, and tigress.

"You asked!" Lucas called after him, and the effort almost took the pressure out of his hydraulic system. He put his hand against the counter and concentrated on not falling over.

"You okay, Dr. Page?" Oscar asked, the Italian accent missing from his delivery. "Because you don't look so good."

"Can I get some Tylenol?"

"I don't think that will do it."

Lucas took a breath to keep himself from yelling and repeated, "Can I get some Tylenol?" He then added, *"Please,"* and even to him, it sounded like a threat.

That shook Oscar loose from his stare, and he pulled a bottle down off the shelf. "Here," he said, and gave it a maraca shake.

Lucas tried to get his wallet out, but Oscar held up a hand. "No charge." He pushed the little red and white box across the counter. "I insist."

Lucas pocketed the Tylenol, nodded a thank you, and tried not to pass out before he got outside.

Leaves rattled down the street as he walked home from the corner. He wondered when they had moved his house—it was farther away. How had that happened? And then a solution presented itself—the one thing he had difficulty getting his students to understand was that objects in the universe weren't moving away from one another; the space between them was increasing—so maybe they had just slipped in more sidewalk between the market and his front door.

After about three years he got to the steps and he stood on the concrete, staring up. Had there always been this many steps?

It took him a day and a half to make it up the seven sandstone steps, which was a miracle considering he was fresh out of pitons, rope, and Sherpas.

He reached out for the knob and wondered if the whole shit-house would just go up in flames when he turned it.

He cranked the knob.

But there was no *kaboom*.

There wasn't even a bark from the dog.

Without the big dummy around to slobber on his pants—after the bloodstains, who would notice a little drool?—the house was depressingly quiet. A few toys were on the floor by the hall tree and Laurie had left her fish sweater on the chair by the console, giving the effect that the place had been cleaned out by a radiation scare.

He walked through the main floor without kicking off his shoes and stopped at the kitchen island, where he managed to get the Tylenol out of his pocket. He dumped it onto the counter and was about to head out back to Dingo's place when the doorbell rang.

It was a lonely sound without the kids chiming in with their harmonic yodel.

Lucas took a breath and opened the big slab of oak, again half expecting a *kaboom*. Calvin-Wade Curtis stood two steps down, staring up, both his hands clutching a camouflage backpack in front of his chest. It was obvious that he was nervous, because he had that idiot smile dialed up to piano key voltage. He stood there staring at Lucas.

Lucas decided that he needed to say something or Curtis would just stand there like Lot's wife. "Hello."

"Wha—? Oh. Yeah. Hello. Sorry. I just—" And he stopped.

"You want to come in?"

Curtis brushed by, contorting comically so as not to touch Lucas.

After he closed and locked the front door, he turned to see Curtis staring at him. "Want some water or something?"

That got a nod.

Lucas led him into the kitchen and pointed at the sink. "There you go."

But Curtis sat down at the island and Lucas took up position against the stove.

"You're interrupting naptime."

The statement gave Curtis purpose, and he unbuckled the flap on his backpack. "This . . ." he said, pulling out a stack of hard drives—five aluminum wedges, "is all the data the lab has on the bombings. Everything from crime-scene analysis to chemical composition to victim histories. All my photos and notes. Everything. I thought there might be something in here you can use."

Lucas appreciated the effort, but Kehoe had been very specific about his new position in the food chain. "Kehoe fired me."

Now Curtis was smiling as if it were a dare. "Yeah, well, I heard about that." The southern accent was back now, and he added an extra syllable to the last word. "But it's not like you lost your security clearance or anything. I checked and your ID is still valid. So, technically, we're not breaking any rules." Curtis stopped smiling for a second. Then it was back. "As long as we don't tell anyone."

Lucas gave his own smile at that, and by the way Curtis's eyes widened, he knew that it hadn't quite turned out. "That's kind of you."

"There's nothing but hundreds of miles of numbers on these."

"Which is exactly what I want." Lucas examined Curtis. "Why are you doing this?"

"Because Kehoe's wrong; that Frosst guy didn't do all this."

"How do you know?"

"Because you said so."

73

Lucas knocked on the door, triggering Lemmy's deep baritone. He leaned up against the railing and held on—if the dog's enthusiasm was turned past five, Lucas would go over like a Jenga tower. Dingo opened the door but only enough to let his head stick out.

"Hey," Lucas said, while holding on to the railing a little tighter than usual.

Dingo tried to give him a friendly smile but managed only a scowl. "For a guy who does spreadsheets, you don't look so good."

"So people keep telling me."

"No, seriously, Luke—you look like shit."

"Thanks."

"You think maybe you should be in the hospital?"

Lucas wanted to tell him to fuck off. To mind his own business. So he made an effort not to yell when he said, "I came to get Lemmy." On cue, the dog's big snout suction-cupped to the window and it fogged over with condensation.

"I can keep him for you."

Lucas would never admit it, but he needed the dog around;

Lemmy was the closest thing to family he had right now, and if he died in his sleep, he didn't want to be alone when it happened. "Has he eaten?"

Dingo nodded. "Walked and pooped. He's gotta pee, then he's good for the night."

"Thanks."

"You wanna come in? I can make you some food. Or you can just crash on the sofa, you know, if you don't want to be alone. Or I stay at your place. Your call."

"I'm going to take Lemmy, then go to sleep."

Dingo opened the door and Lucas gave the dog a *be calm* command. Lemmy came over and sniffed him—which was doggie code for *Where have you been, what have you been doing, and what have you eaten without me?* And as if he could sense that Lucas wasn't well, he didn't go into the usual knock-him-in-the-nuts-with-his-tail spins.

"Hey, dummy," Lucas said, and scratched his ear.

Lucas headed down the steps, throwing Dingo a thank you over his shoulder.

He got Lemmy to pee in the tiny backyard before climbing the steps to the mudroom. When they were both inside, Lucas leaned against the counter and wondered if he'd be able to make it upstairs for the night. He could call Dingo, but that would set off another "Let me stay with you" soliloquy, and Lucas wasn't in the mood for talking.

He stared down at the Tylenol and realized that it would be like putting a cork in a bullet wound. But he found the energy to get a liver treat out of the dog's cookie jar by the sink, and gave it to Lemmy, who took it gently from his fingers, again letting him know that he understood that something was wrong. Lucas didn't bother picking up the Tylenol.

When he got to the study, he pulled a bottle of Laphroaig out of the liquor cabinet—an eight-year-old wedding gift that they had never cracked—then climbed the stairs, one clunky footstep after another. He paused on the landing and resisted the temptation to set up camp right there in the glow of the little elephant night-light. Lemmy was looking down with those sad expressive eyes and probably wondering what the hell was going on.

Lucas finally made it to the bedroom. Erin had left some clothes on the chair and a little open suitcase by her nightstand, but everything else was in its place. He put the bottle down on the dresser by the door and limped into the bathroom. He played chess with the pill bottles in the medicine chest until he found one that fit his needs; the codeine was old and expired, but would provide the much-needed effect. He pocketed it, then walked back out to the bedroom and picked up the bottle of scotch. Lemmy was in the door, still eyeing him with that quizzical look on his face.

"Come on," he said to the dog, and went out into the hall.

He decided on the lower bunk in the boys' room, and he sat down on the edge of the bed. Lemmy came in and flopped his big ass down on the carpet, his hips out to one side, his attention locked on his human. It was obvious he thought there might be a treat in this for him.

Lucas opened the bottle of painkillers and tried to get a pill out with his prosthetic. Thirty seconds of frustration was enough, and he put it to his lips, shaking out a few pills that got stuck at the back of his throat. He put the bottle down on the nightstand, managed to crack the Laphroaig, and washed the codeine down with a mouthful of smoky peat. Then he lay down on the bed, clunking his head on the top rail.

When he was settled in, Lemmy climbed up. The dog didn't have space to do his usual samba before lying down and he paused indecisively before stretching out beside Lucas. He was going to tell the dog to get off, but he was too tired.

The glow-in-the-dark sticker constellation that he and Damien had spent an evening getting just right shone down at him. He had lain on the floor while Damien held up the various-sized decals—there were four in all—and Lucas had done the art direction with a laser-pointer, guiding the boy's hand, until they had strategically re-created all the northern constellations. He saw Draco, the dragon, and its brightest star, Eltanin. The constellation was visible year-round from the Northern Hemisphere, and Lucas wondered if the kids would bother looking up at the sky while they were out at Big Bear—the seeing over that particular part of California was perfect.

But he needed to get some sleep. And tomorrow would be the first day of the rest of his life.

Lemmy started to snore. Lucas closed his eyes, put his arm over the dog, and began to cry.

74

Someone had packed his head with frozen wet compost during the night. It had melted and leaked down, filling the back of his throat with a flavor that might as well have been cooked up in an anchovy's colon—it was tainted with scotch, stomach acid, and something that would probably work in ant traps.

He lay there with his eyes closed for a few moments, hoping the taste would go away and he could go back to sleep. But he burped, almost threw up, and tried to sit up. But Lemmy was on his arm, and all he did was startle the dog, who bumped him in the ribs when he popped up.

Lucas let out a howl.

The dog jumped to the floor.

Lucas sat up and banged his head on the bunk above.

The dog farted.

Lucas fell back into the pillow.

And that was the beginning of the first day of the rest of his life.

He had fallen asleep wearing his eye patch from the hospital, and during the night it had rotated around to the back of his head and was now tangled in the bandages protecting the right side of his face. But there was no blood on Hector's pillow, which meant that he had stopped seeping—so at least there was a silver lining portion to the program.

Whenever he slept with both his prosthetics on, it threw his skeleton out of whack, and he woke up with a little extra back pain, a kink in his neck, and a decent headache. But last night's Molotov cocktail of codeine and Laphroaig had added to the usual problems, and now he had that taste he couldn't shake.

The Lucas Page machine felt a little stronger today. He wondered how long he had slept; the light coming in was from one of those rainy fall days where it could have been eight in the A.M., three in the P.M., or just before dusk. He checked the alarm clock on the nightstand; it was almost two.

He turned and eyed Lemmy skeptically. "Don't you have to pee or something?"

Lemmy just tilted his head in the universal canine expression for *Huh?* and Lucas took him downstairs and into the backyard—all without falling.

It was a miserable rainy day and the dog's breath came out in big wafts of condensation that gave the impression he ran on a steam engine; Lucas half expected the raindrops to sizzle when they hit his fur. Which meant that a cold front had moved in.

While the dog did his business in the dead chrysanthemums, Dingo peeked out from his window overlooking the yard. Lucas didn't wave—he wasn't in the mood for conversation; his propulsion was fine, but he wasn't sure his communications programs were up and running. At least not without the prerequisite jolt of coffee.

Dingo watched him the entire time he stood out back waiting for the dog to finish up his morning constitutional. After Lemmy left a mastodon-sized turd in the flower bed, Lucas waved him inside. The dog clomped up the steps and Lucas slammed the door.

He dried Lemmy off with a towel that hung on a hook beside the door for precisely that purpose, then fed the brute—six big scoops of overpriced human-grade health pellets that Erin lugged home from the store. Which was a miracle considering she was five-feet-one and the bags were the general proportions and weight of a body rolled up in a carpet.

Lucas fired up the coffeemaker and laid out his day. He knew what he needed to do, but not how to do it, and he got lost in his thoughts as the machine chemically converted grinds and water to emotional salve. When the pot was a third full, he filled a mug decorated with hand lettering that read: *World's Greatest Dad—from world's greatest kids (and Hector)! WE LUV YOU!*, took a sip, and went upstairs.

Again, he somehow made it without spilling either himself or the coffee.

He let the shower run and peeled off his clothes. He took out his wallet and the handcuffs he had been carrying since their guy had tried to blow up Saarinen. He didn't bother with the hamper; he shoved yesterday's suit into the garbage can, using the plunger to tamp it down like pipe tobacco. Lucas thought the whole exercise would feel a lot more complete with some lighter fluid and a match. Maybe a Marine playing "Taps" on a bugle. But you had to go with what you had.

It was hard to reconcile eating two suits in a week; he was going through clothes like Super Dave Osborne. Maybe he could bill Kehoe when this was all over if both of them were still alive.

He unspooled the cranial bandages, and it was a slow, painful process. But the shower running behind him was filling the chamber with a thick steam, and even though he knew it was illusory, the warm condensation felt like it helped the process.

When he was done, he leaned in, wiped the glass with a towel, and surveyed the damage.

Erin's Sebastian Krüger analogy wasn't right; he looked more like a Ralph Steadman design—dripping ink and all. There was a new line of creation on the right side of his face—a semicircle that began behind his cheek, circled up over his ear, then back down to the base of his skull at the back. The windshield had taken his ear off, but not completely—it had still been attached in a loose flap that they had sewn back on with tight little blue knots highlighted by red antibacterial ointment. Describing his eyes as black would be a misnomer; the Mascheranda mask left in the wake of his flight through the windshield was actually a mixture of purple, green, and red. The damage around his prosthetic eye was less severe—the scar tissue there had less capillary action and there were fewer vessels to break and flood the skin with dead blood. The bruising would heal in about ten days, but the new scar tissue on the side of his head would take some time. Until then, he needed to get used to frightening little tigresses in convenience stores.

The rest of him wasn't so bad. It wasn't what anyone would call *good*. But he would have taken a much worse beating if the laws of physics had dictated a slightly different collision. Most of the scrapes and scabs were superficial—they'd be gone in a couple of weeks. The bruising on his ribs—now an ugly green and purple—would fade, and disappear. But they were broken, and he knew that they'd feel like a side full of melted rivets for the next two weeks, especially without painkillers. The Klaus Kinski hair was still there, if a little singed. So for the most part, he was serviceable.

After a shower, he finished the somehow still warm coffee, then rebandaged the side of his head. He dressed, putting on a dark suit and black shirt—no tie—with the belief that bloodstains would be less visible. He got his wallet, his phone, and the handcuffs and stuffed them into the appropriate pockets.

He preferred his prosthetic eyeball to a patch—the kids called it his pirate look—but the swelling would make it an exercise in pain management, so Pirate Luke in sunglasses it was. Then he swallowed a handful of Tylenol, stuffed another pocket with paper towels, and left the house with an umbrella.

75

The East Village

"This the place or not?" the cabbie asked a third time, his voice carrying an islands rhythm.

They were pulled over on the right side of the street, and Lucas had to crank his neck around to see the building with his good eye. Rain rippled the image of a typical East Village row house, with a stone stoop, flower boxes on the ground-floor windows, and an army of mix and match garbage cans at the curb.

He wasn't hesitating because of uncertainty over the address—this was definitely the place—he was hesitating because he didn't know if this was the right thing to do. If life had taught him one thing, it was that his luck was contagious. The first big whiff had been when he had killed Kehoe's brother. Sure, it was one of those random culminations of fate that all the caution in the world could not have prevented, but no one could deny that the guy would still be alive if he hadn't been with Lucas. And now Whitaker was on the fence between here and the afterlife. So even though it was a small sample, it was easy to see a pattern.

"Well, is it?" the man asked again, eyeing Lucas in the rearview mirror. "Huh, *mon*?" He was a Jamaican guy, with long healthy dreads and two gold incisors.

"This is it."

He credit-carded the fare, adding a ten-dollar tip that was more an apology for the way he looked than for making the guy stand at the curb for five minutes, and got out without waiting for the machine to burp out a receipt.

He opened the umbrella and stood there among the garbage cans. The rain was coming in at an angle and his pants were getting wet, and the last thing he needed was pneumonia on top of everything else, so he climbed the steps.

The woman who answered the door was tiny—much smaller than Erin. She was dressed in a lilac salwar kameez, and her hair was pulled back in a tight bun. She had a compact disk in her hand and an expression on her face that could have converted to a scream or a laugh.

The little woman said, "Yes?" The sound of cable news delivering ramped-up paranoia was on in the background, at least two rooms away. They were talking about the bomber. And the protests. And the fires and the accidents and the injuries.

"I'm Dr. Page. I was hoping I could speak to your son."

She eyed him skeptically as she ran through some internal checklist, then nodded as a line of code delivered the right bit of information. "Dr. Page, *the teacher?* Oh yes. Yes. Please come in."

Lucas closed the umbrella, shook it off, and stepped over the threshold into the tiled vestibule. The smell of cooking hit him and he realized that other than a handful of codeine, a belt of scotch, a coffee, and some Tylenol, he hadn't eaten anything since the hospital yesterday.

The little woman went to the base of the stairs and yelled, "*Priy!*" up into the void. She then switched to English with "You have a visitor."

Someone upstairs yelled back a response that was lost in the sound of a CNN update.

"A visitor!"

Another mumbled reply.

"A teacher!"

There was the sound of heavy footsteps on the floor, followed by a fast gallop of socked feet down stairs. Bobby Nadeel rounded the newel-post and stopped cold when he saw Lucas.

Nadeel's expression said that he would have been less surprised to see Siegfried and Roy carrying a giant wheel of cheese through the front door. "Dr. Page?" He gave Lucas a once-over. "You don't look so good."

Lucas pointed at a chair in the living room. "Can I sit down?"

76

Lucas spent two hours at Nadeel's house, talking with Bobby and eating dish after dish of his mother's cooking. Each bite delivered a jolt of steam to his drivetrain, and he put down three big plates— which was a miracle for a man who considered coffee to be all the major food groups. When he left, Bobby's mom stuffed a Ziploc of gulab jamun into his pocket.

Nadeel was one of the brightest kids who had come through Lucas's office. Last year, during the Christmas sniper case, Lucas had put Nadeel in the computer lab with two of his other graduate students to collate some data—to find some patterns. The exercise demonstrated that Nadeel was able to think in the abstract, which was an indispensable muscle in the field of astrophysics. The kid had that rare combination of technical genius married to scientific insight that he topped off with curiosity—all necessary components in a good scientist's outlook. Unfortunately, as was true with Lucas, Bobby's people skills needed a little polish.

Tonight, Lucas had given the kid the hard drives that Calvin-Wade Curtis had clandestinely delivered. Handing out restricted data to non-bureau personnel was strictly verboten, but after Nadeel's and the other students' unofficial stint with the bureau last year, Kehoe's people had done a retroactive deep background check, and they still had clearance—*technically*.

The bureau's people were fettered by both protocol and lack of vision; not so Nadeel. So Lucas had tasked him with sifting through the hard drives Curtis had dropped off—with the *very unspecific* goal of finding anything that shouldn't be there.

It was night now, and the cab cut through Central Park on the journey to the West Side. They had come up the FDR to 63rd, then over to Madison, where they headed north to 66th, then across the park. The rain didn't look like it had any intention of easing up and the clouds overhead were blocking out all atmospheric light. Halloween was still a day off, and if this held up, the city of the dead would be the best place in the world for all the spooks and witches and goblins—which these days meant gluten-free robots and princesses and vegan superheroes.

The tunnel of trees opened up and they hit Central Park West, reminding Lucas of the old Ian Hunter song. He wondered if old Ian would still think, "it's the best!" or if he would look around and shake his head at the Starbucks and spatula stores.

The cab turned right, making the eight blocks north on a stream of green lights, while Lucas tried to erase the song from the iPod in his head.

It was a twenty-six-story nod to New York's golden age of architecture, but instead of the belle époque swag of Renaissance Revival, it was classical gothic. Every opening in the building, from the doors to the windows to the passages, peaked in hand-milled lancet arches. There was a round drive out front, and the news parasites were on the sidewalk just beyond it, held at bay by a platoon of private security guards.

Lucas rapped on the bulletproof partition. "Drop me off at the next corner."

"You sure? I can drop you right out front." The cabbie eyed him with an expression that Lucas was getting used to. "Because you don't look so good."

He was starting to wonder if everyone used the same writer for their dialogue. "Here is fine."

After the cab drove off, he crossed the street, slipping by a gaggle of reporters on the corner who were on their phones under a canopy of umbrellas. He walked down half a block until he found the service alley and cut in.

He was about twenty paces beyond the glow of the streetlights when a voice in the dark said, "Sorry, sir, but you'll have to use the front door."

Lucas tilted his umbrella back and squinted into the void. A man in a security guard uniform emerged. He had the prerequisite dark clothes, epaulets, and badge of his kind—but he was wearing a bulletproof vest and carrying a small carbine. He had the shoulders and biceps of a cop, but his head looked transplanted from an orc— it was in the general shape of a turnip, with pointy gargoyle ears. The guy gave the impression that he could chew through a tire. But his voice was relaxed and disconnected; evidently he didn't think Lucas looked like much of a threat.

Lucas nodded up at the building. "I'm here to see the man on the top floor. I can't go through the front."

A second orc emerged from the shadows, this one virtually indistinguishable from the first, only larger. Their type tended to work in packs—probably something to do with making it easier to hunt the smaller animals.

The first orc nodded knowingly. "The TV assholes?"

"Yeah."

The orc gave him a slow up and down. "He expecting you?"

"Nope."

"I'm not a doorman. I'm here to keep people out, not let them in." He was being nice, but Lucas could tell that would stop very soon.

Lucas slowly reached into his coat pocket and took out his badge. "You know Benjamin Frosst?"

The orc nodded. "He was my boss."

"I'm the guy who killed him." Lucas realized that those words might be the wrong ones, but he was going for impact.

The smaller orc said, "And that will make the man upstairs want to see you?"

"I *guarantee* it." Lucas handed his ID over.

Orc One stared at him. Then down at the ID. Then he keyed the mic velcroed to his vest. "Yeah, Zimmy? Call up to the penthouse. I got a guy here wants me to let him up. Name's Lucas Page."

A squawk of static that could have originated in Orc Mountain came back, and Lucas could discern no human words in the warbled message. But evidently the orc's ears were more finely tuned and he keyed the mic again. "I know we're not doormen, but I can't help it if people keep showing up. Just make it fast. It's pissing rain out here and I got four more hours on the clock."

The orc gave the ID back and they passed the next few moments without conversation. The only sounds in the alley were the various drips, drops, and streams of water cascading down from elevation offset by the occasional honking horn or revved engine beyond the mouth of the passage. Finally, the orc's radio made another indecipherable noise that evidently contained meaning because he keyed his mic and said, "Thanks, Zimmy."

His body language opened up and he nodded at some unidentifiable point in the darkness at the end of the alley. "Take the red door, then cut left. Take the red service elevator—not the blue one. Get in, press the button. The doors will close, and they'll check you out over the CCTV before they bring the car up."

Lucas thanked him and he disappeared back into whatever dark alcove he had been nesting in.

Two hundred feet later, Lucas took the red door—a well-lit portal around a corner and hidden from street view. The building was warm and he shook off his umbrella, then took a left. The service elevators were at the end of a can't-miss-it corridor—a red one for the penthouse, a blue one for the rest of the floors. It was a typical service car, painted a pale red that had gone out of style some time in the 1930s. Lucas pressed the only button—a broad brass panel with the letters PH on it—and the doors closed.

As the car shot up through the spine of the building, he felt himself become heavier, and he concentrated on the floor, his focus on a single paw print in the corner. He managed to make the entire trip without toppling over, and when the car slowed, Lucas put a hand out against the wall to keep his footing.

The doors slid open to a white-tiled service area that was larger than the footprint of most New York City studio apartments. There was a single door in the far end, and as Lucas walked toward it, the various locks clinked and clanked. It swung out and William Hockney nodded at him. "Dr. Page."

"Mr. Hockney."

As Lucas got closer, the old man took a step back and gave him a theatrical once-over. The old man said the only thing he could. "You don't look so good, young man." He was in moccasins, gray wool slacks, a high-collared white shirt, and a very nice smoking jacket—evidently he was up to speed on billionaire loungewear. "Why don't you come in and sit down."

The old man walked Lucas through the kitchen—a white-tiled mausoleum with fifteen-foot ceilings, five ovens, and enough tin-lined copper pots hanging over the bowling-alley-sized island to recast the Statue of Liberty. A copper and brass espresso machine sat on the island, polished to a mirror finish. The contraption was bedecked with a dozen valves and thirty yards of piping and could easily be mistaken for a submersible diving bell.

The butler's pantry was next—a glass-cabinet-lined room that displayed at least thirty different sets of formal china—followed by a serving room, then the dining room proper. The table was big enough to land a small aircraft on and sat forty people with plenty of elbow room. You didn't need a history lesson to know that everyone from heads of state to movie stars had rubbed elbows around it.

Whoever said that money could not buy taste had never seen William Hockney's living room. Like Hearst's Xanadu, it was filled with the finest antiques to come out of the major European movements of the past two centuries—it had none of the look-at-me-ism that new-money New Yorkers tended to gravitate toward, eschewing the faux opulence of gold leaf, cherubs, and Louis XVI–inspired crown moldings. Every piece in the room was elegant, tasteful, and very expensive. It was old time, old school, old money.

The doors to the patio were open, four large floor-to-ceiling bronze affairs inset with beveled panes. Out on the patio, there was enough vegetation to launch a well-heeled safari. Beyond the stone banister, the park reached east.

The big surprise in the living room were the bonsai, a shared interest with Saarinen. He knew that the old man had a hobby—his kind always did. But they usually collected classic Rolls-Royce, Old Masters, or pre-Columbian art—objects that had cost associated with them. Diminutive horticulture seemed to be too much of a hands-on pastime for a man like Hockney—he seemed more of a *sit-back-and-pay-people-to-do-things* kind of guy. It was hard to picture him sitting in here on the weekends, listening to Def Leppard in his slippers, clipping miniature branches, sipping obscure whiskey, and letting the stress of counting the zeros in his bank account all day long bleed away.

The centerpiece of the living room was an elegant Japanese shelf—Meiji period—that displayed five of what Lucas knew were perfect and very old examples of the art form; one five-needle pine, two junipers, and two cypresses.

That Lucas was not good with people was no secret, especially to himself. So he thought of the one person he knew who was—

Kehoe—and asked himself what Kehoe would do if he wanted something from William. So he leaned forward and examined one of the tiny trees. "Beautiful cypress." A tree like that took at least a century to cultivate. "Hinoki?"

William managed a smile, however small. "You are nothing if not surprising, Dr. Page."

"I read a lot."

William shook his head. "One does not learn to identify *Chabo-hiba* by *reading a book*. But I appreciate your humor."

"I'm glad someone does." The truth was during his days at MIT, one of the girls he had lived with was a botanist at the Arnold Arboretum at Harvard; he had learned a lot about plants through simple intellectual osmosis.

He reached down and picked up a pair of hand-forged scissors that lay on a piece of silk beside one of the tiny trees. A few clippings were in a small cloisonné bowl; evidently Mr. Hockney had been at work tonight. Lucas slipped his fingers into the handles and felt the craftsmanship in the way they molded to his thumb and palm, as if they had been made for him. They warmed to his touch, and he wondered if Mr. Hockney knew how special they were; these weren't eleven-hundred-dollar hobby scissors sold in a midtown boutique for people with more money than taste—these had been made by a master blacksmith, probably Sasuke, and had to run in the mid five figures.

He put the scissors back down on the embroidered silk and turned to take in the rest of the apartment as William eyed him with interest. "Those two cypress come from the Larz Anderson collection that Anderson's widow left to Harvard in 1949—these two were gifted to my father, and he left them to me. The rest are housed in the Arnold Arboretum."

Lucas wondered if the old man was fucking with him, or if the coincidence was real.

Hockney dropped into an antique club chair covered in zebra

hide. There was a copy of Lucas's latest book on the table beside him, an ivory paper knife sticking out at the two-thirds mark, a highball of whiskey beside it.

"You bought my book."

The old man shook his head. "Dr. Saarinen gave it to me."

"How am I supposed to pay for macaroni and cheese if cheap-skates like you don't splurge on luxury items once in a while?"

The old man raised his whiskey. "Would you like a drink, Dr. Page? I'm afraid that in light of recent events, I am desirous of my privacy and have sent the help home—you'll have to serve yourself." The old man pushed a button—evidently William was big on secret buttons—and a panel slid back, exposing yet another Disneyland for alcoholics hidden away in a wall.

Lucas walked over and poured a Perrier into a tumbler—he didn't feel like fumbling with lemon or ice, so he sat down facing William in one of the safari chairs.

Hockney pointed his highball at Lucas. "I don't know if you're aware of this, but I knew Odelia."

That bit of information was both a surprise and no surprise at all. Odelia Page—the eccentric old lady who had adopted Lucas in the winter of her life—had been a social fixture in New York City for the better part of the twentieth century. The surprise was that he had never heard anyone call her Odelia—not in the fifteen years they had spent together and not in all the time since she had died. She had simply been Mrs. Page, even though her husband had died when she was in her early twenties. "How so?"

Hockney waved his fingers as if casting a spell, and for an instant he was back in time somewhere. "I was trying to climb the social ladder and she was trying not to slip off; she had moved in the circles I aspired to, and I moved in the circles she could no longer afford. I remember when she adopted you—it was the only thing people talked about for several weeks. People thought she was—"

Lucas hoped he wasn't going to say anything bad about her, because he had never hit another human being. But Mrs. Page had been the single greatest influence in his life, and he wouldn't let anyone—not even an ancient billionaire—speak ill of her.

"—making a mistake adopting a child at her age. But I admired her for it. I remember seeing you once when you were new to her world. It was a garden party at the Wassermans.'"

Lucas remembered the party—it was on Long Island, and they had inflatable flamingos in the pool for the children to float around on. There had been a band. And white dinner jackets for miles. Lucas had been with Mrs. Page for only a few months at that point, and he was still worried that if he made any mistakes, she would send him back to the foster home where she had found him. It had been the first time he had danced—she had shown him how to waltz. "I remember the inflatable flamingos in the pool."

Hockney's face went blank for a moment; then his eyes lit up as the memories behind them sparked up. "Yes! That's right. What a phenomenal thing to remember."

Lucas shrugged. "I was six. And it was the first party I had ever been to."

The old man waved his hand again. "I find myself getting more nostalgic as I get older."

Lucas took a sip of his water, put his head back, and closed his eyes. Evidently the cab ride across the island followed by the trek through orc alley had taken a toll and he didn't feel nearly as strong as he had when he left Nadeel's. The handcuffs in his pocket poked his hip, but he was too tired to shift his weight.

William ended Lucas's sleep fantasy. "Now that we have exchanged pleasantries and shared histories, may I ask you why you have come, Dr. Page?"

"There's a Latin saying, *Cui bono?*"

"To whom is it a benefit?"

It was Lucas's turn to smile. A display of a classical education was becoming a rare thing out in the world—all you had to do was look at the conspiracy idiots gumming up the streets around the crime scenes. "So who profits from fucking with you?"

77

The Upper East Side

Kehoe was at home for what felt like the first time in days. In all his years with the bureau, he had never really adjusted to the stop/go mindset the job required. Some of his people were able to turn it off at the end of the day—to simply go home, unplug from the chaos of the office, and settle into family mode. But Kehoe always found that impossible. Not that he didn't relax. He had a well-rounded life outside of work: a good marriage to a woman he still loved after thirty-two years; a sailboat that took him away from the corridors of the city; a cabin on a lake upstate where he managed to spend a dozen or so weekends a year; and his family home in Sonoma that took up ten days every summer, ten days every winter, and the occasional family gathering where the kids showed up with his grandkids.

But he always thought of himself as a bureau man who had a family instead of a family man who had a career. He had given up trying to fight this understanding of himself years ago, but every now and then it came back, and he wondered if he was missing out on things that everyone else seemed to find solace in.

Lately he found himself on the boat less and less. The same with the cabin. And the home out west. With the internet flattening out the world and bad ideas able to circumnavigate the planet at the speed of light, time away from the job was succumbing to diminishing returns. That's one thing that Page was right about: people were becoming dumber and dumber, and they were doing it with open arms and smiles on their faces. All you had to do was look at the conspiracy message boards or any HGTV program—they were peopled by imbeciles.

He was at the bench in front of the piano. The fallboard was down and he was looking out at the East River and enjoying a tea that had just hit the perfect Goldilocks temperature. His wife was out somewhere with her friends—an evening of hoisting cocktails after a day spent in a competitive game of American Expressery at Bergdorf's. He had the patio doors open and the wind was just right, turning the sounds of traffic on the 59th Street Bridge a few blocks down into the perfect score to his thoughts. For the first time in days he felt like he was alone.

Well, alone except for the man with the C-4 and lack of conscience.

They had a lot on this guy—or *these guys*—storage rooms full at this point. But they didn't know how to put it together. It was like one of those puzzles where there wasn't a picture, just a box full of pieces that were all the same color. You needed some place to start or you could just stare at it all day long and get nowhere. Which was not a way to run an investigation.

This was not the first time the bureau faced a bomber. People had been trying to blow holes in the social fabric of Manhattan since the first keg of gunpowder had been ferried ashore on a rowboat.

The first major bombing on record for the twentieth century had been in 1914, when the Anarchist Black Cross group killed four people and leveled an entire city block. Then, in 1920, a group of Italian anarchists detonated a horse-drawn buggy loaded with explosives on Wall Street, murdering thirty-eight innocent people. The forensic evidence had been destroyed when sanitation crews had mopped up the mess—forensics hadn't even been a word back then—and the culprits had never been caught.

Fast-forward two decades to 1940, when George Metesky began a bombing spree that would span sixteen years and include twenty-two separate explosions. Metesky had the distinction of being collared due to some of the earliest criminal profile work undertaken by the bureau.

The late sixties, a decade rife with anti-government sentiment, gave the city Sam Melville, who set off eight devices between July and November of 1969. His spree was cut short after a friend turned him in. He went on to further infamy as one of the instigators of the Attica prison riots of 1971, where he was killed by state police when they retook the complex.

Melville was closely followed by the Weather Underground in 1970, but they managed only to blow up three of their own—so Kehoe wasn't certain that they deserved a criminal distinction; *morons* seemed a more fitting designation.

In 1975, the Armed Forces of the Puerto Rican National Liberation Front subtracted four citizens from the financial district, followed by Croatian nationalists blowing up eleven people at LaGuardia. The Croats hit again in '76, this time killing one bomb disposal technician.

Things were relatively quiet until 1993, when Islamic fundamentalists took their first kick at the can, killing six people and injuring a thousand more when they detonated a truck bomb in the parking garage of the North Tower of the World Trade Center. From that point on, most of the bombings in the city were committed by like-minded religious nuts with the occasional sociopath thrown in just to mix up the statistics.

And now the city could add another spree to the list: the Machine Bomber.

But Lucas's visit yesterday had shaken Kehoe's belief that this thing was put to bed. Not that he doubted the ability of his people—no, he believed in them. But Page was a master at cracks in arguments, and he was smart, which was a lethal combination in the right circumstances. And if there was one thing that Page could be counted on, it was to find the right circumstances.

Kehoe stood up and closed the window.

Then he picked up the phone to call Hoffner—it was time to get back to the office.

78

The Upper West Side

William Hockney let the silence hang in the air as if it grew more valuable with each tick of the clock. The tactic might have worked on others—Lucas had come to learn that most people believed that the opposite of speaking was waiting—but he let it stretch out; he had never been a big believer in meeting the expectations of others. Besides, he often found conversation more awkward than silence.

He poured himself another water, sat back down, and took a sip, grateful that it didn't dribble down his chin. He turned toward the big open patio door; from the change in cadence, he could tell the rain had backed off a little. A cool breeze kissed through the doors—the cold front was taking hold and there was a chance they'd get light snow.

Lucas watched the rain for a few moments, focusing on the way the leaves on the small shrubs outside bounced, and it looked as if they were dancing to the music that Hockney had on in the background—Nina Simone, which surprised him.

"You're the last man standing."

"Like you, Dr. Page, I am a man who defies the odds." Hockney gave Lucas his little cryptic smile again. Back in the day, it had probably charmed the pants off of more than one date—which made it a redundant feature considering all the money he had.

"Are you worried?"

"About?"

"Whoever killed your brother might come after you."

The old man waved it away. "While you were in the hospital, my lawyers had a very fruitful meeting with Special Agent in Charge Kehoe. He is of the opinion that Mr. Frosst is responsible for everything that happened. They assured me that they will find the people who paid him to disrupt my life."

Jesus, Lucas thought, where did these people come from? Seth was dead, his insurance company was down $4.5 billion in claims, he was out another billion in lost revenue from the Horizon Dynamics IPO, and seven hundred plus human beings and a pet dog were dead. If that constituted disruption, Lucas wondered what Hockney considered a tragedy. "And you let them sell you that idea?"

Again, the old man didn't move, and Lucas realized that he had already worked all of this out in his own way. "It is not an unreasonable assumption."

"No one has accused you of ordering Frosst to kill Seth?"

That smile came back. "Only you, Dr. Page."

"Did you?"

William examined him with renewed interest. "Do you think you will solve who was responsible for all these bombings?"

"Yes."

"Then it doesn't matter what I say—truth is truth."

"If Frosst did kill your brother and you ordered it, I solved your problem by putting an SUV into him—they can't tie his actions to you. *Yet.*"

"But?" William Hockney was starting to impress Lucas.

"There's another option."

"That I didn't kill my brother."

He had to admit, the old guy was smart. "If you didn't, who did? And if Frosst killed your brother for some reason unknown to you, it's possible that you were also a target that he didn't get to. Which either makes you safe now that he's dead or buys you time until someone else comes to complete the task."

"You must find this job very tedious, Dr. Page."

"No. Just the people I deal with."

William examined him again. "Of course."

Lucas finished his drink and pushed himself out of the chair that had once been a happy mammal munching grass on the veldt. He hobbled over to the bar, but the panel was closed and Hockney once again had to press his secret button. As before, the wall opened like a prop in a Bond film and Lucas grabbed another Perrier. He went back to his chair, passing the shelf of bonsai and the hand-forged scissors. "But if you had Frosst kill Makepeace and Seth, then the only one who could have sent Frosst after Whitaker and me is you."

The old man looked taxidermied—he wasn't moving at all. But the lights were on behind his eyes. "What benefit would it be for me to send Frosst after you and your partner?"

Lucas had been wondering about that. "I don't know, other than that it was an addendum—Whitaker and I were not targets when this started."

"More tying up of loose ends?"

"Possibly."

"What about you? If Frosst's attack on you and your partner was part of the same grand scheme, you hardly seem to be in any shape to protect yourself."

Lucas took a sip and waved the question away. "I don't die; people around me do."

The old man stared at him for a few moments, and the silence was now a part of their conversation.

"Where is William Junior?"

"He has business abroad." Hockney waved the question away. "Besides, I think it wise that my family spend the next little while dispersed to the corners of the globe."

"Just in case?"

"Something like that, yes."

"And what's next for you, William? I'm sure there are worlds that need conquering."

"I am a little tired right now." He was examining Lucas with some unidentifiable meaning in his eyes. "But what is *your* next move, Dr. Page?"

Outside, beyond the open patio doors, the rain coming down had finally turned to a light snow. It was too warm for it to stick, and it melted as soon as it touched down, but it signaled a change in their luck with the weather: Indian summer was officially over.

Lucas fingered the rim on the glass, and the action made a soft sound that he wondered if the old man could hear. "To find whoever is responsible."

"And then?"

Lucas fingered the rim of his tumbler again, but this time it didn't make any noise. "Use your imagination."

79

The Upper West Side

Some of the small shrubs outside were dusted with white. The help was gone—even his full-time butler and housekeeper had been sent to their quarters on the floors below so he could have his privacy. He thought about calling someone to come up and cover the shrubs, but he wasn't in the mood for any more people tonight—Dr. Page had finished off whatever tolerance for interlopers he had—so he decided to do it himself.

William Hockney buttoned his smoking jacket and went outside. The park across the street was dark, and the East Side was invisible through the fog massaging the city. He knew they kept the Styrofoam covers for the shrubs in a small shed at the far corner of the patio—William oversaw the care of all of his plants; he had inherited the interest from his father. Unfortunately, his son shared none of his love for horticulture. Actually, his son displayed passion for very little, and William wondered what would happen to the many collections he had put together over the years—the paintings, the sculpture, the cars, the objects of virtue. Would they end up at auction, broken up for the philistines to bid on, or would they go to museums, to be enjoyed by schoolchildren? Neither option seemed particularly comforting to William, but he had long ago accepted that each man has only one life.

There were a few triangular puddles on the slate-tiled terrace and he moved slowly. His hip was giving him a lot of trouble lately—he was scheduled for surgery at Cornell—so he took his time. Besides, he liked it out here with his plants. There were in fact very few places on the planet that the old man found as comforting as his garden. When he was with his plants, he forgot the rest of the world. And sometimes even himself, which was a rare thing.

He was almost at the shed when his right foot made contact with the stone and there was a *click*. Not the meek snapping of a twig or the crunch of an insect, but the sharp report of a mechanical device.

Not knowing why, William Hockney stopped. He stood there for a moment, looking down at his foot.

He had no combat experience.

He had never been exposed to any of the baser experiences of life like war.

He was not a fan of popular films. Or novels.

He didn't read the product brochures from any of the arms companies he owned.

But he was certain that he had stepped on some sort of a detonator.

80

The Upper East Side

This time Lucas let the cab take him to his front door. It was coming up on midnight and he was worried that he might turn into a pumpkin. The almost snow was still falling, and for a second he wondered if they had snow in Big Bear, then reminded himself to stop. He needed his meat computer—as Maude called it—for other tasks. Like figuring out who was blowing people up.

The driver eyed him suspiciously, but every denizen of the city knew that at this hour the only people out were those unfit for mass consumption. He glanced back every now and then as if he expected Lucas to keel over.

Even before he was out of the cab, Lucas saw that the embassy next door was having another party. This time they had gas lanterns and valets at the curb. And of course, since it was the French, about twenty people were on the sidewalk smoking, champagne glasses in hand.

Lucas keyed in the front door and was met by Lemmy, who seemed both happy and depressed at the same time; he wasn't used to spending a lot of time alone. Lucas squatted down, his weight over his original hip and knee, and Lemmy hit him in the face with his tongue. They did the *I'm-glad-to-see-you* exchange for a few moments, and Lucas was grateful for the company.

There was a note on the console from Dingo. He had fed the dog, taken him for a walk and a poop. And for Lucas to let him know what else he needed in the way of help while the family was gone.

Lucas was beat, and he felt like his skin was going to slip off his body if he didn't lie down. He took the dog out back for one quick pee, then locked up the house and armed the alarm.

He filled a glass with milk, then took off his jacket and draped it over one of the stools at the island. The handcuffs in the pocket clinked off the wood and reminded him of the bag of gulab jamun that Mrs. Nadeel had been kind enough to give him. He sat at the marble for a few moments, munching on the sweets, gulping milk, and watching the almost snow come down outside.

How was this whole convoluted mess cobbled together? The components all worked on their own, but trying to fit them into any sort of a cohesive story line at this point was a lost cause. But definable problems were like that; you could write a neat and sexy mathematical formula that would answer a particular question, but as soon as you tried to apply the same formula to another—similar—problem, the formula lost its legs.

Fuck it. He popped the last honey-soaked ball in his mouth, rinsed his glass and his fingers at the sink, gave Lemmy a liver treat from his cookie jar, then went upstairs.

Tonight he made the effort to take off his clothes. He also removed his arm. But he left the leg on.

He took another shower, changed the bandages on the side of his head, then crawled naked into the sheets. He thumped the mattress with his right stump and Lemmy hopped up, did his fifty-circle samba, then lay down against his hip.

Next door, Lucas could hear the strains of a string quartet easing itself through a Fritz Kreisler piece that he couldn't quite name because he was already feeling Hypnos tugging at his concentration. Beside him, the dog let out a sigh.

It was impossible to tell who started snoring first.

81

The Upper West Side

He could not remember feeling this cold. Which was accurate, because he had *never been this cold.* He wondered if anyone had ever been this cold. He checked his watch, and the vibrating dial told him that it was past four in the morning now.

Three more hours.

That's all he had to do.

Three more hours.

Then help would show up. He had no idea what he would do after that, but calls would go out, the proper people would be summoned, and the correct decisions would be made.

Three more hours.

He had tried yelling, of course. And the yelling had turned into hollering. Then the hollering had morphed to screaming. By which time his voice gave out.

But there was no one to hear him. The help had been sent away for the night; his brother's apartment—the floor below his—was empty now that Seth had been murdered. And William Hockney had very strict rules about being bothered when he asked to be left alone.

From up here, above the city, no one could hear him scream—not his neighbors; not the occupants of the other buildings; not the people walking on Central Park West at this late hour; not the armed security guards his people had posted in the alley, at the front door, and in the garage; not even the reporters who were lined up three bodies thick down at the entrance hoping to get a glimpse of him.

The snow was still falling, but it was really nothing but slightly gelled rain that melted as soon as it hit him. He was soaked through and shivering.

His leg felt like it wasn't there anymore, except to send him a jolt of pain every now and then. It had started shaking not long after he had stepped on the device. After an hour in, it started to cramp up. Then the numbness set in. And he couldn't shift his weight because there was every reason to believe that the thing beneath his foot was weight-sensitive. But now he was shaking uncontrollably from the combination of muscle fatigue, a bad hip, cold, and terror.

Three more hours.

Three.

More.

Hours.

Three.

More.

Hours.

He was over halfway there. And for the past two hours he felt like he couldn't do another minute. So he knew he could make it until his butler arrived in the morning. Mr. Svensen had not been late a single time in his twenty years of service.

William Hockney had weathered storms that would have dissolved lesser men down to their primordial components. He had battled dragons, vanquished armies, overthrown kings. He was special. Maybe even invincible. So why could he not simply stand here for another three hours? How difficult could it be?

He was old.

He had a bad hip.

He had a pacemaker.

But he had something else—the DNA of titans.

He did not think about what would happen when his butler arrived. He focused only on the goal. Which was to stay alive for three more hours.

82

The Upper West Side
Sunrise

AmFetaMeen walked naked into the kitchen. There were two chicks passed out on the sofa, their arms around each other, a single tit hanging out of a silk blouse. Most of the coke had been hoovered up, but what hadn't now frosted the glass coffee table between the ashtray and bottles of Stoli and rolled-up hundred-dollar bills and cell phones and condom wrappers.

He paused in front of the big window that faced north, and something dropped down from the roof. It took a second for his brain to register that he was looking at a . . . a . . . was that a fucking drone?

AmFetaMeen grabbed a pillow and jammed it over his junk; he had enough trouble as it was. Fucking #metoo had put a serious dent in his income and he didn't need photos of his cock on the cover of the *New York Post* under the headline *DJ Flaunts King Kong Ding Dong Morning After Acquittal*. That would be some kind of bullshit.

But the drone didn't hover in front of his window. It crossed the street, stopped just before hitting the wall of the building, then rose up, hugging the bricks like a spider.

AmFetaMeen watched it, mesmerized. He knew he was still fucked up. Nothing was worse than a coke hangover. Except not being able to scare any up when you needed it. But he felt like the inside of an old shoe. His head hurt. His mouth tasted like dirty ass—the bad kind. But he couldn't stop watching that drone. He wondered if it had anything to do with the crowd of reporters camped out across the street last night. One of the mile-highers in that building must be in some kind of shit, he reasoned. Otherwise, why all the fuckers with the cameras and poor style sense milling around like they were waiting for the food bank to open?

AmFetaMeen scratched his ass, then saw the drone stop at the terrace at the top floor. It hovered, no doubt eyeballing something, and he remembered the telescope.

It was in the corner, with a bra and two pair of panties hanging off it that he didn't bother to clear away. He tilted it up and screwed the eyepiece into his socket. Everything was upside down—he never could get that fucker right side up, even when he rotated the thing 180 degrees—more bullshit. So he moved around to the side and refocused through the eyepiece. Now the image was at a 90-degree angle, which was good enough.

An old man stood on the balcony across the street. He looked fucked up. Like big-timey fucked up. He musta had a stroke or some shit because his face was making all kinds of weird expressions, like he was crying and coming all at once. And he was shaking. Holy fuck nuggets was he shaking. Like a dog taking a shit.

He turned his head. Saw the drone.

Reached out.

Then he grabbed his chest and took a step back and—

What the fuck?

The old man was gone.

Just.

Fucking.

Gone.

A red mist hung in the air.

AmFetaMeen backed up as the drone swung back across the street and out of sight over the roof above him.

Maybe he should call someone. Who? His manager? Fuck, no. The cops? Sure. The cops made sense. That's who you were supposed to call when bad shit happened, right? And being blown up was considered bad shit, no?

Then he looked around at the room—at the coke and booze and passed-out chicks—and decided that the last thing he needed was a bunch of cops poking around.

More bullshit.

Fuck it.

He walked into the kitchen, pulled a bottle of Gatorade out of the fridge, then went back to the bedroom.

But not before giving that bitch's titty a squeeze.

83

The Upper East Side

The insectine chirp of his cell phone woke him up and he rolled over, jamming his eye socket straight into Lemmy's snout. The dog licked him, then stretched as Lucas sat up.

"Thanks, dummy," he said, and reached over the dog for his phone.

It was Kehoe's number. Lucas thumbed the screen. "Dr. Page," he said with forced calm.

Just then, the doorbell rang.

"Why aren't you answering the door?" Kehoe asked.

"Because I'm answering the fucking phone." Lucas hung up and swung his legs out of bed. The sheet was wrapped around his prosthetic and the dog's weight kept it anchored, and Lucas almost spilled onto the carpet. "Jesus, dummy, move!"

Lemmy gazed over at him with big soulful eyes, then stood up and stretched, pushing all one hundred and twenty-five pounds in different directions for a few twangy seconds. Then he deigned to get off the bed.

Lucas lifted his arm off the stool beside the bed, snapped it in place, but didn't stand up; his ribs felt like they were connected to an African beehive. After a few deep breaths, he somehow made it to a standing position without falling over or throwing up. He refocused on the task at hand.

Why was Kehoe here?

If Whitaker was dead, he didn't want to go downstairs feeling like Mary Shelley's creation. His teeth were less swampy than yesterday morning, but he headed into the bathroom to brush out the funk. Once again, he was surprised at the battered character staring back from the mirror. But apparently people loved you for what was on the inside, not the outside. Or at least that's what all the screenwriters said.

By now Lemmy was downstairs barking at the front door.

Lucas pulled on a pair of jeans and a shirt that he didn't bother buttoning, then headed down to the main floor, trying to ignore that his eyes were burning like the batteries in his head were leaking.

He shooshed Lemmy away from the door and opened it.

Kehoe stepped in without being asked, followed by two of his men—one was the monstrous Otto Hoffner, who looked like he had just finished eating a breakfast of car doors. The other was not quite as large, but he made up for it with exaggerated body language and a scowl.

Lucas stood in the entry with his hand on the doorknob. "Did I say *come in*?"

Hoffner and his companion ignored Lucas and walked through the main floor, like a pair of directors trying to figure out where to put the camera. Or home invaders casing the joint.

Kehoe walked into the den and Lucas said, "What the fuck?"

Hoffner turned to Lucas as if he might be a threat and Lucas said, "I'm sorry, moron, is English your second language? I can speak slowly if you want."

From off to their left, Lemmy chimed in with a low-frequency growl that had Hoffner's hand unconsciously inching toward his holster.

"You shoot my dog in my house, you better save a second bullet for yourself." Hoffner took a step back.

"Page?" Kehoe called from the living room.

Lucas decided that he needed to cool off before he started screaming. "I have to take Lemmy out for a pee."

He passed not-Hoffner on his way to the back door and uncharacteristically let his emotions get away from him, swinging his metal hand into the man's thigh. There was a satisfying connection of aluminum with flesh and a grunt. *Fuck these guys.*

He sent Lemmy out into the yard and watched while the dog pulled his morning routine, complete with another chrysanthemum-destroying poop. It was back to raining now, and the small plot of grass was wet. Lucas realized that all kinds of unexamined emotions were bubbling up, not the least of which was a good dose of resentment. Last year Kehoe had polished off his Dr. Caligari routine to get Lucas back. And it had worked. Then he had done it again in Montauk last week. Again, Lucas had bought it. But not because of Kehoe's clumsy attempt at manipulation—no, he had gone back because he missed the work. He missed the way his mind fired up some inaccessible computational software that was available to him only out in the field. He missed the excitement and the stress and the fear and the whole fucking thing. But he refused to be used. Or lied to. And he wasn't going to let Kehoe pull any of that stuff on him again.

When the dog finished, Lucas waved him inside and wiped his paws down, gave him a liver treat from the big cookie jar, and asked him to go lie down on his pillow. Then Lucas went back to the den to rewire their relationship—he was going to put Kehoe in his place. And then throw him and his two flunkies out.

Back in the den, Kehoe was scanning the library.

"Is Whitaker all right?"

Kehoe waved the question away. "Did you go see William Hockney last night?"

Lucas stared at him. "Why?"

"Answer the question."

"My downtime is none of your business."

"I'll take that as a yes."

"You can take that as whatever the fuck you want. Why are you here, Brett?"

"I have a man who can place you at Hockney's last night. You remember a big ugly guy? Head like Shrek?"

He couldn't stop himself from saying, "Beauty's on the inside."

It was evident from Kehoe's expression that he wasn't in the mood for any bullshit. "Hockney's dead. Someone blew him up."

Lucas let the information surge through his chips for a few thumps of his heart, and it upset him. He and William Hockney were not friends. And he most definitely saw the world through a different prism than the old man did. But he hadn't deserved to die like that. At least not for any reason Lucas could think of. That he had known Mrs. Page no doubt added some undeserved weight to the news of his death.

But at least this meant that Kehoe wasn't here to deliver bad news about Whitaker. "You fired me, Brett."

"I was wrong. You were right. It wasn't only Frosst. And it wasn't William Hockney. There's someone left."

"Maybe Hockney committed suicide." He hated himself when he got like this, but sometimes he gave in. "Why are you here, Brett?"

"Why were you at Hockney's?"

"I wanted to talk to him."

"It doesn't look good that you were there, Luke."

"Maybe you should go next door."

Kehoe looked perplexed. "Why?"

"Because maybe someone there gives a shit what you think." He headed into the kitchen.

"Where are you going?" Kehoe asked.

"I can't deal with any more of your stupidity until I've had a coffee."

Kehoe followed him. "How long were you at Hockney's?"

"Ask Shrek."

"I'm asking you."

"Look, get a crew down here, swab my hands. My suit from yesterday is still upstairs. See if I test positive for nitrates, explosive residue, or any other chemicals besides Tylenol." Lucas was work-ing on filling a coffee filter.

"That's not why I'm here, Luke. You didn't kill Hockney."

Lucas didn't bother boiling water for tea—Kehoe wouldn't be staying long. "How can you be so sure? I had both opportunity and motive."

"You have motive only if you believe that he ordered Frosst to come after you and Whitaker. But you already figured out that he didn't—which was why you and I locked horns."

The coffeemaker started wheezing. "There was no locking. You held all the power. And now you can power your ass out of my fucking house."

Kehoe leaned against the counter beside Lemmy's bowl and the dog got off his pillow, expecting breakfast. "There's an old apho-rism that says when you hear the sound of hooves, your average viewer expects horses, not zebras—"

Lucas thought back to the antique club chairs at Hockney's last night, and he suddenly felt sick.

"But you? You expect John Cleese and Eric Idle and coconut shells."

"And here you are."

Lucas walked over to Lemmy's place mat on the floor beside the fridge and picked up his steel bowl. He was supposed to wash it but he wasn't in the mood for doggy maid service. He filled it with six scoops of health pellets, added some warm water, then put it back on the floor. Lemmy was laser-focused on the bowl, and a line of drool itsy-bitsy-spidered out of the corner of his mouth to the tiled floor. Lucas said, "Okay, dummy," and the dog lunged forward.

Lucas turned back to Kehoe. "What happened to Hockney?"

"Someone planted a mine on his terrace. Placed it between the tiles."

"A mine? As in a *land mine*?"

"An S-mine, to be specific."

"What's an S-mine?"

Kehoe held out his hand and Hoffner came into the room— keeping an eye on Lucas—and placed a paper in it. "It's a device that arms when it's stepped on. When you step off, it shoots up and detonates at about three and a half feet, dispersing shrapnel. The results are pretty standard. From what we can figure, Hockney stepped on it last night sometime after you left. It didn't detonate until just after six-thirty this morning." He held the paper out.

Lucas took the page. It was a spec sheet on a specific S-mine. Lucas scanned the basic details, then looked at the technical information, picking out load, timer settings, and chemical composition—as Kehoe had said on the beach a million years ago, it all came down to physics and chemistry. Lucas handed the page back. "That thing's meant to be buried—how do you hide it on a slate deck?"

Unlike the late Samir Chawla, Kehoe did not need to consult notes. "The slate tiles were on a bed of sand. The mine was planted at the transept where four tile corners intersected. The perp hit the corners with a hammer and snapped them off—we found them in one of the planters. Then he scooped out some of the sand and hid the mine."

Which seemed like a lot of trouble to Lucas; with Hockney's fondness for secret buttons connected to liquor cabinets, Lucas could think of less complicated ways to blow the man up—just wire up his Japanese whiskey and wait for cocktail hour. Or just load his ridiculous espresso maker to blast through the roof. There were a lot of less complicated ways to kill the guy. Which again meant that this was personal.

"He stood on that thing all night long?" He remembered Hockney's hip and couldn't help but feel a little sympathy for the old man. "And the mine?"

"Manufactured by ENF—just like the C-4 we've been finding. But we're still collecting evidence."

In this particular instance, Lucas knew that the word *evidence* was a euphemism for *pieces*.

Lucas poured coffee into his *World's Greatest Dad—from world's greatest kids (and Hector)! WE LUV YOU!* mug.

"The C-4 in all the IEDs came from ENF. What does that tell you?"

Lucas raised the mug to his lips. "That whoever is doing this has access to Hockney infrastructure." Lucas felt himself getting sucked back in and he tried to put the brakes on, but the questions were starting. "We had that contraption at the Guggenheim; the two cell-phone-activated IEDs at the internet hubs; the farm in Medusa; the explosions in Forest Hills, Brooklyn, Hoboken, and Staten Island; the humidor at Makepeace's; the bomb at Saarinen's; the briefcase bomb at the FBI; and the land mine at Hockney's. That is a pretty big lexicon."

"Are you going to come back?" Kehoe didn't quite sound like he was begging. But he didn't quite sound like he wasn't, either.

Lucas took a sip of his coffee. "That depends."

"On?"

"Am I working for you this time, or are you working for me?"

84

26 Federal Plaza

Kehoe was at his desk, and for the second time in less than twelve months, found himself acting as his own lead agent on a case because the SAIC had been killed. He was taking notes when Otto Hoffner came in and told him that he had a call from the Manhattan medical examiner's office. He put down the big fountain pen and picked up the call.

"Dr. Marcus, Brett Kehoe."

Marcus didn't bother with formalities. "I found something interesting regarding William Hockney's murder—he had a heart attack just before he was murdered." Marcus had been the ME for Manhattan through six presidential administrations and two bypass surgeries.

"That's a lousy coincidence."

"It wasn't a coincidence."

Kehoe leaned back, as if better posture would somehow clarify things.

Marcus coughed once, then said, "He suffered from long QT syndrome, which required a pacemaker. He had a Johnson

Medical EKJ06 installed at Cornell two years back—I checked. The unit was destroyed in the explosion, but the memory chip was salvageable and we hooked it up to a diagnostics computer to see if it could tell us the exact time of death."

Marcus paused, and Kehoe knew it was for effect. Everyone fancied themselves David Caruso these days. "And?" Kehoe said.

"And 3.4 seconds before the explosion was triggered, his pacemaker caused atrial fibrillation, effectively sending him into an immediate infarc."

"Meaning?"

"Meaning he was standing on the mine, and his pacemaker caused a heart attack that in turn forced him to step off of the mine, causing it to detonate."

Kehoe sifted the information. "Why would it do that?"

"It wouldn't. There is no external force—including a direct hit from an electromagnetic pulse—that could cause that sort of malfunction. There is so much redundancy built into these units that they are—*pardon the expression*—bombproof. I've had linemen working for Con Ed come in here after sucking on 7,200 volts and every organ in their body is destroyed. Skin is perforated; shoes are melted; brain is fried. But the pacemaker is still plug-and-play. I've never seen one shit the bed under *any conditions,* unless the unit itself suffered direct trauma, like a bullet—and three thousand of these come through my office every year. When we pulled the log on this one and ran the code, we found a group of commands that shouldn't be there."

"So it *did* malfunction."

"No. These things receive software updates automatically—like your phone. They also send feedback to the hospital so a doctor—or I should say a medical algorithm—can analyze the data and make the appropriate adjustments. All in real time. But in Mr. Hockney's case, the computer at the hospital sent malicious code."

"I don't understand."

"The software manager at Cornell intentionally sent code to William Hockney's pacemaker that caused him to have a heart attack."

"And you can prove this?"

"The data is in the memory card; this is not speculation."

"So William Hockney wasn't killed by that mine?"

"He was killed by that mine. But only because it detonated before he finished dying from a myocardial infarction that was intentionally triggered by software."

85

Columbia University

When Lucas pushed the door to the lab open, Bobby Nadeel and Caroline Jespersen were both seated at one of the two long tables. Jespersen's head was down and she was snoring in a way that men think is cute and women leave relationships over. Nadeel was deep in the zone and he didn't even look up.

They were in the basement, where the cerebral cortex of the university was housed in a grid of air-cooled passages. The next-generation computational reactor boasted enough firepower to model the most complicated mathematical problems man could conjure. The hardware was on par with that of the Pentagon, purchased through the generosity of a well-funded alumni endowment coupled with a public outreach program to technology companies interested in the next crop of think-tank impresarios and future titans of the tech world.

It looked like every available whiteboard in the building had been dragged into the lab and corralled across the front of the room. There wasn't a square foot of white space left on any of them—

the surfaces were tattooed with three miles of red Sharpie and upholstered in hundreds of Post-its. But by the angle they were at, Lucas could tell they were dead ends; evidently their digital haystack still hadn't paid out—sometimes you had to get your hands dirty to find meaning in all the nothing and even then there was always the risk of low returns.

Lucas felt lousy. He was standing, but so were the whiteboards; verticality did not prove sentience. And he felt like he could use a hit with the paddles.

"Dr. Page?"

"I'm sorry, what?" Lucas looked over at Nadeel and the kid was staring at him as if he had just eaten a handful of car keys. Caroline Jespersen was behind him, in the midst of waking up.

"Are you okay?" Nadeel asked.

"I'm just a little tired."

"You need a coffee or something?"

Lucas took out the bottle of Tylenol. He tried to get the lid off, but he couldn't line up the little arrows, so he laid it on its side on the desk with his good hand and gave it a karate chop with his prosthetic. The cap zinged across the room. Along with half the pills. He scooped up a few, tossed them into his mouth, and looked up as he chewed them to see the kids eyeing him as if he were a lunatic. He said, "Defective cap."

The space was on loan from the computer lab supervisor, a woman named Cecile Rasmussen. Lucas's star appeal was a big factor in the school's fund-raising apparatus, and he never had trouble getting access to the system—bestselling books and appearances on the late-night talk-show circuit had their advantages.

Lucas knew that if he didn't sit down, he would fall down, so he pulled one of the chairs over and slowly ratcheted in so as not to jar his system. Everything felt like it was held together with rubber bands and luck, and he was worried about adding new injuries to the already lengthy roster. "Have you connected those last five bombing victims?"

Nadeel was smart and creative, but Jespersen had an innate subtlety when it came to algorithms—which was a skill that you couldn't teach. Nadeel could sort data, but he needed Jespersen to set him up with the tools.

Nadeel reached into the forest of Coke cans on the edge of the desk and shook a couple until he found one that still had some life in it. He took a slurp that emptied the can, put it down, and gave Caroline the stage with a wave of his hand. "Caroline will tell you everything you need to know about the Jackson Five."

Jespersen stretched, yawned, ran her fingers through her hair, then wiped her index finger across her teeth—all while obviously making an effort not to stare at Lucas. He could tell she was about to ask him if he was okay, but he glared at her and she went straight to work. "Um, yeah, uh, okay—you couldn't find five people less connected if you used an algo to keep them apart. I mean, the random p-value alone makes this statistically impossible, which makes no kind of practical sense for five men in the same age group, with the same type of education, in the same general geographical vicinity. We know that each one participated in the bombings, at least circumstantially. And it appears as if they participated in the bombings independently of one another. Which is not possible. So, like you taught us, we started to look for what wasn't there." Jespersen sounded as if she had figured out a trick question. "And what wasn't there was a social media presence."

Jespersen picked up a cup of what had to be cold coffee and pulled the lid off. She took a jolt, tamped the lid back down with her palm, then spun her laptop around. "We banged our heads against this one all night and couldn't put them in any sort of a mutual orbit. But their lives mimic one another almost completely, and the weird part is they do it in their respective vacuums, culminating with all four of them being murdered on the same day in the same manner, almost at the same time—so they all follow the same pattern."

Jespersen track-padded a command into her laptop, and the wall of monitors came to life in one massive blink of pixelated spreadsheets—the digital equivalent of colored yarn and push-pins. "Up until two years ago from last April, the Jackson Five were all active on social media. Nothing over the top—no Instagram influencer bullshit, no YouTube channels—just regular *Here's-me-and-my-friends-white-water-rafting* kind of stuff. Then it just stops. Dead."

"Just like that?"

Jespersen snapped her fingers. "As if they all found some kind of new religion." She cycled through the spreadsheets she had up. "So here we have the Jackson Five. All five share the same basic profile: males in their early twenties. Donny Rich, twenty-five, blown up in the house he shared with his mother in Medusa. Steven Whiteman, twenty-three, blown up in his bedroom at his parents' home in Forest Hills, Queens. Tony Iannantuono, twenty-seven, blown up in his apartment in Hoboken, New Jersey. Barnabas O'Hare, also twenty-four, blown up in his basement apartment of a single-family home in Castleton Corners, Staten Island. Enrique Cristobel, twenty-five, blown up in his apartment in Brooklyn."

"All had science backgrounds in high school. All good students. All got awards that were published on their school websites." Jespersen pointed up at one of the spreadsheets. "All start university in September, all in the Northeast. All start four years ago except for Iannantuono, who started law school five years ago. Different schools, but there is overlap in four of the five subjects' choice of fields: Rich in cellular botany at SUNY Cobleskill; Whiteman in crop metabolism at Cornell; Cristobel in biodiversity management at Guttman Community College; and O'Hare in crop diversity management at Houghton. Iannantuono is the outlier at Albany Law School.

"None of them had girlfriends. I mean, not a single one. And

I'd bet we're looking at incels here." She looked up at Lucas, who was shaking his head. "What? It's a thing."

"Go on."

She let out a sigh, then went back to the screen. "In April thirty months back, all five go to Las Vegas. They stay at different hotels. Facebook pages show typical student type stuff. Whiteman went to a show—a Beatlemania revival, which is apparently still a thing; Iannantuono went to a car museum; O'Hare went to the Ralph Lauren store; Rich didn't have a Facebook page, so we have no idea what he did. Cristobel played the slots a lot."

Jespersen said, "And from here on out, not one of them has a digital footprint."

"Nothing?"

"They might as well be dead. All five paid for and kept top-shelf internet service with unlimited data plans, but not one ever visited a single website. Never accessed an email account. Never Googled a single thing. Didn't own cell phones. They just stopped participating in their online lives."

"Tor browsers?"

Jespersen shrugged. "Probably. I don't have access to their accounts at their internet service providers, but it's a safe assumption."

Nadeel came back with "How the actual fuck is that even possible? It's like they occupied different universes in the same headspace. Like she said—you'd have trouble finding five other people on the planet less connected than they were—it's as if their lives were intentionally scripted to be unrelated. It's a statistical impossibility."

Nadeel got up and stood in front of the screen. "Three of the four drastically change their career trajectory within two weeks of their trip to Vegas. Rich transfers to computer programming; Whiteman drops out of school and gets his commercial driver's license;

O'Hare goes to a mechanics school specializing in commercial generator repair and maintenance. Iannantuono stayed in law.

"Whiteman was hired by the company that organized the event at the Guggenheim—he's the guy who delivered both the snowmakers and the foil bags. The FBI interviewed him, but there was absolutely nothing to suggest that he was in any way involved. Iannantuono was an intern at Stogner, Pruitt, and Sterlingshires—he was Alexander Stogner's assistant. He was interviewed by the FBI, but he lived such a normal life that they gave him a pass—he's probably the guy who put the bomb in Stogner's briefcase, who was blown up in the FBI building with Seth Hockney. O'Hare worked for the company that maintained the generators at the internet hub on Hudson Street—he was in the building nine different times in the past year. And we know that Cristobel was the UPS driver who visited Jonathan Makepeace on the day he was blown up—so it's safe to assume that he put the bomb in the humidor. Rich never left his hometown."

Lucas saw the pieces slide into their respective places. "So the only thing the FBI could have found that connected them was their deaths. Before that, they were not connected in any real-world way."

Jespersen pointed at her laptop. "Except in Las Vegas."

"So something happened in Vegas." Lucas walked over to one of the monitors and leaned in close, focusing on one of the fields. "And now you're going to tell me that what happens in Vegas stays in Vegas?"

Nadeel started smiling.

"What?" Lucas's Spidey sense started tingling.

Nadeel nodded at Jespersen. "You tell him."

She clicked around on the keyboard and the monitors in the room blinked out, then came to life with a photo of a young man. He was in his mid-twenties and had the bland looks of the single dad/tow-truck driver love interest from every rom-com Lucas had been forced to sit through with Erin. There was nothing interesting about his features, and Lucas knew that if he closed his eyes, he wouldn't be able to remember his face.

"That's Mitchell Stahlberg," Jespersen said.

"And why am I looking at him?"

"Because he took the same trip to Las Vegas as the other victims—same arrival date, same departure date. He had the same general profile as the other five in everything from age to geographical locale. The day he returned from Vegas, he canceled all of his social media accounts. Before he went to Vegas, he was in environmental studies—specializing in watershed management. A week after his return home to Long Island, he switched over to police tech."

"So why haven't I heard of him before now?" Lucas reached out with his prosthetic hand, and his aluminum finger stopped before it touched the screen. A small arc of static zipped to his digit. "Where is he?"

"That's the thing..." Jespersen tapped on the keyboard and the images on the monitors changed to a newspaper article from a Long Island paper. There was a photo of a recreational vehicle on a beach somewhere. Most of the aluminum skin had burned away and the tires were melted; the only features that identified it as an RV were the blackened rims and framework.

"Mitchell Stahlberg blew up seven months after he returned from Las Vegas."

Lucas felt the gears on the machine meshing—the whole contraption was starting to feel like it would soon stand up on its own. The trick was in creating a little structural integrity, which happened only if you had the bearing walls in place.

From somewhere outside his time zone, Bobby Nadeel pinged. "What?"

Lucas looked up at the kid. "*What* what?"

"What are you thinking?"

"I'm thinking that we need to find out who these guys spent time with in Las Vegas."

"How do we do that?"

"Pack up your shit, we're leaving."

86

26 Federal Plaza

Otto Hoffner handed the tablet to Kehoe with the simple statement "Watch this."

It was a video file that had been paused—surveillance footage from one of the cameras overlooking William Hockney's rooftop terrace garden.

It was early morning, and the sun cast long shadows across the roof. Hockney was frozen in the frame, slightly screen left, staring in the general direction of the camera. The tile deck was wet, as were the rows of well-manicured shrubs lining the terrace. Patches of snow were scattered around in an irregular geometry, and some of the greenery was dusted with white.

Hockney was wet, and his clothes stuck to his body, outlining a lean frame and a long upper body. His hair hung into his eyes and the expression frozen on his face conveyed nothing but agony. At this point he had been standing outside all night and had suffered through rain and wind and snow.

The time stamp in the corner was stopped at what Kehoe knew

to be fifteen seconds before the old man's death. He tapped the screen and time began to unfold.

Hockney started shivering in remarkable clarity, and with the added element of movement to round out the image, it was impossible to miss the terror or the pain or the confusion. He had already been at this for seven hours at this point—more or less—and was probably in shock.

The seconds ticked off, and something offscreen caught the old man's attention. His eyes narrowed. He raised a hand. Pointed.

A small drone eased into the frame from the direction he was pointing. It hovered just beyond his reach.

The old man said something.

The drone wagged to the left, then banked back in a movement something like a dragonfly would make. The old man mumbled something else and the drone darted forward, as if threatening him.

But the old man didn't move off his footing—he was welded in place and probably couldn't have taken a step if he tried.

The drone was small, perhaps eight inches square, with some sort of a payload mounted on the front. It hovered in front of him, its focus unwavering.

William Hockney was crying now, big sobs that even without sound were horrid to watch.

And then he shuddered in place, as if his central nervous system browned out, and he clutched his chest.

The drone backed off, to the edge of the frame, and hovered in place.

William Hockney stumbled back in a single wooden stride.

Something beneath where he had been standing launched into the air, exploding from beneath the tiles. It moved too fast to see in any meaningful way.

There was a flash and the old man's upper torso disintegrated in a black mist. Chunks of wet meat splatted all over the frame. One of his legs stood on its own for a second before flopping over into a puddle.

Then the drone turned, disappeared out of frame, and the video stopped.

"What did I just see?" Kehoe asked.

Hoffner took the tablet back. "That's a hobby drone, sir. The guys downstairs identified it as an Aeromax T-221. It's sold everywhere from Amazon to B&H Photo. It costs about three hundred bucks. It connects to a cell phone, and it's relatively simple to use. It has a built-in camera, and you fly it by sight."

"What was that thing on the front?"

Hoffner smiled. "You don't miss much, sir. Our people say it looks like a charge of C-4, mounted into a lens shape for cutting—it was designed to direct the charge forward. It looks like it was large enough that if it had been detonated close enough, it would have cut his head off."

Kehoe leaned back in his chair. "So whoever put that mine on his terrace wanted to make sure he was dead by morning?"

"Looks like, yes."

He hated asking the obvious, because if his people had the answer to his next question, Hoffner would have told him. "If there's a camera up there, do we have footage of whoever planted that thing in the tiles?"

Hoffner shook his head. "The system records to the cloud. It's supposed to be on a thirty-day loop, but it was reset at midnight last night."

"So whoever killed Hockney had access to or was able to hack his security system."

"Looks like, yes."

Kehoe didn't say anything, but this was more proof that Page was right; a neo-Luddite wouldn't use a cell-phone-piloted drone any more than hack a security system. "Thank you, Otto."

Kehoe's desk phone lit up and he hit the speaker button without looking over. "Yes?"

"Mr. Kehoe, Dr. Page is here. And he has some visitors with him."

Kehoe looked up at Hoffner, who rolled his eyes—he and Page were not going to be friends any time soon. "What does that prick want?" Hoffner asked.

"For you to leave us alone, asshole," Page said from the doorway.

87

Kehoe was able to keep the surprise from his face, but Lucas knew him well enough to see it shimmering beneath the surface. He put down the printouts, took off his glasses, and did that thing with his fingers under his chin. "This is—" And he just stopped.

Lucas let the silence hang there for a few seconds before Kehoe came back with "What do you want?"

"I want you to put those kids in the pit and give them clearance. They found all that with off-the-shelf software and a custom-made algorithm. If they had clearance, they'd put your guys to shame." He smiled. "I mean even more than they did." Lucas had given Nadeel and Jespersen the hard drives that Calvin-Wade Curtis had delivered to his house the day he got out of the hospital. And even though the drives contained the entire digital history on everyone and everything connected to the bombings, that was all they contained: digital histories. Nadeel and Jespersen could cross-reference a lot of the data with real-world information, but they lacked clearance to do things like dig through employment records, government archives, or police files.

Kehoe clenched his jaw. Then he forced something inside him to relax, leaned back in his chair, and picked up his desk phone. "Bring them in."

Otto Hoffman escorted Bobby Nadeel and Caroline Jespersen into the office. Nadeel looked positively tiny beside the big man. Caroline was tall, almost six feet, but Hoffman had seven inches on her and outweighed her by a multiple of three.

Kehoe nodded and Hoffman disappeared as much as a guy the size of a vending machine can.

Kehoe stared at them. Then down at the printouts. Then over at Lucas. He leaned forward and put his fingers under his chin again. "We are going to give this a shot. But if there's any fuckery by either of you two, this little social experiment is over—is that clear?"

Jespersen swallowed and nodded. "Yes, sir."

Nadeel was too busy smiling to nod. "So," he asked, rubbing his palms together, "where do you keep the computers?"

88

Lucas took his time going through the police and coroner's reports on the death of Mitchell Stahlberg, former university student and visitor to Las Vegas the same time as the other men. The big difference between Stahlberg's death and the deaths of the five men who had been blown up was the timeline—Stahlberg died seven months after his trip to Vegas.

What Lucas needed to know was how Stahlberg was connected to the Magic Five.

The first few pages of the police report did not give him much more information than the photo of the burned-out RV that Jespersen had shown him back in the lab. The file began with the bored, lazy language of a police officer who had more important things to do (or at least some other place he'd rather be) than fill out forms on an apparent arson. The location was noted—a beach on the north shore of Long Island. The vehicle involved was described: an older recreational vehicle; apparently abandoned; set on fire within the two days preceding the report—probably by kids;

discovered by a couple walking their dog (names given). All basic five-W details.

It wasn't until the second page, upon discovery of a body in the wreckage, that the handwriting became more cramped, frantic, as if something strange was indeed afoot in Denmark.

A quick search of the RV registration cross-referenced with missing persons reports led the officer—one Jamal Rice—to deduce that the body probably belonged to one Mitchell Stahlberg of Sheepshead Bay. Two phone calls to his parents, followed by one to his dentist, had Rice convinced that he had found Stahlberg's corpse. DNA swabs came back five days later, confirming the identity.

The Nassau County Police sent their SCI unit, who discovered that the fire had been caused by a rupture in the line from the propane tank to the stove. They assumed that the camper ignited when Stahlberg lit a cigarette (according to his parents, Stahlberg was a smoker). Foul play was not suspected.

The real insight in the file came when Chad Rice interviewed Stahlberg's parents—Mickey and Judy. They outlined their son's recent bout of anxiety and involuntary mental health evaluation. Which led Rice to interview a state-appointed psychiatrist, one Dr. Alan Abramov, who had handled Mitchell Stahlberg's evaluation at the Rockland Psychiatric Center, two weeks prior to his death.

The police report bullet-pointed Dr. Abramov's findings, and there was no missing the clinical to-the-point nomenclature of the head-shrinking profession in the notes.

Mitchell Stahlberg, male, 25, unmarried, was brought into the Rockland Psychiatric Center by his parents, who were concerned about his mental health. When he was admitted, the patient was in an acute agitated state. He repeated that "they" were out to get him because he had betrayed them, but refused to provide specific details as to who "they" were, or why they would want to "get him." He was treated with 5mg of haloperidol IM for acute paranoid anxiety and calmed down relatively quickly. Since the patient agreed to clinic follow-up later in the week, and weekly follow-ups after that, we discharged him on 1mg of Haldol by mouth twice daily.

Stahlberg's parents insisted that even though their son was obviously sick, he kept the family RV in which he was found in top shape. He had rebuilt the vehicle with his father, a mechanical engineer, and they tested and double-tested the systems all the time. The parents were certain that his death was not accidental.

And yes, he had suffered from bouts of mental illness since he was a child. But they had always taken him for treatment. He took his medication. He had lived a normal—some would say exemplary—life. He had been cured for almost a decade now—there had been no cracks in his composure for almost eight years. They believed that his troubles were behind him.

But Mrs. Stahlberg's statement showed that their son was coming unraveled. He had insisted that he was part of a secret group that was going to destroy society in order to rebuild it out of the ashes; the group communicated via secret email accounts and pre-paid cell phones that were left on his doorstep at night; a mastermind ran the group, and he had an army out there, on the verge of their first strike, when they would lash out at technology, showing their fellow man that the path forward was to side with humanity, not artificial intelligence, technology, or mechanization.

Lucas closed the file and sat there, staring at the folder for a few moments as the pieces swirled around the drain in his head in ever-tightening circles.

Stahlberg came off as a paranoid nut.

A secret group that was going to destroy society?

They communicated via secret email accounts and burner phones?

A mastermind ran the group?

And Lucas remembered the Joseph Heller quote that *just because you're paranoid doesn't mean they aren't after you*. Even Freud had famously said that *the paranoid are never entirely mistaken*.

Maybe it was a coincidence. Maybe there had been a leak in the propane line. Maybe the kid *was* a paranoid nut.

But he had been in Vegas and he fit all the other criteria, right down to the manner of his death.

So how was he connected to all of this? Where did he fit in?

Because there was only one logical reason the rest of those men had been killed—they had completed their parts in the crime.

So had Stahlberg's part been completed?

Or . . . was it something more obvious? Had he gotten cold feet? Had his mental health become an issue?

Because there was one certainty about Las Vegas: all six of those men—who were students at the time and really only kids—had been recruited.

Which led to the next question on the conveyor belt: *By whom?*

Lucas was still staring down at the file when Otto Hoffner came into the office, moving surprisingly fast for a man of his volume and mass.

Hoffner snapped his fingers. "You need to come downstairs."

89

Lucas moved as quickly as he could, which he noted with some pride was slightly faster than he had been able to manage yesterday. He wasn't able to keep up with Hoffner, but the big man hadn't been able to lose him, so that said something about determination. He was led to one of the isolated computer rooms—the ones they usually used for tactical operations—where Hoffner opened the door and waved him in.

There was a single large desk with three keyboards lined up on the otherwise empty surface. In place of a wall, a floor-to-ceiling bank of monitors was acting as one screen surface. The visual real estate was taken up by a single image—a YouTube video on pause.

Kehoe was standing behind Jespersen and Nadeel, and there was no missing the concentration or purpose in his posture.

Nadeel swiveled around in his Aeron, smiling like the only one who got the joke. He pointed at the OLED wall illuminating the room. "I did what you said, and ran through all eight hundred and twenty-six conferences that were happening in Las Vegas that weekend in April, two years back. Half of them were retail fairs—

carpets and cars and stuff like that—so I back-burnered those. I went after anything that might tie in with the general dynamics of this case—medical conferences, insurance conventions, industry and commercial recruiting pushes. And I found this TED Talk."

Kehoe looked over at Lucas; there was no missing that he was impressed. Or at least not regretful for allowing Nadeel and Jespersen into the fold.

Nadeel raised his finger over the keypad, moved it in circles as if conjuring magic from the keys, then hit the return button with his index finger.

Everyone looked up at the screen.

It was professional video, and even on the ten-by-fifteen-foot display, was relatively clear and unpixelated, without visual noise in the dark areas. The setting was an auditorium of indeterminate proportions—the walls and ceiling were blacked out, giving the illusion of vastness. The single word *TED* was illuminated in red, floating somewhere in the background.

The camera swung around, panning over the audience. It was difficult to see the crowd—they were in the dark.

The camera panned back, and a man walked onstage. He was about twenty-five and attired in Silicon Valley formal wear—jeans and a hoodie, both black. He was wearing a headset with a tiny microphone. The applause was perfunctory and polite.

The speaker went into his routine. "My name is Dr. Zachary Sarkozy, and I want to welcome you to my TED Talk on the unintended consequences of failing to prepare for the coming AI revolution."

"Do I have to sit through this?" Lucas was already bored with Sarkozy's lazy delivery.

Nadeel held up his hand. "Okay, forget this tard. Take a look at this." He stopped the video, minimized the screen, then brought up another piece of tape from the same talk.

The new piece of video was paused. It was an image of the

crowd, in the dark and barely discernible as anything other than a group of seated people. "Right there," Nadeel said, pointing at what was the dome of a human head but could as easily have been a sock puppet.

"There *what*? I don't see shit."

"Which is why *I* am here. I started out on the FBI's software, which for some arcane reason is Adobe Premiere Pro, which is not bad off-the-shelf software if you have no imagination." Nadeel side-eyed Kehoe, but no one caught it except Lucas. "It's clunky and has absolutely zero finesse." Nadeel brought the editing console up. "But I downloaded a plug-in my friend Ronnie coded—after Mr. Kehoe's people here were nice enough to open a hole in their firewall—and it sped things up." He highlighted the area of the screen he had pointed at, then fiddled with the brightness, and it was as if a spotlight came on, illuminating a ghost.

Lucas stared up at the wall of image. He would never forget the man he was looking at—the last time they met was in an explosion that had cooked one of them. And nearly killed the other. "That's Benjamin Frosst."

Nadeel was grinning and nodding. "It gets better." He highlighted the figure to Frosst's left, and once again cranked the luminance, converting the form from a shadowy outline to an identifiable human quantity.

There was no missing the high cheekbones, the perfectly groomed hair, or the billionaire tailoring in the gray wool jacket and purple pocket square—William Hockney Jr.

"William Hockney Jr. and Benjamin Frosst attended a TED Talk at the same time our guys were in Las Vegas?"

Nadeel nodded. "It gets better. After finding those two guys, I ran the rest of the crowd through the in-house facial recognition software, but again, your FBI friends are a little behind the times. So once again with their permission, I downloaded a patch that upped their horsepower and I found these—" He pulled up six separate video templates. All were paused on a darkened crowd, a single attendee highlighted in a red circle. Nadeel clicked on all six images—one after another—and the darkened outlines once again morphed into discernible human faces.

They all sat in different parts of the auditorium, but there was no mistaking their identities. "I give you the Jackson Five, along with Mitch Stahlberg. Which I guess makes them the . . . Jackson Six? Which definitely doesn't sound as cool. But you get the point."

Steve Whiteman—the driver for the event organizer who delivered the foil bags to the Guggenheim. Blown up the day Whitaker and Lucas were coming back from their visit to Medusa with C-4 manufactured by ENF.

Tony Iannantuono—the intern at Stogner, Pruitt, and Gibson—who probably handed Alexander Stogner, Seth Hockney's lawyer, his briefcase the morning he flew to be interviewed by Samir Chawla. Iannantuono had been blown up in his apartment in Hoboken.

Barnabas O'Hare—the mechanic with the maintenance company that handled the generators at the internet hub on Hudson Street. He had disintegrated in his basement apartment of a single-family home in Castleton Corners, Staten Island.

Enrique Cristobel—the UPS driver who had visited Jonathan Makepeace at his apartment on Fifth Avenue the morning he had been blown up. Cristobel had also been blown up with C-4 manufactured by ENF.

Donnie Rich—who worked with a text compactor for the local agricultural board in Upstate New York and whose foot had been found dangling on a barbed-wire fence inside a tube sock and a Croc like a Christmas ornament for a vivisectionist with poor fashion sense.

Mitchell Stahlberg—who had been subjected to an involuntary psychiatric evaluation because he believed that he had been recruited by a secret cabal. And had been cooked to death in his family's RV.

Lucas looked at the faces of the dead staring back at him from the screen. Six young men who had gone to Las Vegas; six young men who had somehow been recruited that week; six young men who had all participated in the bombings; six young men who had been erased from the planet—five using C-4 manufactured by ENF, a company owned by the Hockney brothers.

In the same room with William Hockney Jr.

And Benjamin Frosst.

Nadeel minimized the images, leaving the giant YouTube video frozen in place. Lucas walked around the desk, and came face-to-face with William Hockney Jr. and Benjamin Frosst sitting in the front row of a TED Talk two and a half years back on a weekend that all indicators dictated was a fateful moment in the bombing timeline—the actual genesis point where whoever had been planning all of this had crossed the line from theoretical to practical.

Lucas lifted his aluminum hand to the screen, and even though he couldn't feel it, he could hear the sizzle of spark building up as he reached for William Hockney Jr. His anodized finger was half an inch from the OLED surface when an arc of electricity jumped the gap and there was a loud pop.

He thought about the way the bombings had been laid out, about that neo-Luddite letter. He thought about Seth and William Senior's plans for their empire; about Jonathan Makepeace; about Horizon's golden boy, Saarinen, and the jealousy that had fostered; about the C-4 that came from ENF; about William's getting blown up on his balcony; about Seth and his lawyer and Special Agent Chawla and the bureau lawyer being vaporized in the conference room; about Frosst coming after him and Whitaker. All of it pointed to one single person, and it was pure Freudian.

From somewhere behind him, Kehoe said, "The prince wants to be king."

90

Lucas was comfortably packed into the Corbusier cube chair in Kehoe's office. His adrenaline levels had dropped off and the resulting imbalance in his chemical mix was making him sleepy. Which he was trying to counteract with another coffee. Bringing the total for today to ten? twelve?

The war room looked like it was operating at double-speed out beyond the glass wall, as if the HVAC system was pumping oxygen into the building, and no one moseyed, spoke slowly, or sat still.

Kehoe was in one of the terrarium conference rooms across the hall, and Lucas watched him pace the space, working things out in his own inimitable way. The people around him were popping with the same electric juice as he posed questions, coaxed answers, and fed off input.

Nadeel and Jespersen were just outside Kehoe's office, quietly occupying a pair of Herman Miller chairs. Jespersen's head was back, her eyes closed, and she was breathing in a deep rhythmic cycle that said she was sleeping. Nadeel had his hands on his laptop and his knees were bouncing up and down as if Buddy Rich had hijacked his central nervous system.

Kehoe had set every known—and some unknown—American governmental agency at his disposal in motion in his bid to locate one William Hockney Jr. The State Department, DHS, and most likely the CIA had reached out to Chinese officials in their search for the younger Hockney. He was there somewhere; they just couldn't nail down the specifics. Which meant that his mischief wasn't yet contained.

All of his sisters and half sisters had been found—their presence was on file with the appropriate publicists, assistants, and various other handlers employed by the family. They may not have been involved in their father's businesses, but they were most definitely attached to his fortune. Most of them were in Europe, and one was in Palm Beach. None of them knew where he was.

But a man who now commanded an empire and traveled on a seventy-million-dollar aircraft could not stay lost for long, not even in China. There was a paper trail—or digital bread-crumb trail—out there; all they had to do was find the initial morsel. Or wait for Chinese officials to find it for them.

When Lucas had brought Nadeel and Jespersen in with the information that all six of the men had been in Las Vegas at the same time, two years ago last April, it had started a bout of digital necromancy. The bureau people did not like being outdone—again—by a pair of outside nobodies, and they had gone into full attack mode. They sifted through that week with every known investigative filter, intent on one-upping the two graduate students. But after two hours of fine-tooth-combing everything from hotel reservations to rental cars; credit card trails to bank transfers; email and social media posts—including cross-referencing the geotags on social media accounts of anyone even remotely involved in the bombings, including all 781 victims—they had not come up with a way to place William Hockney Jr. or Benjamin Frosst in Las Vegas. Which was quite the feat considering that Nadeel had them on video on YouTube.

Again, it was Nadeel who found it—he had somehow thought to check fueling logs for the independent depots at the Vegas airport. And that's where they discovered that William Hockney Jr.'s jet had spent five hours on the runway after it was juiced up coming back from Taiwan.

Both Frosst's and Hockney Jr.'s passports had been checked, but only as a perfunctory duty—as with many rules that didn't apply to the wealthy, customs and immigration was not a formal exercise, but merely a demonstration. So they were registered as having returned to the country, but their port of entry was listed as LaGuardia Airport in New York the next morning.

Lucas watched as Kehoe paced the room, pushing his people. He couldn't hear what was being said, but it wasn't hard to imagine, and Lucas was glad he had opted out because he needed some time alone in his own head.

Even though the average American had no idea who the Hockney family were, William Junior was a known commodity if you looked in the right publications. He had been interviewed in *Forbes*, *Bloomberg Businessweek*, *The Economist*, *The New York Times*, *The Wall Street Journal*, and countless other financial publications from the newsstand variety to the obscure. The one through line in his thinking was that he believed that the future for the Hockney empire lay not in taking large long-term risks that had the possibility of reshaping the financial landscape, but in taking smaller short-term risks and adapting *to* the financial landscape. It was a complete one-eighty from the way his father and uncle had built the empire, but one, he said, that took the present into account. He didn't come off as particularly bright or insightful, but he didn't need to be—he simply needed to be *smart enough*.

But was he smart enough to orchestrate the string of bombings? Trying to shift blame to a group of neo-Luddites certainly wasn't the move of a genius—although there were plenty of people out there who bought into the whole scam. And what purpose did all the subterfuge serve if the end goal was simply to assassinate his father and uncle? If William Junior had been working with Frosst, how hard would it have been for him to orchestrate their deaths? And how did blowing up the internet hub on Hudson Street fit in with things? If anything, it scooped a $4.5 billion hole in his inheritance.

Kehoe would not miss any of those things—his prime directive was finding bad guys, and much more of his operating system was devoted to it. And he had been at this for a lifetime now, so he would smell out the parts that were rotten. But was his own bias getting in the way? Was he so keen on finding the people responsible that he was grasping at a handful of nothing?

But it wasn't nothing. Not entirely. Sure, most of it was circumstantial. Sure, some of it didn't make sense. But so what? No crime was perfect. There were always mistakes, outliers, unforeseen results, errors in judgment, and personal tics baked into the cake. Things went south because the universe dictated that they were bound to. Not always. But enough of the time.

The image of Frosst and William Hockney Jr. sitting in the auditorium was certainly damning in its own right. It painted all kinds of pictures. But impressions without facts to back them up were nothing more than empty air.

Lucas finished the coffee and leaned forward to grab the insulated stainless carafe on the table in front of him. The junior agent who delivered the coffee had been kind enough to also bring a plate of sandwiches, but Lucas didn't feel like eating—he was too busy trying to find some energy in the caffeine.

William Hockney Jr. did not come across as a long game player.

Especially if he wanted less risk and more short-term investments. Would he have stretched this out to two plus years? If he had, it meant he had been planning it a lot longer. And he did not come off as a planner. And the one thing that the bombings had in common was planning—long-term planning.

Years.

How did William Hockney Jr. meet those six kids? And how did he sell them on the idea of blowing up innocent people? Obviously Stahlberg was a defect in the plan—he had started to melt down. But the rest? They had changed their lives and stuck to the plan for two years, which took dedication. And William Hockney Jr. did not seem like the kind of man to foster that kind of loyalty. The only motivation he had to offer was money. Sure, money made the world go round—it had been the cause of endless wars and untold suffering. But could five average American university students watch as bomb after bomb went off and not get cold feet? Lucas knew university students, and money might get them to take a step in that direction. Of course there were psychopaths out there, more than enough to go around. But what were the chances of finding five young men that fit that profile? After they had all been murdered, the bureau had interviewed family members and friends, and none had a history of mental illness. If anything, they were socially grounded—all of them believed in recycling and supporting environmental causes and reducing their carbon footprint.

Lucas realized that he needed a little perspective, because the investigation was listing to one side, and he didn't want to be on deck when it rolled over. He polished off the coffee and torqued himself out of the chair.

Nadeel looked up hopefully when Lucas came up to the row of chairs.

"I have to go out," Lucas said, but his attention was on Kehoe in the conference room.

Nadeel began to stand. "Can we come?"

Nadeel's voice rousted Jespersen, who opened her eyes and began a tight cat stretch. "Come where?"

"You stay here," Lucas said. "I may need something."

"What about your driver?" Nadeel said, looking around for the junior agent that Kehoe had assigned to Lucas in absence of Whitaker.

Lucas walked away without responding.

91

The Upper West Side

The sky was a seamless gray from horizon to horizon—the park to the east, a dense fog enshrouding the skyline to the west. Lucas stood out on the terrace, taking in the scene as if that might unlock some psychic box where objective truths were stored. He had no idea if being here would do any good, but he knew that every now and then it was enough just to nudge a few molecules to get a new perspective.

William Hockney had died up here after a night of standing on a mine. It was impossible not to imagine the man's terror and fear and, most of all, determination—which was the single truth Lucas could apply to the death. The terror and fear were imagined—reasonable assumptions when considering the reaction of a seventy-five-year-old man with a bad hip to being held hostage by an explosive device. But that's all those two components were—assumptions. But determination? That was a given. A fact. A truth learned from the evidence. Because he had most certainly stared down the Reaper out here for six or seven hours. And the old fucker would have won if the Reaper hadn't resorted to sneaky tricks and blown out his heart with a line of computer code.

Strips of yellow crime-scene tape hung off iron outdoor furniture, the tattered ends snapping in the wind. It was not difficult to discern the blast radius of the mine—the deck, wall, and banister were pockmarked from the shrapnel. The shrubs surrounding the explosion had taken a good hit, and branches and bark had been blown away. The cleanup crew had done a pretty good job, but there were specks of blood here and there and he knew that if he made an effort, he would find little pieces of William Hockney in the bushes, or brickwork, or cracks between the slate tiles.

Two uniformed police officers and a man from the Hockney security company—another orc—waited in the living room. Lucas's badge got him upstairs without the usual phone calls to superiors; right now everyone just wanted this case to be put to bed, and his presence meant a step in that direction. At least theoretically.

Lucas looked down at the deck, to the intersection where four heavy hand-milled tiles met. Their corners had been chipped away with a hammer and the sand beneath dug out to hide the mine. There was no great skill in the job—no great creativity or insight. But it had taken balls.

Which was where his doubts about Junior Hockney came in.

The man possessed bluster and the false security that often comes with being the squab of a billionaire. But for all the education and access to information he had been afforded, he gave the impression that he was barely good enough.

His father had sensed that as well.

Lucas had seen them interact precisely once, and the old man had mentioned him once during their talk the night his life had been taken, and in both instances William Hockney had unintentionally shown that he probably didn't have all that much respect for his son. It was an old story, one that began with Greek tragedy and had been a mainstay in fiction from Shakespeare to Faulkner ever since. And it always ended with the old man in a body bag while a bunch of stooges stood around, chanting, *The king is dead—long live the king!*

But all the great murderers of history and fiction had one thing in common—balls. They may have regretted it afterward, but they all had the courage to do the deed. And Lucas just didn't see Junior having it in him.

Lucas had watched the video where the drone crawled up over the stone banister and hovered in front of William Hockney. It had been set up with an explosive charge, effectively making it a warhead. So the drone pilot—or whoever had ordered the hit—wanted to make sure Hockney died.

But there was something else on the drone—a camera. Which made it perfect for taking a souvenir.

The hole in the deck where the four slate tiles met hadn't been repaired, and the tiles around it were dimpled with shrapnel hits—ball bearings traveling at supersonic speeds. They had torn the old man to shreds, and there had not been much left between his knees and the top of his skull. He hadn't simply been murdered, he had been obliterated.

Did Junior want the empire with such passion that he was willing to mulch his father into meat popcorn?

Lucas's phone buzzed and he answered without checking the number. "Dr. Page here."

"Where are you?" It was Kehoe, and there was no missing the buoyancy of triumph in his voice.

"Upper West Side. William Hockney's apartment."

"Get back here. Junior's plane just entered U.S. airspace about ten minutes ago, a hundred miles out of Southern California. It's on its way back from Beijing for his father's funeral. I'm having it intercepted."

"I'm on my way." He hung up.

Lucas looked down at the hole in the tiles. Then up at the crime-scene tape. And the entire line of internal dialogue he had just engaged in rolled through his head again. Something here was off. Junior didn't have it in him to plant mines. No fucking way.

So who did?

And whom did it profit?

Cui bono?

As Lucas turned to leave, he placed a call on the phone that was still in his hand. It rang twice before Bobby Nadeel answered. "Dr. Page, where are you? I think the shit has hit the fan here—they're high-fiving like they've all gone mental."

Lucas walked by the NYPD men and the orc who had accompanied him into the apartment—they were seated in the herd of William Hockney's zebra chairs, talking shop. Lucas nodded a thank you and headed for the elevator.

"Bobby," he said, "I need you to do something for me."

92

Major Louis "Frenchie" Chasseur looked up, and the abstract blip on his radar became a physical speck, twenty miles out. The speck rapidly grew into an indistinct blob that soon became the outline of a private jet—a Gulfstream V painted in red, with gold lettering on the side. The tail numbers designated it as Hockney 239—it was their bird.

Major Chasseur and his wingman, Captain Emmanuel "Flip" Rodriguez, were both stationed with the 144th Fighter Wing, out of the Air National Guard Base in Fresno. The 144th was tasked with protecting American airspace from Baja up through Oregon, and their purview mandated that they handle interception and escort of tagged aircraft to one of the Southern California airports, which in this particular case meant March Air Reserve Base.

Chasseur and Rodriguez piloted a pair of F-15Cs, each armed with four AIM-9X Sidewinder heat-seeking missiles and four AIM-120 AMRAAM radar-guided missiles. Backing up the array of heat-seeking and radar-guided missiles were the internal

M61 Vulcans—six-barrel air-cooled 20mm Gatling guns. But they didn't expect any resistance from the civilian aircraft they were intercepting. And even if the pilot of the jet refused to comply with their instructions, there would be no engagement—the plane had to land somewhere. And when it did, the pilot would face a list of charges. But that rarely happened; civilian pilots generally followed the rules.

Chasseur and Rodriguez had come around the GV from the west and were now closing distance from behind. They dropped speed to match its 488-knot cruising velocity, and eased into position—Chasseur coming up on the pilot's side of the aircraft, Rodriguez taking its six, a mile back.

They had been scrambled by an order from the FBI that had been bounced through the DOJ to the DHS, who in turn called NORAD, who had authority over the Air National Guard. The interception had been marked as Top Priority, and Chasseur wondered what was so special about this particular jet.

He looked over at the GV, which was about twenty yards to his right, and the pilot was looking at him through the cockpit window. Chasseur waved, and reached out on the standard frequency—121.5 MHz. "Hockney-two-three-nine, this is Griffin-two-one off your left side. Do you copy?"

The pilot of the GV immediately came back with "Griffin-two-one, this is Hockney-two-three-nine, we copy. What can we do you for, gentlemen?"

"Hockney-two-three-nine, we have been asked to escort you to March ARB."

Chasseur looked over and the pilot nodded as his voice piped in through the comm speakers in his helmet. "Understood Griffin-two-one. We'll inform our controller and amend our destination to March Air Reserve Base."

Chasseur radioed the interceptor controller, confirming that they had established contact with the Gulfstream and were escorting it in.

The NORAD controller confirmed that they received the information and wished Griffin-two-one formation a safe flight to the March Air Reserve Base.

Interception of William Hockney Jr.'s private jet was now complete.

93

The security presence was gone, and no one checked his ID between the front door and the elevator.

Lucas wondered if Nadeel would find what he had asked for. Because it was out there. Somewhere. A straight line that ran through the entire narrative. And it started before that week in Las Vegas two and a half years ago.

But how long before?

Because something was missing. And not just something that was supposed to be there—a *known unknown*. No, there was something else behind all this, and it was an *unknown unknown*—a factor that could not be anticipated because there was no way to predict its existence.

It wasn't money. Not entirely. Dollar signs might be a component of the whole thing, but it wasn't the fuel feeding the fire—that was something else. Something personal. It was all over the story, from the bombing at the Guggenheim to the murder of William Makepeace to the attempted murder of Timo Saarinen to the deaths of the Hockney brothers. All of the crimes had sadism mixed in, which meant that this was personal.

The elevator pinged, the door slid open, and Lucas pushed off the wall. The movement emphasized just how tired he was, and he bumped into the doorframe as he stepped out into the hall, the handcuffs in his pocket clinking off the brass doorjamb.

A few paces later he came to the door. He took a deep breath.

He then reached out and knocked.

94

Kehoe said, "Come in," without looking up. When ten yards of Otto Hoffner's shadow eclipsed the light spilling into the office from the war room, Kehoe lifted his head to see the big man accompanied by Page's two graduate students. Weren't they supposed to be on ice somewhere, waiting for Page to return?

He looked behind them, but Page wasn't there. "Yes?" he said.

Nadeel stepped forward, that same big porcelain grin of before upholstering his face. He had a laptop under his arm. "I found something you need to see."

Kehoe pulled one of the standard poses from his repertoire, leaning back in his seat, arms folded over his chest. "Okay."

Nadeel put the loaner laptop down on Kehoe's desk and went into his technological savant routine of massaging the keyboard with the speed, finesse, and accuracy of a concert pianist. He pulled up a group of PDFs and tapped the screen with his finger. "Dr. Page called me about twenty minutes ago and told me to look for this."

Kehoe looked at the forms the kid had pulled up but he didn't feel like peering through a forest of camouflage to find tiny details. "Just what, precisely, are you showing me, Mr. Nadeel?"

"These are insurance policies from 1997."

"Nineteen ninety-seven?"

"Yes, sir, mister—um, special agent in charge, sir."

"And these are relevant how?"

The kid flicked the screen again as if the answer were self-evident. "Dr. Page figured it out. Or I should say he figured out where to look. But he was right, of course. He always is," the kid said matter-of-factly. "Right there. Boris Goldman."

Kehoe looked at the policy, but there was nothing obvious to focus on. "And who is Boris Goldman?"

"A man who died."

"Let's do this the short way, Mr. Nadeel."

"Sorry. Yes. Okay, Dr. Page said that the answer was in what wasn't there, and what wasn't there was a perfect crime—the bomber had screwed up; he had left Dr. Saarinen alive."

Kehoe held up a hand. "The bomb he planted at the internet hub on Eighth failed to detonate."

"That was on purpose; Dr. Page told you that." The way Nadeel said it suggested that Kehoe was either foolish or stupid to think anything else.

"Let's assume you're right."

Nadeel gave him a look, and for an instant Kehoe thought Page was standing in front of him. Were all eggheads like this?

Nadeel continued. "He told me to take the anomaly apart. To go back and look at all the big electrical surges in Saarinen's life. And the largest blip on his x-axis was the death of his son." Nadeel's voice cracked and he took a deep breath to compose himself. "But she found it."

Kehoe shifted attention to Jespersen. She was tall, with a thin face that could have been an inspiration for Louis Icart, but she bit her bottom lip for a second and it wiped out the comparison.

"Saarinen's son died in February 2005—paramilitary rebels blew up the bus he was on, killing all thirty-six passengers and the driver. The bus was operated by Saarinen's employer—an NPO operating through the UN—TLR Solutions. I ran down all the paperwork that was filed with the state department, and the one common denominator was that all the victims had corporate insurance policies. I'm sure your people found the same thing."

There was no missing that she thought they hadn't, and Kehoe ignored the dig at his team.

She continued. "I went back through the insurance histories of all the people on that bus, and I was looking at the policy of one Michelle Lariviere, a French national. Her policy payout had gone into dispute because a week before she was murdered in the attack, she filed for divorce and had changed the name of the beneficiary from her husband to her mother. She had filled out and signed the paperwork, but hadn't mailed it in. The company eventually settled, paying out to the mother because Ms. Lariviere had the change of beneficiary witnessed. All this got me thinking. So I looked up every insurance policy on every victim throughout their lives, and I found something with Boris Goldman." She pointed at the screen. "When Mr. Goldman was in his first year at university, he purchased a term life insurance policy from a kiosk set up on campus. He made payments for three years but eventually let the policy lapse. But look at his beneficiary." She displayed Nadeel's facility with the keyboard as she brought up the form. "Right there."

Kehoe read the name of Boris Goldman's beneficiary. "Benjamin Frosst." He let it all sink in.

Nadeel nodded. "Which means that Timo Saarinen and Benjamin Frosst are connected by the attack that killed Saarinen's son in 1997."

95

Twenty Miles out of March Air Reserve Base, Southern California

Major Chasseur and his wingman, Captain Rodriguez, had escorted the inbound Gulfstream across the last swath of the Pacific before turning northeast, toward MARB. The flight, from first contact until now, had taken a little more than thirty-nine minutes at the GV's cruising speed of 488 knots, and they were twenty miles out from the base. There had been no further communication with the pilot of the GV—there had been no need for any.

"March tower, this is Griffin-two-one flight with you at twenty miles southwest, escorting Hockney two-three-nine."

The controller at MARB came back with, "Griffin-two-one flight, this is March tower, we have you and Hockney two-three-nine twenty miles southwest. No other traffic, runway two-two is in use, wind is two-five-zero at ten, call five miles final."

Chasseur heard the pilot of the Gulfstream acknowledge his landing instructions from MARB, and he looked over at the private jet.

Chasseur waved.

The pilot waved back.

Chasseur was turning back to his instrumentation when there was a bright flash, and the fuselage of the Gulfstream blew open behind one of the wings.

Chasseur was an experienced combat veteran, with more than four hundred combat sorties to his name, and he instinctively veered away from the other aircraft.

As he looked over, the wing peeled off, torquing the fuselage as it ripped away. The aircraft broke in two and hung in the sky for an instant as momentum momentarily beat out gravity.

And then it began to fall.

Chasseur keyed his mic. "March tower, Griffin-two-one— repeat: this is Griffin-two-one, escorting Hockney-two-three-nine, do you copy?" Hockney-two-three-niner, do you copy?"

"Affirmative, Griffin-two-one, we copy."

"Hockney-two-three-nine is going down. I repeat: Hockney-two-three-nine is going down. It was not fired upon. I repeat, *it was not fired upon.* It just . . . blew up." Chasseur began a slow arc around the falling aircraft, Rodriguez on his tail, a mile back.

"Copy, Griffin-two-one. We are initiating emergency response measures. What are your intentions?"

"Roger, March tower. We'll establish a cap and inform you of developments." Chasseur began to bank right. "Two-two, follow me."

As Chasseur started to circle around the fist of smoke that the wind was now breaking up, he saw the form of a man on fire cartwheeling through the debris field, toward the earth below.

96

After knocking, Lucas took a step back; since the trip through the Navigator's windshield, he looked like all the king's soldiers and all the king's men had been high when they slapped his parts together again and he didn't want to scare anyone.

In what could have been thirty seconds or thirty minutes, the big cantilevered panel swung in. Once again, Saarinen looked surprised to see him. "Dr. Page? You look—" He stopped. "Would you like to come in?" He wore a pair of gray pants and a white shirt with the cuffs rolled up. The little bulldog was in his arms, a canine beanbag with fat little feet.

Lucas limped over the threshold and followed Saarinen through the foyer, to the transept where the kitchen and living room intersected. Like the other night, the apartment was organized and staged, but this time Saarinen was not drinking his supper.

The man examined Lucas for a few moments before placing the dog down on the floor. The puppy sniffed at Lucas's ankle before waddling off to the kitchen, where Lucas heard him drinking. Saarinen gestured to the living room.

The coffee table had been moved up against the sofa where he had sat the other night, probably to give the dog room to play, but it prevented Lucas from sitting down. He swung around it and went to the big windows, drawn to the view. Tonight they were closed against the rain, and the city outside looked like a 1940s film—dark, shiny, and mostly blue.

"What happened to you, Dr. Page?" Saarinen's reflection in the window asked from somewhere behind and to his left.

"This is from my run-in with Mr. Frosst."

The reflection over Lucas's shoulder nodded. "Mr. Frosst was nothing if not sui generis. Much like yourself."

"Yeah, well—" And Lucas let the sentence die because he had no idea what he was supposed to say to that.

"Would you like some water?" The reflection asked. "Or aspirin?"

Lucas had to smile. "Do I look that bad?"

The reflection crossed its arms. "You look like you need a rest."

Lucas kept his focus on the museum across the street. The Hayden Big Bang Theater was lit up in suboceanic blues, the domed sphere within the glass cube straight out of a Crichton novel. Water rippled the surface, adding to the effect. "Yeah, well—" he said again.

Saarinen's reflection sat down in one of the Wassily chairs that faced the sofa, his body language conveying the same weary defeat it had the other night.

The reflection of the puppy crossed across the back of the room, from frame left to frame right, chasing a little rubber ball with too-big paws. "What can I do for you, Dr. Page?"

The rest of the murders had been perfectly executed; Saarinen's survival had been an outlier, an accident. The unpredictable element of luck had pooched the calculation. "I know it wasn't the Hockneys. And I know Frosst was only a component. And those five kids blown up on the day Frosst came after me? They were just subcontractors. Patsies. I want the person who set them in motion."

The reflection nodded thoughtfully. "Maybe it isn't the *who* but the *why* that you should be focusing on." Saarinen stood up and went to the Knoll console.

Lucas didn't bother nodding. "I already know the *why*."

The reflection pulled out a pair of highballs that looked like they had been carved out of ice. He placed them on the coffee table, then disappeared into the kitchen, where Lucas heard the freezer open. Saarinen came back with a bottle of vodka and a bottle of Perrier.

"And what is the *why*, Dr. Page?"

"All this time I've been asking the wrong question—*Cui bono?* The right question was *Who does this hurt?* This was about something much more personal than money; this was about revenge."

Behind him, the puppy came ripping back into the room, swerving after the ball like a fat little drunk trying to run down a panicked chicken. Saarinen said, "Come here, *pentu koira*. Let me put you away," and picked up the little bulldog and carried him offscreen.

Lucas stared out at the museum across the street for a few moments. It was amazing how different it looked from up here. It was all a matter of perspective—nudging the molecules.

Saarinen's reflection came back into the room and pulled the table away from the sofa, clearing a path for Lucas to sit down. Then he opened the vodka and poured himself a drink before sitting down. The whole exercise looked odd in reverse, as if something were wrong—more perspective at work.

Saarinen picked up his vodka and resumed his position in the chrome tube and black leather chair. He faced the sofa. "Revenge?"

Lucas turned his back on the city and put his hands into his jacket pockets—which took some of the weight off his shoulders. "Everything about these bombings, from the way the people in the

Guggenheim were incinerated to the way William Hockney stood on that land mine all night long, was personal. Someone was getting back at the Hockneys. Maybe even the world. And—"

Saarinen raised the glass to his lips and Lucas realized what had been wrong with the reflection a few seconds earlier—Saarinen was left-handed.

And, Lucas got it.

All of it.

He had missed it because he was too fucked up by the nature of the crimes to see through it. He told them to look for what was missing. And what was missing was his own impartiality.

He knew who had done all this.

And why.

"Are you all right, Dr. Page?"

Lucas turned toward Saarinen and took a step. His foot landed on the small silk prayer rug where the coffee table had been, and he felt the mechanical click of the mine as it armed.

97

26 Federal Plaza

"Where is Page?" Kehoe asked Otto Hoffner for the third time in as many minutes.

Hoffner stared at the phone in his hand. "He's not answering."

The analyst pit vibrated as the occupants reached out into the digital world via the computerized central nervous system. Each bit of data they collected chipped away the big question mark hanging in the air, and for the first time in days, progress eclipsed motion.

Kehoe stood at the back, watching his people with a pride he hadn't felt in several days. The communal brain of the room was focused on the murder of Saarinen's son in Nicaragua. Most of the visual real estate on the monitors displayed reports from the various departments that had investigated the attack.

The focal point was a photograph of the bus Jukka Saarinen had died on. It occupied a full wall, the grainy image close to a 1:1 scale. The vehicle was on its side, like a beer can that had been left in a fire for too long before being chopped open with a shovel. It was a crime-scene photo, not an image chosen for the evening news crowd—charred bodies were strewn about, arms and legs contorted from being cooked, skulls black, sockets empty, mouths frozen in white-toothed screams. It was impossible not to compare the bodies to those pulled out of the Guggenheim.

A passport image of Jukka Saarinen stared down from one monitor. He had been a handsome kid, barely seventeen, and had spent the last few seconds of his life being burned alive.

Boris Goldman had been an average-looking man with an average haircut and an average life that had ended in tragedy. Through his passport movements, they had put him in twenty-one different countries at the same time—to the hour—as Benjamin Frosst. It was Bobby Nadeel who found the link. "Got it!" he yelled and punched his laptop, which spun around before falling onto the floor, taking a pile of papers and two empty Coke cans with it.

Kehoe allowed himself to roll his eyes as the kid scrambled around on all fours, scraping up his mess. When he had the laptop back on the desk and open, he raised his hand to the central monitor like Babe Ruth pointing at the lights and typed with his free hand. "Check it."

The screen was split. The left-side half displayed a contemporary report filed by the State Department, listing the different groups that could have carried out the attack based on the specific weapon used—a light antitank weapon system. The LAWS rocket had been manufactured by Horsuch LLC, an arms manufacturer based in Ukraine. The right side of the monitor displayed an SEC form detailing a stock purchase.

Kehoe. Looked at the State Department memo, then at the SEC filing, then back.

But Nadeel just screamed out, "The Hockneys own the company that manufactured the rocket that killed Dr. Timo Saarinen's son and Benjamin Frosst's boyfriend."

98

Lucas stared down at his left foot.

Which held down a spring plunger.

That had forced a striker into a percussion cap.

And if he stepped off—

—it would launch half a kilo of high-yield shrapnel-wrapped explosives into the air.

Which would detonate.

Killing everything in the casualty radius.

Meaning him.

So he didn't move. He didn't panic. He didn't swear. What he did do was take a few deep breaths to oxygenate his blood and try to figure a way out of this.

Saarinen stared at him. "Nothing personal, Dr. Page. You just appeared at the wrong place at the wrong time." He waved a hand at Lucas as if he were highlighting a new refrigerator on a game show.

"Yeah, well everyone has to have a gift."

Saarinen drained his glass in two big swallows and stood up.

"I have to get my bag from the bedroom, and then I will be leaving. I doubt we will see each other again." Saarinen went into the bedroom with the slow unpanicked gait of a psychopath.

Lucas pushed everything out of his mind except the spec sheet on the mine that Kehoe had shown him—the propelling charge; the delay; the fuse well; the fuse; the detonator well; the detonator; the ball bearings.

And the big kaboom.

He reduced the device to its basic components—basic physics and chemistry.

The floor beneath his feet was poured concrete slab, which meant that it had been drilled out to accommodate the metal sleeve of the mine housing.

So there probably wasn't a lot of extra room around the sides of the device—no one dug out extra concrete if they didn't have to.

Which meant that if he could get the mine to detonate while still in the floor instead of launching it into the air, the blast would be directed straight up. Or, more precisely, in a fan-shaped pattern. Still deadly, but much less than the eighty-five-foot casualty radius.

But how the fuck could he get it to detonate in the floor? Could he get far enough away to make it matter?

And everything depended on it being the same kind of device. There were endless variants on devices designed to kill human beings, and even the smallest divergence changed the whole equation.

Think, you dumb fuck. There is a way out of this. There has to be.

And then his phone rang.

99

In an uncharacteristic display of indecision, Brett Kehoe stood staring at Otto Hoffner as the big man ran through the report that the Air National Guard had forwarded to the DOJ through NORAD.

William Hockney Jr.'s Gulfstream V had been on approach to March Air Reserve Base in California when it dropped out of the sky. One of the pilots escorting the jet reported that it had exploded, breaking up midair. The debris had plummeted into a residential area—Perris—most of it striking a Walmart parking lot. At least sixty people were reported dead. Fires were still burning. News teams were on site.

More of the same.

As if on cue, one of the monitors in the war room came to life with a smiling reporter standing in front of a burning Toyota. The chyron across the bottom said that her name was Marcy Middelbough, and she was reporting from Perris, California, on an apparent plane crash.

Only there was nothing apparent about it—the tail of the

Gulfstream V was behind her, rising out of a row of burning cars like a prop in an Ozzy Osbourne music video.

Kehoe thanked Hoffner and was about to head to his office for a handful of acetaminophen when one of the junior agents—a woman named Vasquez—came running over. "We found him, sir."

"Him, who?"

"Dr. Page. He's not answering, but the trace you put on his phone places him here," she said, holding up a piece of paper. "On West Eighty-First Street."

"West Eighty-First?" The address meant something, but Kehoe couldn't remember what it was. "Otto?" he said, turning to Hoffman, "what's on West Eighty-First Street?"

The big man's eyes dialed up to two o'clock as he engaged his recall. "That's where Timo Saarinen was staying. It's a Hockney property, sir."

Kehoe pointed at Hoffner. "We leave. Now."

100

"Your cell phone, Dr. Page."

Saarinen held out his right hand, palm up.

Lucas looked down at it. There was a bandage around the first knuckle on his index and myriad scabs on his forearm from the explosion—the one where he had blown up his wife, housekeeper, and dog.

Lucas remembered the husk of the home.

The bonsai blasted all over the street.

Their talk in the ambulance.

Saarinen's voice jarred him back from the scene in Pelham Gardens. "If you do not give me your phone, Dr. Page, I am going to slip an extension cord around your neck, then pull you off the device from around the corner. If you give me your phone, there is a chance you survive. It is your decision. You have five seconds."

Lucas looked down at the man and shrugged. "I guess you got me."

That seemed to please Saarinen. "Your phone."

Lucas reached into his pocket.

He began to pull his hand out of his pocket but paused, as if he was reconsidering.

That caused Saarinen to look up, irritated.

Which was when Lucas came out with the handcuffs.

He slapped the ring down onto Saarinen's wrist.

Then he slapped the second cuff onto his own.

As long as you both shall live.

Amen.

Saarinen began a step back before logic overrode instinct and he froze. His eyes clicked up at Lucas, and his face now belonged to someone else. The calm, the control, was gone. "Are you crazy? How—?"

Lucas didn't smile when he said, "This is where you get to pick a number between one and fuck you."

101

Hoffner cranked the wheel and hit the gas, *Tokyo Drift*-ing the big Navigator around the corner from Chambers Street onto the West Side Highway in a screaming blue cloud.

Kehoe put his hand out on the front seat headrest and tried not to drop the phone pressed to his ear.

There were three bureau vehicles on their six—two cars containing another four agents each, and a midsize sedan carrying Calvin-Wade Curtis and a driver. Kehoe was calling in NYPD and SWAT cavalry. Firemen were on the way. Ambulances.

The column of FBI vehicles moved as one organism, a polished multi-chassis centipede swerving through traffic with, lights flashing, sirens screeching, and determination dialed to toxic levels.

Kehoe finished with the SWAT commander and tried Page's number again.

Voice mail.

So he tried again.

Voice mail again.

Which meant that the phone was off, he was avoiding calls, or he was in trouble.

Why the hell had he gone to Saarinen's?

But Kehoe knew the answer to that—it was just how the guy was built. As much a mystery as his mind was, the way he operated in the world was almost no mystery at all. Which was why it had been so easy to get him back last year. Lucas didn't see the man behind the curtain pulling the levers because he wasn't looking for him; he was looking at the challenge the man was putting in front of him.

As Lucas had stated on the beach in Montauk before signing up for the safari, there is no *I* in *team*. And he meant it—he was not a team player. Half the time he didn't even remember that he was supposed to be on a team. The other half he bitched about having to wait around while the slower kids got up to speed. It was tiring. But put a problem in front of him and he was like some deranged OCD mathematical bloodhound—all you had to do was unclip his collar and watch the fun.

Only now Page was probably in the same room with the man who had orchestrated the killing of more than seven hundred innocent people.

Kehoe wondered if Page even knew it.

102

Saarinen's face had clenched to within a micron of its tolerances, and it looked like his skin might tear, exposing the angry skull beneath.

His right wrist was cuffed to Lucas's left and he had instinctively stepped in close; once you were connected to a mine, there was no ignoring it.

Lucas didn't say anything—he used the time to calculate brisance. Burn rate. Detonation lag. Blast velocity. And a million other little factors he had no means to control, no ability to test, and no way to survive.

Because once again it all came down to what wasn't there—and what wasn't there was enough time. He could never react fast enough to make any of the possible choices meaningful.

Except one.

And it was so weak that it was almost guaranteed suicide.

Lucas ran through the calculations again. The time it would take the fuse to drop. The volume of C4. The explosive yield. The detonation velocity. The number of ball bearings. The speed they would travel. The pattern in which they would disperse. And the time it would all take.

He gave his chances of success somewhere around three and a half million to one.

Which was theoretically better than zero. Or at least sounded like it was.

Saarinen's facial muscles relaxed and he took a few deep breaths. When he spoke, his delivery was once again borderline morose. "It appears as if we are putting Schrödinger's cat to the test, Dr. Page."

"How do you figure?" But he knew what the man was thinking. He also knew he was wrong.

Saarinen sounded like he was irritated at being forced to state the obvious. "Two men handcuffed together, standing on a land mine. Are they alive or are they dead?" There was no emotion in his eyes when he said, "Or are they both?"

"Is that the kind of thinking you pass off as intellect?"

Saarinen stared up at him, puzzled.

Lucas finished the last calculation and Kehoe's words lit up the teleprompter in his head: *basic physics and chemistry.* He said, "In Schrödinger's model, there is only *one* cat."

Lucas thought about the kids.

About the night he had held Erin in his lap out on the deck by the ocean.

How she had smelled.

What she meant to him.

Then he pulled Saarinen in with his left hand as he threw his prosthetic arm and leg around the man.

Saarinen's eyes went wide. "Nonononononoooo—"

Lucas just closed his eyes.

He said, "Three and a half million to one."

And let himself fall back.

103

West 81st Street

Hoffner blew around the last corner in one final snarl of rubber, ripped up the street, and slammed to a stop across from the building. Two fire engines were on site. Along with a bunch of police cruisers, the Special Weapons and Tactics van, two ambulances, and an unmarked police car.

Kehoe stepped out and waved his badge at the cop heading over to tell them that they couldn't park there. "We're taking over," he said, and left him to deal with Hoffner.

Glass and debris peppered the road. One of the parked cars had a coffee table embedded in the windshield. Kehoe stopped in the middle of the road and looked up.

Three large plate glass windows were blown out, one aluminum mullion reaching out into the air. Tattered curtains flapped in the wind that had come up, and there were no lights on in the apartment. And even from down here it looked like a tomb.

His people passed him in a blur of windbreakers and gear cases—escorting Calvin-Wade Curtis to where he would be most useful.

Kehoe was still looking up when Hoffner rolled up on his flank. "The explosion happened just as the first cruiser from the NYPD arrived. SWAT is in the stairwell, but they're taking their time—they're worried about booby traps."

Kehoe stared up at the building for another few seconds before taking his phone out and again dialing Page's number.

And he heard it. Not far away. A personalized ringtone—"Clowns to the left of me . . . jokers to the right . . ."—"You hear that?" Kehoe asked.

Hoffner looked around. "Yeah." He froze for a second as a bus going by on Columbus drowned out the sound. When it was past, he reacquired the song, then headed to the cars parked at the curb. He walked slowly back one spot, then turned and came forward, passing the car with the coffee table planted in the windshield. He walked one car past, then stopped, held up his hand, then took two steps back. He stopped and got down on his knee. Then he got down on his stomach. He reached under the car and pulled something out. He held it up. "Here it is."

Hoffner came over without brushing the glass and stone off his stomach or pants, and held the iPhone out. It was still ringing—". . . here I am, stuck in the middle with you . . ."—but the screen was smashed and it was covered in blood.

Kehoe ended his call and the bloody phone stopped playing the song. He looked up at Hoffner. "You tell SWAT they go in there *now*." He looked up at the blown-out windows. "And they take paramedics with them."

104

Columbia University Medical Center

Let there be sound.

There was sound.

Sort of.

Let there be light.

There was light.

Almost.

Let there be pain.

There was pain.

More than enough.

Then smell kicked in, and he detected cologne almost hidden under the scent of antiseptic.

He tried to open his eyes.

Someone said his name, but it was posed as a question, as if they weren't sure anyone was home at the ranch.

"Page?" the voice asked again.

He forced his eyes open.

A Daliesque silhouette fluttered somewhere in the distance, a shimmering gray flannel mirage.

Lucas blinked, and the form ratcheted one f-stop closer to focus—it had a head now, topped with gray hair that pulsed as if it were electrified. He shut his eyes, allocated all his bandwidth to vision, took a breath, then tried again.

Kehoe was no longer shimmering. And more or less human.

Which was as good as it ever got with him.

Lucas slowly peeled his lips open and his mouth felt like the lining had been replaced with pool table felt.

He reached for the pitcher on the tray, but it was too far away. And he was missing an arm to do it with.

Without being asked, Kehoe stepped forward and filled an institutional adult sippy cup for him. He raised it to Lucas's mouth and his movements were all very perfunctory and precise. But he did have a reasonable facsimile of concern on his face, which meant he was making an effort.

Lucas took a sip from the plastic spout and was surprised that he was able to swallow. He let the fluid drip into his reservoir, then made another go before trying to speak. "Thank you," he said in a voice belonging to Ardath Bey.

He moved his leg. And it worked.

But his right prosthetic was gone.

He tried his left arm. It also seemed to be functioning.

"Doctors said you'd be fine," Kehoe said wryly. "Which is not bad for a guy they wheeled in with someone else's arm dangling off his wrist like a charm bracelet."

Lucas looked at his wrist and there was a dark blue bruise—now turning purple with a green halo—where the handcuffs had bitten in. His arm was peppered with small scabs. He didn't remember stepping off the mine, although he knew he must have.

"They pulled nine ball bearings out of your body, but none of them were life-threatening, which makes you one very lucky man."

"I was under pressure, so I rolled the dice." Lucas pushed the button on the wired remote and the bed whirred slowly up, folding him into a relative sitting position. He picked up the water with his good hand and raised it to his lips. He somehow managed to suck down almost as much as dripped down his chin before putting the cup back on the tray. He was grateful that water didn't shoot out of a bunch of holes in his body like Daffy Duck after a run-in with Elmer Fudd and his shotgun. "Saarinen." He didn't bother trying to form it as a question—his operating system could execute only simple commands.

"You came in wearing his face, chained to his arm. The rest of him?" Kehoe shook his head. "He went from solid to liquid in one big boom."

Basic physics and chemistry.

Lucas looked around the room for his arm and leg. "Have you seen my prosthetics?"

"They're downstairs in a box, but you'll need new ones. They took the brunt of the blast; Saarinen took the rest." Kehoe's body language was slowly returning to normal, which meant the concern and friendliness would soon be gone. "I told them to save them for you."

"Good."

They stared at each other for a few silent moments, and there was nothing awkward or forced in the time. Lucas wondered how many moments like this Kehoe allowed himself.

Kehoe finally asked, "Why do you keep doing this to yourself?"

"I do it to other people, too, but they don't seem to be as robust." Lucas made another run at the sippy cup. The water tasted better than anything he had ever tried before, and he recognized the phenomenon—gratitude.

"So this was all about revenge?"

Lucas didn't waste any energy by shrugging. "I didn't get a chance to ask Saarinen about his motives, but they seem pretty obvious. He was trying to fuck the Hockneys. Probably because they had something to do with the death of his son."

Kehoe nodded as if that had been the right thing to say. "The Hockneys owned the company that manufactured the LAWS rocket used to kill Saarinen's son—Horsuch LLC out of Ukraine."

"And they used Jonathan Makepeace to buy the company."

Kehoe gave him an approving nod. "Very good."

Lucas tapped the side of his head with his index finger. "In the land of the blind, the one-eyed man is king."

Kehoe's face flattened out, and the concern was now gone. "Did you figure out how Frosst factored in?"

"I assume money was the common currency."

"Frosst's boyfriend was on the same bus as Saarinen's son."

Which knocked all kinds of pieces into place. "I didn't see that one coming. Especially with that haircut." He looked at the cup, but he was no longer thirsty. "And Hockney the Younger?"

Kehoe's face made all the necessary adjustments. "Our people from the Air National Guard were escorting him to a base in Southern California when his plane blew up midair."

Lucas wanted to be surprised, but he didn't have any more left in him. "Saarinen was very thorough—he crossed everyone off his shopping list."

"Everyone except you."

This time Lucas did shrug.

Kehoe took a step toward the bed and put his hands on the footboard. "Why didn't you call me when you figured out he was the Machine Bomber?"

"I only figured it out about two seconds before I stepped on that device hidden in his floor."

"How?"

Lucas managed a shrug again, and it felt good to move. But painful. "I kept asking myself who profited the most by the bombings—I was too blinded by my own bias to realize I was asking the wrong question. It wasn't about someone profiting, it was about someone *losing*." He paused to catch his breath, and when he swallowed, it felt like his pump was once again working. "And Saarinen was the exception to the rule, the thing that shouldn't have been there—a survivor. The bomber was way too precise to have screwed up killing Saarinen, which meant he had intentionally been left alive."

"And that was how you figured it out?"

Lucas shook his head. "I suspected, which is why I called Nadeel and had him check out Saarinen's son's murder. But I couldn't get it to gel. Not the way I needed it to. But as I kept seeing Saarinen's reflection in the window as I looked out at the museum across the street, something was off. Curtis said the undetonated IED we found at the Eighth Avenue internet hub had been made by a right-handed individual. The device that blew up Donnie Rich and his mother in that farmhouse upstate had been assembled by a left-handed individual." He took another sip of water and emptied the cup. He held it out and shook it in a gesture that bartenders the world over see in their sleep.

Kehoe came around the bed, refilled the cup, placed it down on the tray table over Lucas's lap, then retook his position at the foot of the bed.

"And what was off in Saarinen's reflection was that he was left hand dominant. And I remembered the scissors at William Hockney's apartment and the bomb upstate, and, well, I got it."

"Scissors?"

"There was this pair of scissors at Hockney's apartment the night I went to visit him. Beautiful hand-crafted bonsai clippers that cost more than a car; maybe three artisans in the world can make something as beautiful as those. And I picked them up and they fit me, which should have set off all kinds of alarm bells because I'm left-handed. So the scissors were made for a left-handed person. And Hockney was right-handed—I saw that in the way he handled his whiskey tumbler. And someone had been using the scissors that night. And there was a paw print in the elevator. Then the next morning you said that Saarinen had visited. I just didn't put it all together until I saw his reflection." He shook his head. "His reflection. Wow. Like I said, I needed a new perspective."

Kehoe was just staring at him and it was impossible to guess what he was thinking. "Impressive."

"Yeah, well—" And there wasn't anything else to add.

Kehoe's face had morphed back into business mode and he crossed his arms. "We found another kid that Saarinen had recruited."

"Alive?"

"Alive. He's an intern at Cornell—cardiology. He downloaded the patch to their system that enabled Saarinen to access their data and initiate William Hockney's heart attack. His lawyer is claiming that he didn't know that's what it was, and we're cutting him some slack through a deal we made—he's the only surviving component of Saarinen's little army."

"How'd you find him?"

"We cracked Saarinen's laptop, which was synced to his phone, which, incidentally, you blew up. We ran down all the numbers in his contacts; Curtis figured he might have planted more IEDs out there with cell phone triggers. Every number in his contacts was a legitimate contact except one, which was a prepaid burner phone. We ran it down, and GPS showed that it was stationary in a parking garage on East Seventieth. We checked cell tower records, and the number had been activated a few weeks before the Guggenheim bombing—it traveled the same route six days a week, the only variance being where it resided in the garage. The phone had never placed or received a call. It was connected to an IED under the seat of an Audi belonging to one Franklin Kisber—a twenty-seven-year-old intern at Cornell. When he found out that he had been driving around with a bomb under his seat—and that he was slated for execution like those five other young men—he decided that sharing what he knew was in his best interests."

"Did Kisber attend that TED Talk in Vegas?"

"No, he was recruited later than the others, just after William Hockney had his pacemaker installed."

"Saarinen crossed all of his Ts and dotted the lowercase Js."

"He certainly didn't leave much to chance."

"How did he recruit those kids?"

It was Kehoe's turn to shrug. "Saarinen met Kisber on 4chan, on one of the message boards. We're not sure about all of them yet, but it looks like your kid, Jespersen, was right—he went after angry young men. The bureau has been following the incel movement for a couple of years now—the general personality makeup is remarkably similar to young Muslim men who become radicalized."

"You're shitting me."

"He made contact, then communicated through an encrypted app."

"And the other kids?"

"Most of his files are encrypted, but there are hints here and there that he spent time on a lot of radical environmentalist sites, and those kids thought they were really signing up to do some damage to the system."

Lucas let that sink in for a few moments. He was continually amazed at how many broken people there were out there. "And Vegas?"

"Saarinen was supposedly in Los Angeles over those three days, but I'm sure with a little more digging we'll be able to place him in Vegas—it's a four-hour car ride."

"I think he was more careful than that. I bet he got them there just to see that talk, and none of them knew they were in the room together. And Frosst and Hockney Jr. were just window dressing for us, when we finally put it all together. Like I said—Ts and lowercase Js." Lucas sucked on the sippy cup again, emptying it. "Which means that when Frosst and Cristobel were in Makepeace's apartment, either one of them could have planted that bomb in the humidor—mutual alibis that were actually accomplices. Wow."

Kehoe stepped out of the conversation for a few seconds to type something on his phone with his thumbs. When he was done, he pretended to be back in the room. "Once again, Dr. Page, you impressed me."

"Nadeel and Jespersen did all the work."

"Which is why I offered them both jobs."

"And what were their excuses for turning you down?"

"Jespersen said she'd be bored working in such a stiff environment—she said something about Caltech, which I understand is one of your old alma maters."

Lucas had earned his second PhD there—working at the Palomar Observatory. "And Nadeel?" he asked.

"He said I couldn't afford him." Kehoe looked puzzled. "Those kids went to the wire for you—how do you foster that kind of loyalty?"

Which was a good question. "I push them to be the fullest people they can. I'm hard on them. And they rise to the occasion."

Kehoe's mouth bent into a small smile with that. "That's an interesting approach."

Lucas almost told Kehoe to go fuck himself, but he had walked himself into that one. "I'm tired. And you have shit to do."

Kehoe nodded at that. "Well, Dr. Page, I appreciate your help. Oh, there's one other thing—well, two, actually. The first is I made arrangements with that school you were supposed to get your daughter enrolled in before last Friday—LaGuardia. They held her place. She got a letter of recommendation from me, and the promise of a lecture from a world-famous astrophysicist once he's back on his feet."

Lucas was surprised by that, and his voice cracked when he said, "Thank you, Brett."

Kehoe waved it away.

"And the other thing?"

Kehoe held up his phone. "What's with your ringtone for me?"

For the first time in days, Lucas managed a real smile.

105

Columbia University Medical Center

Lucas was asleep, or at least almost asleep, when a voice at the edge of the void brought him back from the medicated darkness. "Twice?"

He opened his eyes and couldn't see anything but the ceiling overhead. So he closed them again.

Once again, a voice asked, "Twice?"

Which meant that it wasn't a hallucination. He reached over for the remote on the end of the cord and began raising himself to a sitting position. When he was halfway up, he saw her.

Whitaker was beside his bed in a wheelchair.

They didn't say anything for a few moments, they just examined each other.

She looked good. Or at least better than the last time he had seen her. There was a single bandage around her neck, and her foot was in a cast balanced on a rest. Her plaid pajamas and flannel robe were not in the least bit girlie. The only thing that hinted at how serious things had been for her was the weight loss—she was down an easy fifteen, maybe even twenty, pounds.

"Twice what?" he asked.

Whitaker shook her head as if she was dealing with someone who didn't speak English. "You blew yourself up *twice*?"

"Actually, I blew *other people* up twice."

"I stand corrected—*you* were in two explosions."

"Technically, I have been in *three* explosions."

"I meant recently."

"Well, all time happens at once if you believe in eternalism. Which means that all three explosions I've been in were recent. Simultaneous if you want to quibble."

Whitaker began to wheel herself out of the room.

"Okay, okay. Yes, I blew myself up. *Twice.* Does that make you happy?"

She swung around, and it was easy to see that she had become pretty adept at using the wheelchair. "The time that saved my life certainly does."

"Yeah, well, we all do stupid things."

"What is it with you? Not even in the hospital—with me being all shot up and you having survived two explosions, one that tore off an ear, another that filled you with stainless steel balls—can you be nice. Why the fuck not?"

Lucas shrugged. There were a lot of things he could say—some of them even kind. He opted for "Tough shit."

Which made her laugh. "I give up."

"I'm glad you're okay." He looked over at her. "Really. I am."

"Yeah, well, thank you. Kehoe told me how you got Frosst off me and I owe you one. That was—" And she just stopped as she began to cry.

"Are you all right?" He waved his hand toward her many injuries, hoping to distract her so she'd stop the waterworks.

She wiped her eyes on the cuff of her robe. "I'll need a cane for a while. And I'll probably have a limp. But nothing that will keep me out of the field. The bullet that hit me in the chest went through my right lung, and they managed to patch it all up. I've lost some breathing capacity, but nothing a little exercise and caution won't compensate for."

He pointed up at her neck. "I thought that one was *it*."

"You and everyone else. Frosst used military rounds and it just zipped straight through. It missed the carotid and my vocal cords, and only clipped the vertebra. I got lucky. I can't move my neck very well yet, but the muscles should heal good as new." Her features softened a little more, and there was tenderness in her voice. "And you? Are you all right?"

"Define *all right*."

"You look a little . . . *older*."

"If getting old is the price I have to pay for not dying young, I'll take it."

Whitaker wheeled closer to the bed and engaged the brake. "I have some news."

"Your plastic cactus died?"

She smiled at that. "Remember Owen McCoy?"

Lucas punched into his recall center. "That deputy from the Medusa bombing? The one who liked you?"

"How do you know he liked me?"

"You know how all women can tell what other women are thinking?"

"Men have that, too?"

Lucas shook his head. "Not at all. But for a cop, McCoy was terrible at hiding what he was thinking."

"He saw what happened to you and me on the news and came into town to visit me. Twice. Brought me flowers. *Real* flowers. We've been FaceTiming."

"Does this mean your neighbors are going to have to find someone else to throw into a volcano?"

She grinned at him. "Maybe."

"Well, you definitely have some paid sick leave coming. Maybe you can spend it up in Medusa."

She nodded fatalistically. "God does have a sense of humor."

"Don't start with the God stuff."

"Really? You still don't believe in God after he saved your ass. Twi—*three* times? If there's no God, what's the meaning of life?"

"That's the wrong question." He pointed at her. "Because it implies that there *is* a meaning."

"You never turn it off, do you?"

He thought about that. "I guess not, no."

They were silent for a few moments, and then she reached out and took his hand. It felt odd, but he appreciated it.

"It was Saarinen?" she asked. "All of it?"

"It looks like, yes. He planned this for years. He ran everything, including Frosst. It'll take months to run everything down, but he's the spider at the center of the web."

"And Kehoe filled you in on everything?"

"He was by this morning."

"Yeah, he visited me, too. He was almost . . . paternal. It was weird." She squeezed his palm. "So, what's next for Lucas Page?"

Lucas squeezed back. "That, Special Agent Alice Whitaker, is an excellent question."

106

The Upper East Side

The little bulldog was on its back in his lap, snoring like a small goblin, balls out.

Lemmy sat in the middle of the big Kazak rug, watching Lucas and the puppy. His tail was still and his ears were up in a perfect canine radar array, his head ticktocking from side to side in a slow beat as he tried to figure out the beast piglet in Lucas's lap. They never let Lemmy off leash at the dog park when anyone else was there; he could be rough with other dogs. So Lucas had his doubts about the puppy—who was still just called *Dog*. This was Lemmy's joint, and Lucas didn't know if he was open to new friendships.

"Well?"

Lemmy's head tocked back to the left.

"Does he get to stay?"

And then Lemmy nodded, and for a second Lucas bought it. Then he felt like an idiot for anthropomorphizing an organism that would die of thirst before simply lifting the faucet handle—an action he had seen literally thousands of times. Lemmy's deep learning capabilities were limited. "Well?"

The brute's tail swished for a beat, paused, then zipped back, and he raised his not-insignificant haunches off the floor. He took a few halting steps, his attention laser-focused on the small snoring beanbag in Lucas's lap.

"It's okay, dummy."

Lemmy's shoulders went down and he came forward tentatively, sniffing the air in deep, noisy breaths that sounded like a bicycle pump with a faulty seal.

The dog came to the sofa and slowly pushed his nose into Lucas's lap. He gave the goblin's disproportionate package a sniff, then nosed his belly.

The puppy squeaked, and Lemmy gave him an exploratory lick.

Then he put his two big paws up on Lucas—one on his good thigh, one on his prosthetic—and rose up over the bulldog to lick his human in the face.

"So he stays?" Lucas asked.

Lemmy let out a happy groan and gave the puppy another taste as the front door opened.

The big dog ran off, and Lucas could hear him being greeted with hugs and kisses and a chorus of *Hello, Lemmy!*

Lucas tucked the snoring puppy under his arm like a football and cranked up out of the sofa with his new (but temporary!) cane.

Erin and the Maude Squad were *back*.

As he passed the mirror, he realized he still had to do something about the hair.

Or maybe not.

Acknowledgments

Building a book is never a lone endeavor, and I leaned on a lot of other people during this one. This is certainly not everyone who had a hand in getting me from there to here, but it's a start.

My editor, Keith Kahla, who is somehow still talking to me. Without his help, this book would have been twice as long and half as fun—he walked me through the daunting task of writing a sequel. He deserves cowriting credit on this one.

My agent, Jill Marr, who I have spent a decade slowly winning over by being continually unreachable. She once again managed all the lunacy so I could focus on the writing—she protects my sanity.

Andrea Cavallero, for getting my work into bookstores around the world. And for never getting angry when I refuse to talk to the movie people. Her belief is one of the bearing walls of my career.

Kelley Ragland, Alice Pfeifer, and the rest of the people at Minotaur Books who scramble around in the thankless job of herding writers. They balance out our madness, and somehow make it fit for consumption—which is no easy task.

Sandra Dijkstra, for putting the arsenal behind me. Without her, this business truly would be a poorer environment. Thank you.

Lieutenant-General Yvan Blondin—RCAF (Ret.), for reading an early draft of the manuscript and giving some very solid editorial suggestions—as both a reader and military pilot. I hope I didn't screw things up too badly.

Dr. William M. Bass III, the noted forensic anthropologist, for his patient detailing of the effects an explosion has on the human body. Dr. Bass is not only one of the most knowledgeable people in the world on the subject of crime-scene forensics, but he could do stand up comedy—which is not an obvious combination. He is also the textbook definition of a gentlemen.

John Galligan—I'm not sure this particular journey would have made sense to me without all of the fishing trips I've taken with Dog. I'm a fan.

Once again, my dear friend Barbara Behr, for helping me work out some of the weirdest problems that writing a novel can present.

Charles Anderson, who once again leaned into the task and gave me excellent suggestions.

Louis Lechasseur, for always answering my 3:00 a.m. emails with thoughtful, well-researched replies. And for not laughing at some of my questions.

Stephen Schettini, for his enduring optimism. And for not giving up.

Christopher Snow, who gives me hope for the future—the world doesn't build enough people like him.

Robert Côté for his encouragement, sense of humor, and carpentry skills (he also makes a pretty good *goberge* hoagie).

Kenzo, for helping with the dialogue and always reminding me that he would rather be doing anything other than working on a novel.

My neighbor, Stan, who puts up with everything from burning chicken effigies in my trees to 3:00 a.m. pet grave-digging duty.

All the writers who made this look easy, and have turned out to be the most supportive groups of professionals I could ever imagine being a part of.

My foreign publishers, who have done more for me than I could ever thank them for.

My readers, for taking a risk. Sending a novel out into the world is a very surreal experience, and they make all the late nights banging my head against the keyboard worth it. Thank you. Really.

And once again, I have to thank Rod Whitaker, who made me want to do this.